SABER'S PRIDE

· SPIRITS' VALLEY II ·

SABER'S PRIDE

C.M. BANSCHBACH

Published by Campitor Press
https://clairembanschbach.com/

Cover Design: Franziska Stern/@coverdungeonrabbit
https://www.coverdungeon.com/
Chapter Heading design: Kristin Hildebrand /@artkrisma

ISBN: 978-0-9992203-6-8

To Sarah, Arturo, and the kids.

Sarah. You're the best oldest sister I could have asked for.
Always an inspiration and someone I look up to in many ways.
You're always there to crack jokes, talk faith or life, and always
showing up to be an amazing wife and mother. Love you!

AUTHOR LETTER

Dear reader,

I wanted to leave a note at the beginning because this might be a hard story for some. This is a story that begins with men and women who are careless, where mental and physical abuse runs rampant in a society, and where spiritual leaders turn a blind eye. But it's also a story of one man who decides he's had enough. Who takes a stand with those who want to help, who want to see the change, who want to see peace. Spiritual leaders who repent and turn back to holier ways, of higher beings who show that they have cared all along.

It doesn't make old hurts go away. It doesn't make wounds be forgotten. But within these pages, characters get a chance to heal, a chance to find what love truly is, who can right their wrongs and the wrongs of others. A chance to change their society and make it a better place for those to come. Characters who get to find some peace.

This is a story I have no personal experience with, but I know many do. And it's one I try to treat with respect because no one deserves to be hurt in such a way.

There are a few instances of verbal and physical abuse directed at characters from both a parent and siblings, some flashes of PTSD, and brief discussion of past injuries. A few mentions of past sexual abuse against women by the chief, but no descriptions.

I hope you'll give this story a chance, and I hope you always stay courageous.

PROLOGUE

To understand the weight of what I face this night with the cloak of chieftain newly draped over my shoulders and the wary eyes of the tribe looking back, you must know what it is that brought us here. The history of the Saber tribe.

My grandfather was a cruel man. At least, this is what everyone says. I never knew him. My own father killed him to take the position of chieftain over the villages. And no one stopped him, like they had not stopped his father and the father before them.

We are a proud tribe, and then were bloated on success and victories on the lower plains against the Pronghorn tribes. We wanted a strong man to lead us, and nothing said strength like taking power at the point of a sword.

My father took the ways of my grandfather and perfected them. He took no wife. Instead, four women as he wanted to give him sons. The first was willing. She bore my half-brother Kamil, who willingly ate the scraps our father threw his way and studied intently under his fist.

My mother was not willing. But she bore me and whispered in my ear every night as I grew, teaching me to wait and watch like our sablecats, picking when and where to strike, to fight, and that one might catch more fish with patience and a net, than with anger and a spear.

Another son to a different woman. Emil followed in Kamil's footsteps, willingly obeying his commands and bringing back any murmurs made by the tribe. He is more slippery than a river eel, this half-brother, living in the shadows, watching and listening.

The last, barely a woman herself, and given by her parents as a peace offering to my father, bore the half-siblings I hate the least. Twins. Michal, good with a bow. And Janne, who would have been drowned at birth for daring to be a girl when all he wanted was another male had the *talånd* not acted like a man and told him it would bring the spirits' wrath.

But it did not stop him from shunning her completely. Many in the tribe try to do the same, but she still makes herself be heard. She is as fierce as a sablecat herself, my little sister, and I love her for it.

To understand what it is I plan to do with this tribe, you must know the reasons I have spent all twenty-six of my years in the shadows, learning everything I can, planning three steps ahead. Why I wear my hair short instead of long like the other warriors of our tribe.

My father sowed hate and cruelty like those in the lower village sow seeds. Two of my brothers reaped and sowed this as well. And twenty-six years of living with them, avoiding them, staying one step away from them, has taught me that this is not what I want.

We are a proud tribe, but we can be better. I would see my younger brother and sister live freely. My mother and theirs love and live without fear. I will sacrifice myself to this cause.

But the tribe does not know this. No one does, but me.

ONE

DAVOR

Shouts and boastful cries filled the chieftain's lodge. I did not join in from where I stood half in the shadows, arms crossed over my chest, watching Kamil and Hakkon, the Greywolf outcast, make their case for war. The chief slouched in his chair, fingers tracing over the carved armrest, watching through hooded eyes.

He never gave anything away, but I knew his heart had leapt greedily when the young Greywolf came limping in through the snows, vengeance in his eyes. A new chieftain had been chosen for the Greywolf tribe up in the northern valley—the old chief's bastard son. And it seemed the tribe was divided. Some for him and others violently opposed.

This one had been cast out for attempting to murder the new chief. Hakkon had come looking for shelter from the winter storms that rushed hard over our plains and rivers and geysers, perhaps more violent than his home where they instead drowned the valley and mountains in snows until the spring sun.

But Kamil had latched on to the thought that the Greywolf tribe might be weak. That we could expand our lands past what we had held for generations, past what we had taken from the Blackpaws by their lower lake eight years ago, and claim the entire valley.

For the Saber tribe, he'd cried out. For honor and glory.

But I knew my half-brother well enough. For him to finally claim the place of chieftain much like our father had from his. By violence and death. Who would stand against the man who had taken the Battlelion medallion by force three turnings ago and planned to kill the chieftain and take his place as well?

"What do you think?" A warrior came to stand beside me.

"I think I do not see the point in invading up valley," I replied.

Alik grunted, leaning against the wall with hand settled on his sword. "I do not believe you, Davor."

A mirthless half-smile flickered. Many warriors around us cried out for war, others like Alik and myself stood back, watching. A few sablecats perched in the high rafters, golden eyes watching us below.

"Victories would raise him higher in many eyes," I said.

"He already has the battlelion medallion."

"You think that is enough for him?" Anyone with two eyes could see that it would never be enough for Kamil.

"Chief has not named him heir yet." Alik's voice held a bit of reluctant understanding. In the years we stood together like this in the lodge, bare allies, he knew not to refer to the chief as my father, at least not in front of me.

"That does not matter either."

Our father had long dangled the possibility of any one of his four sons being named chief when it was time. But he had not yet, even though Kamil was nearing thirty years, and me at twenty-six. He declared we must prove ourselves, but he did not want to relinquish the control he had.

Even when he was losing a battle to keep control of his mind day after day. Today was a more lucid day for him. And he was intrigued enough by the possibility of more power that he would pass the war spear to Kamil.

My gaze fell across the spacious lodge, through the hazy smoke left by the hearthfire where my younger half-brother Emil watched me and Alik. A lazy smile flickered across his face, a smug reassurance that he was assessing something about me. I held his look for a few moments before deliberately shifting away. He'd learned how to play that game from me.

If Kamil was looking for battle, he would also be looking for a way to rid himself of any objectors or contenders to him taking the chief's chair. That meant me, and men like Alik.

"Enough." The chieftain finally spoke, stirring and leaning forward.

Kamil's features sharpened in eagerness.

"The snows are yet too deep. But come winter's turning, we will muster the lions and begin testing the borders."

The words sent a ripple through the lodge. My jaw tensed a little more. It was all but a declaration of war. If the chief did not pass the spear by spring, then Kamil would take it and we would ride to war either way.

I left Alik and pushed out into the clean, crisp air. Snows mounded up against the lodges grouped in consecutive squares at the bottom of the slope the chief's lodge had been raised atop generations ago. Breath puffed up before me, obscuring sight of the three villages for a moment.

The upper village downhill from where I stood housed most of the warriors. Once it might not have been this way, but since my father had seized his place and had fed the hot blood of our warriors with battles and wars like he might feed a sablecat raw meat, they had taken over the upper village.

The middle, on the other side of the icy river's curve, held the overflow of the warriors from the lodges, and the hunters and foragers. The lower village, barely in sight as a few flickering lights back on our side of the river, held the men and women who cared for the fields of colorful corn, seen as the lowest of us all despite helping to provide food to the entire tribe.

"You do not call for war?" Emil's voice, as slippery as he was, broke behind me.

"What would be the point of it?" I returned.

He came to stand beside me, drawing his cloak trimmed in red fox fur tighter against winter's chill. He thought it marked him well—sly and full of tricks as Kamil's right hand. I thought an eel would suit him better, the way he lurked in the shadows and slid in and out of darkness to bite the unsuspecting.

"More land, more hunting grounds, room to spread out from these villages."

I held in a scoff. Room for the warriors to roam. Room to make those left in the village even more subservient. If I had to guess.

"What is this?"

The muscles in my shoulders tensed. I had not heard Kamil, though he could move as silently as our sablecats. And I did not like being trapped between these half-brothers.

He loomed on my left side, broad-shouldered and barely taller than me. The rounded battlelion medallion tapped against his chest, the red stone set in the roaring sablecat's eye winking at me.

"Just gathering Davor's thoughts on the council." Emil's smirk shone through his voice.

A sneer curled Kamil's lips. "How could I have forgotten to gather *sage* council from my little brother?" It was a curse in my ears, and he meant it as such.

"But you'd listen to the advice of a Greywolf barely out of training spears and driven half mad by jealousy? Might be a poor decision." I had always been able to play the same game as Kamil. He was brash, confident, his pride easy to prick. Emil, not so much. He absorbed, waited, planned for a more effective strike than brute force.

Kamil's hand closed on my tunic, shoving me back a half-step. Anger flared for a second, then faded in his dark eyes. "Upset that no one listens to the words of a dishonored man who hides in the shadows?"

My heart raged for a few beats before it slowed like I had taught it. "Worried they might think twice if they did?"

His knife pressed against my chest before I blinked again. "One day, Davor, I will cease to tolerate you." The knife point nicked through the layers of tunic and shirt and undershirt before he withdrew.

There was no wisdom in any other reply, so I simply held his gaze for two more heartbeats and then lowered in bare deference.

A scornful laugh announced his departure, and my hate burned bright after them both before I let the winter wind whisk it away. I placed a hand against my chest, finding a slight dampness there. He'd broken skin, but it would need no more than a quick dab of a cloth.

A darker shadow padded up to join me, growling low in its throat. I settled a hand on Luk's shoulder, drawing a purr from the sablecat instead. He leaned his shoulder into mine and I pushed him away, scratching instead under the sharp jawline, careful of the two fangs sweeping down from his upper jaw. Pale golden eyes closed as he pushed into my hand, ears flicking up and down, his purr loud enough to start an avalanche.

But it distracted me, and a bit of calm eased through the storm of anger. I finally shoved him away and dusted bits of black fur from my hands.

"Come." I started down the path from the lodge. I'd been promising my mother a night at her table for days. Tonight seemed good enough and I did not feel like stepping back into the chief's lodge.

The innermost row of lodges held my mother's, just off the square with its large firepit where the entire village could gather. Most lodges held multiple families under their broad rafters. Not this one.

She shared it with the youngest of my father's not-wives—a healer who the chief had graciously allowed to keep training and practicing her craft even after she'd been given to him.

All four women held an odd place in the tribe. Above the others, but not a chieftain's wife. Bearing sons, but no more children. A distance kept between them and their old families. Kamil's and Emil's mothers were both dead, and mine and the twins' had evaded the oppression of the chieftain's lodge to live just out of easy reach, in a lodge no one else dared to share with them other than the injured who came to Inge for healing.

Luk followed in my wake, occasionally snapping at the dust-ings of snowflakes dislodged from the peaked roofs by the trick-ster wind, or returning low growls to the other sablecats who lounged against the lodges or on the broad perches built for them.

Light flickered behind the skins covering the windows. I knocked twice, then once more. Golden firelight spilled out as the door flung open with the energy only Janne could bring.

"Davor!" My half-sister's smile brought a faint one easing from me in return.

"Nina, Davor's here!" she leaned back and shouted around the door.

"Are you going to let me in?" I inquired.

Janne wrinkled her nose and stepped aside, all swirling skirts and unbound hair. Luk settled outside as I stepped up into the lodge.

My mother looked up from the fire, a smile creasing her face. "Just in time. Go wash."

I left my fur-lined cloak on the bench beside the door, setting my curved sword atop it, but keeping the knives on my belt. The table had been pulled out, benches from against the wall tucked underneath it. The soothing scent of fresh baked flatbread filled up every corner of the common room.

A shallow bowl of warmed water waited on the bench beside the fire. I dipped my hands in, rinsing away the day. Scooping a bit more, I rubbed it over the back of my neck, fingers pausing as they always did when they found the scar.

"All right?" my mother asked conversationally, the words between us as she pulled the dinner pot from the coals.

"They are calling for war against the Greywolves."

A sharp inhale came from her, and I focused on drying my hands.

"And?"

"And he will pass the spear come spring."

Names were not mentioned in the lodge. Not there, the small sanctuary any of us might have.

"You will go?"

"I will have no choice."

Her hand brushed my sleeve and I looked down into the dark brown eyes she had given me. Concerned knowing lurked there. I was not the only one thinking I would need to guard my back twice as much in battle where anything could happen.

"And Michal?" She darted a glance at Inge where she and her daughter set out the last of the wooden plates, laughter darting between them.

"Too young yet." Though I'd been commanded to ride into battle against the Blackpaws much too young at seventeen, another way for my father to make me prove myself. But I was a second-born, and the twins were afterthoughts.

Her next look begged me not to say anything yet, and I tipped my head slightly. I stepped back to allow her more room to lift and carry the pot to the table. Janne tapped the table beside her and I slid onto the bench. As the ignored daughter, she'd been free to be raised in the smaller lodge. As the son, Michal had been in the chieftain's lodge for most of his years with the rest of us.

Inge had just started to offer the prayer to the All-Father and Saber spirit, when the door slammed open. Hand on knife, I looked first for my sword, then to the intruder.

But it was Michal himself, stomping snow from his boots, rattling the arrows in his quiver as he did. Inge's face broke into a broader smile and Janne jumped up from the table. I did not share their joy. There was less tension between me and Michal than among the other sons, but it still coiled and snared.

Inge dusted snow from his head and shoulders. His smile died at the sight of me sitting at the table. Mother gently tapped my hand as if worried I'd start a fight with the boy.

"Twice for dinner in one counting. How did I get so lucky?" Inge took his cloak as he set his bow and quiver aside.

Michal darted another dark look at me. "No one to tattle tonight if I'm not at table. Davor never *does* anything."

I simply took a drink of the dark oak ale Janne had already poured out, ignoring the sharp intake from Inge. So Kamil and Emil were off to other lodges tonight as well. Probably mustering up support and feeding ears with stories of glory in war.

Janne sat back beside me, turning a look of pleading mixed with warning not to ruin dinner when her brother had come. Michal took the bench opposite her, casting another look my way, as if he'd been practicing the sneer Kamil preferred.

Like the other warriors, he wore his hair long, bound at the nape of his neck in a leather cord. He'd left his sword by the door along with his bow. He held his own on the training grounds and would likely be joining the ranks of warriors by eighteen. Still too young, but the bitterness he carried all around him lent sharpness to his skills.

"How was training?" Janne leaned forward eagerly as we turned to food. It brought some light back to Michal's face as he answered and gave the news of the coming war.

It prodded at my heart. Not for the first time, I wondered what it was like in other lodges, among other brothers and sisters. If the younger feared the older. If there could ever be more than dinner when it was safe enough to meet with a mother or a sibling.

The wooden cup spun in my hand. War was coming. It was as easy to predict as to say the stars would appear in the sky come nightfall. Kamil's thoughts to take advantage of it for his own gain shone brighter than the sun in midsummer.

I had watched and planned my entire life. But always for

survival and to protect the very few people I cared about.

If Kamil returned victorious, there was nothing stopping him from killing the chief and taking his place. Nothing to stop him from killing me, the twins, our mothers, maybe even Emil to solidify his place. The last three chiefs had not had any contenders because they had killed any competition within a counting of taking the staff.

My cup tremored under a distant rumble. The mountain was talking, muttering to itself as it did every so often. The *talånds* in time past loved to claim it was the Saber spirit speaking to us. Maybe only to curse us.

One warcry went up, echoed by another. Not a call to arms, instead a rejoicing in might. Kamil was out there somewhere, fueling the flames of war with tales of the spirits approving this battle. A quieter noise came back. Luk batting his paw against the door to reassure me he was there.

Our mothers had gone quiet, and Janne blanched under the sounds. Eagerness lurked about Michal. He was ready to act, desperate to claim his place in the tribe. And the look of sadness that creased his mother's face at the sight...it wrenched something deep in me. The same look my mother had once given me when I'd tried the ways of our father.

Mother began to gather empty plates and cups. "Davor." She touched my arm. "Come help me."

She wanted to talk, out of hearing of the others. My gut tightened. It was something important then.

I took the plates she handed me, and followed her around the corner to the cooking fires into the bare semblance of privacy.

"What's wrong?" I spoke first, coming a step away as she braced against the raised bench where bits of the prepared meal still remained.

"We are all right, the three of us," she reassured, but it did not fall easy on my ears. Something was not right. "I saw your look in there." She lifted her chin, looking past me into the common room. "What are you planning?"

I wanted to lean back from her gaze, the assessing one that probed deeper than anyone else cared to look.

She softened. "Nothing yet?"

"What do you think I should be planning?" A hint of bitterness spilled out.

A quick breath escaped her. "For the war."

This time I did move, shifting to lean against the bench, arms crossing as I kept one eye on the broad entrance. Michal and Janne's low chatter reassured that they weren't attempting to overhear.

"Davor." Her brief touch to my forearm drew my gaze to her. "I know you see it. I heard it in the few words you gave when you came in. The packs are riding for war, and whoever comes back will be taking the place of chief. If that is Kamil, you know he will not tolerate any competition."

"One day I will cease to tolerate you."

"You think I should finally try to kill Kamil? So I can get a knife in my back the second I do?"

"No. Killing is the way of Kamil and the chief, and the chiefs before him. You have a different way."

A sharp sound broke from me, closer to bitterness than humor. "I do have a different way. One that keeps me and you safe." The way I had chosen years and years ago.

"The time for safety might be past."

I looked to my mother, at the lines creasing around her eyes: worry, fear.

"What do you know?" I asked.

She shook her head. "I know that I would rather have you alive than myself. I know that once Kamil takes the chieftain's place, he will come for you. I know that Michal is at a tipping point. He wants so much to be a man, but does not know which way to go." Her throat bobbed. There was something else.

"I know that the chief has finally remembered that Janne exists. He summoned Inge yesterday. Makar wants to give Janne to one of his men."

My heart plummeted. "What did she say?"

Mother's arms crossed across her stomach. "What can she say?" Her voice dropped to a whisper. "What power have we ever had?"

A low curse broke from me, and Mother jerked a sharp nod in agreement. But...

"If I make any move, that endangers you, Janne, and Inge."

Her head tilted, and that look was back, seeing straight into the heart of me. "There might not be time to remain passive."

The same old rage burned in my gut, dimming with the tightening of my fists. Shuttering it all away like I'd trained myself so many years ago.

"Just like that," she said softly, understanding there.

"Perhaps I have no power either," I returned in the same tone. She wanted me to do something, but what could I do?

"You do. You are still a chief's son."

I do not want to be. But I had no choice in that much like she'd had no choice in bearing me.

"You have at least one pack leader who sees something in you."

I tilted a look to her. Alik?

"You go to war. Perhaps you can gather more to your side."

"So I can live only a few days more when I get back to the

villages? Maybe survive a counting longer in the war?"

She did not recoil from the seething bitterness that escaped. I immediately breathed and gave a soft apology. Her hand brushed mine, squeezing tight before releasing.

"You are strong, Davor. You could claim a place in this tribe. And I don't just say that because I fear for myself. I want to see you live, find happiness. You help where you can. What if you could do it more openly? I know there are others who do not love the chief and his ways."

"That's a pretty dream you have," I said.

A faint smile creased her cheeks. "Perhaps I'll tell you of the dream I have where my son can come visit me whenever he wants, maybe we live under the same roof again."

I shifted against the bench, one boot scuffing at the floorboard, knowing what her next question would be.

"What would you dream of, Davor?"

So many things. We used to play this game when I was younger and full of more than anger. There had been no point in dreaming for a long time.

She waited for a reply, and I indulged for a moment.

"I'd dream of peace, and no fear. Where words aren't weapons, and knives don't wait around corners. Where everyone in this lodge is free of the shadow of him, and can make their way without scorn."

"And what of the villages? What would you do for them?" Urgency lined her question, and I sent her the same assessing look she had given me.

"What dreams have you been having?"

She did not smile. If anything, she stood taller, stronger. "If you could take a place in this tribe, what would you do with it?"

"Nothing. Because it would never be."

She shook her head. "What if it was?"

"What do you want from me?" The question hissed from me.

"I want you to *live*, not just survive. I want to see a change in this tribe, and I know you can do it. Wars brings many opportunities. Perhaps it holds something for you." She swept around me, returning to the common room.

I stared after her, the words burrowing inside though I tried not to let them. They held a truth that had been lurking deep inside since the chief had declared we'd be riding out come spring. If I lived long enough to ride out with the warriors, I might have a chance to make a name for myself. Take more noticeable power in the tribe. Make sure the lodge weathered the change in power when Kamil surely killed the chief.

But Michal was right. I would have to *act*, step out in defiance, gather my own support from warriors who had never given me much respect through my own doing. Dreaming and doing were different things, and I was perhaps not very good at the second thing.

TWO

DAVOR

I spent the night in the small lodge, sleeping atop one of the benches shoved against the wall covered in extra furs and blankets. Like Michal, I did not spend any extra time in the chieftain's lodge atop the hill.

He stayed on the benches against the opposite wall where Janne also slept. I did not fear anything he might do, but it was not easy between us.

Dawn broke as slivers of light through the animal skins covering the narrow windows. I watched it track a slow path across the floor while my mother's words came again and again to my mind, clinging to me even as I tried to refute them. The lodge remained quiet except for the quiet rustle of embers on the hearth, bringing with it a chill trying to whisper its way under the furs.

The heavy ceiling beams were darker slashes in the shadows above me. Sometimes in the chieftain's lodge they supported a sablecat who watched with knowing yellow eyes as warriors passed by underneath or slept under its gaze.

Not here, under a shallow ceiling and more peaceful rooms. I wondered what it might be like to wake every day in the quiet. To not already be looking for what trouble might be coming from the other benches. If I would feel any safer if I raised my place in the tribe.

I scraped the remainders of sleep from my eyes and sat up, fishing my shirt from where it had fallen at my side. Shivering a little in the cold of the lodge, I pulled it and the overtunic on and slid feet back into boots.

My rising had not bothered the twins. I quietly rolled the furs up and folded the blankets, straightening out my clothes as I did. Crossing to the fire on silent feet, I built it back up, the snaps of flames biting into new logs cracking through the quiet.

"Davor."

I turned at the murmur and Janne's bright eyes peered out from under her blankets.

"Are you staying for breakfast?" she whispered.

I shook my head, hating myself a little at the disappointment crossing her face. She hadn't had to learn quite so quickly the ways to mask her expressions. Not like her true brother and me.

But I crossed over and touched her shoulder. "Tell Nina I am sorry." My low voice did not disturb Michal.

Janne nodded and dug out an arm to catch my hand. She squeezed my fingers and understanding shone bright in her eyes. She did not feel the weight of surviving our father and brothers as much as we did, but she still saw it day after day. It frightened me a little that she might understand me.

I gently squeezed back and freed my hand to leave.

"Davor." Her whisper stopped me again. "Nina told you."

The firelight caught the fear in her eyes. Fear at being bartered away to a man the way her mother had been. No choice in the matter.

"Does Michal know?"

"No." A hitch accompanied the word. "He would do something foolish if he did."

The look she turned to me was reminiscent of my mother's. One asking me to do something about it. But I had no command in the matter, and pushing my way in would only make it worse for Janne and our mothers. It was too dangerous to show caring for another.

"Do you know who?"

Her blankets muffled a sniff. "Just that it's one of Makar's pack."

Kamil's second. A man who enjoyed misery, and who hated me maybe as much as I hated him. And one who would gladly follow Kamil's rise and take whatever he could along the way. His name was enough to have me saying, "I will do something if I can."

I felt her eyes still on me as I went to the door and buckled on my sword. Sweeping my cloak around my shoulders, I stepped out into the dawn.

The sky remained clear, only a few wisps of clouds turned pink by the rising sun. The snow had crusted over under the moon's touch, each step sinking through the new layer and into the softness lurking underneath.

A glance around confirmed I was one of the first out and about. The tribe was slow to stir in the winter months when the cold and snow pressed close. But it would not do for anyone to see me leaving my mother's lodge. It had been a moment of weakness leading me to take a bench there last night.

My path tracked back up to the chieftain's lodge settled on one of the knobbled knees of the towering Half Peak—its internal fire quenched long ago when legend said the Saber spirit lulled it to sleep to give his people a place to settle. If it woke again, it would be because we were somehow worse than we already were.

Woodsmoke coming from the *talånd's* lodge brought me to a pause. Or what was meant to be his lodge. He stayed in the chieftain's more often than not, keeping close to try to calm the chief with herbs and smoke when his mind slipped into a wild rage. Though I'd most often seen the *talånd* at tables instead of anywhere near the spirits' lodge, despite being named as the bridge between us and the All-Father.

Curiosity stirred, I angled my steps instead up a small incline from the chieftain's lodge. The smoke came from behind the lodge at the end of the path. Circling the broad structure, I found a stranger sitting by the fire, aimlessly staring at the low flames. A cloak of light grey wrapped tight around him, matching the streaks in his short, dark hair.

Understanding dawned. The new Greywolf chieftain had exiled their *talånd* as well as Hakkon for daring to join the rebellion against him. I wondered again about the new chief and how he would rule.

The *talånd* stirred as I came forward, drawn to the fire almost like a moth to light. Recognition lurked in his eyes.

"What can I do for the chieftain's son?" he asked.

My entire being rebelled against the title. But I sat across from him.

Hakkon was filled with rage and angry words. But the man in

front of me looked broken. Perhaps I might get a truer account of the tribe from him.

"Your fellow Greywolf calls for war against your tribe," I said.

The wrinkles around his eyes grew deeper. "Hakkon has always been tempestuous. It led me to listen when I should not and here I am." A sigh lonelier than winter winds over the plains broke from him.

"He has bold words. Perhaps you can tell me what we might face in the valley."

The *talånd* stirred, pulling his boots closer to the log and leaning forward on his knees. "You think I would give up my tribe just like that?"

"You did not seem to suffer much from your conscience when you turned on the chief."

He allowed it with a tip of his head. "And the spirits saw me punished for that. Perhaps Etran will be a better chief than I thought."

"What kind of man is he?" I leaned forward.

"Quiet. Steady, despite his place in the tribe."

I tilted my head, confused.

"Reidar took a woman outside the marriage bond and had him. Many were not happy with it or Etran being raised as a chieftain's son and made sure he knew it."

My gaze slipped back to the villages and the chieftain's lodge looming high over all. No one would say anything to my father's face, or to our faces, for fear of retribution, but I knew many did not like the way our mothers had been used. I heard just as much as Emil did. The Greywolves must be bold indeed to be so open.

"But it seems he is just. He could have killed us. His

battlewolf was ready to do it himself despite being wounded protecting him."

Hakkon had not said much about the battlewolf, only that he was untested. And my mother's words grew a little louder in the back of my mind.

"Tell me about the battlewolf."

Would they have any chance to stop our invasion, perhaps kill Kamil? My heart quickened a beat at the thought of Kamil gone. And what that might mean for me. If I could change my place.

"Etran named the chief's true son as battlewolf despite them being at odds these twenty-three years."

This drew my eyebrow up. I couldn't imagine Kamil giving the position to any one of us.

The *talånd* gave a small laugh. "This surprised many as well. But Comran threw himself to the task as he does in all things. He is a restless soul, already esteemed among the warriors. And he has thrown in behind his half-brother."

There was a sort of probing edge to the statement that I did not respond to.

"You will have great resistance from him leading the wolf packs." He seemed grimly pleased about this.

"You think he will be a match for us?" We had been testing the borders for seasons, scrapping with their wolf packs with the borders still holding. We knew their old battlewolf, a gruff warrior who gave no quarter and asked for none.

The mirthless smile shone again in the *talånd's* face. "Comran has never given surrender even when perhaps he should. And I think Hakkon underestimates his cousin as he did when planning the strike against the chief."

The Greywolf might, but Kamil had a cunning streak

alongside the broader cruelty. If the battlewolf could keep his head, perhaps they had a chance.

What would you dream of?

Something took root in my heart. War brought many things. Perhaps I might have a chance if I had the courage to take it.

"That's all?" The *talånd's* voice tilted surprise as I stood.

I pulled my cloak closer around my shoulders. "Packs and weapons mean nothing without the knowledge of the men who make them up."

He sat back and regarded me a little closer. "You are the first to come see me."

"And can I trust you to keep that between us?"

He inclined his head. "I cannot wish you luck against my former tribe. I brought this exile upon myself, a fact I can see clear enough without the spirits' aid. But I can offer a caution." A change slanted over his eyes, and I knew that I should heed the next words for they might be from the spirits themselves.

"Discord has grown among the Greywolves because of the chieftain's actions, but it is rife here, the actions of many causing the spirits to weep and the All-Father to mourn."

A shiver raced down my arms, burrowing to my bones the way the winter wind could not.

"A reckoning will come."

"Is there a way to stop it?" My voice came hushed despite how strongly I tried to ask.

"Tell me if you think it just to stop it?" The piercing gaze leveled at me near stopped my heart.

"Perhaps not all deserve to be caught up in it." My mother, Janne, the innocent also just trying to survive…

"Would you stop it?"

Would I? My mother's words, my own secret wishes buried

deep, the *talånd's* words—it all rushed together in a terrifying mix, settling into a thought so dangerous I should have kept it to myself. I slowly lifted my gaze from where it had fallen to the fire.

"I would see this tribe changed into something different." It whispered from me, lingering in the air like a heavy-weighted promise. One I had never made to anyone. I'd never been enough to protect, guide, make safe for others.

"What would you give to make it so?"

I could not shift from his gaze. What would I? Everything seemed too much. I had never given a part of myself to anyone, to anything.

"I don't know." It was perhaps one of the truest things I'd ever said.

The *talånd* nodded, shifting his gaze back to the fire, compressing into an older man weighted under his own cares and regrets again.

"It will not be easy. But you must know and accept the cost before you start. Otherwise you will fail."

I backed away, retreating from the words. My entire life had been planning three steps ahead, picking the path with the lowest cost, staying safe within my own confines, protecting as I could.

I had miscounted twice and bore the scars from both occasions. The sweet scent of smoke followed me to the chieftain's lodge, the *talånd's* words whispering in my ears over and over.

Words that sounded like he knew something before I did, even if that thing had only been spoken of in hushed tones between my mother and me the night previous. I halted, tilting a look back over my shoulder, then forward to the sweeping beams of the chief's lodge.

If I wanted anything more than watching over my shoulder and keeping to the shadows, I needed to decide how to step forward. If I wanted to protect Janne from a careless warrior, I needed more power than I had. If I wanted to make sure my mother kept living, I needed to become stronger.

If what the Greywolf *talånd* said was true, and a reckoning was coming for the tribe, perhaps I could shield those who did not deserve it.

And the war would be the place for me to start.

THREE

DAVOR

The morning meal had begun by the time I entered the lodge, but the chief did not sit at the head table.

"Davor." Kamil's voice cut over the low chatter.

A break in conversations brought eyes flickering to me, then back to their meals, assuming another spat between half-brothers was coming.

"Father wants you."

Kamil stood at the top of the hall atop the raised platform that held the chief's chair. Wall hangings flanked the doors which led into the chieftain's chambers. I hated the proud sablecat on the right and the warrior holding spear and curved sword on the left.

Glances followed me as I passed between the double row of long tables filled with pack leaders always there to vie for favor, and those who lived in the towering lodge. A stirring on one of the benches brought my attention flicking to Alik for a moment. He inclined his head, some small show of support that I would not respond to because Kamil watched my every move.

"Where's the whelp?" Kamil blocked my way.

"Am I supposed to know the whereabouts of everyone in this tribe? Ask your shadow," I returned.

His hand moved from the door latch to grip my cloak and lean close. "And where were you last night?"

Dark eyes bored into mine, but I did not flinch. "Jealous I might have somewhere more interesting to be?"

Eyes narrowing, he moved even closer. "I heard a rumor you went to the healer's lodge."

"Are you trying to get me to admit that I had a training injury and wanted some salve?" Lying came as easily to me as anger did to him.

"Your mother lives there with the healer, doesn't she?" He watched me for any reaction. "Interesting that you should go there when you banished her from this lodge years ago."

"Is there a point here, or should I worry that you are already following our father's path?"

He shoved me and my foot slid back a fraction to steady. Then his attention shifted past me.

"There he is. Whelp!" he called. My fist tightened in the folds of my cloak, but I did not turn to see the anger leaking from Michal. Instead, I pushed past Kamil and into the chieftain's room.

Emil was already there, sitting at the low table, picking dirt from under his thumbnail with a small knife. The chieftain paced back and forth behind him.

So it was to be a restless day, but perhaps not one of sudden mood swings and forgetfulness that only lent more anger to his heart.

"You are late, Davor." The chief's gravelly voice cut across the room.

"I did not realize there was to be a council."

"He was not here last night, Father." Emil smirked, and his attention shifted to the door. "Neither was Michal." Sharpness lingered in the smile.

Michal scowled back, jerking his shoulder out from under Kamil's touch.

"Where were you both?" the chief asked.

"I had business to attend to," I said.

"What's her name?" The corner of Emil's mouth tucked back up.

My even gaze did not shift with the anger coiling around my heart. "Some of us have more profitable uses of our time than you, Emil."

The tip of his knife dug into the table.

"Michal?" The chief's voice did not lose its sharpness.

The boy looked up, tenseness in his jaw and fists.

"Where were you?" The tone brooked no argument.

"Home," Michal muttered sullenly.

"What have I told you about that?" The chief scowled. "It only invites weakness, and I will not have that in my sons."

Kamil leaned close to Michal, his words still clear enough for all of us. "How is your sister?"

Michal invited Kamil to take himself to the dark woods with haste and received a fist to his jaw in exchange that sent him to his knee. I slid arms across my chest. He had to learn, even if he was getting more clever with his retorts and insults.

Michal lurched back up, swiping some blood from his lips and glaring hate at Kamil who only laughed.

"You will speak to your brother and battlelion with more respect," the chief growled.

Michal's glare at the ground assured he had not yet learned the lesson on how to layer his words and pick his fights.

"I have summoned you all here to discuss each future. Kamil will lead the packs to war when the snows abate."

Triumph leered through Kamil's smile.

"Davor, you will be his second."

Kamil's arms loosened across his chest in surprise. "What? Makar is my *rokr,* and I have no need of another."

I better controlled my shock and the twisting of my gut at Makar's name. Emil's knife ground deeper in the table. The chief looked between us.

"You forget, Kamil, that I have not chosen an heir yet. You will all prove yourselves in this war. Davor is your *rokr.*"

It made Kamil subside only for a moment. "The boy?"

Michal stood a little taller, and my stomach clenched at the way the chief regarded him closely.

"I do not think I want a boy in the packs. Not in war," I said.

All eyes turned to me.

The chief frowned. "You were seventeen when you rode to war."

And I was too young, my heart screamed back. "The Greywolves are more ferocious than the Blackpaws. I want real warriors at my back."

"I can do it," Michal protested, the idiot.

"Kamil, you are battlelion." The chief ignored his youngest's outburst, looking instead to the oldest.

Kamil watched me carefully, but I ignored Michal and his searing glare at me.

"I will listen to my *rokr's* voice." He spat the new title that I had no desire for. "Another few countings on the practice field could do him good." And then he'd be on the frontlines, the promise was clear. Kamil had a chance to rid himself of us, and he was going to take it.

"Good." The chief nodded sharply. "Kamil and Davor, I expect councils with the both of you as we plan for war."

We both brought fists to our foreheads in respect. The chief left and Kamil turned on me. His broader bulk shoved me back against the wall and this time I let him see my anger and discontent with the naming.

"I will allow this for now," he murmured between us. "But cross me again, in anything, and I will take you from this earth even sooner than I might plan. Am I understood?"

My heart counted out five beats before I allowed a faint smile. Doubt flickered in his eyes before I answered slowly. "Perfectly... Battlelion."

He shoved me again with a scoff and left. Emil followed him, sending a probing look at me as he passed.

"Davor."

I ignored Michal's voice and made my way from the lodge, any appetite gone. A piece had been unexpectedly handed to me, like the chief might know I had already decided to make a bid for power, and I needed to think it over. Brisk footsteps followed me across the common room, and back into the clean air under clouds which had begun to form again.

"Davor." Michal grabbed my shoulder, backing away as I whirled on him, yanking out from the hold. His throat bobbed and I eased my grip on my knife.

"You know I can hold my own in the packs." Some doubt and anger played in his face.

"*Think*, Michal." I leaned close to him, frustrated with the quick temper of his youth. "Do you believe that Kamil will place you with a pack leader who cares about you? Who would try to protect you along with his men? No, he will see you on the frontlines where that bow will be useless, and you will fall to a wolf-rider. And then he will be free one less brother."

A bit of horror took over his eyes and he edged away. "So, you are trying to protect me then?" It came with nearly as much venom as if he'd said it to Kamil. "I don't *want* your help."

"Then why are you here?"

He shifted restlessly on his feet, no answer coming.

I shook my head. "War is not what they say it is."

Michal scoffed. "You were my age when you rode out. Maybe I would actually earn respect and position in a pack."

"And then do what with it?" I asked.

"More than you." All bluster, all yearning for something he thought he could find on the battlefield. But I had no better way to show him how to reach manhood. I'd made my own way all my life.

But something prodded my heart. I'd had no one to soften the horrors of war. No one to look out for me in the packs. I'd never thought to ally myself with a half-brother, but with this one, perhaps I stood a chance.

"Kamil has plans for this war. Only a fool could not see that." My voice stayed between the two of us. "Perhaps he is not the only one. Perhaps I would see a better future for our mothers, for Janne."

He scowled, not liking that I was using his sister against him.

"She did always like you for some reason," he muttered.

A smile almost broke through. "You will ride to war soon enough. And I will do what I can there for you if you want."

"To ally with you?" He arched an eyebrow. "I would have no more chance with you than with Kamil. Except from him I might learn strength."

Perhaps he was learning after all.

"Much can happen in war."

Caution lined up his shoulders and he leaned back. "And then what?"

"I am tired, Michal. Of so many things."

His dark green eyes lifted to mine and I think for the first time, he realized how much of the same we were. But he still made no move.

"Then perhaps we'll see if you still live when I join the packs." He spun on his heel, quiver rattling, and strode down the path.

Luk swept up beside me, rumbling deep in his throat as he watched Michal vanish into the village. I rubbed under the lion's jaw. Footsteps approached, and Luk's lips curled back from his fangs. My hand closed about a knife again, bracing as Makar's bulk slammed into my shoulder.

"You are *rokr* now," he sneered, breath puffing in hot bursts between us. "How did you grovel to get that place?"

"The chief gave it to me and Kamil accepted." Not willingly, but Makar would turn from verbal threats soon enough. Might as well get through it. Luk's claws ground into the snow, his growl rumbling deeper as Makar crowded closer.

"Oh, he's already told me. The packs will not accept you, coward." We stood eye-to-eye. A few brighter strands were woven in a small braid through his warrior's mark, and a sablecat fang hung from a leather cord about his neck.

"Perhaps we'll see." An almost alarming boldness crept through my voice.

It only brought a sneer to Makar's lips. "Remember last time you tried to be something you're not?"

The question and memory slithered deep, threatening to crush the spark of boldness.

"Enjoy it while it lasts, Davor." He grabbed a fistful of my tunic. Luk's snarl made Makar pause only for a second. I grabbed the former *rokr's* wrist, halting him a heartbeat more, but he did not release me just yet.

"I still have my place, and will enjoy watching you fail. Maybe even hold you down again when Kamil or your father finally kills you."

With that, he shoved into my chest, releasing his hold and walking away, a swagger in his steps. It wasn't until he had vanished that a shaky breath escaped from me. Luk pushed into my side, rattling threat making way for a purr.

"Davor."

I tensed to fight before I recognized Alik's voice. The pack leader stood two paces away, something like concern in his eyes as he watched me.

"What?" I snapped.

He did not flinch, and did not come any closer. "The news is already rampant. You are lead *rokr* now."

Lead *rokr*. Of course Kamil would not cast his devoted accomplice completely away. And he likely needed someone the packs would actually obey.

I jerked a nod.

"A *rokr* needs a pack," he said carefully and I froze. I did not have a pack who answered to me. Did not have many besides Alik who looked at me with anything other than contempt. Another reason the path I'd contemplated choosing was steeper than Half Peak.

"So you think to pledge me yours?" I tilted a glance at him, but there was no malice hiding underneath his expression. "Think twice before you assign the lowest place to your men."

He nodded. "I already have. I'd have done it anyway if you weren't *rokr.*"

A brittle sound escaped. "Then you have no sense."

Alik gave a faint chuckle, angling to stand beside me where my hand still clenched in Luk's fur.

"I've fought you on the training grounds, Davor. Watched you walk these paths. You're not weak. I think we stand a good chance with you at our head."

Something lodged in my chest. *Not weak.* But not strong either. "No wonder you are terrible at counting sticks and runes."

His laugh echoed again. "What do you say, Davor? Will you take a middle village pack?" This time there was a tenseness in his voice. A distaste for the way he and his men were still looked down on as *less* because they hailed from the middle instead of the coveted upper village. Perhaps he thought I'd scorn him for the same thing.

But I needed a pack, and no one else was rushing to swear their swords to me. And that glimmer reappeared, building into a spark. The faint hope that perhaps I could seize some sort of power in the war. At least see Janne protected before we rode out. The chief had handed me a better position from which to start. And my own pack would be the first step.

"I will."

⌒

Winter crept by, rumors of war growing into full-fledged preparations as ice and snow began to recede from the banks, melting a little quicker under the sun's touch. Janne was forgotten in the promise of war, and with my almost nauseating boldness at hinting to the chief that as lead *rokr*, I might want to see her given somewhere else. But once we returned, her future would be decided for her.

Despite my words with Michal, we still kept our distance, but he threw himself into practice on the training grounds, growing a name for himself more than he already had. It was all I could do to make sure that he would be left behind when the packs rode, hoping to keep him away from war a little longer.

I went to councils with Kamil, my father, and Makar, still claiming a place as the newly formed second *rokr*. The chief did not gainsay it, and looked sharply at me when I did not either. But I was more interested in learning how to tread the new paths of the leadership bestowed on me and navigating around my sudden constant proximity to Kamil to pick fights with Makar.

Hakkon was there as well, trying to push for a faster attack even though he knew better than us the deepness of the snows up valley. Their wolves might be able to navigate it, but at least we all agreed that we would not send our sablecats yet if the valley itself was against us.

After one of these councils where Kamil glared promises of death at me, and the chief brooded in his chair, I stepped out into the clearer air. A sheen of snow still covered the ground, but a few daring flowers had lifted their blue heads through the clumps and shivered together in the light breeze.

It wouldn't be much longer until I saddled Luk and led warriors out.

"We ride soon?" Alik stepped up beside me, staring at the flowers with me.

"Yes."

He grunted and crossed his arms. "Come to my lodge for the meal tonight."

I withdrew a little, but he shook his head.

"Davor, I pledged my pack to you, and you accepted."

Because a *rokr* needed a pack, and I needed someone I could almost trust following my orders in battle.

"The rest of the men need to see you as well. It's easier to fight and die for a man they at least see once in awhile."

The thought of going into a lodge I'd never been in sent shivers down my arms. Easy enough to set an ambush. But Alik's face remained open, no trace of hidden malice I was good at finding lurking in his eyes.

Even I had to admit that he was right. To keep this new foothold in the tribe, I needed to gain the loyalty of men. So I nodded, and tried not to take offense at the way his eyes widened slightly in surprise.

But I was not about to confess that no one had openly invited me in friendship to their lodge to share a meal. I never let anyone get close enough for such a thing, because they could all too easily be used against me or broken themselves.

He clapped a hand against my shoulder and my fist clenched in response as I promised to meet him in the middle village come the evening meal.

As the sun sank lower, I headed for the river bridge. The sense of eyes following me prickled down my spine, but it was not an uncommon sensation, much like the way cold would bring shivers.

The bridge between the upper and middle village had supports sunk into the riverbed instead of swinging loose like the one between the middle and lower village. The railing stood strong despite the runes etched into the wood—names of lovers, youths playing pranks, or small bits of art left by some nameless tribesperson years ago.

Under the even planks, the river pushed at the boulders standing in its way, its constant rushing grumble threatening to wear them away like so many before them. From Hakkon's account, the great river ran more placid through the valley before spilling over the rapids at the border stones and churning its way through our territory.

Soon enough I'd see. I paused, watching it rush downstream, making its way through the open plains down to where our southern border stones gave way to Pronghorn territory. A plume of white misted up into the sky in the distance—a geyser roaring free after pushing its way up from the earth, caring nothing for snow or rain or sun, just that it was free.

A sudden wondering struck—why I was looking at these different things, at the strange stirring it made in my heart. Wondering if I would miss it once we rode north. If I would come back to see it once more.

Many things in my life I did not care for, but these collections of lodges, open plains, pooling hot springs, sudden geysers, and the forest looming to the west with its gentle shafts of sunlight and scent of pine, had a hold on my heart, had wound around my bones. The Saber spirit might have given me anger, but he'd also given me pride in the land.

"Excuse me." A quiet voice broke my reverie. I jolted and turned to see a woman standing a few paces away.

We stared at one another, and my heart gave an odd squeeze.

Marta. This was not the first time we'd come face-to-face, but now there was only caution and maybe a little contempt for me in her face.

She lifted a hand and gestured past me. I moved from where I'd stopped in the middle of the bridge, giving her space around me.

Marta did not move, arms now crossing tight over her embroidered overdress. There was always so much color about her, stitched in her dresses and long tunics. It always drew my eyes unwillingly to her, the times I saw her walking the villages. We were caught in a silent staring match again, before a bit of understanding filtered in.

She would not want to walk past me, where anything could happen. She was headed the same way I was—to the middle village, and she would not want me at her back either.

So I dipped my head in a slight nod and walked away, my steps a fraction quicker than before, giving her more space. But some part of me wanted to look back and see if she did follow.

FOUR

MARTA

He was in my lodge. I sent a glare heavenward as if the spirits actually resided in lodge rafters. First at the bridge when he'd blocked my way, and now sitting beside Alik with the rest of the warriors.

Davor, one of the cursed sons of the even more cursed chief. My glare was only slightly less potent than my sister's where she sat beside me.

"What is *he* doing here?" she hissed in my ear.

The small knife in my hand squeaked against the wooden plate. "I heard Alik invited him. They will be his pack in the war."

"Maybe all four of them will die." Vanda sent another bleak stare at him.

My heart twisted and I rested a gentle hand on her wrist. Her anger faltered, crumpling her shoulders. I gently squeezed and she lifted her head enough to give me a small smile. She knew better than most how careless and violent the chief's sons could be and that there was nothing to be done against them.

The war would take them away. It would not take our father, one of the best hunters in the village. Though I was old enough to remember the Blackpaw war that had claimed him as a scout. Perhaps the packs would not grow lean enough to call him this time.

I'd long thought I wanted a brother as well, but now that war cries were sounding every day, I was more grateful my mother only had daughters who had no interest in the training grounds, sablecats, and spears.

"They will be gone soon enough." I tapped her arm and returned to my meal, though his presence at the other table was enough to sour it in my mouth.

I did not know much about him. No one did. Only what they whispered after he passed, face unreadable, hair cut short with no one knowing why since he'd done nothing open to dishonor himself as a warrior. His father would have made it a public spectacle if he had.

No, instead I knew too much about Emil, the man who had hurt my sister. About Kamil who ruled the warriors and anyone who crossed his path with a fist of hot iron. No one had much hope for the youngest, Michal, either. He seemed many days to be following the path of his brothers.

Davor's gaze met mine across the room, and I was caught back in that strange moment at the bridge when he'd seemed almost wistful, his stern features almost giving away what he was thinking.

I looked away. There was another time I'd been close enough to see into his dark eyes. A time when I thought for a moment that he might not be like his brothers. When he'd seemed…kind. But that was years ago, when his hair was longer, and we were younger, and fewer stories were whispered about him.

I wondered if he remembered it.

Perhaps I would tell Vanda of today and years ago tonight as we curled under our furs on the benches. I would not tell my father. He would hear no word, ill or otherwise, on the chief's sons, only because it might bring fire down upon us from any direction. But the way Vanda's teeth were grinding beside me, she likely would not want to hear it either.

When I felt brave enough again, I snuck another glance from under my eyelashes. Many of the warriors were a little too loud, perhaps covering for the unease they felt at him sitting among them. Only Alik seemed comfortable, but I'd seen him talking to Davor before when I had business in the upper village.

I lifted my head a little. Davor seemed just as cautious among them. Perhaps he was always silent, but he did not do much to interact with the warriors. Instead watching them with the sharp eyes I'd gotten a close look at on the bridge.

With an effort, I turned my attention back to my food. I heard the rumors as much as anyone. Within another counting, they would be riding away. And perhaps in the spirits' mercy, some of the chief's sons would not be riding back.

FIVE

ΔAVOR

"Sleeping on watch. He is part of your packs, Davor; you will administer the punishment." Kamil watched me with a fiendish smile. I turned slowly to the young man on his knees in front of me, armor already stripped off in preparation for Kamil's usual punishment.

His head hung low, and fists curled around the hem of his tunic. His spear lay in front of him, ready for me to pick up and strike against his back as many times as I felt was necessary for such an offense.

"Very well. He has double watch duty for the next three nights," I said.

"What?" the young warrior echoed Kamil's sharper exclamation before ducking his head again.

I shrugged. "You told me to administer the punishment, Battlelion. I have. Though if I see him again for the same offense, perhaps something harsher will be needed."

Kamil stepped closer to me, steam practically rolling off his shoulders like he'd just stepped from a hot spring. "You know my rules, Davor."

I did. And I'd found ways to avoid as many of his punishments as I could over the turnings he'd been battlelion. And had no wish to hand them out myself.

"My packs and I have seen three skirmishes and a full battle in the last three days. We are all tired, Battlelion." I inclined my head slightly. Kamil had taken the warriors and boys too young to ride and brought us into the valley where we found a brash opponent against the Greywolves and their battlewolf.

"And if I was to find you sleeping on watch?"

"Then I would submit to your rules."

"Would you, Davor?" he asked softly.

My gaze flicked to his for a moment, and we both had our answer. He raised his fist and I knew better than to block it. My tongue swept away bits of blood from the inside of my lip as he stalked away, but he had not gainsaid my order.

"Alik."

The warrior snapped to attention.

"See to it he's placed on double watch the next three days."

Alik tapped his fist to his chest once, dangerously close to the double tap given to the battlelion. He had to haul the stunned warrior up by one arm before the man shook free and regarded me with cautious eyes.

"As I said, if I find you in front of me again for the same offense, it will be something harsher."

He nodded frantically, scooping up his spear and retreating with Alik.

"I did not think it would be so amusing to watch you try to

lead." Makar swept around me, and I shifted to follow his path.

"Do we not need men in saddles in order to lead?" I replied.

He scoffed, leaning forward. "We don't need cowards."

My fingers flexed involuntarily, then straightened. "You have two packs to take on patrol, *second rokr.*"

He went still, and his gaze locked on to me. Angry and evaluating in a new way. He surged forward a step and I rocked a little in response. A smirk flickered at my reaction, even as I told myself it wasn't fear of him, it was readiness to get away.

"Remember how we deal with cowards...*Rokr.*" And he strode off.

My grip on my knife handle eased until motion drew my attention to Emil in the shadows beneath the looming pines.

He did not look amused or threatening. Eerily assessing like Makar. "You think Kamil will tolerate this for long?"

It took me aback for a moment. "Worried for me?"

And the younger half-brother I was more familiar with emerged, scorn in his eyes. "No, but perhaps I'll make sure to give a last 'I warned you' before he kills you."

We gave each other scoffing half-sneers before parting ways. But I looked over my shoulder as I did. We had never been close, but there had been a time many years ago, before Kamil and Father got their claws in him, that Emil had warned me of incoming danger.

There was no point in wondering where that boy had gone. He'd vanished when the boy who dared to hope that he could see something good in the world died inside me.

"Davor." Alik fell in beside me. There was true concern in his face. "You should be more careful of the battlelion."

"Telling me to be careful of my own blood, Alik?" I asked mildly.

He tilted his head. "Sometimes I think you might need the reminder."

"If anything happens, it will come down on me. Do not worry."

"That's not…" Alik stopped, and his hand chopped down in frustration. It made me pause, discomfort prickling like a burr under my sleeve. "You've always seemed a fair man. There are three packs under your direct control as *rokr*." He darted a look around. "I can make sure that any discipline is brought to you first."

Daring filled the words and the prickle dug deeper. Circumventing Kamil further, giving me some of the deference due to a battlelion. Did he know the thoughts I'd yet to give full voice to as I struggled to find my footing as *rokr*?

My tongue froze, not sure how to warn him off though another part tried to remind me that I needed allies.

"Do what you think is best for the packs, Alik."

A faint smile flickered across his face before he gave the dangerous salute again. But the next day, Kamil ordered us back to battle. My punishment for what I'd done.

But the packs mounted and looked to me as I settled my spear at my side and gathered up the reins. Fresh red warpaint lined our faces in sharp edges. The Greywolves added white paint to their green to honor their fallen. We had no such tradition. Perhaps not anymore. But some did mark runes for the dead on their bracers or etched it onto spears. Some small ways to carry them to battle again.

Luk grumbled in his chest as I nudged him forward, but he pressed up to a lope, the other sablecats falling in loose lines behind me. Paws were sore, some pads had split, even a few broken fangs throughout the packs. The two packs we joined up with had no such injuries, and their pack leader wore a smug expression as I led the way out of camp.

I did not like this valley. Small streams ran into the wide river meandering its way through. Sporadic clusters of forests, broad plains, temperamental great elk and bison who would charge if you did not approach their herds the right way for the kill.

Not enough open space, mountains leering to the east, towering high with looming peaks threatening to fall over if you stared at them long enough. I wanted plains stretching as far as the eye could see, pools of hot springs, geysers, tamer forests with trees that knew how to cluster together. Free of the grey-wolves' incessant howling and riders with anger and fire in their eyes.

I wanted home, but fate conspired against it.

We limped into camp, sentries raising some eyebrows at the amount of wounded we brought with us, contrary to Kamil's usual orders to leave the wounded to find their own way back. The Greywolves had just as many victories and defeats as we did, but thanks to Kamil's orders, our ranks would dwindle quicker.

I helped some down from saddles, getting them to ground where the healers pushed in.

The pack leader who had mocked with a smile before riding out, paused in front of me, face drawn under his warpaint. His jaw worked a moment before he nodded.

"Thank you."

"How many did you lose?" I asked.

His hands clenched tight and a ragged breath escaped with the admission, "Half the spears, but most of the archers made it through. We would have lost more if…" He faltered, looking away.

If Kamil had been leading.

"Get your packs taken care of. I'll see what I can do to make sure you get a day of rest."

He saluted, and moved off, a little more purpose in his stride.

"And what of us?" Alik asked wryly, coming to stand beside me as we looked out over the wounded.

I raised bloody hands, regarding them for a moment, before wiping them against each other and dislodging some of the drying flakes.

"I will see what I can do." But I did not have any more hope than he did that Kamil would forgive us for losing a battle.

It did not take long to face his fury. I stopped only to wash some of the blood from my hands before going to face him. Alik clung to my heels, though he was not needed to report.

Kamil stood in the center of the tent circle, arms crossed over his chest. Sablecats lounged about or crouched in the trees—perches they had gladly taken to once we had entered the valley.

"Davor." His voice growled deeper than some of our burlier lions.

"Battlelion." I gave the double tap salute to my chest. "Scouts drew us to a battle with the Greywolves, but they took the field this time."

Kamil's eyes narrowed. I held steady. This was not the first time I'd reported a loss.

"I see you brought back wounded, *Rokr*."

"Yes, Battlelion."

"Cowards who could not hold their weapons in a fight?"

This time my back teeth slid against each other. "Men who were too wounded to keep fighting. We had a chance to bring them back and I took it."

"That is not our way." He was in my face, fire in his dark eyes. *Not your way.*

"With respect, Battlelion, how do you expect to win a war without men?" It snapped from me. "If I left every wounded man, there would be no one left to fill the saddles, to raise spears."

"We send for more." He shrugged carelessly. Like the chief had in the Blackpaw war and I could—*would not* watch the rampant death happen again.

My anger broke free, and I shoved forward a step. Surprise sparked in his eyes as for once, I challenged him.

"So you would strip the villages bare of boys and men who do not ride with the packs? Who will be left then? Will you drive us to extinction for a traitor's war?"

Hands latched onto my shoulders and pulled me back. Kamil's chest heaved with anger, it burned out of his eyes. My armor pressed too tight around me as I tried to regain any sense of balance. Deathly silence reigned around us; even the sablecats sat alert, ears pricked forward.

"I spoke out of turn, Battlelion." But even my slightly deeper bow could not save me.

"Take his armor."

I flung up a hand, pausing the warriors who reached for me, and undid my sword belt and breastplate. Kamil glanced pointedly at the ground when I finished.

Gritting my teeth, I knelt.

"Where is your spear, *Rokr?*"

"Left in a greywolf on the field, Battlelion."

"Then your sword will do."

One breath in, slowly out. Then I unsheathed my sword and handed it to him, my mask back in place. As his hand closed about the hilt, my heart wavered. There was a curious light in his eyes as he weighed the weapon, and, as the point swished down to press under my jaw, I wondered if I had just handed him the blade to kill me.

The same thought played across his face, followed by a deadly smile. He was thinking on it. But instead, the tip skimmed around my jaw to brush over the scar on the back of my neck.

"I am starting to wonder, Davor, if the cowardice you show in retreating from battle is the reason you lost your warrior's mark years ago."

I said nothing. We both knew how I had lost it. Even if no one else in the tribe did.

He circled around to my side. I flinched as he suddenly leaned down beside my ear, breath hot against my cheek as he whispered, "I am going to enjoy every second of this. You have had this coming for countings, Davor. I hope you remember your place."

Then he straightened and the flat of my own blade crashed against my back. The impact threw me forward and I caught myself with one hand, fingers digging deep into the grass and dirt as he struck again and again.

Blood filled my mouth as I bit through my cheek. The force of the iron reverberated through my bones. The world shrank to the blades of grass, the grains of dirt sliding through my clenching fingers.

Until finally, my sword fell down in front of me.

"Remember," Kamil whispered again before he strode off.

Slowly, slowly, I released my hold on the earth, and lurched to grab the sword hilt. Each breath stabbed hot spikes through my chest. I spat out blood, breaking getting back to my tent into smaller tasks.

Sheathe the sword. Take the breastplate. Hands shaking. Standing, staggering forward.

Warriors stared, but as my gaze swept around, they found other things to do. Alik appeared in my narrowed vision. He reached out, then backed away at whatever he saw on my face.

Step after step, across the circle, to the tent where Luk waited, concerned growl in his chest. I pushed through the tent flap, and my armor fell from my hands. Staggering forward one more step, I collapsed down to hands and knees, nausea from the blinding pain finally breaking free.

My chest heaved dangerously, but there was nothing to release, only several pained breaths. A sob clawed its way free before I shoved it back down. I should have taken Alik's help, but that was not something I knew how to accept. I should have gone to the healer's tent for something, but instead was curled halfway onto my furs just trying to breathe through it.

Dampness pooled at the corner of my eye, and I hated myself for it.

"Davor?"

I flinched away, until I registered Alik's voice saying, "Easy."

"What?" Pain stoked the fire inside at being seen so helpless.

"Were you planning to just sleep off that beating?"

"Why?"

The small lamp he'd brought illuminated his face and the slight puzzlement there.

"I would do this for any friend or man under my command."

A bitter laugh escaped. "Is that what we are, Alik? Friends?"

He shook his head, a bit of frustration in its sharpness. "I do not talk to you because of your wit, Davor."

I just stared at him. Perhaps the pain was making me hallucinate him. Perhaps this was another trick from Kamil like he'd played over the years.

Alik sighed. "Fine. Then put me as the man least likely to kill you."

He reached for my arm, and I did not resist as he undid the bracer and set it carefully aside. My other forearm was freed in short order.

"Your shirt needs to come off."

This I did balk at, but Alik didn't allow me to say anything, working around my limited strength and pulling off the tunic and shirt.

My body shook even more by the time they were piles on the ground.

"On your stomach." His voice stayed even and almost kind. I didn't have the strength to do anything but obey, and dragged an arm up to brace my forehead against.

"I collected as many cloths as I could for compresses. This will be cold." His warning was not enough to prepare me as ice pressed against my back. A groan wrenched up from deep in my gut.

"He cut you a few times, the bastard."

We're all bastards, I wanted to say, but the world was spinning and fading in and out.

Silence accompanied the slow spread of cold down my back.

"You're not a coward."

Darkness swept in, cutting off any reply I might have made. Trying to be something other than that was how I had gotten here. Like the last time I'd tried to use my ranking, it had not ended well.

But the words followed me through wild dreams, keeping a bit of warmth deep inside against the cold surrounding me.

SIX

DAVOR

Warmth had replaced the cold by the time I peeled my eyes back open. I tried pushing myself up, stopping as the stiffness in my back gave way to a warning stab. Settling back down, I looked across the tent.

A bucket with cloths draped over the edge stood in the center of the space, and on the other side...my heart stalled. Another figure lay wrapped in a cloak and snoring softly. Getting an arm propped under me, I pushed again, making it a little further before a grunt escaped.

The roaring pain had subsided to a steady throb, but moving was not helping.

"What are you doing?" Alik's groggy voice asked.

I froze, torn between relief and caution. "Why are you still here?"

He sat up, rubbing his eyes. "Wanted to make sure you wouldn't do anything stupid when you woke up."

Sparks flickered and caught, spreading light through the tent.

"How do you feel?" he asked. "And if you say fine, I am not going to believe you."

My brows flattened in a glare, but I lowered back down to the blankets.

"Can I check?" He lifted a hand towards me.

I nodded, and hid my face in my arms as he came over and gently peeled away the blanket covering me.

He made a sound I couldn't quite identify. "This is worse than I thought."

"I thought you were trying to help."

One of his easy laughs sounded. "Still am, if you believe it."

A hiss escaped me as a cautious touch pressed against different spots on my back. "I'll get more water for another round of compresses to keep the swelling down. The healer should have something by now to spread over afterward." A rustle accompanied the words and then his next admonishing, "Don't move."

Daylight speared through the tent and vanished again. I lay in silence. There was no reason for him to help me. Other than I might keep taking the brunt of punishment for him and his men.

He'd called me a friend. I did not make friends. I made agreements. Exchanges. Understandings that when I needed something they would be there.

I was not alone long enough to keep puzzling it over. Alik swept back in, and frigid cloths draped over me took away some of the sting. He worked in silence, and I almost slipped back into sleep.

A tap on my shoulder brought me stirring back to alertness.

"I am going to spread this paste, then we'll get some bandages on."

The strong scent of herbs filled up the tent and I wrinkled my nose against it.

Alik coughed. "He makes that potent, doesn't he?"

Under his touch, I felt every welt my sword had left, and the tougher ridges of old scars. Odd warmth gave way to numbness, and I more easily sat up when Alik tapped my shoulder again. He shook out some bandages, fiddling through wrapping them around my chest.

"Healer said getting up and moving would help a little. And figured you would need to eat, too." He reached around and dragged my pack closer. "I'll leave the water to wash."

Alik pushed to his feet, stooping a little under the low ceiling.

"Alik." My hoarse voice halted him before he left. "Thank you."

He tipped a nod and left me alone. I struggled through washing away the remnants of my war paint from my face and changing into clean clothes. A dark tunic went over the shirt of deep grey. I'd never worn much brighter, preferring to use everything to my advantage to pass unnoticed.

My armor I left, except for bracers, and with a certain amount of disgust, buckled my sword and knives back on.

I swayed on my feet, closing my eyes and breathing in strength, before drawing my features into their familiar mask and stepping out.

Luk rose to his paws and I rubbed under his jaw, taking some comfort from his throbbing purr. He carefully rubbed his cheek against my forearm, rough tongue sweeping out to dab at my hand.

"I'll be all right," I whispered reassurance. He'd seen me

through worse. He pressed his forehead against my shoulder, growling a little, then his cold nose swept over my cheek. "Go on." I gently nudged him, but he just followed me, padding along by my side when Alik waved me over to the fire.

A few other pack leaders sat around, sharing a meal. They said nothing as I stiffly lowered myself down to a seat. Alik's lion paused from its intensive grooming to return Luk's sniff before they both settled back.

I took the bowl Alik handed me—stew with chunks of bison meat. I'd barely taken my first bite when one of the pack leaders leaned forward, darting a glance around before focusing back on me.

"Did you mean it, *Rokr*?" he asked.

"What?"

"What you told the battlelion. You won't leave wounded behind."

The focus of the others landed on me and I almost squirmed under it. Alik sipped from his bowl, watching me just as much as the others. It was one thing to do it in the heat of battle, another to decide the morning after being punished for it.

But the bit of iron that had appeared since taking the *rokr* title grew a little more. I wasn't going to watch men left to die and their friends and brothers who actually cared left to mourn something that could have been stopped.

"If we leave wounded behind, we will have no packs left within the next month."

"We just tools to you as well then?" A bit of harshness lined the face of another pack leader.

My fingers pressed against the bowl. "Tools do not have families or homes to return to."

"Like you do?" he scoffed. The first pack leader smacked

his arm, nervousness plain in his eyes.

The speaker did not flinch from my gaze.

"My family does not have much fondness for each other."

Glances were thrown around, but it's not like the tribe didn't know. Maybe not everything, but they knew enough.

"This is no way to fight a war. This is no way to live," I said.

The pack leaders nodded, some staring at the fire. Alik spoke next, looking to me like he might guess what plans stirred slowly in the back of my mind.

"And are you going to do anything about it?"

The brazenness of the question out in the open, where warriors passing by could hear, almost made me flinch. He said he did not think me a coward, but deep down perhaps I was.

I could have challenged Kamil for the medallion. But I had not. I could have stood up in many different ways over the years, played my hand at any time. But I had not. Instead, I hung back, laid my own plans, ensured my own survival.

The men around the fire leaned forward, their focus on me, something like hope in their eyes. They had family to return to, had friends within the packs. Perhaps they too wanted something different. And the hushed dream I had admitted to on a winter's night grew a little brighter.

"I would see this tribe live without violence or cruel carelessness against one another. But it will not happen overnight."

Alik tipped his head as he leaned forward to ladle more stew into his bowl. "You need more support."

I turned sharply to him.

He shrugged. "You are not the only one who would see something different in this life." His look turned distant. "I have long thought that I do not want to bring children into…this." He gestured around.

One of the men gave a sad sort of smile. He had marriage cords around his wrist, perhaps children in a lodge back home.

"You can count on us here," he said. "Many still agree with the battlelion, what he said about you. I do not think that." Though he cast a wondering look at my short hair.

Coward, Kamil's voice mocked.

I swept the spoon slowly through the broth. "War brings many things. Perhaps it can bring change."

"Perhaps it already is," Alik said. "There might be more than you think who would want to see it."

There was something in his eyes that had me looking away. Something I had never seen directed at me. Belief. Hope.

I already knew that this path would have nothing but pain and blood for me. But there were a few more fools who believed in it. Perhaps I did not have to do it entirely alone.

SEVEN

DAVOR

"*D*avor." Makar's voice cut through my concentration. I flexed my fingers around the cleaning cloths and saddle leathers in my lap before looking up.

"Battlelion wants you." The sneer on his face promised nothing good.

Perhaps I should have been grateful that Kamil had given me two full days to recover from his punishment before calling me to gloat.

"Where?" I asked, still pointedly cleaning the saddle's seat.

"War tent." He kicked dirt up onto Luk's bridle sitting clean on a blanket beside me. I swallowed a retort, setting the saddle aside and shaking the dirt free with a few sharp jerks. It all went back into my tent, and Luk yawned mightily, his jaws parting in what might be a frightening cavern of sharpened teeth and swooping fangs to some.

"Don't be late, coward," Makar called over his shoulder.

My back and shoulders protested movement, but I kept my spine straight as I made my way across camp to Kamil's tent.

"What do you want me to say, Kamil?" Emil's voice rang through the flaps, sharp in frustration. "I cannot make favorable reports appear out of thin air."

"Mind yourself," Kamil sneered. "I want a way through to the river."

"Then maybe you should stop leaving men behind and you would have enough packs to take it."

A crack sounded. "Find it for me."

The flap swirled open, and Emil almost crashed into me. A red mark smeared his cheek under eyes rimmed in exhaustion. Dirt and old blood covered his armor. I'd barely seen him over the countings, as Kamil had him and the scouts out without rest.

For a moment we regarded each other warily.

His lip curled. "I heard I missed an opportunity to tell you that I warned you."

"Sounded for a moment like you agreed with me."

Emil scoffed. "Always thinking you're right, aren't you?"

I usually made sure I was. "You should get some rest."

The sneer crept back over his face. "Do not start pretending to care now, Davor. It does not become you." And he pushed past me.

I paused a moment, afraid to puzzle out his meaning. Neither of us had cared for the other in a long time. Shaking it off, I entered the tent. Kamil leaned on a low table, a map etched on cured hide spread out in front of him.

"Worthless," he growled to Makar. "I cannot trust him with one simple task." He slammed a fist down on the map, jostling the cups on the table.

I came closer. "Battlelion."

"Davor." He did not take his gaze from the map. "Able to walk, I see. Have you learned your lesson, yet?" His head tilted up to fix me in stormy eyes.

"I am here to serve, Battlelion."

"And grovel." He leaned fists on the table. "As much as it normally amuses me, it does not today."

I waited in silence, hand clenched tight around my sword hilt. He punched the table again and straightened, dragging a hand down his face.

"Emil is failing. Hakkon has nothing useful to give right now. And that cursed battlewolf has us at a standstill across the valley. We need more men."

I kept my mouth shut and his warning look faded to approval.

"Davor, you are going to go get them from the village."

"There were not many packs left behind," I said carefully.

He snorted a tired laugh. "I know. You are bringing back others who can fill saddles. I want huntsmen too. Emil complains he cannot find ways through the valley even with Hakkon's information, so we will bring men who can. Perhaps he can find another way to be useful again."

A flicker of unease hit me. Perhaps things between my half-brothers were not as I had assumed for years.

"Make sure you bring the whelp out as well."

Michal. The thought of his eagerness to fight, prove himself, pricked at my heart. There might be no chance for him to avoid the paths of Kamil and the chief out here.

"When do I leave?"

"Now. Makar has picked a small pack to go with you." A smirk flickered again. "And make sure you give Father a full update on the war. He'll want to know."

Bastard. So Father's wrath would fall on me instead of Kamil when he heard the news.

"And what should I tell him?" I asked, the almost frighteningly stubborn bit of me pushed back.

Kamil's glare sharpened. He slapped a roll of birchbark paper on the table. "It's all there."

I saluted and swept it up.

"I want you back with as many men as you can muster before the counting is up."

Not much time. We were already three days into the nine, and it was almost two to get back home.

"And, Davor?" He halted me before I could open the tent flap. "Make sure you get a new spear before you go."

Red smeared across my vision for two heartbeats before it faded back to the sight of the elk-hide tent.

"Yes, Battlelion."

I returned to my tent, signaling Alik. He met me before I ducked inside to get my armor.

"Kamil is sending me home to gather more packs."

"How long will you be gone?"

"He's ordered us to be back before the counting is up."

"Will you make it?" Alik rested a hand on my shoulder. I eased out from under it.

"I will be fine." But I already dreaded putting my armor on. I hesitated a moment more.

"Is there anything you want me to take back to your lodges?" It seemed the sort of thing a friend might ask. If we even were friends. We weren't enemies, and that was more than I'd ever had with anyone other than my mother or Janne my entire life.

He gave a half-smile. "I do not think you know what you're asking. If every man sent something, your lion would not be able to carry it all and you." But he sighed and looked out over the camp. "I could send a list of the dead, but it seems unfair to make you tell the families on your own. Who are you bringing back?"

"Every pack left, and anyone able to ride a sablecat."

Alik vented the curse weighing on my chest.

"He's also ordering hunters into the field."

"And who is to look after the villages?"

I raised an eyebrow, and Alik cursed again.

"I will be back as soon as I can." It seemed a poor promise, but Alik nodded.

"Ride safe."

By the time I managed my armor and a small pack, he had Luk saddled and waiting for me. And I did not like how relieved I was that he silently accompanied me over to where Makar waited with my new pack.

"Some of my best men, *Rokr*." Makar swept a hand to the five warriors riding with me. "They'll protect you." His hand slammed into the back of my shoulder, and darkness flooded my sight for a moment.

When I could see and barely breathe again, Makar had backed away with a smirk. "Don't worry. I'll make sure we don't notice your absence, *Rokr*."

I turned, inhaling shortly before getting myself with bare grace into the saddle. His short laugh seemed to be echoed by some of the warriors riding with me. Gathering up the reins, I wheeled Luk around, meeting Alik's stony look. I shook my head imperceptibly, warning against something stupid.

Makar made to shove past him, but Alik stood fast under the intended disruption. He held Makar's sneering look for a few heart-stopping moments, defiance and scorn not even hidden in his expression. Makar moved first, striding back into camp. Alik turned to me, tapped fist to his chest, and gave a nod.

I spurred Luk into motion, not waiting to see if the men followed. And hoped that Alik and his pack would still be standing when I made it back.

⟜

The village lights blinked like large lightwings in the twilight. Our sablecats pricked up their ears and paws, loping along at a faster pace. I did not stop it, eager to climb from the saddle and find some place to ease the ache pounding through me with every stride.

Either Makar had sent his best men or his worst, maybe hoping that we'd be ambushed on the way back and all of us killed. They'd made no move against me, but I'd barely slept the entire ride back, keeping one eye open amid the unknown.

Sentries challenged, then welcomed us back with glad cries once I gave the replies. We halted inside the upper village boundaries. I gave the dismissal and turned Luk up to the chief's lodge. I did not think my feet would take me there themselves.

Luk gave a coughing chirp when my boots thudded to the ground, and I grabbed hold of the saddle to keep myself from falling.

"Stay." I touched his shoulder and forced my way inside.

Torches lit the common room, some of the benches still filled with warriors eating or nursing more cups of oak ale. They watched in interest as I made my way around tables, stepping over one man passed out on the floor already.

Despite the late hour, the chief still presided at the head table. Michal sat beside him, a lone figure beside the fading chief. He'd taken the place Kamil usually occupied at the chief's right hand, a new straightness to his posture I didn't know yet how to interpret.

"Chief." I brought a hand to my forehead.

He barely stirred, but Michal leaned forward on the table, taking in the sight of me with eager eyes.

I shuffled forward a step, barely hiding a wince, and tried again. "Chief."

He looked up at me and blinked once, twice. "Davor." Then, as if my name signaled something in his mind, he sat taller and coherence came back to him. "What are you doing here?"

"Kamil sent me back for more packs and to give you a report on the war."

"Come with me." He shoved back from the table. "You too, Michal."

Michal regarded me as I braced a hand against the table for a long moment before following the chief into his chambers. There he read the report I handed over, and admittedly had already read. But it seemed even Kamil did not dare lie to our father.

The chief's face darkened with every word until he threw it across the room.

"By the Greywolf whelp's account, this war should have already been won!"

Michal flinched from his place by the door, leaning back a little from the anger in the chief's voice. Perhaps he was finding that our father's sole attention was not to be craved.

"It seems he underestimated the battlewolf. He is a fierce opponent," I said.

"Kamil is strong enough to counter that, and you crafty enough to assist him. That is why I sent you as his second!"

I stared at the chief. He had truly thought we would work together?

"You are failing me again in many ways, Davor."

This time I flinched. "I am doing what I can, Chief."

"No excuses."

I kept my head bowed. "He is asking for more packs, more riders to fill saddles. And huntsmen to help the scouts."

The chief scoffed. "I will give the order. I want this war won before mid-spring."

That did not give us long. The season had already set in, taking a little longer to dig itself into the higher valley.

"Yes, Chief."

"Michal."

He snapped to attention at the door.

"You will ride back with Davor. Make something of yourself in this war." The same warning smattered with pride directed to me at seventeen winters when I was sent off too young to war, was there again for Michal. And his youngest son saluted, excited promise in his eyes, looking to the chief with an almost nauseating respect. Just as eager to please the chief as I had been.

"Council tomorrow, Davor."

I saluted again and made for the door as the chief turned away, already muttering under his breath. The longer we stayed, the more likely we were to have to weather an outburst. Michal knew the signs as well as I did, and we both made our retreat.

"Still alive then?" he asked once safely back in the main hall.

"Disappointed?" I asked.

"Surprised."

To my own surprise, a faint smile tugged at my lips. "You are not the only one."

Michal rolled his eyes. "You haven't taken control of the packs yet? No surprise."

I refused to let the open scorn of a youth prick me.

"Rushing into things is how you get yourself killed." I began to make my way back across the lodge.

He scoffed but continued to dog my steps. "Where are you going?"

"To take care of my sablecat."

Luk still waited obediently outside, crouched down on all fours, tail flicking gently back and forth at the new moonlight casting shadows through the clouds. He rose at my clicking command and nudged his head too hard into my side. A curse whispered from me, and I grabbed the saddle to keep from falling.

A light wind picked up, bringing with it the sweet scent of the plains in spring, tinged with pine from the forest. Home.

I abandoned any thought of staying in the chief's lodge that night. Every part of me ached, but where I was going, some of it could be fixed. Luk did not protest as I turned him and headed back down the hill.

"Davor?"

I ignored Michal's questioning tone, afraid that if I stopped, I wouldn't be able to make myself keep going. He followed in silence, not saying anything as two days of riding without sleep or trusting anyone to help with the welts on my back caught up with every step. Breaths tore ragged from me, but I pushed on.

Finally, my hand slammed against the painted doorframe of the healer's lodge. Michal searched my face, sudden doubt in his wide eyes.

"What's wrong with you?" he asked.

I couldn't yet remove my hand from the door, turning my attention to the grain of wood between my fingers.

"The reception of Kamil's strength you so desperately crave."

He had no reply, and he did not press the weakness. A faint

sound caught in my throat as I finally straightened, tugging Luk's reins.

"I can take him." Michal held out a hand, the look still there shouting that he knew what had happened and didn't want to give voice to it.

Wordlessly I handed the leathers over. If he tried anything, Luk knew how to protect himself. I knocked on the door and it swung open to reveal my mother.

She gasped and pulled me inside, wrapping her arms tight around me until I could no longer bear it and twisted away from her hold.

"Davor?" she questioned softly, one hand pressing against the side of my head. I did not dare to look her in the eyes, knowing if I did, I would lose hold of the things I'd held close over the last countings.

"Do you need Inge?"

I nodded. "Please."

Her hold transitioned to under my elbow and she guided me to a bench against the wall. Once there, Inge appeared, Janne hovering behind her, concern in both their faces.

They helped set aside my armor and weapons, saying nothing as I kept a knife at my side. Sweat-soaked tunic and shirt were next, and as I slowly lay down on my stomach, my mother grabbed my hand and squeezed. Janne's small gasp drove into my heart.

Inge's voice stayed even as she sent Janne for healing supplies. Mother kept hold of my hand, settling fingers gently atop my hair.

"You'll be safe here tonight, Davor," she whispered as she leaned close to drop a kiss against my head. It had been so long since I'd spent enough time around her that she could be so open towards me that it almost brought tears to my eyes. I squeezed her hand in return, and her shaky breath told me she understood all I didn't want to say.

EIGHT

MARTA

"You can't go!" I leaned close to my father. But he only smiled and gently nudged me away so he could continue filling his pack.

"The chief ordered it, Marta. And the battlelion commanded first. I have no choice."

"It should never have come to this." Fury trembled through my jaw. Mother stood nearby, eyes already red from holding back tears. Vanda sat on the bench, arms crossed tight over her stomach. She didn't remember as keenly as I did watching Father ride off to war eight years ago.

And I didn't think I could do it again. Couldn't sleep beside Mother every night he was gone, sometimes waking each other up with our tears. Couldn't stitch another name into a remembrance cloth for a new widow or orphan or sibling who looked lost without their brother. Only because we had no news from the packs other than to call more men had I not already stitched some.

"Marta." Father guided me gently away from the others. The lodge was so empty already without Alik and his pack. Meals quiet without their boisterous noise. But now that Father and some of the other hunters were going…

His hands gently rested around my upper arms.

"Marta, I need…" His voice caught and it was all I could do to not burst into tears right there. His grip tightened and then eased. "I need you to stay strong. Look after your mother and Vanda like…"

Like last time.

"Father, I can't…"

He brushed my shoulders, then gently set hands against the sides of my head, tipping me forward to press his forehead against mine.

"You can. The Saber spirit gave you the heart of his lions."

I never felt it. Not when I was more comfortable with a needle in my hand, or basket on my hip listening to stories being told to me over barters or trades.

"What if you don't come back?" I whispered between us.

"I will make no promises."

I wanted him to.

"Perhaps I will find my way to Alik's pack." He lightened the words. I sniffed.

"I'm not convinced he has anything but air in his head." But I managed to match his tone. We shared a short laugh. He moved, bringing something out of the small pockets on his fur-lined tunic and held it between us. A well-worn scrap of blue cloth embroidered with prayer runes, white antlers, and yellow violets.

"I still have this from last time."

A small smile spread over my face as my fingers brushed the cloth. My stitching had improved from eight years ago, but yellow violets were still my favorite.

"I've always thought it brought me good luck. Perhaps it will again."

The prayer cloth blurred in front of my eyes, and I threw myself into his arms. He would not leave until the morrow, but better to get these goodbyes done in private before he rode away.

"Be careful," I whispered.

"Be strong," he returned. I pulled back and planted a kiss on his cheek, mustering a smile in promise.

Vanda was next, folding into Father's arms as if she were not nineteen but a small child ready to hear stories of the days the spirits walked the earth. Finally releasing her, he set his pack against the wall by our benches as if he was just getting ready for an early morning hunt.

He and Mother left for their small room deeper in the lodge and Vanda and I wordlessly turned to bed like the other families. She curled on the bench first among the furs and blankets. I was slower to fold my dress away, my thick knee-length shift still keeping out most of the cold.

"Marta." She sniffed and rolled closer to the wall. Silently I gathered up my own blanket and squeezed onto the bench beside her, tucking an arm over her and pulling blankets over us both.

"I wish things were different, I wish they weren't so cruel, I wish..." She trailed off into a sob.

I hugged her tighter. "I know. Me too."

I slept fitfully all night, waking sometime in the early morning before the sun had even thought to start its rise. My cheeks were tight with tears that had slipped out during the night. Better to cry them in private than to show Father when he left.

Vanda still slept, her breath coming and going in a steady cadence. I carefully eased out from under the blankets and dressed in the dim light coming from the hearthfire coals. The floorboards were cold beneath my feet and I wished for spring to come into its own faster.

My fur-lined boots squeaked gently against the floor as I tiptoed to the door, pulling a cloak around my shoulders as I went. A layer of frost lingered on the ground and on the peaked roofs of the middle village, but the green grass and flowers that had already bloomed did not recoil from it.

Dim light had broken over the horizon line, growing brighter every minute I spent slowly walking the paths through the village. By the time I made it to the bridge, a few golden rays had begun to poke their heads up. Even by that hour, there should have been guards patrolling, or hunters moving out.

But today, guards and hunters would be stealing as much time as they could with wives or families before riding out. And some would not be returning.

Tears threatened again and I sniffed, pressing a cloak-covered hand under my nose to stave them off.

The sight of a figure on the bridge was enough to drive them all away. I halted, my toes neatly at the line where packed earth gave way to weathered planks.

Davor was back. He was the one who had brought the order.

But he stood in almost defeat, hands braced against the railing as he stared down the river. As if he could sense my glare, Davor looked up and from half the bridge away, I was caught in his somber stare.

I wondered again if the stories were true. That if you could gather the courage to talk to Davor, second son of the chief, he might find a fair answer or solution for you. Or that he was just as careless and cruel as his brothers. Either way, they all agreed. He made agreements, and many times came to collect.

And part of me feared he might think I owed him for our meeting years ago, and what it might mean if he came to collect.

But as before, there was no recognition in his eyes.

"Are you all right?"

It took a moment to register that the deep voice had asked it of me. And then I realized how I must look. Hair loose and trailing over my shoulders, eyes scratchy and red rimmed, and cloak tugged tight around me.

"Yes," I automatically said before my anger caught up. My chin lifted higher and perhaps because my mind had not yet fully woken, I decided to tempt fate. "Perhaps you have just never seen what happens after you drag men off to war."

He looked away, back over the river shifting away from shades of grey under the fresh sunlight.

"Have you lost someone?"

My throat tightened, thinking again of the mourning cloths. "Not yet. Tell me, how long do you expect hunters and *boys* to last on the battlefield?" My feet took me onto the bridge.

He did not shift, made no inclination that he would punish me for my words. Instead he sighed, as if the thought pained him as well.

"I did not want this," he said.

A laugh scoffed from me before I could stop it. "I hear you are second to the battlelion. How could you not want this?"

Something flickered across his face as he faced me again. "Perhaps the only thing the *battlelion* and I have in common is that we both want this war over and the other dead."

I leaned back from the sharpness of his voice. His fingers

curled in a fist on the railing and my heart stammered a beat. But he did not move.

"Believe me when I say that I want many things and taking more men and boys from these villages are not it." He did not sneer over the words, and it seemed he knew well how many on the training grounds were still too young to be riding off to war.

And I did believe him. Believed him like I did years ago when he'd softly offered to help.

"Who is going from your lodge?"

My arms pressed tighter over my stomach. Was this how he would punish me for my words? Hurting Father? But there was only curiosity there.

"My father. He's one of the tribe hunters." *One of the best,* I did not say. Who would keep hunting when he was gone? Some wives or young sons could take up bows and fill in, but not for countings on end.

"They are to go with the scouts. Perhaps they will be safer there than with the packs."

I blinked at the words, evenly spoken, but trying to be reassuring.

"That does not mean they should go."

"I know." He paused. "I will do what I can to bring as many back from this war as I can."

"And then what?" There was so much unspoken about him.

A bitter half smile flickered. "If the spirits have any thought for us at all, perhaps something different." And he turned and walked back across the bridge and into the upper village.

I stared after him, his words still swirling around me in the light breeze. I didn't know whether to hope or fear what those words meant. But it seemed that war would follow the packs home.

NINE

DAVOR

Sablecats milled about in the open spaces between the chief's lodge and the upper village as packs and hunters gave one last farewell to their families. The chief had come out to oversee our departure. I stood with Luk as far away as possible, a new bruise on my ribs after the council the night before.

His anger at our apparent failure had not abated.

Inge and Janne had braved the crowds to come say one last farewell to Michal. He stood by his young sablecat, carelessly shrugging away their concern. Already trying to become a warrior.

"Davor." Mother's quiet voice warned me before she appeared at my side. Luk sheltered the two of us from the eyes that might care.

I stiffly turned to face her. But Inge was a gentler healer than

Alik, and I had supplies in my bag for later. Mother rested a hand on my forearm and the other against my head. Closing my eyes, I pressed my forehead against hers.

"Be safe," she whispered.

I nodded, afraid to open my mouth and tell her a lie.

"Will you be all right?" She pulled back a fraction and looked at me with eyes that could always see to the heart of me.

All I could do was nod again, mouth twisting in a poor smile. Her eyes welled with sadness and she pulled me forward again, gentle hand around my neck and other against my shoulder, as much of an embrace as she could give without hurting.

But it still did, stabbing away at my heart, making me wish all the more for something different as I had every day since I'd made a public display of banishing her from the chief's lodge to try to keep her safe. She'd forgiven me instantly, knowing my reasons, but the guilt of my actions still plagued me. I wouldn't miscalculate again.

She released me and familiar cold rushed around me again. With one last shaky smile, she left me standing beside my lion.

Turning away from the sight of her retreating figure, I pulled myself into the saddle and settled my spear. One glance over the hunters and I knew which man was Marta's father.

He had the same proud tilt of his chin, same full cheeks, the same confidence. There was no sign of tears on her face as she embraced him one more time. Not like the women beside her. Mother and younger sister if I had to guess.

Then, as if she felt my stare again, her gaze met mine and she squared up in almost defiance. I wondered if she remembered how we first met years ago. Maybe even forgotten what I did afterward. But there had only been disdain in her eyes at the bridge for the side I presented to the tribe. Not like years ago when there'd been something like trust in the brief time we'd walked side-by-side.

I could not blame her for that. The spear pressed tighter against my palm. It would be easier to carve a place among the warriors. They respected strength and cunning. But it would be harder to gain a higher foothold among the villagers. If I returned alive to even try it.

I blew two longer blasts on my horn, the signal to form up. Michal mounted and urged his sablecat forward until my look had him staying paces away from me. The pack leaders got their men into position, and I nudged Luk forward, raising my spear in deference to the chief as I passed, and then pushed up to a lope, for once eager to get back to the fight.

It brought me strange relief to see Alik and the pack still alive when I returned. It looked as if they had been given a few days' respite while I was gone. Weariness did not cling to them as tightly as it had days ago.

Kamil took the news of the chief's decree of victory by mid-spring with a sneering curse. Emil stood on the opposite side of the table from Kamil, arms crossed and one hand holding the hilt of a knife sheathed across his chest. He shot Kamil an unreadable glance, and I caught a glimpse of whitened knuckles around the knife hilt. The battlelion then regarded Michal who had also been summoned.

The boy stood tall, one hand carelessly gripping his quiver strap.

"Well, whelp, where shall you go?" Kamil prowled closer.

I angled slightly where I stood in front of Michal to keep them within my vision. The boy didn't say anything, just stiffened as Kamil leaned in.

"I have room for an archer in my personal pack," Kamil said.

Michal straightened, still not seeing what would likely befall him. He would be assessed for any potential use, and if not, he would fall in the next battle. My heart stepped up its rhythm, urging me to get Michal through this war. If only for his mother and sister's sake.

"Perhaps the scouts, if they want scraps," the battlelion continued, circling him.

"Perhaps Davor should take him," Emil spoke up. Kamil looked to him, mild anger there. Emil shrugged off the differing looks we both gave him.

Kamil regarded me and my blank features. "You did speak out against him coming."

"I have no time to watch over boys on the battlefield," I said.

Michal stiffened, righteousness beginning to ripple from him. I'd hear about that later.

Kamil's lips tilted up at the corner. "I've overseen some of his training myself, Davor. Do you doubt me?"

"No, Battlelion."

"What do you think, whelp? Should you go to Davor's pack?"

"Maybe I don't trust his leading," Michal spat.

Emil smirked, a pointed thing at me. Kamil's amusement rumbled through the tent.

"I think that settles it. You get the whelp, Davor. Try not to kill each other. Or perhaps do me the favor already."

Our gazes locked in a now-familiar battle for several heartbeats before I lowered first. Not yet ready to challenge.

"Now that you are back, Davor, you can lead a patrol northeast. See if you can push to the river and report back."

I tapped my chest twice, and shoved Michal out of the tent

ahead of me. He shook off my hand and scowled as he matched my stride across the camp full of frantic energy as the newcomers tried to get sorted in camps and sablecats jostled and growled at each other.

"Alik," I called as we approached.

He saluted and sent a look from Michal to me, wordlessly asking why I had brought the youngest with me.

"We've been assigned one of the new riders to the pack. Make sure he has a place, and get ready to ride. Battlelion has ordered us to test the river."

Alik saluted again, but gave another pointed look at me. I tilted my head, reassuring. I felt as fine as I was going to until the bruised welts healed.

"I'll take a spare lion if there is one. Luk needs some rest."

He nodded and beckoned Michal on. The younger's scowl dimmed as he passed me, the same curiosity there. I knew he'd seen the mess of my back in his mother's lodge, but I was not interested in discussing it.

The river boundary had held firm under wolfrider spears days ago. I did not think it had changed. We'd see battle before the sun touched the horizon.

Alik's second brought me a fresh sablecat and I transferred a light pack to its saddle, giving Luk a reassuring pat as he growled in offense at the sight.

My gaze fell over the camp again, looking for the trackers and hunters. We had a few scouts who rode with us. Alik might naturally pick out Marta's father if I sent him to get fresh scouts. But I did not want to drag him into a sure fight this soon.

What am I doing?

I shook myself, trying to figure out when I'd started thinking about her, and why. Why I'd wanted to try to promise something to her. When I looked back up, Michal was making his way to me, leading a fresh sablecat, determination on his face.

"You don't think I can do this?" he asked. There was a space restless energy gave way to anger and I wondered if he knew any other place.

"Did you not want to live long enough to prove yourself a man?" Weariness pushed around me, and the healing bruises were starting to cry out against the constant rub of the breast-plate.

His head tilted in confusion. I did not have the energy to continue any argument he might want.

"Alik is a good pack leader. Listen to him and you might make it out of this war alive. You have nothing to fear from me."

"What about you?" His quiet question stopped me as I gathered up the reins. Despite myself, I tilted a look back.

His green eyes held something nearly foreign to me. Sympathy. Understanding.

"Go form up." I harshened the words a little, but he did not react to it. Instead, he saluted with the tap over his chest like Alik, not knowing yet what it meant.

But as I mounted, I wondered why Emil had helped me. He had some game to play separate from Kamil's more direct machinations, that was clear enough. But why?

The sablecat growled as I tightened up the reins. Its discontent mirrored in my chest. I did not want it any more than it wanted me. And riding into battle with a feeling like that could be disastrous.

Three packs formed up with me, most giving the salute and something like welcome on their faces. Michal was at the back with the small group of archers. I lifted my spear and we rode out, scouts loping in front of us to check the path we were taking to the river.

We did not get within three miles of the river before we found battle. It was sharp and quick and I withdrew the pack before more damage could be done.

We retreated a safe distance to wrap bandages around the wounded. Alik pressed a comforting hand over Michal's shoulder as adrenaline faded and he retched beside his lion. I did not move closer though the sight of Alik gently talking him through a few breaths prodded at my heart. There had been no gentle support after my first battle, though my reactions had been much the same. The way Michal looked gratefully to Alik stung more.

It came so easily to Alik, unlike me, and the mocking barb of *not good enough* came. Though just as quick came the returning thought that Michal would not want anything from me. And that came with a different sort of sting.

Back at camp, Kamil expressed his displeasure and left me with a bleeding nose. I ignored the looks, stopped the bleeding, and collapsed to sleep in my tent, barely out of my armor before I did.

The resistance still given across the valley gave me some small hope that the Greywolves might yet prevail. But that died less than a counting later when Kamil rode back into camp, raging. His sablecat was dead, but not before it had killed the battlewolf.

TEN

DAVOR

"We are close to taking the river," Kamil said without looking up from the map spread on the table before him.

I edged closer to look at the lines strewn across the tanned hide. We had several miles to go before reaching the broad waters. And when we did, we would have control of half of the valley.

No remorse showed in Hakkon's face. No sorrow for the wolf-riders who lay dead at our swords and spears. Instead, eagerness for the victories shone brightest. The spirits would judge him, perhaps harsher than I already did.

"I want packs out, Davor. Start pushing the lines toward the river. I want a new camp by counting's end."

My fist tapped twice against my chest.

"Emil can go with you."

I pulled up short.

Kamil gave a short grin. "It seems he needs to prove himself as well."

Unease threatened, but I sharply nodded and strode from the tent. Alik mustered up the warriors and I ordered out another two packs on different routes. They obeyed readily enough, content with my leading after countings of war, and then I was free to find the last member of our patrol.

Hesitation dogged my steps to the scouts' camp. I found Emil behind his tent, standing with his lion. The sablecat had its head pressed up against his chest as Emil's forehead rested between its ears. One hand fisted tightly in its fur.

It was a moment no one was meant to see, hidden in the shadows of the trees surrounding camp. And it almost made me turn away, pretend I couldn't find him for the patrol.

"Emil."

His head whipped up and there was a glimpse of something in his eyes before it shuttered away into his usual sneer.

"What?"

"Kamil wants you on patrol with me."

He shifted between his feet, still holding steady against his lion. Head shaking, he looked out into the trees, the muscles tight in his jaw. "Now?"

"Yes."

Emil retrieved his saddle, pausing only to glare until I left him alone.

A bit of unease stirred through my pack when he joined us minutes later, but nothing was said. Alik cast a glance of distaste at him which Emil returned without hesitation. I led the way out.

The path lay clear across the land we'd already taken. Our lions growled as they found the scent markers left behind by the greywolves and we crossed into their territory.

Michal loped off with the advance guard and I couldn't help but be a little proud of how confident he rode after several countings of war. The packs had started to look at him with more warmth when it was clear he was giving all he could and did not exhibit many of the traits of the rest of us, even if his anger was painfully evident most days.

Another bit of resolve came to keep giving him a safer space to keep proving himself.

Alik pushed up beside me. "Why is he here?" He tossed a glance over his shoulder to where Emil rode.

"Kamil ordered it." I stood taller in the saddle to see over the rolling hillocks ahead of us.

"And you don't think he's going to try to kill you while we're out here?"

"Perhaps." I settled back to the saddle. "Are you going to stand back and watch it happen?"

A snort came from Alik, as if he didn't realize I might have meant the question a little. "You're the closest thing we have to a real leader out here, Davor. We might make sure you stay with us a bit longer."

A glance to him showed a grin despite the more serious tone. I found myself faintly returning it.

The quiet didn't last long. Michal came racing back with word of a pack ahead. We formed up and I placed Emil on the flank. It made the skin between my shoulder blades prickle with the threat of a knife, but forged on.

We met the Greywolves with a clash, neat lines devolving quickly to chaos. My spear sank into a greywolf haunch, and it tore away, limping and collapsing. Whirling Luk, I searched out a new opponent and my heart leapt up into my throat. Michal was on the ground, sword in hand against a spear and mounted Greywolf.

He batted away each strike with grim concentration, gaining a short respite when his lion darted in and swiped with bared claws. I drove heels into Luk's side but Emil reached him first. Alarm spiked even higher at the sight, but Emil's lion charged the wolf, his focus on the warrior. Michal retreated, grabbing at his sablecat's leathers.

Too close for weapons, the Greywolf used his spear and slammed the haft against Emil's chest. It knocked Emil off-balance, breaking his attack enough for the wolf to spin and ram its head into his side, throwing him to the ground. Then the wolf and his sablecat were a tangle atop him for a breathless moment before they kicked free of each other. Halfway there already, Luk leapt faster at my command, but the Greywolves were retreating.

We circled up, some riders facing out as the others saw to wounds. I dismounted and edged around Emil's sablecat where he curled on the ground, sharp breaths tearing from him.

I reached down, but he wrenched away, pulling a knife out. "Don't touch me!"

My hands steadied in a sign of peace, and he gradually lowered the weapon, not easing as his lion came to crouch protectively behind him.

I sank down and he pulled back. "Do you need help?" I asked.

"Not from you," he sneered, but still did not move from his protected position.

A shadow fell over us and I half-turned to see Alik standing there, impassively watching Emil. The pack leader looked to me, but when I did not say anything or make any move to leave, he crouched beside us.

"Injured ribs?" he asked.

"Get away from me," Emil hissed.

Alik didn't flinch. "You want to make it back to the camp? I'll happily leave you here."

Emil scoffed but didn't relax his hold on the knife as I offered a hand to help him sit up. I reached for the straps of his breastplate, undoing them and getting a punch to my shoulder as the pressure eased. Alik scowled but Emil only cursed again the warrior gently pressed the injured area. A warning rumble started in the sablecat's throat, dimmed only by Luk's returning growl.

I wondered why Alik knew so much about healing when he led packs, but he offered nothing as he took bandages and wrapped them around Emil, bracing his ribs.

He said nothing as he left, and Emil and I stared at one another again.

"Why?" The harsh question lingered between us.

I avoided it by cinching up the armor straps again. "We cannot win a war without men."

"No, why? Kamil does not understand what you are doing. It just makes him angry." There was a familiar weariness lurking in Emil's eyes.

I rocked back on my heels. It felt tenuous between us, but the sort of uncertainty where there might be understanding but not betrayal. "Because I am playing a different game than him."

"And what do you hope to gain?" His eyes narrowed. "You think to take the medallion? Maybe even the place of chief?" His suspicion faded to sneering amusement.

I gestured around to where the wounded were beginning to mount up, pack reforming into a loose group. "Perhaps I want something different than war."

His laugh came bitter and sharp as he leaned his head back

against his lion. "We've been at war our whole lives. You cannot change that."

But I was starting to try to shake free of that truth. It was a hard one to divest, but I wanted a more peaceful, safer life, so much that I could almost taste it through the blood and dirt in my mouth. And looking at him, I wondered at this moment. It had been so long since anything but hate and sharp words had passed between us.

"Mount up," I called as I stood. "We're going back."

A sharp laugh came from Emil, halting me. Others paused, but I had attention only for him.

He looked at me from where he slowly gained his feet with the help of his lion. "Do you intend to kill me here or later?"

A weight sank heavy in my gut, and I did not reply.

Emil shook his head. "Playing games, Davor, only works if you are paying attention to others around you."

"So tell me why he would throw away one of his pieces." I did not flinch. The pack was silent around us, but our focus never wavered from each other.

The sneer came back, but it was not just for me. "When he tires of things, he casts them away, no matter the use."

I had no answer, but he was not finished.

"And when he sees no value in a thing, how long do you think it lasts?" This time his glance flicked to Michal.

The silence stretched out, sablecats barely twitching as they waited for an order, sensing the tension lingering between us.

"Well." I stirred. "I have never been good at playing his games."

Emil scoffed, shaking his head as he edged his sablecat away from me. "You might play, Davor, and learn a thing or two."

He reached to grab the saddle, and his knees buckled with a muffled cry. Michal was there in an instant, one hand on the reins to stop the lion's surprised jump, the other under Emil's elbow to keep him from hitting the ground.

Arms shaking, Emil released the saddle and grabbed Michal instead. Slowly, he re-settled his feet, Michal taking most of his weight, arm shaking under the strain.

They stared at each other a moment, then Emil shoved him away. It took two tries to get his foot in the stirrup, then he hauled himself up, falling forward onto the sablecat's neck. Michal still had hold of the reins and he did not relinquish it until Emil sat taller and tightened the leathers.

I said nothing, just mounted and led the packs back. At the camp boundaries, my stomach flipped, wondering how Kamil would take the sight of all three of us riding in. And which one he hoped wouldn't have returned.

Though watching Emil slumped in the saddle, I might have had my answer. I gave the dismissal order, taking a few moments to nerve myself up to enter the war tent. The rest of the pack peeled away from Emil, leaving him alone beside me.

"If he wants me, tell him to go to the dark woods." Emil spurred away, heading for the scouts' camp.

I'd rather not.

A faint noise had me looking over my shoulder. Michal hadn't moved. He watched Emil leave and then met my gaze. He swallowed hard.

"Would Kamil really…?"

I tilted my head and Michal's shoulders slumped. In his quick glance down there was just acceptance.

"You helped him." I nodded after Emil.

Michal's green eyes snapped back up to me. "So did you."

I said nothing, waiting. There had been some understanding between them for a moment.

"He's not always…sometimes he's not…" Michal looked down, fiddling with his reins. "Sometimes he tries to help. The way you do."

"What?"

A faintly annoyed smile flickered. "I'm young, Davor, but I'm not stupid."

"No, you're not," I said.

His head ducked, and when he lifted it again, there was something almost like respect there.

"You meant it then? When you said you'd do what you could here?" He shifted between his feet, hand fluttering between his quiver strap and sword hilt.

It had my heart jolting a little. Like I might actually be hoping for something between me and a half-brother that was not hate.

"I did. And I am learning how to actually *do* things."

Michal's head jerked up as I used his past accusation, but I only had a small and rueful smile for him. One that he faintly returned.

"I'm ready to try another way," I said softly.

"Me too." The words came small. He darted a look around before bringing a fist to his chest, now knowing what it meant after being with my packs.

I offered a small smile. "I think we already are."

Michal's lips tucked up into something similar.

"Go on." I nodded after Alik and the others.

But he didn't move. "You're going to report to the battlelion?"

"Go on," I said a little more firmly even if my heart didn't feel as stern. He obeyed, but with a glance over his shoulder.

Gathering a breath, I headed for Kamil's tent. Luk growled as I dismounted, sensing my trepidation.

"Davor." Kamil's voice stopped me before I stepped in. He stalked towards me, knife in hand and chunk of dried meat in the other. "Where's Emil?"

I eased fingers out of a fist. "He took an injury. I ordered him to go rest."

"Ordered?" Kamil's eyebrow arched. "How did he take that?"

"Not well."

He half-laughed and carved a bit of meat away, tossing it to Luk who snatched it midair. "And the whelp?"

"With the pack."

Kamil stared at me a moment. "I am trying to decide, Davor, if you are just stupid or if you do not have the stomach for war."

"I'm here, aren't I?"

"Perhaps stupid then." His knife sliced another piece of meat.

"What honor is there in killing a boy or a man half-wounded?" I asked.

"Perhaps I meant for you not to make it back." A sly smile flickered.

"Perhaps it is a day for disappointment then."

Kamil stalked closer, wiping his blade clean as he tossed the last meat to Luk. The sablecat ignored it, focused on the new threat approaching me.

"Perhaps it is. Although, I had wondered if we could have made an agreement, the two of us."

My mind screamed for me to give way as he came in close.

"Emil has many uses in the villages. But here, I have been sadly disappointed in him. You, for once, are following orders. Could this be the start of something new?" The tip of the knife swept up to settle against my cheek.

"I am here to serve...Battlelion." My eyes never left the cold wells of his. The knife pressed harder, and warmth dribbled down my skin.

"So you are," he said quietly. "Then perhaps you should follow orders more directly and maybe you will not end up with a spear in your back in some unfortunate battle."

"Perhaps."

The blade threatened to dig a little deeper, then the pressure released. "I'll take the whelp off your hands. Make sure he learns the ways of war properly."

Words died on my tongue, but I had nothing to give him as Kamil whirled and set off across camp towards my packs. I could only grab the leathers and follow.

Alik and the others paused in the midst of caring for sablecats as they saw Kamil. Salutes were given and Alik's gaze bored questions into me.

"Whelp!" Kamil called.

A flinch rocked through Michal's shoulders, but he turned and slowly made his way over. He stood a few paces away from Kamil and gave a salute.

"Alik." It almost surprised me to hear my second's name coming from Kamil. "How have the scraps been performing?"

Alik flicked another look to me, but I was still scrabbling for something. If Kamil was trying to get me to show a hint of caring or other perceived weakness, I couldn't give it to him. Otherwise it might be worse for Michal.

"He makes a good scout, Battlelion. He's proved his skill with the bow many times in the last countings."

A faint look of pride spread across Michal's face before he focused on the ground between his boots again.

"Good. Then he'll join my packs. I have need of more scouts."

Michal's head flew up and he looked in near horror from Kamil to me.

"Battlelion," Alik tried.

"Will that be a problem?" Kamil glanced from Alik to me.

I focused on Kamil to avoid the uneasiness on Michal's face. "No, Battlelion."

Kamil's eyes narrowed in slight frustration, but he did not change his mind.

Alik moved first. "Get your things," he told Michal.

The boy backed away, trying one more time to reach my gaze, before twisting away. I moved Luk over to my tent while Michal packed. And when he led his sablecat after a triumphant Kamil, I could only hold the younger's gaze for a moment before looking away.

It was the same look of anger I saw whenever I stood by and let Kamil or the chief have their way. For all my words, for all my dreams, I was still just a coward.

ELEVEN

DAVOR

"What happened?"

I jumped as Alik's hands slammed down on the saddle in front of me. Luk twisted his head, growling at Alik, but the pack leader ignored him.

"Davor?"

I finally looked at him across Luk's back for a moment before yanking the saddle leathers free. Alik cursed and I'd never heard him invoke the spirits so harshly. He ducked under Luk's head to come around.

"You let him?" The accusation rammed straight through me, and it brought my head back up. But Alik wasn't finished with me, and the disappointment in his eyes was perhaps the harshest.

"I don't often agree with the snake, but Michal is just a boy. And after looking out for him these countings, you let him be taken right into the bear's den."

I dragged the saddle free and threw it down, whirling back to Alik, my own frustrated anger finally finding its voice.

"Did you want me to refuse? Make an argument? I have survived my brother for years, Alik. And if he thinks something is important to you, then it is cruelly disposed of. Fighting for Michal would just make it worse for him."

Alik's gaze did not relent. "Is that what you're telling yourself?"

My lips twisted, tasting every bit of the bitter laugh that escaped as I divested Luk of his bridle.

"Perhaps it is. Perhaps it is the latest lie I am telling myself because I *cannot...*" My hands fisted against Luk's side. I dragged in a breath and a little bit of control to quiet the way my voice had risen. "Perhaps I am just a fool, Alik, and I am wishing on stars for something to change when it never will."

He did not stop me as I strode away, weaving through the trees to find somewhere quiet to sit and think on my failure.

I was not alone for long. Footsteps announced Alik coming towards me. I tipped my head back.

"Not finished?" I asked.

He hooked a hand into the collar of his breastplate, scuffing one foot against the thick grass. "No, I came to apologize."

My confusion must have shown on my face because he shook his head.

"It's what friends do, Davor."

An odd feeling pressed up against my chest and I turned my attention to the grass and small white flowers poking through. The thought still spilled out. "I do not have friends."

"I know." He grunted as he settled beside me.

"Then why are you here?"

I think I preferred it when he was yelling at me.

"Because for all that I said, I did not do anything to stop Kamil either." He sighed and swept up a few grass blades. "I was angry with myself, you, Kamil. I saw a scared boy and did nothing to help."

"It's not you he is testing. It's me."

Alik shook his head. "That doesn't matter. What matters is that I did not stand up for him. Just like no one has stood up for you or many others in the tribe."

I focused on the yellow center of the flower beside my boot. Why would it matter to him? I didn't want to ask, not sure I wanted the answer.

He shifted and bits of torn grass fluttered to the ground. "My family has lived in the middle village for three generations. We've given warriors to the packs with each one. Except my brother. He wanted to heal. So he apprenticed and stayed clear of the training grounds that called to me every waking moment."

I tilted a glance from the corner of my eye. Alik stared straight ahead, focused on something out of sight in the trees ahead.

"In the war with the Blackpaws, we both rode out. Him with the healers and me with the packs. And in those packs was a chieftain's son who had no business riding to war so young. I was barely old enough myself and had just earned a spear. Nowhere close to sitting in the chieftain's lodge as a pack leader, just hearing the stories and knowing to steer clear of the upper village."

I sat frozen, watching another grass blade fold under his fingers. This was a story of the two of us, and I did not know what to make of it.

"But one day, the chief, desperate for more warriors to fill saddles, ordered the healers to mount up."

I swallowed hard. I knew this part of his story.

"The chieftain's son tried to argue against it, saying we needed their skills for after the battles. We all knew it because the chief punished him for it in plain sight. And the healers rode to war. In the battle, the son tried to protect my brother. I saw it happen. But my brother hated spears and swords, and the warrior was one against three lynx riders."

Alik's voice trembled, and he squeezed his eyes shut for a long moment. "I saw him die and you try to protect him. We got him off the field together, and I remember you saying you were sorry over and over before you passed out from a wound."

My hand strayed up to my left shoulder where a lynx's teeth had left their mark.

"Later I came looking for you to see if you were all right. My brother would have wanted it—me to tell you thank you for trying. That's the way he was." His smile came shaky. "It didn't matter to him if a person succeeded or failed, just that they tried. I saw you take a blow from Kamil like you barely felt it. But it was the rage in your eyes that scared me the most. The war ended not long after."

I searched my memory for the years since the Blackpaw war, wondering if I remembered when I had let Alik start talking to me. He'd persistently tried even though I had failed him and his brother. Perhaps I was waiting for revenge that had never come.

"I snuck up to the chieftain's lodge one night, and saw some of the stories were true. I already knew what sort of man Kamil was from the training grounds. Saw what sort of man the chieftain really was in the war. And I saw the streaks of their cruelty rampant through that lodge in many of the pack leaders. And you absorbing what was thrown your way but not giving it out again."

I shifted to try to shake the feeling pressing around me. No one saw that about me. They only saw cowardice.

"So pity drew you my way?" The sharpness of my voice did not wound him.

"No. I wanted to see what kind of man you really were. You made it hard to even get close to you to say anything." He lifted a wry eyebrow. "I wanted to hope that maybe the chieftain's line wasn't all bad."

"And have I proved you wrong yet?"

He tossed the tightly folded grass blade away. "Not yet. I could have stood with you many different times over the last years—today—but I did not. I left you to face many things alone. That's not what friends, or decent people, do."

I picked at a callous on my palm, turning his words over and over. "Why would you want to be friends with me?"

"Because you care. You always have. And maybe I still believe that you could make a change."

"I don't even believe I could," I said softly.

"Well." He turned to face me a little more fully. "That's what you have me for." He held out a hand.

I stared at it for a long moment, my heart wanting it, but my head telling me it was a trick, some way to try to trap me. And for once, I listened to my heart.

Alik smiled as my palm met his. He shifted and pulled me to my feet.

"Come on."

He led the way back to camp and the low fire with the pack leaders friendly towards me gathered around. And hope started to flare back to life again.

TWELVE

MARTA

"I'm going to the gathering, Vanda. Do you want to come?" My hands did not hesitate in packing items into the woven basket.

My sister paused in clearing dishes from the tables. "Perhaps later. They'll need help with cleaning from the hunt."

Despite being the daughter of a huntsman for twenty-four years, I did not like blood, but it did not bother Vanda. She often helped our father when he had hides or kills needing to be cleaned. And now that he was gone, those who were still hunting needed help more than ever.

"Anything we need?"

The gathering was the day every counting that the villages came together in the wide field between upper and lower and traded wares or supplies. A place where there was usually laughter and peace that sometimes could not be found within lodges or villages.

"Only if Zora has any berries from her secret stash."

We shared a bittersweet smile. Father loved the breads flavored with the berries that Zora somehow made even sweeter through their drying. But he was not here, and we'd had no news from the packs in the countings since he had been ordered away. Across the lodge, Mother moved in the same sort of quiet haze she had since he'd left.

Vanda came closer and we watched her for a moment.

"Should I ask her if she wants to come?" I whispered.

Vanda shrugged unhappily. "I don't think she's really left the lodge since they rode out."

"Last time it took a while before she was more herself." The bitterness lodged back in my throat. Vanda leaned her shoulder against mine, and I tipped my head against hers.

"I can better help this time," she said. "Maybe we'll go for a walk along the river. The cornflowers are blooming already."

My arm snuck around her, and we stood for a moment. "And what about you? How are you doing?" I asked.

Vanda settled more against my side, like we were just children again. "I'll be happier when the war is done and he's back."

"Me too." I sighed, and released her.

"Have fun." She kissed my cheek and spun away, picking up the plates and taking them to go wash in water barely heated from the river's iciness.

As expected, Mother refused my invitation, quietly patting my cheek and telling me to enjoy the morning. I gave her a smile and kiss and picked up my basket, hurrying from the lodge before I could wish for vengeance on those who had taken Father.

The village had been quiet these last countings, no echo of practice swords or spears from the training grounds. No sounds of sablecat growls or roars as they scuffled or trained with riders. No shouts of men and women to each other in greeting as they went about their day.

It already felt like I was walking through ghosts much like eight years ago. It took a moment and the sight of cornflowers bobbing in the patch of sunlight beside a lodgehouse to shake me from the thought. My steps picked up as I headed for the bridge.

A figure stood on the bridge, staring out at the river. My heart jolted in my chest thinking it was Davor again, back with more cruel news. Just as fast, I wondered why my mind had gone to him immediately.

As I came closer, I found I did not recognize the man, wrapped in a plain cloak, and greying hair cut short. His shoulders slumped under some weight.

"Are you all right?" I asked, shifting the basket on my hip, ready to back away or move closer. But for some reason I did not think I had anything to fear from him.

He shifted and turned to face me. Wrinkles deepened around his eyes as he gave a smile.

"Better for having seen the river." His eyes held a deepness I had seen in one other man before.

"You're the Greywolf *talånd*."

His smile faltered. "Was. But it seems the spirits have not cast me off from their care completely. I had a thought to come to the river today, feeling that I might get answers for questions and dreams turning over in my head. And I think I have some."

I tilted my head. "Are all *talånds* so cryptic?" Our own tended to speak around things when he came to the villages.

The *talånd* laughed. It had a nice timbre to it, and I relaxed a fraction more.

"A question often asked by the young. But I'll tell you what I often had to tell a young man of my tribe when he wanted quick answers. The ways of the spirits are never easy, never straightforward. Something is coming to this tribe, and I wonder that I am here to see it."

I shivered despite the warmth of the spring morning, but no breeze whipped up off the river to explain it.

"Why are you telling me this?" Me, and not someone else. But I did not think the chieftain would care to hear news like this.

"Because every man and woman in this tribe will soon have to make a choice. And you are the first I have seen this morning, and that makes me think you are important."

"I'm nobody, really." I shifted again. Perhaps less than no one. One who was better contented to embroider the beauty of the land into cloth, listen to the stories told in the gatherings and around the fires. A woman of twenty-four who had refused two marriage proposals from men I barely knew and who had only one use for me. And I would not be relegated to that, left powerless like so many other women in the tribe.

"No one is really nobody. We all have a purpose." It seemed like the sort of thing elders kindly told men or women who were deemed to not be serving in the ways expected of the tribe. But from him, I wanted to believe it.

He tipped his head and wandered off the bridge. I watched him go, before shaking free of the strange feeling his words had left me with and continuing to the gathering.

The last unease left me at the sounds of chattering and

laughing. I switched the basket to my other hip and quickened my pace. The wide field was filled with tables and benches hauled out in the early morning hours from lodges to give places for wares to be displayed or villagers to gather and exchange gossip.

The grass grew shorter in the wide square after generations of gatherings and the sections dedicated to the training circles. The even ground spilled into the river where it ran a little quieter and shallower against the sandy banks.

I slipped through the milling men and women, children running wild with baked treats clutched in their hands. A few sablecat cubs chased them or pounced on anything that moved, all oversized paws and fangs they sharpened on any hard surface.

"Marta!" A call drew me over to my first stop. "What do you have for me today?" The older woman leaned forward on her table. I set my basket down and drew out a few of my favorite pieces.

Strips of cloth embroidered in bright colors. Some in shapes that struck my fancy, some following the winding pattern of ivy around trees, and some with flowers of all colors. Lene pulled out one filled with blues and reds.

"This would well suit the neckline of the dress I'm making my daughter."

"I likely won't have more red thread for a while," I said. We got the red die from the Coyote traders who moved between the tribes in the valley and down through the lowlands without fear from anyone. But the deep red dye came from the Blackpaw side of the valley and with war and the traders away south for the spring, my supply was already low.

Lene traded me a few more lengths of finely woven cloth from her lodge. She and her daughters watched over the process of harvesting the plants from the protected side of the hills, drying and cutting, then pounding to get the fibers to be woven into cloths on their looms.

A few more stops to trade smaller ribbons with prayer runes for safety or protection and to quickly add a name to them. Some to be worn around the wrist or to be burned in an offering fire to the All-Father or Saber spirit, asking protection for a warrior out with the packs.

I stopped at an empty bench to rearrange my basket with my supplies and the items I'd gained in trade. I eased onto it to let my feet rest a moment and pulled the basket into my lap. Others called my name in greeting as they passed and I stayed where I was, content for the moment.

I went to the upper and lower villages often enough. People knew my skill with the needle in both and I traded often for things for the lodge. But there was never quite this much openness. It was like the field was the one place we could all trust that there would not be violence or trickery.

A stir cut through the crowd, and I tensed. A woman spat at the feet of a younger woman, and a man bumped rudely into her shoulder but she kept walking, sending them both seething glares which were ignored as much as her.

But what surprised me most was that she was headed for me. A leering man with the smoky forearms and heavy apron of a blacksmith stopped her. The woman said something back to him that had his face darkening in anger. Her hand strayed to the knife on her belt and he raised a fist, but I had already started moving.

"There you are!" I said brightly as if I hadn't almost witnessed violence. The man lowered his arm in surprise. She jolted away from me, but I set a gentle hand on hers. "I've been waiting. Come on!"

We retreated back to the table, and she edged away from me.

"Are you all right?" I asked.

She crossed her arms over her stomach and regarded me a moment before nodding. There was something familiar about her narrow features and stormy eyes, and judging from the looks many were giving her as they passed us, I was starting to have an uncomfortable realization of who I'd helped.

"Thank you," she finally said. "Are you Marta?"

"I am. You were looking for me?"

She nodded. "I'd heard that you have some of the best patterns. I'm not very good with a needle, and my mother is a healer and better at stitching wounds than cloth."

I tugged my basket closer. "What are you looking for?"

"Prayer cloths for my brother."

I offered another smile and pulled out the few I had left—narrow strips of cloth marked in runes and small sablecat heads. "Is he with the packs?"

She nodded, lips twisting a little as she bent over the cloths, studying intently. I watched her just as closely. Darker fabrics made up her dress and overtunic, worn around the elbows, a few rips mended in the cloth with slanted stitches. Not what I would have done, but then I tended to cover holes with flowers or brighter colors. Her hem could have done with a pattern around it. The red thread would have suited it well.

"These two." She selected two cloths with runes of protection and I offered my smile again. "I have some things to trade." She dug in the small leather bag slung across her chest. "Herb packets from my mother. If you burn them, they help you calm."

I immediately thought of my mother. "One will do."

We made the exchange, and she cradled the narrow cloths in her hands. "I noticed…you can put the names on them?"

I nodded, tucking the herb packet into my basket, and pulled the needle free from the skirt of my overdress and some thread from the pocket. I usually did it in white for remembrance.

She handed over the first one.

"Michal," she said, and the bit of unease prickled the back of my arms again. But I stitched the runes.

"Same for this one?" I reached for the second. But she hesitated, and looked around.

"No…" Her voice lowered to barely a whisper. "Davor." Wide eyes looked up to me as my hand jerked back involuntarily.

My fingers curled around my needle as I wondered what might become of me for helping Janne, the outcast daughter of the chief. Giving her prayer cloths for her brothers.

"If you do not want to, I can do it." It rushed from her.

It was one thing to save a young woman from violence in a way I wished I could have saved my own sister, but another to help her ask protection for two of the chief's sons. Even if neither of them had been the one to harm Vanda.

The Greywolf *talånd's* words echoed back to me, and my hand eased forward again. Relief shone in her eyes as I made the first stitch, forcing myself to think of the prayers and not a curse on him instead.

"I did not think you might want one for Davor." It slipped from me. I'd turned his almost promise over and over in the sleepless nights since Father had left. Wondering if he'd truly look out for the hunters or instead follow the ways of his brother.

Her green eyes turned sharp again, her hands tucking under her arms as if stopping herself from grabbing it from me.

"Many underestimate him." It came with a challenge, but I made the last stitch and tied it off. She took it from me, movements wary again. I tucked the needle back through a fold in my skirt, gathered my basket back up, and made a choice.

"Did you have other business here?" I asked.

Janne shook her head, but the glance she cast back through the crowd was almost weary.

"Can I walk with you?"

It took her off guard, and I think she nodded just out of reflex. But she stayed close to my side as we wove through the crowds, and this time many smiles or greetings died as they saw who walked pressed up by my side. Our path stayed unimpeded to the edge of the market, and she paused, cloths clenched tight in her hands.

"Thank you." She lifted her hand a little in offering.

"You're welcome." I managed another smile. "And if the herbs work, can I come to find some more at your lodge?"

She nodded, eyes wide.

"My father is out with the packs," I said. "My mother has not been sleeping well."

Janne's smile came wobbly. "My mother has been restless as well since Michal has been gone."

"Your twin?"

"I tell myself I'd know if something happened to him. We're close. I think Davor might help look after him, but—" Her shoulders rose and fell in a shrug.

"He really would?"

Janne's look turned protective. "Davor isn't like the others."

I wished I could believe her, but coldness surrounded him just like the others. Except for that moment at the bridge where it seemed there was a shred of the man I'd glimpsed one day in the forest.

"Thank you for the cloths," she said stiffly, and turned in a ripple of skirts and braids, and made her way back into the upper village.

I looked back, but the crowds had closed again, and I suddenly did not feel like trying to dive back in. Instead, I headed back to the bridge, pausing once in the middle and wondering over Janne's words and the *talånd's* predictions. That and Davor's face when he said he'd hoped that something different might come when they returned from war. If they returned from war.

The chill returned to brush down my back and I hurried away from it.

Thirteen

DAVOR

I eased a finger under the bandage tightly wrapped around my forearm. Kamil's tent loomed large in front of me. For one blessed counting my packs and I had been gone from the main camp, scouting and pushing the Greywolves back.

The three new packs Kamil had assigned me on the mission looked less warily at me now that we were back. The sneers had quickly faded under the quiet support from Alik and his pack, and when I continued to order wounded taken from the field, and did not wastefully throw men at a losing battle for pride's sake. When infractions weren't punished with physical violence, and instead with extra duties, because I would not beat a man for a mistake.

Even though this time I had good news to bring, I still gathered a short breath before stepping in.

Kamil was not alone, and my heart plummeted down to my

toes to see Michal standing at the table, arms tight across his breastplate, and eye blackened. Emil turned as I came in and his glare seared through me, though not as harshly as the anger fresh in Michal's eyes.

"Davor." My name came lazily from Kamil. "Look at us all here. One happy family."

Makar was the only other one in the tent and he smirked from his place beside Kamil. I had not missed that expression over the last counting either.

"We're at the southern bend of the river." I turned to reporting instead. "I left two packs there to keep patrolling."

"Good." Kamil's tone turned sharp and commanding. He could be a battlelion when he wasn't playing games. "Losses?"

"Two dead, many wounded. They did not give the river easily."

"How soon can you ride again?"

I bit the inside of my cheek. My packs needed *days* to rest, let wounds start to heal before we found battle again. I felt like I could sleep for a counting. Challenge lined Kamil's eyes, and I returned some of it.

"Two days."

His eyes narrowed. "You have one."

I tipped my head. He circled the table and I stiffened as his arm draped around my shoulders in a friendly manner, drawing me closer to the map.

"Always so suspicious, Davor," he chided, but his gaze tilted towards Emil. The younger stared back, face blank. Kamil gestured to the map.

"We need to strike north. You're the first to reach the river; what do you think?"

Though I wanted to shake his arm free, I let it stay there as I studied the map. Some carved wooden pieces settled on the hide, marking the places we thought their camps were and small stones marking the borders.

"There." I pointed to a place where small tributaries came together before spilling down into the great river. It was well on their side of the stones. "That's where we should aim for. Send five packs. If you can get the wolves in retreat, keep harrying until they fall back, and leave riders to secure the rivers."

"And then?"

I nudged a few stones with my finger, creating a precarious bend in their lines. "Then it's easier for us to strike east and push them towards the river."

"Perhaps not a complete fool after all, Davor." My shoulders shook slightly under his nudge.

My other hand did not ease its grip around the knife on my belt.

"As the mind behind this, you should be the one to lead it." His hold slipped free, and I inclined my head. If I failed, the blame would be squarely on me. If I succeeded, he'd have to find another way to kill me.

"You and your packs take the day of rest, then I want you riding out."

I snuck a glance at Michal, who still hadn't moved.

"I want fresh scouts, and another pack with me," I said.

Kamil arched an eyebrow, but conceded with a wave of his hand.

"I'll take Michal." Iron filled my voice, and the challenge there almost frightened me.

Kamil's eyes narrowed, and he searched my face, looking for the reason. I inclined my head slightly.

"He makes a good scout. And perhaps I am finding the stomach for war."

A faint smile crept through. "Take him then." He waved to Michal whose glare did not abate. "And we'll see when you return."

I saluted and pushed from the tent. A hand grabbed my arm, pulling me around, and I caught Michal's fist. Rage burned in his eyes with a tinted redness around the green iris.

"Kamil hasn't killed me yet, so now you will?" he gritted.

"Go get your things." I released him and kept walking.

Alik limped over to join me as I returned.

"We have one day," I said. "Then we leave to strike north."

He sighed and looked over the camp. "One day is not enough."

"I tried to get us two." My shoulders slumped a little.

"You need some rest, too." He tapped my shoulder and it did not make me shy away like I had from Kamil.

"Not yet. I claimed new scouts and a new pack to go with us. I want them now before Kamil does something."

Alik nodded. "I'll go with you."

Together we made our way over to the scouts' camp.

"I got Michal," I said quietly.

"Good." Firm approval lined in his voice. "How is he?"

"It looks to have been a hard counting for him." I couldn't lift my gaze from the ground passing under my boots. No harder than countings I'd spent with Kamil out on patrol or during the Blackpaw war, but that was different. It wasn't someone who'd made a safer place for me and then abandoned me without a fight.

Alik cursed softly.

"Will you look after him again?" I asked.

"Why not you?"

A scoff broke from me. "He hates me. Wouldn't you?"

Alik shrugged. "You cannot make change if you do not try."

I shook my head. "I think being friends with you will be too annoying."

He laughed and clapped my shoulder, as a smile tilted the corner of my mouth. It died when we found Emil waiting for us by the scouts, the familiar disgust back in his eyes.

"I need new scouts," I said.

"I know." He spat at my feet. "I won't even stop you like he wants me to."

I regarded him warily, but when he made no other move, Alik and I passed around him. I tilted a look back, but Emil had already moved on.

"I know a few of the hunters here. They're good at what they do," Alik said. I nodded, letting him pick out three men, one of whom was Marta's father. There was an odd sort of relief at seeing him still alive, and I shoved thought of her away again.

My paltry offer of assurance on the bridge might now come to an end with my plan. We were heading straight into battles and with the condition of my men, the scouts would have to be pulled in as well.

Emil did not stop us as we left, and I stopped at the nearest pack to tell them to ride with us the next day. The pack leader gave a tentative salute of fist to chest even though I hadn't ridden with him yet.

As I swept a glance over the camp again, realization struck that there was a divide in the camp. The scouts held their own corner, but there was a division between the packs who rode with me—and those like the pack leader who had just saluted—and warriors I knew supported Kamil wholeheartedly.

I swallowed hard, watching what seemed a dangerous thing.

Alik paused beside me. "You see it?"

I nodded, afraid to give voice to the hope stirring. If my eyes were to be believed, I might be able to summon half the packs to my side if I made a bid for something higher than *rokr*.

"I told you," Alik said.

I had no answer, and instead kept walking back to our camp. I wouldn't bother pitching my tent. We were just leaving in the morning.

The new scouts settled in among the packs in a tight group. I hung back, seeing to Luk as Alik spent a few minutes talking and sharing a few laughs with the men. My hands stopped in pulling the saddle away as Michal arrived in camp, leading his sablecat.

...if you do not try.

I stepped around Luk and called, "Michal."

He stopped, shoulders set, then slowly turned to face me. A bit of fresh blood streaked beside his mouth, a raw bit of warpaint highlighting the anger in his face. For me.

Try.

"I am sorry," I said softly.

He lurched forward. "I am not interested in being bartered back and forth in whatever game you and Kamil are playing."

"I..." But I didn't know what to say that would not sound like some other plot.

"I shouldn't have listened to you." Refusal twisted up his lips and he walked on. There was no point in even cursing the rejection. I might not have believed it either if I was him.

A few of the warriors greeted him, and his guarded posture slipped. Alik tapped his shoulder and brought him over to the new scouts to introduce. The pressure in my chest eased when Marta's father made room for him in their small circle.

Morning came too fast, and with it, Kamil, reminding me of our orders. My men wearily stood and began saddling sablecats. I did the same, wondering why they still bothered to follow me when it was clear we might have the worst lot of the packs.

Alik grimaced as he hauled himself into the saddle. "I think we got more rest last counting away from camp than we do here."

I raised an eyebrow. "Maybe we'll take a few extra days."

He frowned in thought. "Not a bad plan."

Except that we'd be riding deep into Greywolf territory and would have no safe place to camp and rest.

The scouts rode up, the three we had left from our original packs and the new huntsmen. Michal rode at the back, still not looking at me.

"We're heading north to a rivers' crossing. The Greywolves still hold it," I said. The huntsmen all wore old looking armor, perhaps drawn out of trunks for the first time in eight years.

"Names?" I asked them.

They gave them readily, all eyeing me curiously as they did. My scouts rode relaxed, though some stifled yawns. My attention flicked back to Marta's father. Dariy. He seemed a decent man; no doubt Alik would have said something otherwise. Marta's anger at his leaving proved that as well. And I jerked thoughts from her again.

Try.

"Michal is young, but he makes a good scout and hunter. I want you all to teach him what you can."

Michal's head flew up, eyes narrowed as he tried to sort out what I'd said, searching for some other meaning. There was not much I could give him that he would even want. Perhaps from them he could learn another way to be a man. Dariy twisted in his saddle to look at him, then back to me, evaluating.

But they all saluted, the huntsmen eyeing the others warily at the bold tap they gave.

"Move out." I did not give them time to think on it.

We followed them from camp, and I felt the burn of Kamil's warning glare for miles afterward.

I slumped in the saddle, hand trembling against my side, hot blood leaking from a wound scored under the breastplate's edge by a Greywolf spear. I clutched at Luk's fur, unable to find the rein leathers. He rocked forward and I almost lost my seat but Alik's stern "Hold on, Davor," had my fingers gripping harder.

Luk's fur abruptly shifted to the darkening sky peering down through towering branches. Alik's face appeared, and the pressure of my breastplate released. My hand was moved, and something prodded my side. I lurched upright until a hand slammed into my chest.

Alik pulled my shirt up, fingers slipping in blood as he prodded at the wound. I cursed him and several of his ancestors.

"It's a clean cut through the muscle," he finally said.

"Stitches?" a new voice asked, and my head slowly turned to take in Dariy as the one holding me down.

"We need something quicker. Get this in the fire." Alik handed a knife to someone just out of sight.

My head hit the ground and another groan pulled from me as Alik's hands pressed back to the wound.

"Just hold on, Davor."

I didn't have any reply, just trying to do as he asked as the sky swam in and out of focus.

"All right. Hold him." Alik's voice had a strained edge to it.

With an effort, I craned my neck back up to see him holding a glowing blade in one hand. Part of my mind finally fought back, and hands pressed down harder as I tried desperately to wrench away from the threat.

"Bite down." Dariy shoved something in my mouth, and I tasted leather through blood and panic.

Alik tilted a glance up at the sky and his lips moved before he brought it down. I screamed even before it touched me and then until it stopped.

The knife handle was pulled from my mouth and a ragged breath followed. Dampness trickled across my cheek. Alik's hand fell to my shoulder, and he was leaning close.

"I'm sorry. I'm so sorry."

My fingers unclenched from something and closed around his forearm instead.

Cold pressed against my side and I twisted again. Alik's hold stayed gentle as he kept me from moving too much.

"Breathe."

I pulled air back into my battered lungs as the cold began to lessen its sting. It happened twice more, then Alik helped me sit up and Dariy wrapped a bandage around my middle, obscuring the burn from view.

They prodded at another cut on my thigh before dousing it in water and wrapping another bandage.

"We need to get riders back out," Alik said.

We'd taken miles from the Greywolves as we'd forged past the rivers' crossing, only stopping our pursuit of their steady retreat when I'd been wounded.

I nodded, working my jaw to appease the aching joint. "Give me a few minutes."

"Davor, no." Alik shook his head, something like resigned

amusement in his face. "You've done enough. Stay here and rest."

I stared at him a moment. "Don't engage them. Patrols only."

He tapped my shoulder and helped me lie down, propping my head against something. Warmth pressed over me, and I slipped in and out of consciousness until sometime later I stirred more awake. Stars peeked down through the foliage over me. Another shift and I saw Michal standing nearby, sablecat's leathers in hand. His expression stayed unreadable in the dim light of the moon and the fires.

"Come to finish me off?" Maybe then I could finally find some rest.

He shook his head and came slowly over to sit just out of arm's reach. His sablecat sank down on haunches beside him. Luk's soft chuff drew my attention to my other side where the lion sprawled beside me.

"Kamil said I should. If I had the chance." Michal pulled his knees up to his chest, resting arms atop them.

"You listening to Kamil now?"

He scrubbed under his nose, turning his head slightly to glare at me. "Kamil at least understands the ways of this tribe."

I stared at a star appearing and disappearing with each rustle of the branches. "I told you. I don't care for Kamil's ways."

Michal scoffed. "So you keep to the coward's way?"

It sent a flinch through me, the way it was meant to. Maybe he had learned a thing or two.

"It's clear you're out for yourself now, Davor. And I don't think yours is the place for me." But he didn't seem quite sure, still glaring at me from what I could see in the darkness.

"That's for you to decide for yourself." If anything, he seemed to stiffen even more. "If you want to go back to him, you can. If you want to stay here, you can. There's no danger from me."

There was no reply from him, no move to walk away, or maybe try to take me in my current state. He adjusted his boots against the ground.

"How do I know you're not lying?"

"I have broken many promises. I'm trying to fix at least one of them."

His eyes gleamed bright, and I held the angry stare, silently promising I wouldn't give him up this time. Michal broke it off first, sniffing and raking fingers through the grass instead.

I lifted the blanket, pressing my free hand against the bandage barely hiding the pain stinging and writhing its way into my side. Another curse softly whispered through my teeth.

"Do you need anything?" Michal's quiet question had a bit of truce.

I looked around from my poor vantage. Around dim fires were bundles of sleeping warriors and sablecats.

"No." We all just needed rest. "Is Alik back?"

"Not yet."

I settled back, telling myself that it had only been a few hours. There were plenty of prayer cloths around warriors' wrists in the packs. Maybe the spirits would watch over them, even if they never did much for me.

Michal hadn't shifted, picking at his collection of grass and pine needles when it was clear I wasn't moving.

"Are you all right, Michal?"

He tossed the bits away. "Why do you care?"

But he still hadn't left, and I wasn't sure why. "Perhaps my way is making sure as many of us make it home from this war as we can."

"Even your brothers?" His scoff was almost as sharp as Emil's.

"Maybe the ones who aren't interested in killing me."

His brief laugh held something almost like humor. "So I should suddenly trust you then?"

I shifted again, wincing at the fiery jab into my side. "You decide. But I am going to sleep."

He didn't leave, and we stayed in silence until I finally slipped back into sleep.

FOURTEEN

ΔAVOR

I woke to more warmth and the stronger smell of wood-smoke. A grimace contorted my face as I pushed up to an elbow. Luk stirred beside me, stretching his large limbs, paws spreading wide. A low chuff broke from his throat as he yawned. Pink tongue licked around his curved fangs as he turned to me.

He let me get a hand around his neck and moved gently up to his feet, bringing me most of the way with him. I leaned heavily on him, waiting for a burst of dizziness to pass. An extra blanket fell to my feet—one I didn't remember from my packs.

Michal still lay nearby, half curled atop his sablecat who lay sprawled on its side. One paw curled back protectively towards Michal, and he shivered a little in the morning air. Taking Luk's support again, I scooped up the blankets and limped over to Michal, carefully draping them over him.

His sablecat blinked, then rested its head back, content that I was not there to hurt its rider. Luk padded along beside me as I staggered to the small stream running quietly through the small forest we sheltered in. Every step prodded at my thigh and side.

I stared down at my rippling reflection, barely recognizing myself. Blood and dirt smeared across cheeks thinned and rimmed in exhaustion and warpaint. My fingers plucked at the shirt stiffened by the dried blood that stained my trousers down to the top of the greave still in place over my boot.

Luk huffed as he bent and lapped up water. I used his shoulder to help lower myself to the bank. The icy waters shocked me fully awake as I dipped my hands underneath and grabbed a handful of sand from the bank to scrub them clean.

My bracers came off and sleeves rolled up as I cleaned my arms, then my face and neck. Once done and my thirst sated, I sat back, that effort leaving a strange exhaustion in my muscles.

The camp was slowly stirring. Shapes moved, emerging as warriors or sablecats in the growing light. Quiet murmurs started joining the ever-present rustle of the pines and aspens clustered around the water.

Someone cleared their throat and I looked up at Dariy. He held something and I pressed a hand over the knife at my side.

"You all right, *Rokr*?" he asked.

I nodded warily, not about to show that I wasn't quite feeling up to the short trek back to my pack.

"I have some baltar root. It's good for burns." He offered the item in his hands, and knelt a pace away, keeping my gaze. "I can do it for you, if you're not familiar with its use."

I had no idea if he was telling the truth about the root or not, and I wished Alik was there to confirm or deny. Although he seemed to trust the hunter.

"I swear by the spirits that it'll help." Dariy lifted his wrist, showing several prayer cloths tied around his wrist. Someone more devout than me.

I finally nodded and he gathered two stones from the river and set about grinding the root down.

He directed me to sit on a larger rock, and Luk lent his strength to help me up. Dariy finished and came closer. Hesitating, I pulled up my bloody shirt and let him loosen the spotted bandage.

"You helped last night."

He nodded. "I think you bruised my arm the way you were holding on."

"I'm sorry."

A smile creased up around his eyes. "Can't blame you."

Dariy dipped a cloth in the river and pressed it gently against the red, warped skin I winced to see. Water dribbled over the ground root, and he stirred it with a finger, thickening it into a paste.

"This might sting for a moment."

He dabbed it over my skin. Flashes of yellow from the cloth around his wrist caught my eye. Intricate patterns and runes sewn in to beg protection of the Saber spirit and All-Father.

"I've never seen prayer cloths like that." My mother hadn't been one to frequent the spirits' lodge either, so I'd never thought much of tying them around my arm.

He paused and tipped his wrist to look at them. "My daughter makes them." I didn't miss the glance he shot at my bare wrists. "She's one of the best stitchers in the entire tribe. Don't feel safe unless I've got one on."

I winced as he found a tender spot, but the paste had started to bring a cool to chase away the lingering fire.

"I am sorry you were dragged out here."

He rocked back on his heels, dipping his hands back in the stream to clean them. "It's the way of it. I served in the last war as well."

My mind was all too happy to conjure up his daughter's angry, tear-streaked face.

"It shouldn't be the way."

He dried his hands on the grass and set about retightening the bandage. "You really aren't like the others, are you?"

His steady eyes tried to see past the walls I'd built up.

"Alik speaks highly of you, and his trust isn't so easily earned as people think."

"You are from the same lodge?" I asked, even though I did know.

He nodded. "Ours is newer, built for overflows of families. My girls grew up alongside Alik and his brother." He paused and I wondered if mention of the brother, dead to another war the chief ordered, might make him regret helping.

"It seems that some of us might be getting back if we follow your orders." He stood, hesitating before tapping a fist to his chest. "I'll keep an eye out for more root. You'll want to keep some on that for a few days to keep down the sting."

"Dariy." He halted, surprised that I remembered his name. "Thank you."

He tipped his head, a deeper nod that made me shift in discomfort, and walked away.

Luk nudged my arm, and I let him push underneath. He cautiously sniffed at my side, mouth dropping open for a moment at the odd scent of the root paste. I scratched the side of his jaw, only to get him surging up to lick my cheek with rough tongue.

"Go on." I pushed him away. He came right back with damp nose into my face.

"What?"

His gold eyes stared into mine for a moment, an odd sort of understanding there before it flickered back to the animal instinct that normally showed. I caught the look occasionally and it would make me uneasy. The Saber spirit had given us the bond with his animal generations ago and sometimes it seemed that they understood more than we thought. That Luk might understand many of the things I'd whispered to him or screamed in the lonely woods. Maybe telling the Saber spirit how I sometimes cursed him.

Luk pressed his head against my chest and a ragged breath escaped, helping me shake free of the feeling. He withdrew and I scooped up my bracers and buckled them back on. I leaned on Luk again as we made our way back to where Michal was stirring. He pushed the blankets away and stared across the camp with bleary eyes.

"You get some rest?" I asked.

He nodded, and warily moved away from his sablecat, hands patting at his weapons before closing around the bow and quiver he'd set aside. His lion heaved to its feet, stretching and yawning then coming to nose at his hair. Michal scowled and pushed it away as if afraid to be seen showing some sort of affection to it.

Luk padded over, sniffing at Michal's face then circling around to push against the other sablecat. They shoved for a moment, thunderous purrs breaking as tails twitched and paws batted with sheathed claws. Luk reared up with front paws raised and crashed down on the other.

Michal huffed in irritation as they started scuffling. He stood and pulled his gear away from the mock battleground.

"Davor!" Alik strode over, trailed by his sablecat in leathers. It looked at our battling lions with vague aloofness. "Good to see you up."

His clap to my shoulder sent me unsteady on my injured leg.

"No thanks to whatever you did." I managed a faint smile.

"The thanks I get for my quick thinking." He shook his head. "Michal, you look a little better than awful."

Michal ducked his head. "I'm all right."

Alik's look to him was the same as I'd caught him giving to me—something like faint exasperation and understanding. With a jolt, I realized that I'd finally recognized that Alik went through life with lighthearted pronouncements that held no underlying meanings, and Michal had not had time enough with us to understand this. And it made me want to keep trying to show Michal this side of life.

"Reports?" I asked.

"We chased their packs another few miles before turning back. It's been quiet here all night from what guards have said, but I don't like it." Alik scanned the trees around.

"I don't either. Can we make it back to the rivers' crossing?" The landmark had yielded almost too easily to us before we'd chased the Greywolves this deep into their territory.

"I will give the order." He nodded and strode off.

Luk broke off his fight at my whistle. I stifled a groan as I bent down to retrieve the saddle. Michal was still standing there, watching me.

"Do you need help?" he blurted.

Part of me almost snarled a reflexive *no*, but the new part of me that had started to emerge away from the villages nodded. He kept eyes down and stayed away from me as he slung the saddle over Luk's back. I took over tightening the leathers as he slipped the bridle on.

He buckled my pack to the saddle while I stared down at my

breastplate. Blood still covered part of it, but the thought of tightening it over my wound had no appeal. I might regret it, but I carefully picked it up and loosened a strap over the packs to tie it down.

My sword and knives I rearranged over my belt to sling across my chest instead. Michal saddled up his sablecat, and I did not miss that he kept a wary eye on me.

He paused, mouth opening a moment, before he slammed it shut and spun away, pulling his sablecat after him.

I watched the weariness of warriors and sablecats as they broke camp and prepared to move out, and made my decision. We were going back to the rivers' meeting and staying there for a few days before going back to the main camp.

Alik returned to my side as I struggled up into the saddle. He passed over folded flatbread wrapped around fresh cooked elk meat. I laid my spear across my lap and tapped a signal against Luk's shoulder to remain still while I halfheartedly tried to eat.

"Scouts are going out to make sure our way back is clear." Alik eyed my lack of armor. "You all right?"

I nodded, still trying to choke down another mouthful. My stomach rebelled against the food even though I'd barely eaten anything since the morning before and had lost blood since. Finally I stopped and handed the rest down to Luk who snatched it from my hand with an eagerness that reminded me we needed to let our lions free to hunt for themselves for a day.

Alik said nothing though I knew he wanted to. We moved forward and I hunched over my injured side before my body adjusted to Luk's gentle padding gait.

I led the way through the mounting warriors, returning nods and pausing beside some of the more seriously injured. Taking questions after my own health was a different matter and I awkwardly brushed them off despite the clear evidence of injury still all over me. And more than once felt Michal's evaluating gaze on me.

Fires were doused and scattered, and evidence of our stay wiped from the ground. Dariy rode back first with reports that the way before us was clear. The stronger warriors flanked the wounded in a protective square as we made a slow, steady retreat back to the safety of our new boundaries.

Alik and his sablecat tirelessly circled, joining me when scouts came back. It took twice as long to return as it had to cover the distance the first time with the Greywolves on the run. But no howls split the air and no flashes of grey showed on the horizon.

An uneasy thought came that we might have struck a harder blow than I realized with taking the river. There was no quick retaliation like there had been before the battlewolf fell. Had their resolve fallen with him? How much longer would it be before we saw their lodges?

Hakkon still labored under the thought that he would rule the valley, missing entirely the look on Kamil's face when he promised such a thing. There would be no Greywolves left once Kamil was done with the valley, and no Hakkon once he had served his purpose.

I nearly fell from the saddle once Luk came to a halt in the camp. The pack leader left in command gave a salute and I almost pulled back from the concern in his eyes for me.

"Choose some scouts and guards," I told him and Alik. "We are staying here for a few days to let everyone rest."

They exchanged a glance, but it was more of relief than doubt.

"Are we sending reports back?" Alik asked carefully.

"Tonight." I flashed a tired half-smile.

"So rebellious." He tapped my shoulder. My smile faded and

my stomach knotted at the word. Rebelliousness brought attention. I was not that.

I limped away to find an open spot. It seemed too much effort to pitch my tent, so I undid the bedroll and kicked it out. Luk growled as his leathers came free and he nosed at the pile I left them in.

I couldn't manage to care. I slowly lay down and pulled a blanket over me. The comforting feeling of Luk pressing up against my back let my muscles finally relax.

A gentle shake had me opening my eyes into the dim light of evening. Alik nudged me up to sitting. A waterskin was shoved into my hand and I drank as he changed the bandages. I barely heard that he had sent someone back to report our victory to Kamil before lying back down and slipping back into sleep.

The next time I woke, it was to gentle morning sunlight and Luk's nose in my face. Muttering an incoherent grunt, I pushed him away. He scrubbed his head against my shoulder, a purr rumbling in his chest.

"Go 'way," I said halfheartedly. The thrumming only deepened, and whiskers tickled my face.

I tilted my head to glare at him, but once he saw he had my attention he flopped to his back, giant front paws tucked up. Rolling my eyes, I reached out and scratched his chest. His golden eyes closed, and his purr continued.

A reluctant smile crept over my face. It shattered when a voice shouted, "Where is he?"

Luk rolled to his paws, ears flat and growl ready at the threat. I tossed away the blanket and had pushed halfway to my feet when Kamil's boot to my side sent me back down.

"Get up," he sneered.

I obeyed, scooping up a knife as I did. Kamil's scornful gaze raked up and down, taking me in. Alik stood a few paces behind, wary concern in his face.

"You had a victory here days ago and only just sent someone to inform me?"

"We only returned yesterday, Battlelion." At least I thought it was yesterday.

"Did you think to claim it for yourself?"

"What?" My tired mind barely comprehended his question.

Kamil scoffed again. "You are right. That might be too much for your simple mind to think."

My hand clenched tighter around the knife.

"With respect, Battlelion, the packs are exhausted. We needed rest."

My head snapped to the side, and I stumbled a step against his strike.

"Respect?" He sneered. "You've never had respect, Davor."

Not for you. I straightened. The warriors who had ridden with him stood with hands on weapons, most taking in the confrontation with smugness. But a more reassuring sight was my packs also waiting. A dangerous feeling settled through the air and I finally understood why Kamil feared I might claim the victory for myself and not for him as battlelion.

"Where's the whelp? You've had your fun, now he'll come with me."

"No." My voice lashed out with startling force.

Kamil turned back to me, eyes calculating.

"He stays with me," I said. "As do the other scouts I chose."

His hand shot out, thumb jamming into my injured side. I clamped fingers around his wrist, trying not to break against the pain stabbing through the wound.

"You are trying to play games, Davor," he said softly.

"Perhaps I will just kill you now. Maybe get rid of your friend."

My teeth scraped together, holding words or cries back. My arm shook and his smile let me know he felt it. He dug deeper. Sweat trickled down the side of my face. His head tilted to the side, a new look in his eyes that sent cold rushing down my arms.

"Or maybe I'll let you keep the whelp, these packs, even your place as first *rokr*...if you beg for it."

Darkness flitted across my eyes, and my world shrank down to Kamil's satisfied smile. I had nothing to counter with, and nothing to do but at least try to keep Michal from his clutches this time. The pressure released and it sent me collapsing to a knee. Exactly where he wanted me.

"Say it, Davor."

Bitterness welled on my tongue, and I kept my eyes fixed on the ground, not willing to look up and see his satisfaction at my humiliation as I searched for words I could stomach to say in an even tone.

"I am asking to keep my men and my place, Battlelion. As well as *all* of the scouts under my command."

He hummed. "Not good enough."

I lifted my head, and he met my burning gaze with warning.

"*Please.*" It gritted from me and a smile spread over his face.

"Not low enough."

Rage flared in my heart, but I placed a hand on the ground, fist curling into the grass, head ducking lower.

"Please."

He leaned down, keeping his words between us. "Better, Davor. Enjoy your position a few days more."

He was so close and the knife burned hot in my hand, but my body stayed still. His way was murdering those who stood in his way, who made him angry. I'd never played that way, and no matter how deep my hate ran, I still could not.

"You and your men will have three days to rest." Condescending generosity filled his loud voice. "Then I expect to see you for new orders... *Rokr.*"

"Yes, Battlelion." The words scraped from my raw throat. His last scoff barely warned me to angle in time as his boot clipped my chest. I caught myself on an elbow, the motion sending shock waves through my injured side.

This time a small sound escaped, and his laugh echoed in my ears as he strode away with his pack. Quiet lingered for an agonizing moment before Alik's boots appeared. He crouched and I lifted my battered face, bracing myself for the pity. But there was only concern past the tightness of his jaw.

I looked away, finding Michal staring at me where Dariy stood protectively in front of him. Disbelief covered his features.

A touch against my side had me drawing back. Alik raised his hands.

"Can I check it?"

But I was moving already, pushing up to my feet and stumbling away through the trees, retreating. The only thing I knew how to do well.

I found a spot beside the churning river and half-collapsed against a tree. Stifling a cry, I tugged up my shirt to see fresh blood spotting the bandage. I let it fall back, easing out my injured leg.

The river rushed by without a care for the roiling turmoil inside me. Bitterness coated my tongue from the words I'd said to Kamil. Humiliating, but not as much as the last time I'd begged.

With a sobbing curse, I stabbed my knife into the ground, the iron gouging through the earth.

Four strikes, then I released the handle and drew in a shaky breath. My hand raked through my short hair, another reminder of all the things Kamil had taken.

I could have challenged him. I didn't have the strength to best him in a fight right now. I had saved Michal. I'd surely lost any respect I might have gained.

Another curse whispered from me. The familiar whirl of questions circled through my head. Things I should have done, reasons I had not. The *why* echoing behind them all. Why had I not been stronger? Braver?

A whisper of sound drew my head up, hand clenched tight around the knife hilt. Michal stood, arms crossed, and trailed by Luk. Silence stretched between us until he lowered to sitting, drawing his knees up to his chest.

Luk padded forward and eased down between us.

"Why don't you fight back?" Michal blurted.

The river reclaimed my attention.

"Father, Kamil, sometimes Emil… You never do."

My hand strayed back to my side and the ache that had started to pound. I rarely did. Rarely openly.

"If you fight back, it marks you as a challenge," I said softly. "If you don't, they often overlook you."

"But how can you let them…let *him* do that to you?"

The rough bark of the tree pressed against the back of my head. "You think it doesn't make me angry every time?"

"I don't know. You never show anything."

He hadn't shifted from his position, arms wrapped around knees and one hand gripped tight around his forearm, questions in his eyes.

"It does. But this is the path I chose a long time ago, Michal." More than exhaustion slipped out with the words.

"Why?"

Why indeed? Because showing no emotion left nothing to be exploited. Because it was better to be underestimated. But the truth lingered not too far down.

"Because maybe I am just weak, a fool, or a coward."

I'd heard them so many times, there must be some truth.

"No." Michal's vehemence brought my startled attention to him. "No, you're not." He pushed to his feet, fists clenched. "And I am not either."

He whirled and vanished through the trees. A curse whispered from me, the forest blurring for a moment before it steadied. It took a long time before I mustered the strength to stand and limp my way back to camp.

Alik met me and wordlessly changed the bandage. Dariy contributed some more baltar root to soothe the burn. He offered nothing other than a slight nod. I pulled my other shirt from my pack and slipped it on, hiding every time that I had not, or had not been able to, fight back.

The pack leader opened, then shut his mouth. "I'll bring some food."

While he went to the cookfires, I dared to look around. Most had turned to their own business—food, tending wounds, or many returning to sleep. Even the sablecats were curled up in tight balls beneath the spreading trees. But none of the glances thrown my way were ones of pity or scorn.

I still pulled away, sitting cross-legged and pulling my armor into my lap to start cleaning. Alik thrust a plate into my face. I scowled up at him, but he did not relent, holding it until I set aside the half-finished task and took the food.

He settled beside me with his own plate. My wish that he would keep quiet was not granted.

"Do you mean to challenge Kamil someday?"

My jaw clenched tighter around the bite of food. "Losing faith in me?"

"No," he said with certainty. "But I am wondering how you mean to do it and play along with his whims at the same time."

I pushed the hash around the plate, appetite suddenly dulled. Did I mean to challenge him? Emil's words echoed back. Did I dare to reach one day for the place of chief?

"We've all felt Kamil's wrath in some way." He kept the words between us.

"Have you, Alik?" My sneer cut back, but Alik did not flinch.

"We know what he does when he feels challenged," he said calmly. "That's why no one does. It's fear more than anything. But you are not afraid."

"It's becoming clear that you don't know anything about me."

"Then why did you stand for Michal?"

I sought out the young warrior among the scouts, sharing a meal and easy conversation.

"He wants to be a man. I want him to see a different way from Kamil," I finally said.

Alik nodded, gaze not breaking from me. "That seems a weighty thing."

"I should have tried years ago."

"Then what would you do if you had the medallion?" He leaned a little closer. "Had the chieftain's staff?"

I set aside my plate and pulled the armor back. "Dreaming again?"

He shook his head. "Do not tell me you haven't thought of taking it?"

My hands paused, fingers clenching around the cleaning cloths.

"I have," I said softly. "But as you said, it is no easy thing going up against Kamil." And my father would be another matter. I would not kill him to take the chief's place, not like he and my grandfather had done.

"And maybe even harder if we win this war and there is no reason for the *talånd* to not hand over the staff when Kamil rides back to the village."

Alik opened his mouth, but I cut him off.

"I will not start a war between our packs right here. You think any outside of these"—I swept a hand around the encampment—"would just accept me? They've lived a good life under Kamil these last turnings. No reason for that to change."

"We need to work on your optimism." Alik's eyebrow arched, but he settled back without further argument.

"Maybe it's your patience that needs work."

His easy laugh broke free. "True enough. But you have the support of the men here, I've made sure of it."

This time my brow arched, but he waved it off. "Just simple conversations, Davor. Some people know how to have them."

"Are you sure they did not agree just to get you to stop talking?"

"Someday, you'll come to appreciate me."

"It's not today." But a faint smile emerged. Alik laughed again and pushed to his feet, scooping up my plate as he did, and left me to work in peace.

FIFTEEN

DAVOR

Countings passed, more miles and victories gained, until it seemed like nothing would stand in our way. The final death stroke lingered when my packs and I caught the Greywolf chief in a skirmish, brought him back, and subjected him to Kamil's whims.

I stayed on the far side of camp, away from the war-tent and the sounds of Kamil's and Hakkon's cruelty. And as the three days of Kamil's ultimatum passed—the chief's death or the tribe's total surrender—my hope faded. The divide among the packs had grown sharper, but if I made a move while still in Greywolf territory it would send death streaking through our ranks, and I would not do that.

I needed the Greywolves to attack, but there had been no sign. If they fell, so did I, and any hope to take a higher position in my tribe.

Even the valley seemed to rage against this, bringing a late winter storm and coating everything in sleet and snow.

I emerged from my tent the morning of the third day, a clouded breath bursting from me as I stood in the soft new snow. They had left the chieftain bound to a tree, laughing around the comfort of a fire as they'd made bets on how quick he'd die. I did not want to see his frozen body and the final strike against any of my plans.

I'd been ready for a few minutes in the pre-dawn hours, to release him and take him the Greywolves myself, maybe bargain for my life and Kamil's death, but I would not have been able to myself, and I would not endanger my men with the plan.

"Davor!" Kamil's voice was filled with fury as he stormed over. My hand fell to my sword.

"He's gone. Two sets of prints and a wolf."

I could only stare. The chief was alive. Someone had come for him.

"Get packs ready to ride, Davor. The tracks are headed to the river. Meet us there."

I took a breath, hands fisting to still the jittering starting to ripple through my muscles. This was it. Maybe not an answer to the prayer I'd dared give thought to in the darkest hours of the night, but a chance. I just hoped they had enough of a head start.

"How many packs?" I asked before Kamil strode away.

"All but a small guard for the camp. Makar is barely fit to ride, so you will lead. We're finding the chief and wiping them out once and for all." His mouth set in grim determination.

I saluted and turned to Alik who'd stumbled to my side, barely awake. "Muster the packs."

He read the rest in my face, tipping a nod. They'd be with me if the chance came. I set off across camp, giving the orders to the rest of the packs to muster up and follow my spear. The packs staying behind were the wounded who would do us no good in battle. Makar's searing glare as he clutched the sling binding his injured arm followed me every step of the way.

Shouts and chaos gradually gave way to mounted warriors gathering in their packs. A shiver ran down my arms and I twisted in the saddle to see Emil across the camp, watching me with cold eyes. Perhaps I was not the only one with plans in the snowy dawn.

We gave nothing away to each other, but as I turned again and lifted my spear, my back prickled with the uneasy feeling of waiting for an arrow or sword to strike me down.

Alik and his pack fell in behind me, bringing some small sense of security. The rest formed lines and Michal rode out with the scouts to clear our way to the river. One set of wolf prints did not mean there might not be more out there.

We'd almost reached the river, the sun rising higher to scatter golden specks across the snow-coated fields, when Kamil's shout brought me reining in.

His sablecat plowed to a halt, skidding on hind limbs on the snowy ground. A sablecat with empty saddle followed and several riders sported wounds.

"They got away," he growled. "The cursed battlewolf isn't dead! They had a lynx with them."

The battlewolf? A lynx? Perhaps the spirits had decided to care for a moment.

"Battlelion!" Dariy pointed out across the field where a small pack of wolves raced away. Kamil lashed his sablecat forward and it roared a warning as it leapt across the half-frozen ford. Heart in my throat, I followed, lifting my spear and bringing the rest of the packs forward with the action.

Paws thudded, spraying up snow around us. Kamil outpaced me, though I barely checked the reins.

Then a figure broke from the Greywolf pack, hauling himself up onto a wolf. The wolf stretched forward, ears pinned back and teeth bared. I pulled back on the leathers and Luk fought the command, hackles rising at the threat of the charge. But the rider had only one target.

I shouted a halt as he leapt from his wolf, taking Kamil around the waist and throwing them both to the ground.

Sablecats roared as warriors hauled back on the reins. Kamil and the Greywolf scrambled to their feet. Red coated the Greywolf's face and neck, and it took a moment to realize his face had been newly cut in the pattern of the Battlewolf warpaint. Kamil had found them after all.

"Just can't stay down, can you?" Kamil snarled.

The battlewolf wrenched his sword free from the scabbard on his back. "You should not have hurt my brother."

The words echoed across the plain, savage promise within them.

Hope sparked anew. Kamil had finally angered the wrong man.

I gave another order to hold, the challenge between the two of them clear. The Greywolf pack was circling back up, and two lynx stood within their ranks.

The clash of iron on iron brought my attention back to the fight. Cold fury radiated from the battlewolf, but it moved through controlled movements. Kamil fell back until he finally blocked a strike and moved to the offensive.

Their battle brought them closer to me, and the battlewolf shied away, catching a glimpse of Luk from the corner of his eye. In the brief moment of distraction, Kamil looked to me.

And I looked back.

I snapped my spear out horizontally and shouted an order to keep holding.

The packs obeyed and understanding and rage filled Kamil's eyes.

"You traitor!" he shouted at me. I did not flinch. Did not rescind the order. Twenty-six years burned to be repaid.

The battlewolf launched forward again, his sword screaming vengeance with every strike. I leaned forward in the saddle, following each motion, pleading with the spirits.

Then Kamil's sword fell to the ground. He drew a knife, stabbing at the charging battlewolf. Who grabbed Kamil's armor and stabbed up underneath it.

It was almost like I felt the blow as well. My breath left me, and my heartbeat thundered in my ears. Though I'd just been hoping, praying for the battlewolf to triumph, imagining the moment I might be free from Kamil, it still sent shockwaves through me when his body fell to the ground.

The battlewolf staggered, his sword dripping blood onto the snow torn apart by their struggle.

"Davor!" Alik's hiss snapped me back to the present. Some of the packs shouted, starting to urge sablecats forward.

But a darker mass swept up around the Greywolf packs in the form of more wolves and, unbelievably, Blackpaw packs, their lynxriders arrayed for battle, blue paint streaking their faces.

Luk grumbled, shifting and lifting paws, waiting for the signal.

I lifted my spear, gathering attention to me. Then twisted it point down and struck it into the ground. I checked from the corner of my eye to make sure that the lines held. One of my packs shoved back at an overeager mass of riders toward the middle, keeping them in line.

Dismounting, I spread my hands wide and approached the battlewolf. Abrupt silence fell. Each step crunching forward in the snow seemed to echo louder and louder until I stood a few paces away. The battlewolf held his sword out, signaling his men to hold.

"Battlewolf." I tapped my chest with closed fist.

It took him a moment before he gritted out around tight jaw, "Who are you?" Blood beaded around the hasty poultices barely holding his cheeks together.

"I am Davor." I gathered a short breath, feeling the target on my back growing bigger, the improbability of what I was about to attempt. "And I will claim the battlelion's place over the Saber tribe."

His eyes narrowed and he shifted the grip around his sword, but I shook my head.

"And I would call a truce with you and your chief."

My gaze slipped past him, hoping to see the chief still standing. The battlewolf followed my gaze and we both found him, standing with arm cradled to his chest, flanked by two warriors.

At our look, he started forward, one of the warriors keeping step with him. He stopped next to his battlewolf, both of them barely holding themselves together. I could take them both without worry, but instead I touched my fist to my forehead.

"Chief."

He gave a sharp nod.

"If you agree to a truce, I will withdraw my tribe from the valley."

Outrage stirred through some of the warriors who could hear, but none moved. Except one. Hakkon stirred forward.

"Coward!" he shouted and charged me. I flung my hand up.

Alik stood in his stirrups and threw his spear, taking the traitor through the back.

Alik settled back, spitting in contempt. The half-brothers in front of me stared in shock.

"We have no use for a traitor." I did not have to force the coldness in my voice.

"No one will challenge you?" the chief asked.

I smiled thinly. "I have no doubt they will. But it will happen away from this place."

Once a fight could happen without inviting Greywolves and Blackpaws into it as well.

"Then I accept a truce. You will take your warriors and leave this valley immediately."

I gave a small bow, for once not minding the action of deference to a conquering warrior. I had my chance thanks to the battlewolf. And maybe I could dare to take it further, keep pursuing the change I so desperately wanted. I now held the position second to the chief, and had the support of at least half the warriors.

If courage did not desert me in the next hours, I would regather my pieces and start casting for the place of chief.

"When we make it back to the villages, there will be much upheaval. It will take time to sort through it, but if I come out the victor, I would discuss a treaty with you, Chief."

He studied me a moment and it seemed like he understood some of what I'd faced my entire life.

"Then I will look for you on midsummer at the border stone," he said.

I bowed again and backed away to stop by Kamil's body. Sightless eyes stared up at the clear sky. It took a moment to nerve myself up to pull the battlelion medallion off. The iron circle hung heavy from the braided leather cord, and I could not help but think of all Kamil's misdeeds and those of the battlelion before him.

It slipped over my head, thudding against my chest with a weighty promise of new duty. I half-expected an arrow or spear to fly at my heart with the action. But none did. Just Saber warriors looking at me, as I looked at them.

Alik nodded and tapped his chest with a fist. My packs followed suit. I strode forward, passing Hakkon's body and spitting in contempt. He would not be mourned.

I grabbed Luk's leathers and pulled him around to mount, pausing when I felt Emil's eyes on me. His head tilted as he watched me, eyes narrowing as if I was a new puzzle. I swung into the saddle, breaking his gaze and finding Michal instead, who sat with hands clenched around his reins, staring at Kamil's body.

"Michal."

He flinched and turned to me, sitting wary in the saddle. I pulled my spear from the ground.

"Let's go."

He tapped a fist to his chest and rode after Dariy and the other scouts. Luk wheeled to follow, but I kept him in place a moment longer.

Michal wasn't the only one to stare at Kamil's body. Emil now sat hunched in the saddle, expression unreadable as he took in the bloody sight. A bit of loss surrounded him and he suddenly seemed different, smaller, less sharp, without the shadow of Kamil falling over him.

Then he stirred, straightening, and tightening up the reins, and the more familiar Emil was back. But as he turned, I caught sight of his face. There was something newly jagged about him, and the freshness of it almost frightened me.

Greywolf and Blackpaw packs followed us to our camp, where Makar stiffened in rage when he saw the medallion around my neck and no Kamil. He lurched forward, good arm reaching for the medallion until I grabbed him and shoved him away. Something new and calculating grew in his eyes as he looked me up and down.

And he mockingly gave a double tap to his chest when I gave the order to start breaking camp and retreating from the valley.

I turned away, meeting the unforgiving gaze of the Greywolf *rokr* who had stood with Etran during our truce. His wolf shifted, lips curling back from fangs as I did not move. Luk rumbled at my back and the wolf's snarl deepened.

Warriors paused around me, ready for something, possibly me to order a fight with fewer opponents facing us. But I did not even need the Blackpaws glaring down from their lynxes to spread my hands peacefully and snap my fingers to Luk to stand down.

The allied packs waited on their animals with weapons ready as we worked. Then trailed us as I led the way back across the hard-won miles, not stopping until two nightfalls later when we passed the first border stones and left the valley behind.

SIXTEEN

DAVOR

We rode for another two miles before I called the halt. The western forest spread its way past the mouth of the valley, coating the land until it gradually gave way to grass plains. We camped in the shelter of friendlier pines and oak. Aspens grew closer to the river, still not settled in its banks after the rapids at the valley entrance.

The constant churn of the water masked some of the quieter sounds of camp being set. I beckoned Dariy and another scout over.

"I know you need rest, but I need messengers to go ahead to the villages," I said.

It had taken five minutes of riding away from our camp in the valley for Makar to start solidifying his position among Kamil's old packs. But what worried me most was that I had barely seen Emil.

I needed my own message to get through to the chief and the villages before they decided to send something else and gain his ear first.

Dariy followed my glance across the fires starting to spring up through the trees. The light sparked off sablecat eyes where they settled into the darker spots away from the flames.

"We'll make it, Battlelion." He tapped his chest.

I handed him a birchbark scroll. "Dariy." I stopped him. "Give it to the chief, and then go home."

He studied me a moment longer and then nodded. The chief would not be happy with the news, and I did not want him taking it out on the messengers. Not when it would be another day's ride before we reached the villages.

Dariy and his companion slipped out of the camp, my men already on guard.

"What tales are you sending home to your father?" Makar swaggered over to me.

"The chief will want to know that his battlelion is dead and we are coming home," I said evenly.

"Only because you had us turn tail and run like cowards." His voice rose.

"Two tribes full of vengeance were arrayed against us. We would not have won."

"We would have died in glorious battle!" Makar lifted his hand and murmurs of agreement rang out.

"And left our villages defenseless if the Blackpaws decided to finally take vengeance for eight years ago. If the Greywolves thought killing Kamil was not enough for the dishonor of their chief. What happens come Autumn if the Pronghorns decide to try and take more grazing land?" My gaze slipped from him and swept around camp. Some of those who had just called for death in battle now sat back, shifting in their seats at the uncomfortable truth.

"Clever words to disguise the heart of a coward, Davor." Makar pressed closer.

My hand curled around one of the knives in my belt.

"You did not even challenge Kamil for that medallion you wear so boldly."

"It's hard to challenge a dead man."

"Maybe I'll give it a try." A faint smirk toyed at his mouth— one I'd seen for so many years from him and those thinking that I had nothing to offer, nothing to challenge with.

For the first time in a long time, I let the constant churn of anger in my gut rise higher, coating my heart with its heat, spilling out in my own dangerous smile.

Makar's smugness faltered under the look and the sudden press of cold iron against his neck, and I could see him rethinking everything he knew about me. I leaned a little harder into the blade set right over the large vein.

"Want to try your luck right now?" I held his gaze unblinking until he shifted away with a scoff.

"So you'll challenge a wounded man?" He *tskd*.

"You speak of courage, Makar. You have never once challenged me with sword, only words."

His face darkened, and he shoved forward again, not blinking as my knife touched his neck again.

"Guard your back, Davor." His words hissed between us. "Once I am free of these bandages, I will take what should have been mine." He flicked a gaze up and down, scornfully assessing. "Or maybe I'll just wait for the chief to kill you when we get back, and take everything for myself."

I didn't flinch. And I wondered if Kamil knew he would have

had a threat from his trusted *rokr* if he'd lived long enough.

Makar gave a mocking salute, and backed away. A breath eased through the camp, and I tried not to let my own burst forth.

I returned to our fire where Alik stood, hand on sword hilt.

"And I thought things were complicated enough before," he said.

The medallion hung even heavier around my neck. "I think the war just began."

And one I was at a disadvantage in because I had no idea how to be battlelion. I went to Luk who had patiently waited for me and began to unsaddle him. His ears flicked to the trees a few paces from us, his upper lip curling slightly away from his fangs.

The saddle thudded to the ground, and I laid a hand on my knife. A figure appeared in the shifting shadows, and I loosened the blade in its sheath at the sight of Emil.

"What is your plan, Davor?" He leaned against the trunk, hands tucked over his chest.

"Here to make your own threat?" I kept one eye on him as I pulled the bridle from Luk.

Emil's gaze flicked past me, then settled on me again.

"Davor?" Alik's voice held cautious question. I risked a glance over my shoulder to see my second warily eyeing Emil.

Emil hadn't shifted his position from where he was screened from the rest of the camp by the trees. I flicked my hand to Alik and he backed off with a frown at me and a darker scowl at Emil.

"Maybe I will just stand back and watch you fail." Emil shrugged. "Maybe long enough for you to see me turn my back on you first."

I scoffed. "When have you ever thought about helping me?"

A sneer curled his lips. "Perhaps the last time you gave any thought to anyone other than yourself. Don't pretend like you care, Davor. A piece of iron can't change a man."

"Are you going to challenge me or not?" I asked, avoiding the sharp edges of his words and the way they threatened to cut me.

"I've never wanted it." His look of loathing was directed at my chest, but it just as quickly turned up to me. "I just want to know, now that Kamil is out of the way, what you are going to do at the villages. You said you are playing a different game. I think you have no idea what you've just gotten yourself into."

I did not care to admit that what had once been an impossible dream was turning into a daunting reality. But I had tendrils of a plan and a future that still beckoned.

"I want to see something different come of all…this." I swept my hand around. "Something better for the tribe."

Anger contorted his face and he pushed forward. "That is *scata*, Davor. That is scata!" His fist in my chest knocked me back a step. "Do they know?" He jerked his chin towards the campfire. "Do they know that at the first sign of trouble, you'll run? That when pressed, you'll give them up? Don't lie to them, to Michal, and pretend to *give a damn*!"

His wild rage seared at my heart, and I knew this was not about the medallion or anything else, but about him and about me. And I had no one to blame for that but myself.

"Perhaps once, but there is only so far someone can run before they tire," I said. "Are you not tired of all this, Emil?"

He shook his head, jaw tight. "So what? You have the medallion. What do you think Father will do to you when you come back to the lodges and not Kamil? Unless…"

He rocked back on his heels, studying me, then scoffed a laugh. "You are going to take it from him?"

"I'm not killing him, Emil. But I'm going to make sure he passes it to me."

A strangled sound broke from him, and he shook his head. "Just when I thought you could not be a bigger fool. There is nothing for a man in this tribe unless he takes it by the force of his blade. If you don't have the heart for that, Davor, then there is a long line of men ready to take it instead. Starting with Makar."

"And where are you?"

"You know many things about the tribe and the villages, Davor, yet you know absolutely nothing." The weariness I knew so well crept up around his eyes, turning him years older than his twenty-four. "Play your games, fight your own battles, and don't come running to me unless you want to hear me say 'I warned you' right before you die."

And with that, he turned and vanished back into the trees. A chill seared through me even though the snow and the cool from the winter storm two days ago had long vanished.

I already knew I was going to be facing the task alone, but it did not make me feel any easier to know that Emil would not hinder me. Luk settled down as I set my bedroll out and arranged packs and leathers more neatly. The smell of food drew my attention back to the fires and the men clustered around.

A bit of shame pricked. I wasn't completely alone, and the sight of Alik easily moving through the packs had another piece clicking into place.

He'd chosen to follow me. That part was almost as frightening as the tasks that lay ahead. Michal sat with the scouts, staring down at the bowl clutched in his hands. Under the weight of my stare, he pulled his gaze up. There was nothing to give him away in that look, but I vowed then I would not turn my back on him, on any of them. No matter what came.

SEVENTEEN

DAVOR

Lights twinkled through the trees, flickering in time with the roaring of the tributary river as it rushed its way around Half Peak to dump into the great river before it curved between our villages. Our sablecats pricked up ears and tails, scenting home.

I did not share their eagerness, instead wishing that I could ride for the other side of the village and the comfort of the woods. Get away from the eyes staring at me every minute, and the heavy weight around my neck that had sunk deep into my chest, feeling like it was keeping me from drawing a deep enough breath.

We reached the outskirts of the upper village and cries went up. Welcome and families already trying to pick out their warrior from the packs. I gave the order to disband, most gladly obeying that order.

Makar passed close by and gave a sharp smile. "See you in the chief's lodge…Battlelion."

Ready to see what the reckoning would be. The invisible bands pressed tighter around my chest.

Alik didn't shift from my side, and neither did his pack, even though most were casting longing glances to the gathering tribespeople.

"We'll go with you," Alik said.

"No." Even though part of me wanted to beg for him to stay at my back. "Go find your families."

Alik didn't move, and neither did his men.

"We'll go with you."

Some faint expression I knew betrayed how sick I felt crossed my face and I did not have the strength to argue as I turned Luk uphill to the chief's lodge. Michal fell in with me. He did not need an order to know that the chief would want him there.

Emil was dismounting in the open space before the lodge by the time I reached there. His look seared through me, but he waited for me to slide down and force my feet forward.

The medallion tapped ominously against my breastplate with every step up to the lodge, through the doors, and into the great common room, mocking every thought that I could stand against my father and keep the place of battlelion in the tribe as I tried to reach higher.

The chief sat in his carved chair at the head of the room, the fire in the great hearth blazing behind him. Dark furs draped the chair, and the necklace of chief glittered where it rested against his chest—sablecat teeth interspersed with small bits of metal inset with the same red stones as the battlelion mark.

A few tribespeople sat at the tables or on the benches on the outskirts of the hall, remnants of dinner still strewn about. From the chief's posture, it did not look like a good day and most had probably vacated to get as far from his easy wrath as possible.

"Chief." I touched fist to my head, coming to a halt at the foot of the steps leading up to his chair.

He stared over steepled fingers, dark eyes cast into shadow. "I see you wear the medallion, Davor. Where is my son?"

"Killed on the field by the battlewolf."

He leaned forward. "And where is the victory I was promised in the upper valley?"

My hand clenched at my side, sudden heat in the room chasing away the numbing chill. "They allied with the Blackpaws. We would have been wiped out in one battle."

"That would be preferable to the failure I see standing before me." The chief's voice scored through me, and my teeth ground together.

"And you, Emil? What have you to say to this?"

Emil cast me a hateful look as he came to stand beside me. "Kamil fell in battle, Chief. Davor claimed his place."

Just facts, but it only made the darkness grow on the chief's face.

"Michal."

I glanced quickly over my shoulder to see Michal coming forward, clutching the strap of his quiver. I extended a hand to keep him behind me. I didn't know what the chief would do in his mood, and I had a vow to keep.

Michal obeyed the gesture, knuckles whitening around the strap.

"Everyone out." The chief pushed to his feet, but his gaze was locked on the three of us.

"Chief, I—" Makar pushed forward, barely quelled by the chief's returning shout.

"Out!"

A curse welled inside me as riders and tribespeople obeyed without question. Most going outside, but some disappearing deeper into the lodge. Makar gave a sharp smile before slamming the door behind him.

The chief strode down the steps, vengeance clear in his eyes. I backed up a step, pushing Michal farther away, but he was focused on Emil.

"You were in command of scouts. You planned the ways into the valley." A blow landed and Emil staggered back into a table. "You have failed me yet again."

My gut twisted at the sight of Emil pinned between the table and the chief, half curled away, a familiar motion of arm shielding his head as fury rained. A knife gleamed in the chief's hand. Something precarious snapped inside me, and I moved. Grabbed his wrist, pulled him away.

The chief came around under my force and sudden stinging pain to the side of my face had me stumbling. His fist battered again and my vision swam before I finally dredged up a fighting instinct. I twisted, but his knife scored across my arm.

I blocked another swing, grabbing his wrist and pummeling until the knife clattered free. Firelight glinted off the rage burning in his eyes, and I quailed before it.

His free hand clamped over the knife wound. My other hand found his wrist but my foot caught on the steps and knocked me off balance. One fury-filled shove and I fell, smashing against the steps. His boot jammed me into their hard edges and a stunned breath wheezed from me.

The chief stalked up the steps. My body jerked with desperate gasps. Michal was by Emil, a hand reaching out to him. But his gaze snapped past me, and his mouth moved in warning before terrifying heat found me.

The chief stood over me, burning brand in hand. A scream burst from me before he plunged it down. My wounded arm curled up over my head, but the fire still found me.

Just as suddenly, it ripped away, and hands were extinguishing the flames eating through my sleeve. Michal dragged me up, face twisting in effort. I collapsed back to my knees, staring in confusion at the sight of Emil grabbing the brand from the chief, tossing it away.

The fury grew brighter in the chief's face, but a knife appeared in Emil's hand.

Before I could cry out, he plunged the blade through the chief's throat. Blood gushed and the chief's face slackened in surprise.

Emil yanked it free and stabbed twice into his chest. I lurched to my feet, halfway up the steps as the chief crumpled to the ground, blood soaking his body and beginning to spread.

Emil stood over him, dripping knife in hand, chest heaving, and loathing in his blood-spattered face.

"What...?" My hoarse voice broke the sudden silence.

"I *hate* him." Emil spat.

"Emil..."

He whirled on me. "You wanted him to keep living? You want something better but were ready to let him keep doing that?" He pointed to my arm where nauseating pain was beginning to eat away.

The weariness came back, and he curled his wrist up to look at the bloody knife. He regarded it a long moment and tossed it down by the chief.

"Take it then."

"Davor." Michal's point brought my attention to where the log had fallen. Its flames had begun to eat into the dried wood of the wall and floor, reaching up to snare at the bottom of one of the wall hangings. The woven threads caught eagerly and began to wither away from the fire.

For a moment we all stared at it. Then Emil looked around at the common room, the wall hangings, the aged wood holding up the lodge. The memories we all had stored in the corners, in the chief's room only a few steps away.

He looked to me. "Let it burn."

As if in response to his words, the flames leapt up the tapestry, roaring suddenly in their attempts to reach the ceiling. The wall behind caught, lending further fuel. Smoke began to escape in billows, ensnaring us in a bitter fog until we stumbled away.

And all the while our father stared through sightless eyes.

A surprised shout brought us all out of our near stupor. A tribeswoman stumbled from one of the back rooms, eyes wide at the sight of the fire now crackling among the ceiling beams, catching on the thatching.

I stirred. "Get everyone out."

She nodded, her voice rising with every shout.

"What about him?" Michal nodded to the body.

"May he rot forever in the dark woods." Emil spat again and for once, I agreed with him. A warning creak sounded above us, and we ran for the door as one of the smaller support beams fell in a shower of sparks.

A roar followed and the fire blossomed into something even angrier, maybe fed by the miserable memories and spirits lurking around. We stumbled out into chaos.

Warriors and women ran, some for buckets to bring water

from the river. Others making sure everyone was out of the rooms and away from the fire poking its ragged head through the thatched roof.

"Davor!" Alik was at my side, pulling me farther away. "What…?" He looked over me with wide eyes. Dampness trickled down my cheek and my shaking hand came away smeared in blood.

"Where's the chief?" Makar pushed forward with the *talånd* hot on his heels.

"Dead." Emil's voice held some hoarseness from smoke.

Makar looked sharply between the two of us. "How?"

The blood on Emil's hands and smearing up his bracers seemed painfully obvious. I was clearly bleeding from somewhere.

But Emil spoke before I could. "He was angry. Grabbed a burning brand and it caught a hanging. Flames caught in seconds and a beam fell."

I stared at the almost lies.

The *talånd* turned to me. "Is this true?"

"He was responsible for the fire. It caught too quickly to do anything."

"You are burned too." He reached out in sympathy and I stepped away.

Makar's suspicion hadn't faded, but the *talånd* seemed to accept it.

"As the chief had not named an heir formally, we will discuss it tomorrow at the spirits' lodge." He encompassed all three of us living sons and Makar in his look. He had already gained the ear of the *talånd* in the minutes since we returned.

Makar strode off, joining up with another man. The tribespeople who had tried to bring water now stood back with buckets in hand, just watching the flames soar to light up the sky. More and more people were gathering from the upper and middle villages. Warriors had come running from lodges, half in armor. The head of the lower village arrived, panting and looking up in horror.

Another tremendous crash announced the collapse of the great support beam. A woman screamed and others took steps back.

Emil turned to me, face smeared in soot and redness rimming his eyes. He grabbed my sleeve and the anger melted away for a moment.

"Be better." And he strode off into the darkness.

I stirred, finding a pack leader with a bucket dangling from one hand.

"I want alternating shifts. Make sure the fire doesn't spread," I said.

"Battlelion…I heard the chief is dead?"

I nodded. "He didn't make it out."

He looked back to the fire, then to me, lifted his chin and tapped fist against his chest. It seemed more like a promise.

So many people still lingered about. The ones who had lived in the lodge needed places to stay, things to be replaced. But the shifting firelight blurred across my eyes. I staggered and Alik was there to catch me.

"I need…"

"No," he said firmly. "You're coming back to my lodge."

"No, I…" I needed to find my mother.

"Davor."

He steadied me again. I found Michal, still standing there, red light scattering across his face.

"Go find your family," I said. He nodded and I thought I even saw some worry there. He swallowed hard, looking to Alik warily.

"I'll let her know," he blurted.

"I'll be there tomorrow." But the world shifted again, and my arm had started to throb mercilessly.

Michal backed up a few steps, then darted away, his sablecat bounding after him into the darkness.

"Come." Alik gave his second an order to help watch the fire, and kept gentle hold of my arm as we started down the hill.

"What happened?" he asked softly once we were away from the confusion, light from the blazing lodge following us across the bridge.

"He…he was going to…we stopped him. First time I've stopped him." A curious sound burst from me.

Alik's hold tightened but he kept me moving when all I wanted to do was sit down.

"Emil killed him." The quiet confession seemed to echo even over the roar of the fire.

This time Alik did stop. "That's not what he said."

I tilted my head, so many things trying to burst out that I had no way of knowing what would escape.

"I don't think he'll challenge me," I said.

Alik moved us on. "But Makar will."

Another sound escaped with my nod. Alik didn't say anything, just kept guiding me on until he swung open a door in front of us and I stumbled, blinking, into brightness.

EIGHTEEN

MARTA

My knees bounced and fingers worried at the prayer cloth around my wrist. The raised threads rubbed under my thumb. We'd all rushed outside at the first cries of fire to clearly see the blaze of the chief's lodge from the middle village. Father and other men had raced to assist, while the rest of us tried to be patient, to wait and see if any wounded needed help. Or worse.

If a battle had broken out in someone's bid to seize new control from the chief.

Father had just returned, and I could not bear to lose him to some battle in the village. It would be worse than him dying on some faraway field. Mother paced back and forth, biting at her thumb. Vanda had her feet tucked up on the bench beside me, braiding and combing out a small section of her long hair over and over.

I was about to go see what I could find out, when the door swung open, and two figures stumbled in. Women and the men who had stayed behind jolted to their feet, more unease sweeping around when we recognized Davor in Alik's supporting hold.

They said nothing as Alik helped him sit on a bench at the table. No one else came in after, and no sounds broke past the door bobbing gently against the painted frame. Alik did not seem harmed, but blood coated Davor's left cheek, and he held his left arm awkwardly against his chest, the sleeve torn and burned to show red skin underneath.

And even though it had been the subject of intense conversation since Father had returned in advance of the packs, the sight of the battlelion mark sitting atop his breastplate sent unease squirming through me.

Alik reached for Davor's arm, but he moved away, trying to push up.

"I shouldn't stay here."

So he saw the mistrustful looks everyone was giving. Or maybe not, the way his eyes were unfocused, and his movements jolted.

"Davor, it's all right. There's room here." Alik tried again, but he shifted restlessly on the bench.

"No. No, I…"

"Davor. Breathe."

Davor leaned forward on his knees, hands burying in his short hair, and uttered the roughest curse I had ever heard. It sent my ears burning, and more scowls his way from mothers who clapped hands over young ears perked in interest at the new word.

"What happened?" one of the women asked quietly as Davor didn't move.

"Chief's dead," Alik said.

A faint whisper ran through the lodge.

"Word is he set the fire to the lodge and didn't make it out." But Alik cast a look at Davor.

My hands gripped the edge of the bench as I leaned forward. Those around me exchanged uncertain glances, some whispering prayers that seemed a little too thankful to be about asking the spirits for rest upon the dead. Not that I blamed them.

"Has the *talånd* named someone yet?"

"Tomorrow." Alik tipped his head at Davor who still sat in silence. He would throw in behind the chief's second son. Father hadn't said much about what had happened in the war, other than the packs had started to split. And that seemed like a dangerous thing.

Alik dropped into a crouch in front of Davor. Another breath shuddered through the new battlelion.

"Davor." There was a cautious gentleness in Alik's voice. "Can I look at your arm?"

Davor lifted his head, blinking and coming back to the lodge. He straightened and began to pull at the laces of his bracer. The lodge door swung open, and he and Alik both pivoted that way, hands on knives.

But Father stepped through. His face cleared when he saw Davor, and he stepped over.

"Battlelion." He tapped his fist once to his chest.

I frowned. That was not the customary salute, and my father had never once felt inclined to give it to the chief or his sons.

"Dariy, the fire, is it…?" A hoarseness coated Davor's deep voice.

"Contained," Father reassured. "Some at the far end from the starting place might even be salvageable. *Ach*, but that looks like it hurts." He pointed to the burn.

"You have any root?" Alik asked, taking Davor's arm and undoing the armor.

Father moved past him and beckoned to me. "Bring some water, Marta."

Other mothers besides my own glared at him in rebuke for sending me so close to a chief's son. My fingers curled into my skirt, but I rose and retrieved fresh water from the barrel in the corner.

I paused, then shifted the bowl against my hip and dipped a mug into the barrel. Father took the bowl from me as I approached, one hand tapping my shoulder in thanks. Alik stepped away to lay Davor's breastplate on the table, drawing my attention back to the battlelion.

"Here." I extended the mug so fast, the water sloshed dangerously close to the edges.

Dark eyes slowly rose to my face, and I braced under their scrutiny. But it did not burn. Instead, it reminded me of the first time we had met. He took the mug, careful not to touch me, and murmured, "Thank you."

"Marta, good to see you." Alik leaned back in.

"Glad you're back safe." I gave him a smile. Over the last few years there had been plenty who had nudged us in each other's direction with not-so-subtle smiles. But he'd always been more of an older brother to me and Vanda. Something we'd sort of awkwardly confessed to each other four turnings ago when forced to walk along the river together.

"Can I help with anything else?" I asked.

There was an aggressive clearing of a throat behind me, but my father barely looked up from grinding down baltar root.

"He doesn't bite." Alik waved a hand. "You don't, right?" He directed it at Davor, whose lips flattened as he cast an annoyed look up. It made him look suddenly human, and a small laugh caught in my throat.

I retreated and took a seat on the bench again. Warriors began to come back through the door, and families reunited. Vanda leaned against my shoulder, both of us smiling at the sights, and feeling the sorrow for the ones who would wait forever for the door to open.

But my gaze kept sneaking back to Davor. Alik's movements were quick and sure. He'd learned well from the healer, going for lessons in a desperate way to still feel connected to his brother after he'd died. Finally, he went to his trunk and pulled out a clean shirt.

Davor shook his head as Alik handed it over.

"I can't take your things."

Alik waved his hand. "*Borrow* until you figure out if you have anything left other than what's in your bag."

Davor winced slightly. A bit of pity flared. I hadn't thought of him losing his home with the fire.

"And some of us like color, so I won't miss this one." Alik bobbed the dark grey shirt in front of him. The half-hearted glare came back.

"It's what friends do."

Davor swiped the shirt from him with an annoyed huff and Alik grinned in triumph.

"What is Alik doing?" Vanda muttered, pulling me from the curious scrutiny.

"I don't know. Father seems to be all right with him," I returned under my breath.

Vanda scowled at both of them. But the warriors had begun to gather around the table as food was pulled out to serve up a second dinner. None of them seemed uncomfortable with Davor in their midst, and some even let their children climb onto their laps. Not like countings ago when he'd sat there for the first time. Instead, he exchanged some conversation with them and seemed more at ease. And gave the children some sort of look I couldn't quite interpret—almost like wistful kindness, and it softened something about him.

It made me wonder again about the war and the words from the Greywolf *talånd*. He'd predicted change was coming, and it seemed like it was already in front of me. And I did not know yet what to make of it.

NINETEEN

DAVOR

The soft sounds of a lodge asleep underlay someone's snoring on a bench against the opposite wall. But it was more than the rumbling sound that had kept me awake for hours. More than lying on a bench in a strange lodge surrounded by people I barely trusted.

Dim firelight from the hearth reached for the rafters. A ladder in the corner led up to a sprawling loft where most of the young children had disappeared when parents sent them off to bed. Someone had carved runes and jagged pictures into the wall beside where I lay. My fingers stumbled over the roughness of the cuts then fell back to my chest.

It was so different to watch warriors hold their wives close, reaching out to comfort the families who were a member short and giving mementos taken from bodies before we'd buried them in forests far from here. Almost terrifying to watch children run and clamber around with no fear in their faces, greeting Alik as some sort of adopted uncle. A few had even given me tentative smiles before mothers ushered them away with dark glances in my direction.

I couldn't blame them, even if their husbands now regarded me more easily. I rubbed my thumb knuckle across my forehead, trying to banish the slight ache lingering hours after I'd struck the side of my face against the steps.

It felt like there should be some sort of relief that the chief was dead. That Kamil was dead. Instead there was a terrifying sort of emptiness stretching in front of me, enhanced by the weight of the medallion resting atop my chest.

What am I doing?

The thought rebounded mercilessly in my head. Years of staying back, keeping to the shadows, doing whatever I could to keep away from the chief. Now he was gone, and I somehow thought I could take his place.

My knuckle pressed harder against my forehead. With a restless sigh, I sat up, pushing away the borrowed blanket and furs. The thicker coverings over the windows had been taken down with spring's takeover and the thinner skin let through the hint of dawn.

I slid feet into boots and fastened my greaves back over. Bracers and breastplate went back on, habit leading my hands in the dimness.

"What are you doing?" Alik's sleep-filled voice drew my gaze where he propped up on an elbow.

"I need to go." I drew my pack out from under the bench.

"Davor." He shook his head, sitting up and tugging at his shirt twisted around him.

I didn't argue, just tipped my head.

He sighed and rubbed his face. "Where?"

"I need to go find my mother." She would be worried frantic, even if Michal had reassured her like he'd promised.

Alik stiffened. "Why?" Suspicion laced his voice and regret stabbed through me. He only knew what he'd seen.

"I had to get her out of that lodge," I said softly. "I *had* to, and that was the only way I knew."

A murmured curse came from him. "Spirits, Davor. I'm so sorry."

I shifted. What did he have to be sorry for? He wasn't the one who'd forced his mother out in a show of anger and only dared go see her when his half-brothers and Makar were out of the villages on patrols and the chief was not paying attention.

"Where is she?"

Mistrust flared for a moment before I quelled it. "Inge's lodge in the upper village."

"The healer?"

I nodded, grateful he hadn't called Inge what so many others were content to call her in and out of her hearing, even if they were happy enough to go to her when they needed healing. What my mother often heard as well.

"I'll go with you."

"No."

"You think I'm just going to let you walk out of here by yourself with Makar and Emil lurking about?"

A faint smile tugged my lips. "How do you think I've navigated these villages by myself for years, Alik? I will be fine."

He slumped back against the wall with a huff of surrender. "All right. Then I'll meet you there to go to the *talånd's* lodge."

"You don't have to." Awkwardness shifted through me. This was going to be something different than riding into open battle.

"Friends, Davor," he reminded me.

My hands fiddled with each other before I picked up my bag. I wished I knew how to be that better for him. He said nothing more as I stood and moved over some of the sleeping forms on ground pallets, and slipped out the door.

Luk emerged from the pile of sablecats lounging against the lodge walls. My saddle and bridle were tipped up against the wall and he grumbled as I tacked up.

"Only for a few minutes," I reassured.

He followed on silent paws as we traced a way across the bridge and through the backways between lodges in the upper village. I paused one moment to look uphill.

The chief's lodge was a pile of smoking timbers fallen atop themselves. Barely a third of it still stood, edges charred, and roof caved in, looking eerily reminiscent of the way the mount behind it stood with half its spire gone. It stirred at the same emptiness inside. I wanted change, but what was I supposed to be outside the rules I'd forced myself to live in for the last twenty-six years?

I moved on, backtracking around another lodge where smoke had begun to curl. A few sablecats lifted heads in idle curiosity as we passed, but some recognized me and Luk, and did nothing more than yawn.

Inge's lodge stood on the inner edge of the broad square flattened in the side of the mountain's knee. Luk followed me into the small walkway between the house and the sweatlodge that contained a small hot spring. He huffed as I undid the leathers again.

I waited in the lodgeway until the scent of smoke stirred and tendrils crept up from the chimney before I circled around and knocked on the main door.

A glance around ensured there was no one out and about to notice me or Luk left behind the lodge. The door cracked open and Inge's greeting died at the sight of me. Then a smile bloomed and she pulled me in.

My mother looked up from setting the table. A faint cry escaped, and she ran around the table. I wrapped arms around her, resting my head against her shoulder, letting a breath finally escape.

"I'm sorry I didn't come last night, I…"

But she shook her head as she pulled away, her hands cupped to my cheeks. "Michal told us. I'm just glad you are safe. I was so worried."

"I am all right." I pulled her back into an embrace, a little gentler this time.

Her small sigh told me she didn't quite believe me, but she stepped back and touched the medallion against my chest.

"We heard about this."

It felt heavier than before. If I played my pieces right in the next few hours, I would not be wearing it for long.

"What are you planning?" Her head tilted. She'd given me her shrewdness, so it was no surprise she saw it already.

"I want to know, too," Michal's voice cut in. He pulled his shirt on and raked a hand through his long hair before grabbing the leather band to tie it back.

"I want a hug first," Janne butted in. Mother smiled and stepped away as Janne hurried over in bare feet. The force of her affection almost knocked me back a step, but a smile tugged at my face for the first time in a long time.

She knocked a fist against my chest. "It looks better on you."

"There's very few who think that, so thank you."

Her knuckles thumped my armor again and bright color

caught my eye. As did the sight of my rune.

"What's this?" I tapped her wrist where two strips of cloth were tied. She held up her hand to better show.

"Prayer cloths for Michal." She lifted the edge of the second. "And one for you. I got them from Marta from the middle village. Clearly they worked."

She danced away before I could deny anything. Or wonder at the fact Marta had traded her for prayer cloths with our runes on them. Mother smiled gently and touched my arm, guiding me over to the table.

Inge paused beside me. "Michal said you were hurt last night," she murmured.

"Alik took care of me," I reassured.

Her brow creased, trying to figure out which healer I meant. "Do you need me to look later?"

I nodded, my arm already starting to ache again. She patted my shoulder and moved past. Michal dropped onto the bench across from me, and leaned forward on elbows.

"What are you going to do?"

"What are you?" I countered.

He appeared taken aback. "Me?"

I lifted my shoulder. "You have every chance with the *talånd* in a few hours."

Disgust swept over his face. "I don't want it. But you do." New astuteness glittered in his eyes.

A decision snapped into place. Openness spread between us, and there might be a place for two half-brothers to truly ally in it.

"I do," I said. "And what I said countings ago is still true. I want to change the path of this tribe. To not keep his spirit alive and infecting the villages."

"You think you could?" Inge interrupted. Her hand pressed tight over her stomach as she watched the two of us.

My gaze slipped from her and back to Michal who asked the same question just as loudly in his younger eyes.

"I am going to try." It felt almost like a promise.

Michal's jaw tensed but he never shifted from my gaze. "You proved yourself a different kind of leader in the war. I want to help."

"It is not going to be an easy road."

"It never has been."

I hated how old the words sounded coming from him. I tipped my head.

"Allies then?"

Michal's small nod came a little grim, but I did not think he truly saw what was ahead for us. For me.

A small sound brought my attention up to my mother. She stood next to Inge, her eyes piercing through me, and I knew that she saw what lay ahead, even if she had tried to set me on this path countings ago. But pride lit up her features.

"When do you go to the *talånd's* lodge?" she asked.

"In an hour. Alik will be coming with us," I told Michal and he relaxed a little. I felt the same relief.

"I want to go too." Janne slid in beside Michal.

We both shook our heads. Janne opened her mouth to argue, but her brother took her hand.

"Janne, the *talånd* won't consider you, and Makar is going to be there."

Her shoulders collapsed inward at the name. He'd never done more than belittle her very existence to her face as far as I knew, but I knew all too well how much power words could have.

"If I can get the *talånd* to name me, then I am going to have an even bigger target on my back," I told her. "And Michal will as well if he backs me. I don't want that to extend to you."

Stubbornness lined up her shoulders again, but I cut off her retort by reaching over and flicking a finger against the prayer cloths on her wrist.

"Don't really want to test these either."

A frustrated smile tugged her lips. "If you asked the spirits for help yourself, Davor, you might find a few things easier."

I shrugged it away. "That's what I have you for."

Janne rolled her eyes, but subsided. Inge raised an eyebrow as she set food on the table in front of us, the expression shouting she agreed with her daughter.

Mother claimed the seat beside me, and we both patiently waited for Inge to offer thanksgiving to the All-Father for His blessings. I stared at my bare wrists, half-wondering if some of the desperate words I'd directed His and the spirits' way in the last countings had been answered in some way.

But I shoved away the thought. There still wasn't evidence of the mercy Inge and Janne liked to claim the spirits had.

A certain lightness spread over the table as we began to eat. Even Michal was quicker with a smile or reply than the last time we'd sat there together. It might have been the absence of the threat of Kamil or the chief forever looming just outside the safety of the lodge door. Or maybe it was the strange new alliance between him and me. Either it gave me the confidence to step back out once Alik knocked on the door and we turned our steps to the *talånd's* lodge.

TWENTY

DAVOR

The Greywolf *talånd* occupied a bench outside the lodge as we approached. He sat taller than in the days shortly after his arrival. A lighter cloak wrapped around him, and his head tilted back to the early morning sky, lips moving soundlessly.

At the crunch of our boots on the path, his eyes settled on me and I paused.

"Battlelion." He dipped his head. "I hear a decision is to be made this morning."

"There is," I confirmed.

"And have you weighed the cost?" There was a mix of sympathy and challenge in his gaze.

"I have." Many times in the hours since the medallion had slid over my head.

"Then may the All-Father and His spirits bless you." He

nodded like that was all that was needed, and settled back.

"What's that about?" Alik murmured as we continued on. Michal craned a look back over his shoulder at the Greywolf.

"Thoughts from an old man," I replied and stepped into the lodge.

Our *talånd* stood at the head of the room where a low table sat before a large wall hanging depicting the Saber spirit and smaller images of the other spirits who'd long been named as giving favor to the tribe. The All-Father's runes were embroidered into a prayer that wrapped around the entire picture.

The center of the room held a small spring that bubbled gently in the inset square. A shadow moved by the low hearth, and Emil glanced at us before returning to sliding the blade of a knife under his nail.

"Battlelion." The *talånd* greeted me with his easy smile that always seemed more conciliatory than anything.

I nodded sharply and took a stand across the room from Emil. My half-brother swept another glance over us again, then back to me, something unreadable there. Like us, he'd come in full armor, and there was an extra knife or two strapped to the belt across his chest.

Voices marked the arrival of Makar and two other men. It looked like he'd been busy last night, making his own promises. One of the men glanced at the medallion, but Makar's lust shone for something higher, and he tugged at the sling holding his injured arm like he might try to fight for it then and there.

They kept in the center of the room, completing the third camp. The *talånd* placidly looked out on this and stepped around the table.

"The tribe has not been faced with such a decision in many generations," he began, avoiding the fact that the last two at least had seized power at sword point.

"I have been up through the night begging for guidance. And there are some things to be considered first." He looked to Emil and to us. "Your father was blessed with many sons."

My teeth clenched tight. "Blessed" was maybe not the word I would use.

A scoff tore from Emil, but the *talånd* continued like he did not notice.

"I would ask of each of you what you seek here?"

Emil shifted. "The place of chief has never been for me. I don't need to stare into smoke and pretend to see things to know that."

The *talånd's* face tightened in disapproval of such open disdain, but turned to Michal and me. Michal stirred and for a moment, my heart stalled, my mind telling me that he would just as quickly turn back on his word.

"It is not for me either, but I will support Davor's claim," he finished in a breathless rush.

Emil's knife paused and his gaze seared through me again.

The *talånd* turned to me. "You wear the battlelion's mark, yet would lay claim to the chieftain's position?"

I wanted to ask him how he would have resisted Kamil if the oldest had ridden back and murdered the chief. But it seemed like the secret of Emil's deed stayed between him and the three of us standing together.

"I will pass the medallion on if I hold the place of chief. There is not room for a man to hold both," I said.

Makar's face twisted and I fought down triumph. Now he'd be bound by my words as well.

"And as the oldest living son of the chief, I claim his place by right of birth."

The *talånd* nodded and turned next to Makar.

"I held the confidence of the chief and of Kamil, both of whom did not favor Davor, thinking him too weak to lead within the tribe." Challenge locked our gazes in battle with each other.

"Then why was I named head *rokr* to the former battlelion in the war and you were not?" I returned evenly.

Red rushed up Makar's face and receded just as quickly. "Perhaps it was pity that drove them to give a coward a chance to redeem himself."

Emil kept picking at his nails, darting a glance up at me under lowered brows.

"He's not a coward." Michal lurched forward, my heart flipping at the raw anger in his defense. Emil's glare burned into me.

"Your word doesn't count for much here, whelp," Makar sneered.

A growl caught in Michal's throat and only my outstretched hand kept him in place. Alik tapped his shoulder and he subsided, but his eyes tried to bore holes through Makar's heart.

"Bringing the scraps to fight for you, Davor?" Makar sneered.

"It's a truly bold man who hastens to deride any man he deems weaker than him," I said. "Michal has proved himself many times over on the battlefields."

Makar crossed his arms, his anger returning.

"Enough." The mild voice of the *talånd* cut off whatever insult he was preparing. "Perhaps the fate of the tribe will be better served away from the men I see before me. Such strife will only lead to more and this might be the spirits' justice."

I was shaking my head before he even finished.

"Do not pretend like you care about justice," I snapped. "Not when you supported a man who murdered his way to the position. Not when you stood by and did nothing as he took whatever woman he wanted with no bonds. When you barely stood up for a young child to keep her from being killed just because she wasn't a boy. Don't you *dare* spout the will of the spirits when you knew as well as anyone what went on in that lodge and there was no word of rebuke to him or to anyone else."

My anger had risen enough to almost choke me, but no one stopped me, cut me off. The *talånd* did not blanch away, instead a stubbornness taking over as he shook his head, like he denied all my accusations.

So many years and things were clamoring for a sudden voice and only a harsh breath contained them all again.

"And what would you do, Davor?" Makar sneered. "You are the coward who pulled us from battles, stole our victories in the upper valley. Let the chief's lodge burn and the chief die. What makes you think you have what it takes to hold his place?"

"The pride of this tribe is warped," I said. "If spirits watch over us, I don't know how they stand it. Not when misery lurks in every corner of these villages. I would see us turn to a different way than the bloody paths we've stood on for too long."

Everyone stood taken aback by my words, but it might have been the strength and vehemence with which I said them. My voice had never held so much before, not publicly. Emil's knife paused but even the weight of his stare did not quell the anger rushing through me.

A faint creak jolted through the breathless silence, and the Greywolf *talånd* emerged into our midst.

"Davor speaks well," he said. Our *talånd* bristled, but the Greywolf kept on.

"Division threatens when men try to thwart the will of the spirits. It is only due to their blessing that the Greywolf tribe did not succumb to something worse when Reidar took the matter of heir into his own hands."

Makar scoffed. "He still named his bastard chief, and they would have fallen to our spears if not for this coward." He spat the word at me.

"His two sons came together to save their tribe on their own strength. I see before me a man willing to do the same here. I do not think you have to look outside the chief's line for strength." The Greywolf cast the challenge directly to the *talånd*.

The *talånd* drew himself up tall, hands clenching at his sides before he turned to me.

"You speak boldly, Davor. Perhaps you do have some hidden strength."

It needled me more than I cared to admit.

"I will support your claim as oldest of the chief's line. You will be anointed at the end of the counting, but—" A challenge rose in his eyes, and I found myself almost recoiling from the promise there.

"If you truly want to be different, to follow the paths of the spirits, then you will know that tribe law speaks of a chief supported by the strength of a wife. You do not have one as far as anyone knows. You have until the ceremony to bind yourself with a woman to keep the claim you have laid, or it will go to someone else."

I refused to flinch at the way the words pummeled me. Makar laughed. He was already married and so would be able to take the position if I did not meet the requirements. From the look in the *talånd's* eyes, this was his vengeance for my words. And he knew well how perfect it was. I wanted to be different, but how was I going to find anyone willing to stand beside me?

TWENTY-ONE

DAVOR

It took a moment before I found my voice, suddenly quieter after my rage. "Very well, *Talånd*." I tapped a fist to my forehead in respect, though curses seethed inside me.

Makar's hateful smile stayed in place as he gave me the battle-lion salute and backed away, but not before he beckoned to Emil.

Emil paused for a moment, and I did not like the look he gave me—something like pity—before he moved away and joined Makar. They went from the lodge together.

"Anything else, Battlelion?" the *talånd* asked smugly.

"No."

He did not quail before my look, and I swept past the Greywolf who drew his cloak around him, shaking his head at the *talånd*. He reached out, but I avoided the touch and stepped into the open air.

Michal hurried around in front of me, backing away as I kept walking.

"What are you going to do?"

"I don't know!" I snapped and he shied away from it. It ground me to a halt, and I tried to tame the anger inside.

"Davor." Alik stepped up beside us. "It's a cruel trick he played back at you for speaking the truth."

My teeth might be ground away by the end of the day under the force of them pressed together.

"I said I'd stand with you. I'll do what I can to help here too."

"How, Alik?" The biting sneer did not make him step back. "How are you going to help with this?"

"Davor." Alik placed a hand on my chest, halting me. "I might know someone already. Please, just trust me."

But I pushed around them and left them alone on the path, cursing everything on the way.

It did not take long for my mother to find me. She settled down with a faint sigh beside me on the log I'd wedged between two stones long ago. The small sanctuary was inset into the rocks on the eastern side of Half Peak, a ten-minute hike from the chieftain's lodge through tall pines and aspens. It looked down to the roaring, tumbling waters below, a torrent crashing through the trees in a narrow gorge where it whipped around the mountain before dumping into the curving river. She'd found me here more than once over the years. Her hand rested over mine where they clenched together.

"Michal told me."

A bitter laugh broke from me. "I'd thought gaining the position of chief was going to be the impossible task."

She nudged her fingers between my fists and scooped my hand into hers. I pushed up from where I leaned on my knees and the rocky outcropping scraped against my back.

"Davor…"

"I am not forcing anyone. I'm not."

"I know." Her hands tightened around mine. "Maybe… maybe there could be someone willing."

"Willing only to avoid what they think I'll do instead? No one believes any of us will be different than him." I'd seen it often enough in the eyes of the tribe. Even if I tried to find some way to help, there was always the doubt.

"What's to stop them from believing I'd steal their daughters as well?"

She had no answer for me. She'd lost dreams of a life, of a family, when my father had taken her.

"Don't give up," she finally pleaded.

I had four days before the end of the counting. And three to convince some soul to bind themselves to me on nothing more than a promise that I wanted to be different than my father. It would be easy enough for someone to bring their own plots to such a marriage. Easy enough for Makar, perhaps Emil if they made an alliance, to strike down an innocent to weaken my position.

I'd never considered marriage for myself. And even if I had, this was not how I'd want it.

"Davor."

I finally looked at my mother, and mustered a promise that I wouldn't give up yet, though each word tasted like ash.

When I finally returned to the lodge, the sun was tracking toward late afternoon. After my mother had left me, I'd spent even more time pacing, thinking, and planning, and trying to tame the rage still festering at the *talånd's* decree.

The door softly shut behind me, and Alik and Michal shoved up from the table where they had clearly been waiting. I leaned against the door, crossing my arms, and interrupting whatever Alik was going to say.

"I don't want to bring anyone else into this."

"Are you just going to give up then?" he demanded.

A scowl creased my face. "And who will be rushing to join hands with me, Alik?"

He grudgingly admitted that I was right.

"I'm not forcing anyone," I softly echoed my words to my mother, and Michal's sudden stiffness eased.

Alik softened again. "I know you wouldn't."

A curse escaped me again and I slumped to the nearest bench, elbows resting on my knees.

He settled beside me with a light sigh. "I'm assuming you don't have anyone in mind?"

My lips flattened with my glare at him, and a faint and honest grin appeared before he sobered.

"If I found someone, would you at least speak with her?"

My hands worked together, tendons standing out sharply across my knuckles. Another choice taken, another piece added that only added risk and no security. A stranger brought into my life.

But…the truth remained. I wanted the chief's place, and this was the surest way. I could not yet change laws or traditions from where I stood now. I had to carve out my place and hold my claim.

And that meant complying with the *talånd's* order.

"Yes."

Alik's hand rested on my shoulder, and I tilted a look from the corner of my eye.

"Trust me, Davor. I'll be back." He vanished through the door and a faint noise drew my look to Michal. He'd taken a seat at the nearer table bench, hands gripping the edges.

"You're going to marry someone?"

I was almost afraid to interpret the look he gave me. One already disbelieving me.

"To take the chief's place, yes."

He scoffed, shaking his head and turning away.

"Michal." My quiet voice halted him. "I am not going to... use anyone the way he did. If there even is a woman out there who would agree, she would be safe."

He eased back a little.

"What do you want, Michal?" I asked when he said nothing.

Michal unlatched his grip from the bench, hands coming to fiddle with each other.

"What do you mean?" he countered.

"You agreed to ally with me. We fought beside each other in the war. But what do you want with all this?"

"I...I want Mother and Janne...Nina..." He darted a glance at me with my mother's name. "I want them safe. I don't want Janne bartered off to one of Makar's warriors or anyone else."

"She told you?"

"No. Makar did. Countings ago. When...when I was with Kamil's packs. He was trying to make me angry. It worked." His gaze came to settle on me more squarely. "And last night Janne told me that you were going to stop it if you could. But you already did, didn't you? Otherwise, she would have been married off before the war."

I paused, then tipped my head in acknowledgement.

"He and his men aren't touching her." That was a promise we could both agree on. He nodded sharply.

"I want you both to have your own choices. Decide who you want to be in this tribe. So, what do you want?" I asked again.

"In the war, and in the *talånd's* lodge, you said many things. And you did look out for me in some way."

I wondered how hard that was for him to admit. But he was not done.

"I want…" His knees bobbled and his hands clenched tight. "I want to not be afraid."

Red coated his cheeks and he focused on his hands, shoulders setting like he was bracing for my scorn.

"Me too." My words had him looking up, and I gave a faint smile of understanding.

"I never thought I'd agree with a half-brother." A slightly wider grin split his face.

"Me neither." I straightened. There was one more thing. "I will need an heir."

His face darkened faster than an oncoming summer storm. "You said—"

I shook my head. "I do not intend to have a natural heir."

"Then—?"

I looked to him again, and understanding flashed. He slumped back against the table. "You would trust me enough?"

"Who should I name instead? Emil?"

A smirk flickered, and his fingers were back to picking at the bowstring callouses on his fingertips.

"You have a claim by blood if anything happens to me. It could stop whoever killed me from claiming the chief's place by right of the sword. I want someone willing to keep forging a new path after me."

"What if you don't marry?"

"Then it goes to Makar, and I survive as long as possible. Keep this if I can." I tapped the battlelion mark. "Change what I'm able. And find some lawful claim to take the chief's place from him."

He sat in silence for so long that I almost started fidgeting. Then he looked up, and it seemed he had matured years in those minutes.

"I'll do it. I'll be your heir."

TWENTY-TWO

MARTA

A light breeze kept trying to throw strands of hair across my vision. I finally broke off a piece of thread from the coil in my pocket, tied my hair back, and returned to stitching a new hem on an overdress.

Its future owner played in the dirt with three other small children her age, heedless that the amount of tripping and scuffling on knees was the reason for the new skirt. I smiled and watched her brush wild hair from her face. I'd finish the hem and add in leaping foxes and twirling vines atop it. She'd love it.

Their laughter was a welcome break from the gossip swirling endlessly in the lodge. I'd finally taken my work outside to the bench to avoid it. Word had gone out that morning that the *talånd* would be naming a new chief by the end of the counting.

Rumor was it would be Davor. Providing he could find a wife before then.

No one knew if that was the truth, and even in the last hours, some women had claimed to be marrying him only for the bold lie to be exposed.

I might almost pity him if that was truly what the *talånd* had declared.

The children's laughs turned to shouts of greeting. A look up showed Alik striding down the path. He barely acknowledged them, focused on something else. He'd been preoccupied since he'd first returned with the news about the chief's naming, then vanishing until now.

He stopped before me, and I shifted the dress away from the puffs of dust he stirred.

"Marta, I need to talk to you."

"About what?" I kept stitching.

"Marta." The tense urgency in his voice brought my attention to him and nervousness pricking through my fingertips.

He beckoned me away from the children who'd stopped to watch us. They followed the lessons of their elders and listened in whenever they could.

I set aside the dress and tucked the needle through a fold in my skirt. We stepped away and he waited until the young ones turned back to play. He crossed his arms.

"Hear me out before you say anything."

"That's not promising, Alik."

He looked pleadingly to me. I dipped my head and waited.

"The rumors are true. That Davor has to wed to be named chief," he said.

"Why are you…? *Oh.* Oh, no, Alik." I shook my head firmly, turning to walk away. "No."

"Marta!" he pleaded.

"How could you ask me that?" I hissed. "He's a chief's son."

"Davor is not like *him*." Alik's voice rose before he composed himself.

"How many women have turned you down before you came to me?" My arms pressed tight over my stomach.

"None." He shook his head. "He'd change the *talånd's* demand if he could, and I've been trying to figure out a way—"

"And you thought of me?" It stung a little. Thought of the woman who had turned down two offers and hadn't had another in two years because spurned men tried to tarnish my reputation with those who'd listen. Maybe I'd become the one no one wanted, so why not offer me up to the son of a chief?

Maybe even he wouldn't want me.

"I'm not going to be *used*, Alik!"

"He won't." Alik's hands extended, almost pleading. "He won't."

My scowl didn't abate. Maybe once I might have believed it about Davor, but not now.

"You didn't seem afraid of him." Alik sighed. "The other night. You weren't scared."

I paused, retorts dying on my tongue. Hadn't I been?

"Marta," he said more gently. "He's a good man, even if he has practically walled himself off with thorns. He wants to make this tribe better, to right many of the wrongs of the chief and Kamil, and everyone before."

I scoffed in disbelief. "And you believe that? They are almost as good at lying as they are at hurting."

"Not him," Alik persisted. "Trust me, Marta. Not him. War shows the truest parts of a man, and he does not lead like Kamil did. I wouldn't pledge my sword to a chief's son if I didn't believe him."

"Why do you?"

"He tried to save my brother years ago." Raw pain welled up in Alik's eyes. It had been so long since it had shown that I ached to see it again. It stole any answer away.

"If he does not marry before the naming, then Makar takes the place of chief. Davor dies and probably me too for daring to support him. Makar is just as ruthless as the chief and Kamil were. I know you don't want to see that."

I glared, letting him know I hated the low blow. I seethed often enough at the treatment of men, and especially women, in the tribe, the way the lower village and even most of us here in the middle village who were not part of warrior families were looked down on as *less*. The way I wished for more children to innocently play in the paths and out in the fields. How I tried in small ways to make it better and safer for the weak, but it was like placing a pebble in the river and expecting it to change course.

"What has Father said to this?" I asked.

Alik smiled wryly. "I came to you first."

I half-laughed. Intelligent plan.

"Would you at least talk to Davor?" he asked. "He barely consented to me coming to you." It came with a bit of wryness that made me curious.

"Very well. But I want Father there."

A relieved breath exploded from him, and he grabbed my hand. "Thank you."

"I'm just talking to him," I stressed, but Alik was already nodding.

"I'll go get him. Thank you."

I watched him run off and tried to will away the trickle of dread growing wider and wider inside me.

⌒⌒⌒

"What is this about?" Father asked as I paced back and forth across the smaller back room I'd claimed for the meeting. This one had a door for more privacy instead of just a hanging. Once Davor walked in, there would be plenty of ears trying to hear.

"It's…you'll see." I resumed my pacing, gnawing at my thumbnail.

"Marta." Father's voice bordered on the tone we didn't dare refuse. Alik's knock and entry saved me.

I took a step back at the sight of the man behind him. *Why did I agree to this?*

My father's glance between me and the two men turned understanding, furious, then controlled. I bit hard enough on my thumb I thought I might taste blood.

"Alik." Father's voice only increased the skittering in my gut. "Close the door."

Alik sent a pleading look around the room before obeying.

Father pinched the bridge of his nose, taking a deep breath. "Battlelion, I have some respect for you after the war. Which is why I will listen for a few moments. Alik, you're lucky that I've known you since you were a child, which is the only reason I am not skinning you right now."

Alik gave a faint smile. "Believe me, if my father knew about this, he'd beat you to it."

But Davor had gone still, glancing almost sharply at Father as if he really believed the threat. It made me pause.

"I take it the rumor about needing to be married is true?"

Davor jerked a sharp nod. "Do not worry, your daughter would be safe with me."

"Were you planning on giving me a reason to worry?" Father's question brought him up short and he shook his head.

"Marta." Father turned on me next. "I'm assuming you knew about this since you called me here?"

I pulled my thumb from my lips and started picking at the nail with fingers instead. "Alik asked. I said I would speak with...you." I mustered the courage to look at Davor.

"Why?"

The quiet question had my fingers twisting around each other.

"Because I know Alik. And I believe him when he says that he trusts you. That you want to be different for the tribe." I forced my hands to still and press against my skirt. "Father and the other men, they speak well of you, of how you acted in the war."

I'd been turning over everything I'd ever heard about him over and over in my mind as we'd waited.

"And what do *you* think?" he asked.

"I don't know," I admitted. All I knew were stories of him. What people said, but words could be changed, could be twisted. I had only a few brief moments of time with him in recent memory, and one bigger moment that almost frightened me to look back on.

"There is no obligation here. No demand. You are free to say no if you choose, or if there is someone else waiting for you," he said. "I will not steal your life from you like this."

I looked to Father. If he truly thought there was trouble waiting for me with the battlelion, then he would be fighting tooth and nail to keep me from it. Alik would not put me this close to danger either. If a man's true nature was revealed in war, they both seemed calm enough beside him.

"If I were to say yes?" I had to force the words to come evenly. Even knowing that the men from my life would see me protected, I still did not know him.

His fingers curled up to his palm and then straightened.

"This is no temporary thing," he reminded. "There are those who already plan to take the medallion or the chief's place from me if they can. A marriage would only bring you right into the middle of the fight, though I would do everything to keep you safe from it." His glance swept from me to Father, the same grim promise never leaving him.

I believed it. Was starting to believe maybe he did want something different for the tribe. But words could be skewed or carefully said. There was one more thing I needed.

"Why did you do it?" I blurted. "That day in the woods?"

Alik and Father stiffened, gaze whipping to Davor. They didn't know what I was talking about, but he did. I saw it in the softening of his shoulders.

I'd been seventeen, alone in the woods to gather plants and flowers to make more dyes. An unseen vole's burrow had turned my ankle badly and I'd been helpless on the ground when he'd appeared. We'd stared at each other for a terrifying moment, and I could have sworn there had been traces of tears about him.

He'd started to come towards me, and I'd scooted backwards, tearing my palms against the ground. Then, with a gentleness I didn't know a chief's son could possess, he'd crouched, spread his hands, and said he would help me if I wanted.

I'd believed him, and he'd used a bit of cloth from the scraps I always had in my bag to wrap a splint around my ankle. Then let me lean on him all the way back to the lodge. When I'd tried to turn around and thank him, he'd already gone.

"You needed help."

"And after?" My arms tucked back over my stomach.

After, when I'd been able to walk by myself again, I'd mustered up the courage to go find him and thank him. But when we came face-to-face in the upper village with him looking fresh from the training grounds, he'd looked at me with no recognition, practically shoved me from his path, and snarled at me to not look at him again. I'd run all the way home.

His gaze dipped to the floor, then slowly back to me. "Plenty of people had seen me helping you back to this lodge. If Kamil or the chief, even Makar then, thought there was something between you and me, they would not have hesitated to hurt or use you in some way."

"Oh."

"This is why I do not want to bring anyone else into this," he said to me and the others in the room. "Perhaps the *talånd* would change his mind."

"I doubt he will," Alik replied.

I thought of the children outside, of Vanda, targeted by another of the chieftain's sons. Davor had not threatened me into this decision. He'd even almost...asked? Perhaps he might make it different, safer, for others like Vanda. Even for his own sister who'd cared enough about him to trade for a prayer cloth with his rune. Perhaps I could help make it happen at his side.

I'd never thought myself to be one who would seek power or to change her standing in the tribe. But perhaps I'd hoped for something like this every time a man came to ask for my hand. The thought of having a weight behind my actions and attempts to help was something I did not want to refuse.

"Davor." I surprised myself, and him, with the bold use of his name. "I do not know anything about being a chieftain's wife."

Hope sparked in his eyes, and a faint smile touched his face, turning him to something gentler. "I do not know anything about being a chieftain."

But he was willing to try.

"When would you need to know my answer?"

"Now," Alik said apologetically. "There would be a wedding tomorrow at the latest."

Tomorrow. I swallowed hard.

"And where would I stand in your life?" I'd been content enough in my life, my place in the lodge so far. But I would not be shoved in some back corner, used up however he wanted, cast aside for some other woman if he felt like it. Even if he claimed otherwise, his blood had damning actions.

His dark eyes were not as frightening as they had been even minutes before. Nor was the way he was studying me. Like he saw me, the way the other men who'd sought my hand had not really seen.

"I would have someone stand beside me and help me lead as best I can for this tribe."

Words could be twisted, but spirits help me, I believed him. And even if he turned out to be full of false promises, perhaps I could use my position as *dronni* to create some good in my own way.

I looked to my father, and he nodded, a bit of resignation in the motion. But he would not abandon me to misery if it came to it.

"Yes."

Davor actually seemed taken aback. I stepped forward and extended my hand. His hand closed about mine, and our fates were sealed.

TWENTY-THREE

DAVOR

She said yes.

Even hours later, it did not seem real. Even more strange that it was her, the one person who'd flickered in my mind when Alik had asked if I had anyone before I'd immediately dismissed it. I'd thought she only had scorn for me, but there had been nothing but honest evaluation about her and her words.

The *talånd* had taken the news with a disgruntled face. But I had not told him who he would be binding me to. I wanted to keep her safe for one more day.

She and Dariy had understood that at least, though the rest of their family would be there at the ceremony.

Michal and Janne had taken the news with eagerness. Both that my plan still might succeed, but I think Janne a little more for a sister. Especially after she blurted that Marta had treated her with kindness before. But Inge and my mother had looked at me with sympathy and some reluctant understanding. At least there would be some honor in Marta's position with marriage cords around her wrist.

I don't think she truly understood what she'd done by agreeing to marry me. What she might face every day.

"Where are you going to stay?" Mother asked.

I scraped my thumb knuckle across my forehead as I leaned on the table. I had no answer. I had not really expected anyone to say yes. And with the chief's lodge a pile of burned timber, there was no place for a chief or his *dronni* to stay.

"Our lodge is open." Alik sat across from me. "Tomorrow and after you take the staff."

I shook my head. "I think it would be dangerous to move the chief to the middle village."

His face twisted in a frown. "I should argue the middle village is just as good as any, but the chief's home has been on that hill for generations. What are you going to do about the lodge?"

"Rebuild it?"

"Bring all three villages together that way. There are plenty of craftsman in each, and many in the middle and lower villages who have felt slighted for years."

I raised an eyebrow at Alik who tapped his fingers against the table. "I keep an eye on my village. You're not the only one who pays attention to things."

"This still does not solve tomorrow night," Mother broke in.

The wedding night.

And I was not putting Marta, or myself, into any lodge in the upper village. Not surrounded by people I didn't trust, or those who would easily side against me.

"You can stay here." Inge came closer, hands tucked into the pockets of her overdress. "Tomorrow night, and after. Until the lodge is rebuilt."

"No, Inge, this is your home, and I don't want to bring danger here."

"And how do you know you can even trust her?"

Alik bristled, but Inge cut him off before he could defend Marta.

"I have known Davor longer than you. Anyone who hurts him answers to me first."

I stared in bemusement at the two of them locked in some sort of battle over *me*. Mother smiled faintly. Then Alik bowed his head in deference.

"You win." But there was a bit of a laugh in his voice.

Inge softened. "As for you, we need to work on your healing skills if you're going to be around."

"They're a little more rough than ready," he admitted, and I could attest to that. "And that will depend on the new chief."

I allowed a faint quirk of humor. "I had hoped you would take this off my hands." I tapped the battlelion medallion.

His grin faded to shock. "Me? Battlelion?"

"I need someone I can trust. And the packs who support me looked just as often to you."

"Are you sure? No battlelion has ever come from the middle village."

"I have already said I am doing things differently, haven't I?" I tried for a lighter tone.

He exhaled. "I'll do my best."

"That's all I need, Alik."

There were just a few more things I needed before the day was over. Before I found myself bound to a stranger, and before I took the mantle of chief on shoulders already tired of fighting.

But this time I had allies. I only hoped I was not dooming us all by every one of my actions.

⌒

Mother and Inge fretted all the next day about what I was to wear. Alik was ready to drag his entire trunk to the lodge and make me borrow something. In the end, we cleaned what I had from my packs and Mother mended a few rips with neater stitches than I would have, and I pulled them on.

Had my trunk survived the fire, it would not have yielded much brighter which was what they wanted. And I did not much feel like wearing the colors and finery reserved for the chief and his line. I did not want any reminder of him to further stain the ceremony.

I spent more time cleaning and oiling armor and weapons. A few visits to lodges had assured me that rumors continued to fly. There might be some unwelcome guests at the spirits' lodge.

If she even showed up.

Another curse escaped under my breath, and I yanked harder than needed at the laces of my bracer. I just had to get through this night and then the next while making sure the *talånd* would name me, and then survive every day after for as long as I could.

A wife had not been part of the plan.

Part of me wanted to hold a knife to the *talånd's* throat until he relented, but a word with the Greywolf confirmed it was part of our tribe's scrolls. A law which had been ignored by the last two chieftains and who knew how many before that. But I'd made sure that children were not a requirement of the law.

The last of my armor settled around me, feeling even more disjointed from me than it normally did. The bare reassurance from my weapons was destroyed as soon as my mother appeared in front of me with the somber pronouncement that it was time to go.

She offered a small smile as she straightened the collar of my tunic, tugged at my sleeves, and touched the medallion resting against my chest.

"I know this is not what you want, Davor, but be kind to her."

My throat tightened as for once I didn't quite know what she thought of me. "I will."

"This will be as hard for her as it will be for you." She squeezed my hand, telling me something I already knew.

"She will have nothing to fear from me," I said softly, and Mother blinked back tears. She nodded and slowly released my hand.

"We will make her feel welcome here," she said.

"Thank you."

She mustered a smile and gently touched my cheek. "I'd hoped I might someday see this happen for you. I pray some good might come of all this."

"Pray?" I scoffed, already moving from her touch.

"Things have changed so fast, and the future seems so uncertain. Perhaps Janne's belief is finally wearing off."

I gave a faint smile. Some days it seemed like Janne could will a falling star to stay in the heavens.

We were a somber group walking the path up to the spirits' lodge. I had not been to many weddings, but they were usually a more cheerful affair.

Alik met me at the door. With a look oddly reminiscent of my mother's, he critically looked over me and tugged at a sleeve.

"You look about as cheerful as a shade."

My mouth flattened in a line.

"You are marrying a friend of mine, Davor, and this is a wedding for spirits' sake. At least look like you're not attending the funeral of a loved one."

I only frowned more at him.

The *talånd* met us at the lodge door. His brightly colored cloak stitched in runes and decorated with redhawk feathers was pinned at the throat with a brooch carved from sablecat teeth. He beckoned us in.

"We just await your bride, Battlelion."

My gaze rested evenly on him, not letting him see my doubt when he seemed to take delight in projecting his own.

A knock sounded and the *talånd* ushered me forward to the low spring inset in the floor. Alik stood a few paces away, and behind him, Mother, and Inge and the twins.

The *talånd* opened the door and spoke the traditional words of greeting to an approaching bride.

Marta's low voice rang with the same certainty as when she'd said yes the day before. I willed myself to turn as she stepped in, the *talånd* taking her hand from her father's and leading her to me.

Her family filed in behind her, and so did the men of Alik's pack. I glanced sharply to Alik. He leaned closer.

"They would not hear different. She is of our lodge, and they think highly of you. She will have a willing guard from among them for as long as she needs."

For the first time, I relaxed a fraction. I had overlooked the men so easily, but here they were, all giving me the same tap of a fist to their chests as they took up positions on the outer edge of the room and two stepping back outside to the door.

The *talånd* halted in front of me, and I finally looked at Marta. Like all brides she wore a cream-colored dress stitched in red, a belt of new leather around her waist. Her hair tumbled free across her shoulders, for tomorrow she would be able to wear it in different braids as a married woman.

She met my gaze readily, though there was a faint quiver to her jaw, a slight tremble in her cold fingers when the *talånd* placed our hands together.

I almost yanked mine away, not ready to go through with this thing that was only the *talånd's* vengeance. A question sparked in her dark eyes, but I kept my hand in place.

The *talånd's* eyes bored into Marta as he asked if we both came willingly to this ceremony, and it seemed he looked longer at her. Until her chin lifted, and her voice came stern. For some reason, it almost made me smile.

Our hands fell apart and we stepped around the spring on opposite sides before coming back together, letting it rest as a barrier between us and the rest of the gathering. The *talånd* joined us and I extended my left hand, my weak hand, to leave my sword free to defend. Her right hand, her strong hand, came under mine to support and lend her strength to my weakness.

The *talånd* wrapped a red cord around our hands, tying us together as first I, then Marta, repeated the vows in the sight of the spirits and of the tribe.

"Flesh and bone, heart and blood, I bind myself to you, that through darkness and fire we may come out together, in joy and laughter we may abide. My heart will reach for none other than you in this world. If you leave before I do, I will hold your spirit close. And in the All-Father's lodge may we find each other again for all eternity."

He cut the cord and we brought the pieces away. He gave me a piece of leather cord and she handed me a woven band of the same length, runes and sablecats and some sort of flower stitched through it. I added the red cord to the others and the *talånd* held them as I braided them together, tightly and evenly.

It went to her next and she wrapped it twice around my left wrist before threading the ends through an iron loop and knotting them securely.

She did the same with another leather cord, her bit of red, and the dark woven band I'd stitched runes of strength and honor onto. Her slender fingers braided the cords together opposite what I had done, tucking from the inside out. I took it from her, and she held out her left wrist.

Carefully so as not to brush her sleeve or her hand, I wrapped it twice around, threaded the iron loop, and tied off.

And it was done.

"Blessings on you both," the *talånd* said. "Davor, I will see you tomorrow for your naming to chief." The placid smile was back, but a sneer was not too far underneath. I had exposed something with my words.

He stepped back and we turned to lead the way from the lodge and receive the subdued congratulations of our families.

Barely a word passed between us through the meal prepared in a smaller building just downhill from the spirits' lodge. It was hard enough to think of anything with the marriage cords wrapped snugly around my wrist, her sister glaring at me from a few seats away, and the undercurrent of concern that any moment someone might burst through the door, weapons drawn, ready to come for me, and by extension, her.

But nothing stirred, and no warning came from the warriors rotating guards at the doors. Finally, the meal was done, and everyone rose. Marta went to her parents. Her mother tearfully pressed a kiss to her forehead. Dariy solemnly rested hands on her shoulders before they embraced tightly. Her sister whispered something in her ear as they hugged.

Mother's touch on my arm startled me. She offered a slight smile.

"We'll see you tomorrow."

I nodded, looking past her to Michal who straightened in resolve. All four of them would be going to Alik's lodge for the night. I didn't like them so far away in the middle village, but they and Alik agreed it might be safest, though perhaps no one had any way of knowing yet what they actually meant to me.

And now I had an extra piece I hadn't gambled on to guard. Her fingers were cold under my touch as we left the lodge. Once out of sight, I dropped her hand. Alik and another warrior trailed at a safe distance. They would make sure we got to Inge's lodge safely. Another pack from the upper village who had promised swords to me would be keeping a watch as well.

We reached the small lodge without incident, twilight hanging heavy over the village and only a few tribespeople out. Luk settled by the door, raising his head slightly as I let her step inside first.

The fire burned low on the hearth. Covered bowls rested on the stones beside it. Food for the morning. I latched the door and turned.

Marta stayed five paces away, arms locked tight over her stomach, the uncertainty back. My mouth suddenly felt dry and I wanted to escape, but I did not move and kept my voice even. Perhaps I should have told her this before our cords were woven.

"I expect nothing from you other than to stand at my side in view of the tribe. Other than that, I will accept whatever you are willing to give."

She stared at me, lips pressed tight before her words escaped. "And what if I am never willing to give you what a wife will to her husband?"

I refused to flinch, to move from the almost promise in her voice. "I have already spoken with Michal. He will be my heir as chief. And after him the place will go to whatever children he or Janne choose to have."

She shifted, taken aback by the answer. Like she had not expected me to have a plan in place.

"There is a room which you may take for your own, or one of the benches out here. Whatever you choose will be your place among us."

It would be an odd household: me, her, the twins, and the two almost wives of the old chief.

Her hands slid up and down her arms, as she looked past me to the small room I had indicated.

"And you?" she asked.

"I will take whichever you do not."

Her eyes flitted around. Furs piled atop the benches, and trunks were tucked against the wall between them. Carved runes announced their owners.

A door warded off the small room, but she eased back another step.

"The benches will be fine."

I nodded. "Very well. These are empty." I pointed to the ones against the wall closest to the entry. "It's farther from the fire, but there are extra furs as needed."

She said she did not mind. I stoked the fire, twisting as I heard the scraping of her trunk—delivered earlier that day—against the floor over to the bench, but she did not ask for my help, and I did not offer it.

Marta sat, still warily watching me as I straightened.

"Good night." I nodded and took myself to the smaller room and shut the door gently behind me.

TWENTY-FOUR

DAVOR

After a restless night, I rose and dressed. Paused a moment at the door, where no sound disturbed the main room. The door creaked warningly as I edged it open. Marta was a bundle of furs on the bench, and I stepped over the creaking board that ran down the center of the floor and through the back door.

Morning was a grey affair, hovering on the edge of sunrise, and even darker in the narrow walkway between Inge's home and the sweatlodge. I sank down to the bench set against the lodge and rested elbows forward on my knees.

The red braided through the marriage cords mocked, with guilt following quickly on its heels for having dragged Marta into such a thing. What did I have to offer? I did not even think I could truly give any part of myself to someone.

She seemed too good a person for someone like me.

"You do not look like a man blissfully married."

I wrenched up, knife drawn in an instant. Emil leaned against the corner of the sweatlodge, arms crossed, and dark eyes watching me.

"What do you want?" I asked, gathering my wits about me, trying to determine how long he had been there.

He shrugged, shifting so he was sheltered between the two lodges, so it was just the two of us six paces from each other. The wall supported him again.

"To talk, Davor. Is that so surprising a thing?"

I scoffed and slid the knife back into its sheath but stayed standing.

Emil picked at his thumbnail for long enough that I almost asked again. Then he raised his piercing gaze to me.

"Why did you stop the chief? And don't give me some *scata* about being different now."

Reasons why and the too many years left between us competed so harshly inside that all that came out was, "I don't know."

He gave me a flat look. "Yes, you do."

"Why did you?" I countered. "You could have let him keep coming after me."

There must have been something strange on his hand the way he studied it before saying, "Let's just say we're even then."

"Is that all you came here to say?"

His upper lip curled as he crossed his arms. "Makar knows you married. He will not challenge yet. Not until he is healed and can better defend his place. And the packs are too divided. He thinks to garner more support in the next countings. Leadership has always been taken by the sword in this tribe. Many might support him if he does the same."

My guard slammed back up. "Did he send you here?"

Emil scoffed a laugh. "He does not know. He thinks himself clever and secure, riding on Kamil's name with the packs."

"And you?" I asked cautiously. It still made no sense for him to be there telling me such things.

"You want to play at caring, at making people believe you can change, make them love you. Maybe I just want to be free."

I did not know where to start with his words, so I settled on the last one. "Free?"

"I told you, Davor." A bleak look flitted across his face. "You know nothing."

"Then where do you stand?"

"Wherever the most information flows. As much as it pains me to admit it, I'd rather see you in the chieftain's position. Makar would ruin this tribe. He thinks to lead the packs back up valley once he takes it from you."

It brought back my promise to the Greywolf chief. If it was not me at the border stones at midsummer, would they bring their wolves in vengeance against us?

"So why come to me with this? Why not just help him?"

The sneer lifted his lip. "I have no interest in serving a fool."

My hand spasmed.

"Tell me why," he demanded again, and there was no yielding in his eyes.

Frustration welled up, mixing dangerously with pure anger. Why did he care? Why did *I* care?

"Maybe I am tired of this. Tired of looking over my shoulder. Tired of waiting for change, of waiting for someone to step in and stop it, because no one ever has. Not for any of us. I finally saw a chance and I took it." Like in the *talånd's* lodge, words were spilling from me, the dam broken for a perilous moment, and I could not stop.

"And I know that there's nothing worthwhile about me, nothing about me to love, but maybe I can make it different for someone else. So maybe others don't spend their life just *waiting* for something to be different."

"So why now?" Anger seeped from him. "Why not sixteen years ago?" His eyes seared a path across my face. "Why not thirteen years ago? Or any moment in any of those years?"

This was about him, and about me.

About a moment in time sixteen years ago when our father had come and so had Kamil, angry and violent and careless with a knife even at thirteen years old. And the more innocent eyes of an eight-year-old Emil had looked to me for help, and I had turned away, unable to face the punishment for defiance. I had learned it well even then.

They'd dragged him away, brought him into their games, and that was the last time we had stood together.

"We were children, forced to make impossible decisions."

"Is that what you tell yourself?" he hissed, slamming a hand into my chest and pushing me back. "You *abandoned* me. You talk of waiting for someone to step in, of making a change, but you turned your back on *me*. You made me into this just as much as they did."

Of thirteen years ago when I'd let him take the blame for an action I committed, unable to take the consequences of it.

Wild rage crackled through the air between us, flowing and ebbing from one to the other. Perhaps there was no room for anything else in us but anger. Perhaps our father had done his work well.

He broke away first, his laugh a scoffing thing. "You are not a fool, Davor, but sometimes I wonder if you have a heart."

It rammed through me, tremoring in my chest. Perhaps I did not and that was why I felt nothing but anger.

"I will help you keep the position and defeat Makar. But after that, you and I are done." He shook his head. "I am finished playing the games of chiefs."

Before I summoned any words, he was gone, and I was alone with more confusion swirling inside.

TWENTY-FIVE

MARTA

I carefully folded away the wedding dress, my fingers tracing over the stitching one last time before it settled into the bottom of my trunk. It was not how I imagined a wedding day. Not how I imagined the man I'd tie myself to, for the few moments I'd considered such a thing.

The trunk lid settled gently closed and I smoothed the skirts of my simpler overtunic and dress. I brought only what I already had. None in our lodge knew what might be appropriate for my station if Davor were to take the staff. There had not been a *dronni*, a chief's wife, in two generations. Longer than the memory of anyone living.

And—I cautiously moved towards the hearth—I did not know where he was.

I'd slept fitfully all night, but his door had not opened once he'd closed it. The covered bowls yielded flatbread, spring berries, and dried kernels for hash. A water barrel stood in the corner, and a wealth of wood stacked by the hearth. It did not take long to nurse the flames back to health and mix water in the kernels and set it to boil.

The creak of a door sent a jolt through me, and I nearly dropped the bowl of berries all over the floor. Davor stood just inside the back entrance, hand still on the latch and watching me cautiously.

"Good morning." My voice creaked out barely above a whisper. It would be easier if I knew what he truly wanted, but nothing slipped past his stern features. Not like it had in the moments before we'd joined hands in my lodge.

He nodded.

"Food will be ready in a few minutes. If you are hungry." My hand fluttered towards the table, realizing then that I had no idea where any plates or cups were.

Davor disappeared around a corner and emerged with the wooden plates and earthen mugs. He set them out across from each other at the table, and filled the cups with water.

The soft clatter of bowls against the table filled the silence between us. The bench scraped against the floor as I hesitantly sat, him sitting a few seconds later. No prayer cords circled his wrists, and I'd sensed some scorn from him towards the *talånd* yesterday. Though it seemed mutual.

He said nothing, but waited as I bowed my head and mumbled a quick thanks to the All-Father and Saber spirit for the meal. I couldn't bring myself to thank them for anything more than that.

My spoon scraped over and over through the hash in my bowl without picking anything up. Davor stared at his plate as he tore a chunk of flatbread into smaller pieces. He seemed not quite in the room with me.

"Are…are you all right?" My voice wavered a little.

His attention darted to me, watchful for so long I almost looked away, then he nodded. "You?"

"I am fine." I didn't know whether to thank him for the courtesy of last night, or to ask when he might get tired of waiting and take what he might see as his due. Surely he would want an heir if he ascended to chief, no matter what he had said.

But he still barely looked at me. The marriage cords felt tighter and tighter around my wrist as I finally started to eat. For better or worse, we were bound to each other, and I'd walked into the lodge with both eyes open.

Davor said nothing either, but I'd not heard him speak overmuch except for the few times we'd traded words. Perhaps he just did not.

"I…I know of you, but I don't know much about you." I set my spoon down and my fingers wound together in my lap. Dark eyes focused on me again. "I'd…I'd like to know something."

There was much I wanted to know, but I did not think asking those things would yield answers.

"What would you like to know?" Caution rang in his voice as he rubbed his fingers together to shake crumbs free.

"Do you have a favorite food?"

His head tilted and confusion flickered. "That's what you wanted to know?"

A small laugh broke from me. "I thought it was an easier question to start. Food connects people more than many things."

His features softened somewhat. "Pine cakes."

I smiled. "When I was younger, my mother threatened to never make them again because my sister and I would steal them hot from the hearth." I rubbed my hands against my skirt and dared to pick up my spoon again. "I will happily eat currant bread all day."

Davor tipped his head again, and it seemed he would remember it. I choked down another bite in the silence that fell again.

"Alik has talked about how you want to make changes for the tribe."

A faint crease appeared between his eyes, and I worried that my words might irritate him. But he only nodded.

"That is what I hope to do once named chief. It will not be an easy path."

My thumb rubbed over the edge of the spoon handle. "I know, and I'd like to help."

"How?" But it did not sound condescending. Instead, there was a new sharpness in his eyes.

"I talk to many people, and they talk to me. And…and I would like to see things different as well."

"What would you want to see?"

I swallowed hard, wondering if this was some test or if he would go and do the opposite of everything I said.

"Women to feel, and to *be*, safer. Justice for those who have been hurt and used. Children to know love and safety, villages coming together without division, no more war." The last one came as a whisper. That would be harder as there might always be border strife between us and our neighbors.

But he only nodded. "It seems we want many of the same things. Though I have ears in many places."

I half-smiled. "Men love to talk, but there are many things

women only speak of over flatbread dough or weaving around a fire."

His features eased again and there was almost a flicker of a smile. I wondered what he might look like if he let it free. I might be bound to a stranger, but I could freely admit I found him handsome.

Short hair curled a little at the nape of his neck and at his forehead in a way the rest of the men's did not with their longer hair. Broad jaw and cheeks, but across his left cheekbone a fading bruise and small healing cut still there from whatever had happened during the fire days ago. And dark eyes holding depths of things.

I jerked my focus from those eyes, conscious I'd been staring for a moment when the crease appeared again. Heat crept up my neck and I willed it away.

"Allies?" he asked.

"I should like to be friends at least." I wasn't going to be shoved off in some corner and brought out only for tribe matters. I wanted to at least know, and possibly like, the man I'd bound myself to.

The word seemed to take him aback. *He walls himself off with thorns.* Alik's declaration was starting to make more sense. I didn't think he was happy with having to get married. That might make two of us, but perhaps he did not hate me.

His attention fell back to his plate. "Friends, then."

It didn't stop quiet from falling between us again, but it didn't feel so cold to me.

"What do you need me to do today?" I asked after another few bites.

"Whatever you would normally do. I will be making sure the *talånd* follows through on his promise to name me tonight."

I shivered a little at the iciness of his tone, the anger I'd sensed with the *talånd* last night even closer to the surface.

"And tonight?" My hesitation crept through again.

"Stand with me." He shifted his cup against the table. "Once people see us together, you might find things not as easy as they have been for you." Apology filled his voice. "Many might try to shame you or fill your ears with stories."

I thought back to Father's words and the way he'd acted toward Davor. "Is there anything I should feel shame for?"

His lips twisted in bitterness. "Walk with me long enough and you might hear."

"Well." My hands tucked into my lap to twine around each other. "I'd rather take the word of Alik and my father over others in the tribe. They speak well of you."

Davor's fingers curled in and eased out. He reached to his belt and my heart stalled as he pulled out a sheathed knife and set it on the table between us.

"All the same, I want you to take this."

I stared at the knife, bigger and heavier than anything I'd ever used to prepare a meal. A bitter taste touched the back of my tongue. A hunting knife whose iron had likely tasted blood in war.

I didn't reach for it. "I don't know how to use it."

He nudged it a little closer. "The pointed edge goes away from you."

A tentative smile curled my lip at the lift in his voice.

"Sometimes the promise of a weapon is enough to deter people."

The smile died just as fast. What did he think might happen? I reached out and brought it into my lap. The leather-bound handle was worn in a few spots, speaking to frequent use. I unsheathed it. Like my father's blades, the iron was clean and sharply edged.

"Here." He stood and beckoned to me.

Hesitation filled me as I joined him. He took the knife and gestured to my belt. I undid it and watched as he threaded the sheath onto the belt and handed it back to me.

The new weight against my hip felt odd, a piece apart from me. He nodded, satisfied.

"Do not hesitate to use it if you feel threatened."

I swallowed hard. What did he expect to happen? Was he that hated through the villages?

"As for the rest of it, our arrangement last night will hold."

The heat threatened to creep back up to my cheeks. But the same sort of awkwardness appeared around him too.

"No one in this lodge will judge or speak of it."

Before I had any reply for him, he turned and slipped out the back door, leaving me alone.

I gathered the dishes together and washed and dried them with one of the cloths left on the hearth. Hating being unsure of where to put anything, I left them on the table in a neat stack. The door beckoned, but after his somber pronouncement and the dagger weighing on my hip, my feet stalled until finally I willed myself to step out.

The sun was well on its way up, and the upper village stirring.

"Marta!" Vanda bolted up from the bench outside and rushed to me.

I stared at her in confusion. "What are you—?"

"Are you all right?" Her hands on my upper arms and desperate look in her eyes cut me off.

"Yes."

"Are you sure? Did he…? I barely slept at all last night!"

"Vanda." I gently freed my arms and took her hands. "I am fine." My voice fell between us after a cautious glance around. "Nothing happened and I have my own separate place in the lodge."

Her shoulders collapsed with a relieved gust of a sigh and she pulled me into a tight hug. "I just didn't want you to be hurt...I didn't..."

"I'm all right." I rubbed her back the way I did when she would wake from a nightmare or lean into my shoulder while we shared secrets with each other.

"Why did you marry him?" she mumbled into my shoulder. It held the exhausted argument we'd engaged in from the moment she'd heard until I'd walked into the lodge with the *talånd*.

"Because if he is to be chief then perhaps I can do some good at his side."

She lifted her head. "What if he does not let you?"

Our stilted conversation had allayed some of my fears. "I think he will."

Vanda shook her head. "You are too trusting, Marta."

I smiled. "Careful, you sound like an older sister."

She just hugged me again. "I just don't want to lose mine."

"You won't," I whispered.

Her arms tightened around me before she released me. "What's this?" She pointed to the knife.

"He gave it to me." I didn't admit how off-balance it made me feel.

Vanda's expression shifted. "Why does he think you need it?"

I lifted a shoulder. I didn't want her to worry, but it wasn't as if she was a child needing protecting from the world.

"I think there is going to be trouble ahead."

Vanda crossed her arms, shivering a little in the early morning air. "Alik and the others are whispering the same."

"I'm going to do what I can to make sure the weak stay safe." The words sounded bold, but in my heart they rang more empty. If he did not become chief, or did not hold the position, then what would become of me? Davor had said he'd named Michal his heir, but what might people assume about me and him?

The cold found me, but in the face of Vanda's small smile, I stood a little straighter.

"Go home and tell Mother not to worry." I gave her another hug. She held tight, drawing it out before placing her hands on my shoulders.

"Stay strong."

"I will," I promised, and then I was alone, arms curled over my stomach, staring out at the village that was my new home.

The earth had been flattened for the lodges long ago, but it still looked down slightly on the middle and lower villages. I turned around, my head tilting back to take in Half Peak and the ruins of the chief's lodge.

There had been talk of rebuilding it, and the thought sent another shiver down my arms. When it was built and if Davor took his place as chief in it, where did that leave me? It did not seem like a *dronni* would be able to sleep on the benches without awkward questions being asked.

Movement sent me stepping back towards the door. But it was a warrior from my lodge. He took up a stance six paces from me, met my gaze, and gave me the curious salute they'd all been giving Davor.

I didn't know if a guard was his or my lodge's doing. Either way, it brought some reassurance to me and helped me lift my chin a little higher to meet the day.

TWENTY-SIX

DAVOR

I *'m going to be sick.*

Alik rested a hand on my shoulder.

"You'll get through it," he reassured even though I'd felt the blood drain from my face long ago and nausea stirred at my gut like the ceaseless churning of the river.

I wished I had his confidence, but the entire tribe had gathered in the open spaces at the foot of the mount where the *tâkns* stood and a path wound through the grove to the spirits' lodge. The poles carved with the histories of the tribe and the spirits towered over every new event of the tribe.

Fires had been built throughout the field as the sun began to set, and torches ringed on tall poles. A collection of four in a line stood at the base of the head *tâkn* where a low platform had been built, and where the *talånd* waited. The eyes of the roaring sablecat atop the *tâkn* seemed to watch me.

We stood on the fringes of the gathering. Michal stayed with his mother and mine, Marta with them. She stood tall, the brightness of her clothes a beacon drawing my eye to her. Her hands were clasped in front of her where her fingers twisted the marriage cords around her wrist.

I flexed my left wrist against the tightness of mine. I'd avoided her all that day, going to different lodges with Alik, making sure I had the support of the packs who'd looked to me in the war, gathering more information, and seeing where the thoughts of the tribe lay in regard to Makar.

It seemed, like the packs, the villages would be split nearly down the center. I caught glimpses of Makar throughout the day, but nothing face-to-face. And I did not see Emil again.

My challenger was in the front lines, and when he felt my gaze upon him, he turned and favored me with a smile. Smug and knowing and holding vengeful promise. His injury gave me time. If he wanted to take the chief's place, he would have to be the one to kill me, like my father and his before us, or the tribe might not accept him.

I kept my face blank and held his eyes until the *talånd* climbed up on the platform and raised his arms, drawing all attention to him.

"Tonight, we gather to mourn a chief," he began.

A shift drew my attention back to Makar, but it was Emil who had moved. His glance flicked to me, and it seemed that more than just our secret lurked between us. How many years had he held his hatred of the chief, hidden it, obeyed, like I had?

"He has been called home to the All-Father."

The *talånd* made it sound like the chief would be feasting with honor at the All-Father's table. I did not turn the direction of the spirits often, but it would be a poor world and afterlife indeed if they favored men such as him.

"The sun has set upon his name, and will rise tomorrow upon a new chief of the Saber tribe."

Some shouts of approval rang out. Perhaps they would change to different sounds once the *talånd* made his choice.

The thought did nothing to calm the churning inside. I shifted restlessly, the battlelion medallion scraping against my breastplate with the motion. In just a few minutes it would be Alik's responsibility, and I might have something worse.

"Tonight, I call…"

My heart stalled with his pause, and for a moment it seemed like he might change his mind, call Makar, or someone else, from the glint in his eyes, but then he raised his arms higher.

"Davor, the second son of Chief Kirill, to take his place as guardian of this tribe."

It took another thunderous heartbeat for my feet to remember how to work. A deafening hush had fallen over the gathering. Even those who supported me were silent. Perhaps it was one thing to follow a man in battle, and yet another to follow him into peace. If that's what they believed I would bring.

Or perhaps with the mention of the chief's name, the stain of him had fallen over me and all of us as well, and they believed I would follow the same bitter paths as him.

Men and women fell back as I made my way forward and joined the *talånd* now standing impassively upon the platform.

"Davor, do you swear to lead this tribe in honor and faithfulness before the All-Father and men?"

My mouth dried as I looked to him. Behind him the sablecat was emerging in the night sky, the constellation on the rise with spring. Perhaps the spirits might look kinder on me than man did.

"I do." No going back now.

"And do you swear to give your life, your blood, to the defense of this tribe when its enemies come?"

The question seemed pointed, but it was no mystery that enemies abounded.

"I do."

There was no chieftain's staff anymore, burned up in the lodge, and I'd refused another to be made. He took up a bowl of red paint.

"Kneel."

For a moment, my knees seized at the command. Then, slowly, my right bent and took me to the wood before him.

He dipped his fingers in the paint and drew the lines of chief on my face. My eyes shuttered closed as it smeared chill against my skin.

A broad stroke across my forehead, bisected by a short line in the center. Three vertical lines on my right cheek, a swooping band under my left cheekbone and shorter line underneath it.

The *talånd* set the bowl aside, raised his hands, and sang strength and blessings upon me and my new rule. He draped a cloak trimmed in sablecat fur across my shoulders, and stepped back, beckoning me to turn. For a moment more I hesitated, a prickle warning down my spine.

I was chief now and all a contender had to do was draw a blade and try to take it. The *talånd* lifted his hand again, and this time I obeyed.

Turning, I faced the tribe. The sun's light lingered as a band of orange on the horizon line. Stars came out to look down on the spectacle, ghosts of warriors past watching and speculating from the All-Father's halls if indeed they cared.

The living stared back, firelight glinting off their upturned faces and the eyes of sablecats sitting or lounging about. My mother's gaze held pride, the same as Inge and Janne. Michal seemed grimly pleased, and Marta? I could not tell from the way she looked at me and the wedding bands spinning faster around her wrist.

At my look, her hands fell to her sides, and a faint bob at her throat betrayed her before she moved forward. Her cold fingers wrapped around mine as she joined me on the platform and for the first time a noise ran through the crowd.

My heart quailed before the many eyes turned on me. The hate, the discontent, the disgust. *Why should the coward be named chief?* my mind mocked. *Change*, my heart reassured through its thudding. But I was not used to being so visible, and the weight of my new role suddenly crushed down around me.

Marta's hand squeezed tight around mine, an unexpected re-assurance breaking through the panic. I looked to her, wondering if she'd felt the tremble. Her chin stayed high, posture confident as she looked back. Dark eyes locked onto me, reminding me of my promises and the keeping of them.

The *talånd* stepped up to my side again. "We lost a battlelion as well in the last countings, a grievous price for this tribe to pay."

I hoped my face did not show the disdain rising in me. Was there anyone who would truly mourn Kamil?

"Davor, will you name a new battlelion as you now hold the place of chief?"

I released Marta's hand and pulled the medallion off from around my neck. It seemed there was a whisper of relief through the tribe as I did.

"Alik." My voice obeyed my will and stayed steady.

The pack leader joined us on the platform, though now his confidence seemed to have vanished as he knelt and accepted the medallion over his head. It settled against his breastplate with a light thud.

He rose to his feet and I dipped my fingers in the paint the *talånd* proffered. My hand stalled again as I prepared to paint the lines of the battlelion on his face. I wondered if I might change them so that I did not have to see the hated pattern on Alik's face.

In the end, I traced the four diagonal lines across both of his cheeks, then on impulse added a small line down the center of his chin.

The *talånd* glowered a little, but there was an understanding glint in Alik's eye as he unsheathed his sword and held it, point down, between us. My hand rested on the pommel as he swore allegiance to me and the tribe. He re-sheathed the sword and took the new spear I gave him. The *talånd* sang strength and honor over him, and then it was done.

Warriors began to shift and come forward, to swear allegiance to us as chief and battlelion. But there were too many who did not, Makar smirking at me as he stayed back. He touched the sling around his arm, and tilted chin up in defiance.

When he was healed, he was coming for me.

Emil shifted at his side, and across the distance between us, his eyes extracted a wordless promise from me. The one he'd demanded the night of the fire.

Be better.

I did not know what games he was playing, but he'd sworn to help me keep the position. And spirits help me, in that moment I believed him.

The moon had risen by the time the oathtaking was finished. Perhaps in a different age, there might have been a celebration feast. Instead, the tribespeople dispersed back to the villages, sablecats padding along with them. Some stayed behind to extinguish the torches and tend the fires until they were embers.

Alik promised to meet me the next day and he left for his lodge with a company of warriors. Four more trailed us as we made our way back to Inge's lodge. Michal and I went first, making sure there was nothing to fear inside the lodge. The women joined us, and the door was shut on the night.

There seemed no words to say as I washed the paint from my face. No one said anything as Marta sat on her bench and I retreated to the small room.

Once inside, my hands braced against the wall, breath jerking in a few gasps and stomach wrenching like it might reject the bits of dinner I had choked down hours before. It stayed down and I stumbled forward to sink onto the bed, leaning forward with hands clenching in my hair.

I had done it. Survived my father and Kamil. Taken the place of chief. But my own mocking doubt might be worse than that of the tribe. If there was one thing I was good at, it was surviving. Only now, I could not do it *and* stay invisible. I had to go against years of habit, find a way to lead, and to protect those I might dare to call family. Protect Marta, even though I wondered why the strength of her hand around mine still lingered long after our hands had fallen apart.

TWENTY-SEVEN

DAVOR

Morning came too soon. I had lain awake most of the night, planning what to do for the first day as chief. In recent years, the old chief had barely left the lodge, deferring most of the rulings to the village heads, and only dealing with the bigger decisions. Or leaving it to Kamil.

I walked the villages often enough that I knew what some might need, but it might be a different song with me walking in as chief and not as I had in the past with deals on my tongue.

I dressed slowly, deliberately. The *talånd* had wanted to form another necklace, but I had refused. There was nothing but hate in me for the chieftain's mark and I did not want its smothering weight for the rest of my life. As yet there was nothing for me to wear that would mark me as chief, other than the cloak and my blood and the fact that everyone had seen the naming last night.

The others were awake and preparing the table for breakfast

when I stepped out. There was barely a pause other than from Marta where she moved with slower movements, Janne at her side showing where things were to be found within the lodge.

My mother greeted me and gave a pointed look over at Marta. But we had nothing for each other besides a slight nod. Mother's lips flattened but she said nothing. Though something must have passed between her and Nina, for when we prepared to sit at the table, the space left for us was beside each other. Janne and Michal sat across from us, and from the look Janne flashed us, they were in on the plot as well.

"What is your plan today?" Michal leaned forward, elbows on the table until his mother tapped his arm and he withdrew, but the question was still there.

The others looked expectantly at me and for a moment I almost wilted away under it.

"I need to speak with the village *sjandsens* first." To see where their alliance truly lay and hopefully before Makar had gotten his hooks into them as well. "You'll come with me."

Michal did not look pleased at this, despite his agreement to be heir.

"There will be some warriors around." I looked to the others. "Makar will make a challenge at some point, and I want all of you protected."

Silence fell over the table at this somber pronouncement and Marta shifted at my side.

"What of my family?" she asked.

I winced internally. They had not been high on my mind when planning for guards.

"Alik and your father will make sure they stay safe." I turned to give her this news and there was some thanks in her eyes.

"And what should I do today?" She did not waver.

"What would you normally do on a day like this?" I asked.

She rubbed her hands against her skirt. "I have embroidery promised to some in the lower village that I was to deliver at the end of the counting."

Today.

"I will go to the lower village first then with you."

I did not want to tell her to listen and ask what the opinions of others might be when we were there. If she even wanted me to go with her. But she nodded her acceptance and turned back to her food.

Mother appeared pleased and I did not look longer at the sight than was necessary.

The meal finished and I waited for Marta to gather her things into a bag that she slung across her chest. Michal dragged his feet before pulling his bow and quiver on. Like me, he did not wear armor, except for bracers buckled over sleeves. I did not like going without armor, but I did not think it would be a reassuring sight for the new chief walking about fully armed and encased in leather.

I stepped out first and the warriors standing guard around the lodge ghosted forward from their spots and saluted with fist to chest. If they followed the rotation Alik had set, they would be fresh as of an hour ago and ready to join us or any of the lodge where they might choose to go.

Luk rose from his spot by the doorway. It seemed he, too, understood that danger might come and so had refused to go any place other than the door. He pressed up against my side with a purr, then turned solemn gold eyes to Marta.

"He's yours?" she asked, keeping hands tucked against her waist. There was no nervousness, just caution for a lion she did not know.

"Luk."

The sablecat glanced at me with the sound of his name. I snapped fingers twice and he sank down to haunches, still watching her. At my nod, she extended a hand and Luk reached his head forward to sniff.

"Have you had him long?" she asked.

"I picked him from a new litter five years ago." I felt closer to Luk than to the sablecat before who had split his paw too badly on a border patrol along the Pronghorn border for me to keep him.

"Father's is older. And the other lions at the lodge don't seem to like many who aren't related to their warrior."

"That's often the way," I said.

But Luk pushed forward, scraping his head against her hand. A smile bloomed across her face as her hand brushed across his sleek head. A throaty purr broke from him. Once I might have thought him a traitor for giving affection to someone else, but part of me was pleased instead that he liked her.

"And you, Michal?" Her smile turned to him.

Michal came more alert under her focus and whistled. His sablecat came tearing around the corner, barely slowing before slamming into him and knocking him back a pace.

Marta chuckled and accepted a proud introduction to Michal's sablecat. His first and with him for the last two years.

The lions fell in behind us with one of the warriors keeping pace off to Marta's left side as we took the narrow path carved from the upper lodges through the large field to the distant lower village.

Quiet lingered between us except for the soft crunch of boots and occasional snaps of sablecats at bugs jumping from the low grass. The training grounds settled alongside the river and there were already packs of warriors out. I spotted Alik walking with another warrior.

He looked up at the same moment and jogged over to us.

"Battlelion," Marta greeted him with a bit of a tease. He flashed a smile and tapped a fist to his chest when he looked to me.

"Going somewhere without me, *Chief?*"

"I did not think you wanted to hear me talk with the *sjandsens*."

He tilted his head. "Sounds like a more miserable day than the one I have ahead of me."

I shifted a little. "Anything yet?"

He looked back over his shoulder. "Some pushing already. Makar sent a pack out to train today and they are making no bones about their disagreement with you and me." A faint smile appeared at the way my concern must have shown. "I can handle it. Meet tonight?"

I nodded agreement. We had already planned a system to find each other by the end of the day, exchange reports, and make new plans. Time to see if we'd survive until then.

He left and we continued onward, Michal now up on my right side.

"When do I go for training?" he asked.

"Alik and you can decide tonight. I don't want you out there unless he is as well."

"I don't need protecting," Michal protested stubbornly.

I arched an eyebrow, but he was not quelled. "Until everything is settled, this will be the way."

"Do you think Makar will wait long to challenge?" Marta asked quietly from my other side. Michal studied me just as intently.

"I do not know." And I did not like that it was my answer. I did not like not knowing.

Her bottom lip caught in her teeth for a moment. "Where do you want me to find you when I'm done?" she asked.

"The *sjandsen's* lodge if I do not find you first."

We entered the first row of houses in the lower village. It smelled different there, fresher and more earthy. Less of leather and iron, and more of sweet grass and husks of colored corn. There were not many sablecats around, and very few perches for them among the lodges. They were more used to plow harnesses than to saddle and leathers.

Some children paused in their play to stare with eager eyes at Luk and the other lion. But just as fast it faded to suspicion when they saw me and Michal. They pulled off the path and to the lodges.

Men and women moved about, their clothes a plainer design with wider pockets on overtunics and broad belts to hold scythes and planting sticks instead of swords and quivers. The same expression fell over their faces when they recognized me. It was not an unfamiliar sight to me, but Marta slowed a half-pace when it also turned to her.

Finally she stopped, and excused herself quietly. I paused, telling myself I wanted to keep an eye on her as much as possible before leaving her in the charge of the warrior. But something else tugged at me, making me wait as she approached a woman grinding corn in a river-rock mortar and pestle.

The woman paused, a smile starting then fading as she looked past Marta to me. I did not hear what passed, but Marta's shoulders stiffened as conversation seemed stilted. She handed over a small bundle of cloth with glimpses of bright thread stitched through. The woman disappeared inside and then returned with a bag that she thrust at Marta before attacking the corn in the basin with a vengeance.

A bit of anger and frustration lined Marta's features when she returned to my side.

"Everything all right?" I asked, even though I knew what had happened. My shadow was already staining her.

"You did warn me," she said wryly.

My fingers curled, bracing for the hate that must surely follow.

"But I will be all right."

My fist slackened in surprise, and she offered me a small smile.

"I might be done sooner than normal, so I will meet you at the *sjandsen's* lodge?"

I nodded dumbly, trying to make sense of her civility.

"Are you sure?" I finally mustered words.

She made a shooing motion and turned to Tinek, already asking his name as she marched off into the village.

"I like her," Michal announced.

I cocked an eyebrow, and he shrugged in answer.

"She doesn't seem afraid of things."

Of you.

"No," I agreed slowly. "No, she does not."

TWENTY-EIGHT

MARTA

It stung much more than I thought it would. He had warned
me, and I'd shrugged it off, thinking the opinion of people
would not be so easily swayed by the sight of marriage cords
or the man beside me.

But I'd been wrong, and he'd been right.

Men and women who had greeted me easily for years now
turned a shoulder or completely away from me as I passed. The
warrior said nothing at my side, but his look carried almost the
same weight as Davor's had.

A few offered a fist to forehead with a respectful, "*Dronni.*"
Others said it with more of a curse and the implication that they
meant something far, far worse.

At my second stop to deliver embroidered cuffs and collar
for a wedding dress, the future bride's mother stepped in front
of her. Before they'd been eager to bargain for my skills, keeping

drinks and food on hand as we talked for hours on design.

"We do not want them anymore," she said.

Her daughter opened her mouth to protest but the elder waved her hand.

"You think those bands make you something more? We all know what you are to him."

"And what is that?" I snapped.

Her brows raised suggestively and despite myself, red rushed to my cheeks. I had no answer.

Tinek stepped up to my side, but I stilled the warrior with an outstretched hand. A simple gesture had never held such power before, and I blinked at it.

"The chieftain has no bearing on our arrangement," I said. "Nor on your daughter's day."

Her lip curled. "Maybe he might make it so if his eye wanders this way. Bands will not save any of our daughters. It never stopped anyone else of his blood." Her fingers twisted a curse.

Heat rushed through me, maybe more so that I'd had the same thought many times since Alik had broached the subject with me.

"You have nothing to fear," I finally said.

"Mother," the daughter said in a low voice.

"Take them." I held them out. "And our bargain will be complete."

The woman's brow arched again, but she did not turn down the chance to be free an exchange. The collar and cuffs were swept from my hand as if she was afraid to touch me and pushed back inside.

The daughter hesitated. "Am I to offer congratulations on your marriage?" she asked in a low tone, cautious of the warrior who had fallen back a step.

I offered a small smile. "He is an honorable man from what I have seen. Not like his father or brothers."

The young woman relaxed a fraction. "You are safe with him?"

I tipped my head. "And the tribe will be as well. He wants only peace and security for all of us."

Her arms crossed over her chest. "I do not know if I can believe that."

"I did not think so either," I admitted. "But I am starting to."

She nodded. "You were—are—respected for your skill, Marta. Many felt shocked and betrayed at seeing you beside him last night."

My fingers curled around the strap of my bag. I did not know what to do with this news other than reflect, again, that he had warned me.

I forced my chin up to look her steadily in the eyes. "I intend to see protection given to those who need it, care given to those who lack it. I did not enter into the marriage or this position lightly. But we are both agreed, the chief and I. We want to set this tribe on a different path than the last chieftains have led us down."

Tentative belief flickered in her eyes, but she said nothing else.

"Congratulations on your marriage." I stepped back and fled from the lodge.

"You should not have surrendered so easily," Tinek said.

I glanced to him. He walked at my side, watchful eyes roving around us.

"What do you mean?"

"With the woman. You let her out of your bargain. Spirits know we have not had a *dronni* in a long time." He said the word respectfully and a bit of my confidence came back. "She issued you a challenge. A warrior should not back down."

"I am not a warrior." The thought made Davor's knife on my hip weigh heavy again.

A faint smile tugged Tinek's mouth, smoothing out some of the wrinkles around his eyes. "You are of a different sort than with bow or sword. You say you want the same things the chief wants. He now fights a different battle, and you have pitched in to his side."

I mulled this over. It was a war I did not know how to fight. Though it seemed I needed to learn.

"And what do you think of the chief?" I asked.

"I dismissed him readily enough before the war," he admitted. "Many did. But he proved himself on the battlefields, and showed he had none of his brothers' cruelty."

"How?" I had not heard details from Father or Alik other than they respected him. But Tinek seemed more willing to talk.

"Kamil would often leave wounded behind on the fields, even ordering it. Davor would not let that happen. He always brought them if we could, and he helped with it too. Took a beating from Kamil for it, but kept giving the order."

Despite myself, a small sound escaped as my heart twisted. A beating?

A faintly chagrined look crossed Tinek's face as if he'd broken a promise not to speak of such things. His next words came rushed as if to draw my attention from what he'd shared.

"The chief is not harsh with mistakes. He is shrewd on the field and off. Brought our packs through battles many a time. Did not push for a victory in the face of sure defeat. None of us hesitated to swear to him."

"And what of Michal?"

I'd never seen the youngest much, but there were rumors and whisperings that he might follow the path of his father and brothers. Though that might not be true as Davor was proving to be much different than I thought.

"Good archer, scrappy in a fight." Tinek nodded. Qualities a warrior might notice first. "Chief took him under his wing when he came to the packs. Lost him for a counting to Kamil before bringing him back. Seems he is content to follow the chief for now."

I rubbed my thumb along the bag's strap. From what I had seen, Michal readily looked to Davor. He'd been named heir even. But there was something swirling about the two of them that I could not yet pin down, though it had abated in that moment with their sablecats. It still made me nervous to be around both of them together.

We stopped at the last lodge, one on the inner square of lodges. The man who greeted me did not falter. He waved us inside, looking slightly askance at Tinek who offered nothing back.

Inside was a mess of children of all ages running around, some straightening up the lodge from breakfast, others splashing each other as they washed dishes. Older girls tried to sort the chaos as Feliks smiled ruefully.

"Marta!" One call sent the lodge into stillness, then bursts of greetings. Smaller children ran over to fling arms around my waist before turning back to their chores. The older girls waved, and the boys looked more interestedly at Tinek and his weapons and armor.

Feliks whistled and some calm descended on the lodge. "We have a *dronni* here today. How do we greet her now?"

Hands went to foreheads, and I smiled. None of them seemed to realize what some outside did or thought with the title. But this lodge of orphans or unwanted children followed the lead of the man who was trying to raise them all with his wife, brother, and sister-in-law.

The adults came through from back rooms, one of the women with an infant on her hip.

They made the sign again until I wanted to wave my hands for everyone to stop. For a moment, I wondered if this was how Davor had felt last night on the platform. I thought I'd imagined the tremor in his hand as we stood there, but perhaps not.

I pulled the last thing from my bag. A blanket for the baby coming any day from the look of the sister-in-law. The girls pressed close around to exclaim over the stitching until a different sort of heat flushed my cheeks. I'd prayed for strength and health for the baby as I'd stitched. Sometimes I thought the spirits maybe blessed my needle the more for it.

"When are you coming for another lesson?" one of the girls asked.

"She might not have time with her new duties," Feliks's wife cautioned.

I smiled. "I should be able to come as usual."

The third day of every counting, I came to the lodge for an afternoon, showing the girls stitches and trying to instill in some the patience for it. They would need everything they could to draw a husband with no father to help make a match.

Feliks and Ione beckoned me apart. "He would let you?" he asked, concern as bright as his wife's.

"He would. Perhaps he could even do something for the lodge as well."

Disbelief twisted Feliks's lips, but I pushed on.

"I will speak with him."

The last war had created the lodge. The one just finished had brought new faces. It was the only one of its kind in all three villages, orphans practically exiled to the lower village if they did not have a relative willing to look after them instead.

I took my leave before I could make more promises I did not know if I believed. Out of sight of Davor and after seeing the change in the villagers' opinions towards me with one act, doubt wormed its way in despite efforts to smother it.

We traced our way to the *sjandsen's* lodge. Usually I would stop at some other lodges for more trades or work, or have others seek me out. Not today.

The door to the lodge was open, Davor and Michal's sablecats lounging outside. I did not have the courage to step inside, so I took a seat on the bench against the wall. Tinek stationed himself nearby. After a moment, Luk heaved himself up and came to settle at my feet, head up and alert as he sat there.

It brought a slight smile to my face, like the sablecat was also standing guard for me.

Murmurs of voices came from the lodge, and I leaned back against the sun-warmed wood to listen if I could. The lower rumble of Davor's voice sounded and the clearer reply of the *sjandsen*. There was not much to hear, so I took the needle from my overskirt and one of the plain remembrance cloths I always had in my bag, and started to stitch.

"Excuse me, *Dronni.*" A soft voice drew my head up. A young woman stood there, tentative smile in place. A loose braid fell over her shoulder, tied off by a strip of red cloth. A bit of thread marked a barely visible rune, and from the worn edges, I assumed it was from someone well-loved.

"You are waiting for the chief?" she asked.

At my nod, she extended a cup. "While you wait."

Her sleeves were rolled up, and her overdress was soaked in patches from the washtub at a nearby lodge.

"Thank you." I took the water.

"Is…is everything all right?" I did not miss the glance she gave to Tinek.

I managed a smile of reassurance. "Yes." I paused, the hurt at the reactions flaring again. "Not everyone shares your kindness at my new name this morning."

She didn't turn away from the slight bite in my voice. Just gave a sympathetic tilt of her head, and her fingers brushed the cloth in her hair. "If you need anything else while you wait, I'm just there." She pointed to the pile of clothes waiting to be scrubbed. "Our lodge will be open to you."

I thanked her again, a bit of confidence coming back. She returned to her washing, and I turned back to stitching.

I worked until a shadow fell over me. A glance showed Davor, eyes and expression largely guarded. Michal cast an angry look back through the door, but nothing else was said.

"Are you ready to leave?" Davor asked.

I tied off the thread and slid the needle back through its usual fold in my skirt. As I stood, I caught the look Davor gave Tinek. Questioning.

The warrior inclined his head. I wished I spoke this silent language to know what was said. Davor focused on me as I stood, adjusting the strap over my shoulder.

"How was it?" he asked.

I fidgeted a moment longer, not sure if I wanted to admit to how shaken I'd felt earlier or if I wanted to pretend that it did not bother me.

"How was the meeting?" I countered.

A faint shift crossed his face, but still nothing to give away. "Fine."

I did not think it was.

But we began to walk and left the lower village behind. He did not say anything as I stayed at his side as his steps turned to the lower bridge. No order to go back to the upper village and the lodge. The sablecats crouched low over the swaying bridge, padding their way on cautious paws, tails flicking as they crossed.

It wasn't until we reached the boundaries of the middle village that he looked and seemed taken aback to find me still there.

"I thought I might stop to see my family?" Two days outside the familiar lodge had seemed like a year with all that had happened in between.

"Yes." He nodded to Tinek, and he and Michal broke away, leaving me gripping the strap of my bag in anxious hands. As we walked further into the village, winding the way to my old lodge, my fingers clutched harder. There seemed something different in the air, some laden promise, and I found myself worrying for him and Michal.

TWENTY-NINE

DAVOR

The first indication that something was wrong was the sight of Emil walking towards us. He didn't pause, but his eyes met mine for a telling second. My hand wrapped around my sword hilt, and I kept moving.

Moments later, one of Alik's pack fell in with us.

"Chief, Makar is here," Artem said, voice low.

"Where?"

"At the *sjandsen's* lodge."

"Doing what?"

Artem shrugged. "We don't know, but he brought a few men with him."

"How many do we have here?" I searched out the narrow spaces between lodges and those moving about the pathways.

"Two packs. We have a warrior going to warn Alik."

"Don't pull him from the training grounds," I ordered. A chief might need a battlelion to back him in a fight, but I did not want to trap the both of us together so soon.

Artem lifted his chin and two other warriors came forward. I gave the order for one to follow up the message to Alik. The other I ordered to take Michal away.

Michal protested, but I shook my head. "If he's striking, I don't need him taking you out as well."

He glared, but thankfully did not argue.

"Go find Marta and make sure she made it to the lodge. I'll meet you there once this is finished."

"Be careful." The urgent care took me aback for a moment. I was not used to seeing it in any brother's face.

"You too."

His sablecat loped after him, and Luk prowled up beside me, hackles raised and growl lurking in his throat.

Artem walked with me as I kept making my way down the wider path to the official's lodge. Nothing and no one stopped us, and I entered before I could second-guess myself further.

Makar sat at the table with the *sjandsen*, sharing a friendly-looking cup of ale.

"Ah, Chief." Makar raised his mug, the smile in place. If he was surprised to see me there, he did not show it.

"Makar." I eased forward, but no warriors lurked in the common room. Artem backed off to the doorway, hand still on his sword.

The *sjandsen* looked between the both of us, nervousness edging around him. I did not blame him. Perhaps he did not fully know what he had come between.

"You seem surprised to see me here," Makar said.

"Perhaps I am."

"Come now, Davor. You should know I hail from this village. Is it so bad a thing to come to visit?"

"When I've never heard a good word from you regarding this village? Yes." I took the head seat at the table, forcing them both to turn slightly to look at me. If I was to be chief, I had to act like one.

A thin smile crossed his face, but I turned my attention to the *sjandsen*, staring for an uncomfortably long moment before he scrambled to his feet and got a mug of spruce ale for me.

"Chieftain." The fist to forehead came hurriedly. "What can I do for you?"

"I know a chief has not been here in years. I want to know the true state of the village."

"Do you not think he has cared for the village?" Makar broke in as the *sjandsen* opened his mouth. So it was to be words first, gaining more support while he healed, undermining my already tenuous position, weakening if he could before he reached for a sword.

No one would mourn a chief who was not strong enough to lead.

"I know he has. I've walked these paths often enough."

The two of them paused, forced to acknowledge that they might not know how much I did.

"But I know there are things that need to be brought before a chief."

The *sjandsen* swallowed and anxious fingers tugged at his cup. "Nothing that I cannot address, Chief. Nothing to bother you with."

But his gaze darted to Makar.

"I would advise you to rethink that." A bit of a growl crept through my voice.

Makar did not look worried in the least, meeting my gaze with a challenge. The *sjandsen* sat back, trying to withdraw from the silent fight.

"I do want your best craftsmen." I turned back suddenly to him and he flinched.

"Why, Chief?"

"I plan to rebuild the chieftain's lodge. And bring the villages together to build something new."

The *sjandsen* sat a little taller. He at least seemed more receptive to this thought than the official in the lower village, convinced I was just going to steal away his men and women.

"A worthy endeavor," Makar praised, sending a crawling feeling down my spine. "Perhaps the *talånd* would want to bless the site and make sure nothing evil lingered from the fire."

His glance was sharper than a Greywolf spear, shouting that he did not believe Emil's story. And I wondered again what Emil was doing for him.

"A good thought. Perhaps I will see what else the *talånd* knows."

Makar did not seem worried by that either. Whatever vendetta the *talånd* had raised against me was not done it seemed. And I had not even met with him to see what other duties a chief might have in deference to the spirits. The old chief certainly had never done anything, but surely there were traditions to be upheld somewhere.

"I must congratulate you on your wedding, Chief. You honor us by choosing a *dronni* from the village." The *sjandsen* broke between our silent struggle again.

"Yes, how fortunate you were to find someone to wed. How does she feel about being your wife?" Makar's question held a knowing sneer.

The official paled and withdrew from me.

"I have no doubt she will bring strength and honor to her role," I said after a moment.

"So you intend to keep her there?"

The carved hilt of my knife was leaving an imprint on my palm. "I do. Perhaps I should worry, Makar, that you are taking such an interest in my wife. How might yours feel about that?"

He smirked. "Perhaps she worries for other young women who might attract your attention once you tire of Marta."

Her name from his lips sounded wrong and left a ghost of a chill around me. But perhaps it was the aftershock of anger at his well-directed words. Feeding into the *sjandsen's* fear, bolstering the rumors that I might be a chief like my father.

"I am not my father, Makar. I have nothing but contempt for how he used the women of this tribe. And I will see that it does not continue."

"Bold words from a man who forced a woman into marrying him."

"An offer she accepted of her own will."

The *sjandsen* still sat back, gaze darting between the two of us, his internal debate splayed across his face as plain as day.

"Did she?" Makar's question held more than threat. But he shoved back from the table and I followed the motion, hand still on knife. Makar offered the sneering smile again.

"I look forward to seeing what you will try to do as chief. But there is no place for weakness or cowards in this tribe."

He left behind the almost challenge to snag at me. Artem looked to me in question.

"Follow him for now."

Artem saluted and the door creaked behind him. The *sjandsen* shrank back as my attention turned back to him.

"Now that we have some privacy, let us discuss the village again, shall we?"

He nodded frantically, and we set to business.

⌒

What seemed like hours later, I left the lodge and turned my steps to find Marta and Michal. I did not get farther than three steps from the *sjandsen's* lodge before Alik blocked my path, arms crossed and frowning.

"You were just going to walk right into potential trouble?" he asked.

I sighed and kept walking. "I have some battles to fight on my own."

His scowl did not let up. "That doesn't make anything better."

"What do you want me to do?" The frustration budding at the top of my chest escaped before I could rein it in. "I cannot go running to you any time there might be trouble."

He sighed. "I know. But that does not stop me worrying for what might be happening when I'm not there to guard your back."

A few children darted across our path and I did not stop to see what their stares or the looks of their parents might be as we passed.

"You're not alone, Davor," he reminded me, but I was tired of hearing it. I was ready to not be seen again.

I said nothing more until we reached the lodge. Michal bolted up from the benches outside.

"You're all right!"

I nodded, relieved to see that he was unharmed and had done nothing worse than kicking up his heels for an hour. The door flung open, setting me back on guard, but it was only Marta.

"You're back." She settled back on her feet instead of finishing her charge out the door.

"I am fine." It came with a bit of a snap. She did not flinch away, but a faintly guarded look fell over her.

Alik cleared his throat, but I was already mustering something different to say.

"How is your family?" Like it had been years since she'd seen them and not just two days.

But it brought the brightness back to her face and eased a little of the restlessness in me.

"Are you going to keep the chief outside the lodge?" Dariy's voice interrupted.

Marta flushed and stepped aside, ushering us in.

"Chieftain." Dariy tapped his fist to chest. His wife and other daughter were slower to give the more formal greeting of fist to forehead, but their looks lacked the sharpness of before. Perhaps Marta had reassured them on some counts of the way our marriage was to be.

"Settling in?" he asked.

"That remains to be seen," I said wryly. "I've just come from the *sjandsen's* lodge, but I'd rather know how things really are here and what might you say to a chief who would try to do something."

Dariy nodded. "You have time for an ale or two?"

Alik chuckled. "Should I get some of the others if you're serious about doing this now?"

I paused. It might offend the *sjandsen* if I went immediately behind his back. But he'd been hiding things. Things I knew that happened right under his nose or under his orders after walking less-used paths in this village for years.

"I think there is time."

"You might regret that in a few hours when they don't stop talking." Alik tapped my shoulder.

"If they would even talk to me."

Dariy backed away. "I think they would. The warriors have been spreading your name about. Some of us have something like hope."

A soft movement at my side brought my attention to Marta. She stood with arms tucked over her stomach and her look was thoughtful, assessing as she looked at me. Not even my returning scrutiny made her withdraw.

Alik headed out the door and Dariy ushered me to sit at one of the long tables set in the middle of the common room. Some of the women looked askance at me, and nudged the few children away.

"Do…do you need anything?" Marta hovered for a moment as I took a seat. Her fingers twined about each other.

"No. Thank you."

I almost asked if she wanted to sit with us, but she backed away and disappeared with her mother and sister around the corner to the cook fires.

"Chief." A cough grumbled in Dariy's throat. "Marta said you've been…kind over the last few days. I wanted to thank you."

Kind was perhaps generous.

"I will make sure no harm comes to her. From anyone."

He nodded, rubbing a hand over his chin. "I know you will."

We lapsed back to silence, Michal fidgeting on my left side until others began to slowly filter in. Some were hunters who had been called out to join the scouts. Others wore simpler tunics or wore runes of leatherworkers or smiths. Ten in all, and those who had not fought in the war glowered at me from under heavy brows and took seats farthest away.

Even with the hunters filling in the other spots, there was a gap between me and Michal and where Dariy still sat with us. Alik filled up part of it, but no one else made a move to do the same.

My skin crawled under the stares of so many and it took a moment to bring my voice out.

"I have met with the *sjandsen*. He has told me some of what troubles this village. I would hear more."

No change in the looks turned on me.

"He is here in honesty," Alik reassured. "Have no fear of retribution."

I should have thought to lead with that. But a shift ran through the men. Before anyone could speak, Marta was at my side, placing a mug of ale in front of me. A light touch on my shoulder as she did, and then she pulled back. Her mother and sister handed out drinks to the others.

She had planned well, and the small motion did not go unnoticed. The men relaxed a little more with it and the promise of ale.

Little by little they spun a story of hunters going home empty-handed if they did not bring back enough meat from a hunt to satisfy the *sjandsen* and those in the upper village who did not deign to hunt for their lodges or turn their sablecats loose to hunt for themselves. Of leather workers forced to create armor instead of things for families or something other than war. Iron confiscated for weapons instead of for use for farmers or cooking implements.

A village used to making do with what they were left with, much like the lower village. I knew how wealthy the upper village was in many ways with warriors used to having the villages and the chief bow to their needs in a tribe fashioned over generations for nothing but war.

I sat mostly in silence, listening, especially as the ale loosened tongues further and more was aired. I did not have time to settle petty differences between some lodges or families, but the bigger things, I did need to know, and the back of my mind was already turning solutions.

When the rest of the lodge began to come back in, surprised to see such a meeting at the table, the talk began to halt. Alik caught my look and began to dismiss the men.

Dariy was last to rise as it was his lodge. His hands twisted his empty mug around.

"I do not think you realize what you have done in listening to them today."

"What do you mean?" I asked.

"My grandfather was the last to talk of a chief coming into the villages regularly to hear his people. Even if you promised nothing today, you have made a change already."

Faint humor twitched my mouth. He might be the only one who noticed what I did and did not say.

"I still make no promises, but I will be back next counting if not sooner to at least change the way the hunts are divided. There are plenty of bowmen in the upper village who can go hunt, and sablecats who can provide for themselves."

A sort of pleased frown took over Dariy's weathered face. "That will be a fight, but one a long time coming. But if there are any willing to come off their high mountain, I will help train them."

"Better man than me," one of the other hunters from the lodge scoffed as he gathered up some of the mugs to hand to his waiting wife.

Dariy tilted his head, but did not withdraw the words.

"Will you stay for dinner, Chief?" Dariy's wife asked, her voice coming a little breathless in nervousness.

Marta sat on a bench against the wall, watching me. I wondered if she had been there the whole time. She made no argument for staying or leaving. Michel still moved restlessly beside me, so I shook my head.

"Perhaps another time."

Her mother offered a faint smile, but like the others she didn't seem as violently opposed to me anymore. Perhaps there might be some hope after all.

Michal darted to his feet and was at the lodge door before I'd barely stood and handed her my mug with another murmured thanks. Marta kissed her mother on the cheek and accepted a hug from her father before joining me.

The warrior now on duty moved with us as we headed for the bridge between the upper and middle villages. At my nod, Michal and the warrior moved ahead. I intended for Marta to go with them, but she paused with me in the middle of the bridge.

Sunlight slanted in golden rays as it tracked its way to the west. The river tossed and clattered its way under the bridge, glittering spray coating the edges of the boards. New cloths bound about the slender railing struts fluttered in the light breeze. Mourning cloths or prayer cloths in thanksgiving for warriors come back. Some carried bloodstains from men who had placed them there after returning alive, or in remembrance of the fallen warrior who had once worn it.

"May I ask you a question?" Marta asked.

I looked from the rippling cloths to her. Her long hair caught in the same timid wind, and the sunlight tinged the depths of her eyes a deeper brown.

"We met on this bridge twice. It means something to you."

There was not much of a question there. I turned back to the river rushing its way past the villages and onwards to whatever faraway lands it traversed after it left our territory.

"It's a place of quiet," I said. "A place to remember what I want."

She stepped up beside me, hands settling on the railing. "This is what you want?"

"Some of it."

I did not have the heart to remind her that our marriage was something I still did not want. A glimpse of color drew my eyes down to a cloth. There was a familiarity to the pattern, the bright colors. My thumb and forefinger caught it.

"This is one of yours." I shifted so she could see.

"Yes." She offered a smile. "I made many of them this war and the last. Janne has two of mine."

The ones with my name and Michal's name on them. I wondered how she had felt stitching my name onto it. If it had come with a prayer or a curse.

Marta leaned her hip on the rail to look more directly at me. "You really meant it when you said you wanted something different? Change within this tribe?"

"Yes." Even though the work raising itself before me before even nearing that dream was enough to make me shy away from chasing it.

"Then perhaps I will be glad that fate threw us together so you can do this."

"Even after today?" My brow raised.

Her lips tilted into a half-smile and her look turned over the river. "It was not so bad. And the men began to change their mind readily enough. Perhaps it will not be like this for long."

I wanted to believe in her hope, but she did not know me well enough yet. She would likely not be in disfavor long. I was another story.

She moved away, her steps turning to the far side of the bridge, and I again did not have the heart to shatter what hope she had just dared to grab. Some of it might have even transferred to me as we made our way through the upper village and back to Inge's lodge where dinner waited.

I let the hope linger for a few dangerous hours before setting it away. There was not much room for it in my heart and it was a fool's errand to keep it where anyone might smash or steal it.

Finally, my door shut behind me and I had some blessed silence and an absence of eyes watching or weighing every little thing. Under the light of a candle, I scribbled things I had learned or heard that day on a piece of birchbark until charcoal stained my fingers.

One day down and so many new pieces to move and shuffle. And sitting on the opposite edge of the table, Makar, yet to play his full hand.

THIRTY

DAVOR

There was no *sjandsen* in the upper village. That duty fell to the chief. And so my second day as chief was filled with discussions and visits to lodges, maneuvering around pointed questions. Years of practice helped other comments roll off my shoulders with only a fraction of the sting intended. Michal stirred at my side every time I did not respond.

But he did not know that I always remembered.

Alik had different battles to face in the upper village. I was a son of the old chief, but he was a battlelion from the middle village and in some people's eyes, there might not be much difference. At the sight of the anger and frustration in his eyes, I wished I had something to offer, but I did not think he would want to follow my way of dealing with it.

By the time I turned home, tension knotted through my shoulders. I paused at the door, not yet wanting to go inside where there was no chance at quiet. It would not do for me to disappear to any of my usual spots, not without a guard, and I was not willing to share my secrets with anyone. So I sent Michal inside and went around the back where blessed silence lingered between the lodges.

I sank onto the bench, my head tilting back against the wall. Luk padded up to me, settling his chin in my lap. His throbbing purr began to tease apart some of the knots.

"Regrets already?"

I jolted with a curse. Emil leaned against the sweatlodge, a smirk in place, but it lacked its usual sharpness.

"What?" I grumbled, sinking back. Luk slowly settled after a longer stare at Emil.

He lifted a shoulder. "You've looked even more withered than usual these last few days."

My glare did not perturb him. "Should I be honored by how much attention you're giving me?"

His grin tilted again, but it did not seem like he had come to hold something over me.

"You are frustrating Makar."

It almost made me smile. But he was doing enough of the same to me.

"Did he think I was just going to roll over and show my stomach so easily?" I asked.

Emil shrugged again. "Perhaps many did. That's the side you've shown for years."

There was the sharpness.

"So why are you here?"

"He will not be content with exchanging words in lodges forever." Emil tucked his arms across his chest. "Once he heals, the real fight will begin."

I stared at the wall across from me. I was already so tired of fighting, of blood, of pointed words. Luk pushed his head against my stomach. Makar had to be the one to kill me if he wanted to take the place of chief. It was the unspoken rule of the tribe for the last three generations. And after he did, he'd have to be strong enough to defend his place from any objectors. Unless he killed Alik and Michal along with me.

"What is he planning?" I asked, not really expecting an answer.

"He is trying to figure out what you care about. Who you care about. If he does not succeed with words, he will start striking wherever he can."

Tactics I was not unfamiliar with after being on the receiving end before.

"Wish him luck for me."

A half laugh came from Emil. "He might figure it out before you."

He returned my look with a slightly pitying one. "Are you so afraid of caring?"

"Like you have so much experience with it?"

His scoff was at least familiar, putting us back where we had always stood. Or so I thought.

"Perhaps I do, Davor." He pushed away from the wall, but paused once more. "I would not trust the *talånd* either."

I scratched Luk's ears and his golden eyes shuttered closed as I gave voice to the thought nagging the back of my mind ever since he'd agreed to name me. "You think he might want to try to take the chief's place for himself?"

Some respect showed in Emil's face. "You noticed that as well." He ran a thumb over one of the knives strapped across his chest. "I think you set him against you with your words in the lodge, and by finding a wife."

I nudged Luk's head from my lap so I could lean forward on my knees and scrape palms together.

"The old chief...he never did much with ceremonies at the spirits' lodge. Surely there are things a chief and *talånd* must do." It had begun to needle me how much I did not know about what a chief needed to do. It was not as if there were memories for easy access from anyone about how a chief might act.

"Father never cared about the *talånd*. But he still kept him close and gave him privileges. Perhaps his way to assuage the *talånd* for caring nothing for his duties."

"I do not think that bothered the *talånd* overmuch." Ever since I could remember, the *talånd* had never been far from the chief's lodge. There were smaller lodges for the spirits in the middle and lower villages, but I was hard pressed to find a memory of him going there.

"He has never had an apprentice."

Emil's thoughtful statement brought my head up. I considered the new piece laid out before me. A *talånd* who might have a taste for power and what his position might offer with no care for duties that came with it.

"And he gravitates towards Makar."

That worried me more. But perhaps this was a piece more easily dealt with. And there was another I could go to for the matters of the spirits. Unless he just wanted to see the tribe tear itself apart.

My stomach began to nag at me with hunger, and I pushed to my feet.

"Thank you."

Emil seemed taken aback by the words. It took a moment before he tipped a slight nod and vanished around the corner.

I turned inside to face the surprised looks of the others when I came through the back door instead of the front. Marta and Janne sat at the table together, cloths and needles in hand. Marta echoed Janne's smile though it came more cautious.

It sent a warning spike through me. Makar was looking for someone to hurt in order to get to me, and I was suddenly looking at a lodge full of people I did not want to lose.

"Just in time." Mother saved me from sinking back into my thoughts. She shooed Marta and Janne from the table. I turned away so I would not see Marta tucking her needle into her skirts and carefully folding up the cloth in a way that was almost starting to feel familiar. Janne pulled Michal after her to help set the table and Marta turned to the cook fire with Inge.

I retreated to my room to set aside my sword, but kept knives strapped to my belt and under my left bracer.

"Where were you?" Michal's voice as I came back out rang with some slight accusation.

"Stealing a few minutes of quiet," I said almost wryly. He softened, and I wondered if it was really concern there.

"How was the day?" Mother asked.

"Long," I admitted, still turning over Emil's words from before. "Janne, you care about the spirits."

She paused to arch an eyebrow at me.

"What do you think of the *talånd*?"

Janne set cups on the table, stacking and unstacking them. "I suppose I should feel thankful that he saved my life when I was a baby, but...he makes me uncomfortable sometimes." It came rushed and with an apologetic look to her mother.

"Why do you ask?" Inge set down the pot of her mouthwatering fish stew.

"Just a thought." I shrugged.

Marta cleared her throat, looking a little nervous as I turned to her. "My grandmother…before she died…she used to tell us of the ceremonies each season. The way the *talånd* would come to the spirits' lodges in the other villages."

She darted a look to the others as if afraid to be admitting this. "I think I learned more of the spirits and the All-Father from my family and those in the lodge than I did from the *talånd*."

I rubbed my chin. That's what I had been afraid of. Mother looked shrewdly to me. She knew I did not care much for the *talånd* or the spirits. Though perhaps I needed to at least look their direction once in awhile if I could prove to myself that they cared anything for the matters of men.

"What are you thinking?" Mother set down the plate of perfectly browned flatbread.

"Trying to see where loyalties might lie." I did not want to bring them into the plots of those around, but they were tied up in this just by existing beside me. They needed to know some things in order to be prepared.

"I do not think you should be looking to him for any help." Inge raised her hands and sent a look skyward as if to ask forgiveness of the spirits she was closer to than any of us in the lodge.

Though it might have been because she saw birth and death, and had brought many back from the tenuous point right before entering into the afterlife—a chaotic place that might make more sense if you believed in something that resided beyond and cared about what might happen on earth.

"Could you even name a new *talånd*?" Janne's brow wrinkled.

"No, but I might insist he take an apprentice." Though there was no guarantee that he might not raise an apprentice to be the same as him.

"There's a boy in the lower village who is always going to the spirits' lodge there," Marta offered. "He might take the chance to be apprenticed."

She did not flinch from my regard.

"When is the next time you needed to go to the lower village?" I asked.

Her hands rubbed against her skirts. "I usually go the third day of every counting to a lodge to teach some girls needlework. I wanted to ask you anyway if it was all right that I still go."

I nodded, another thought taking shape in my head. A meeting had been set for tomorrow among craftsmen who had expressed interest despite the resistance of the *sjandsens*. The two men were a matter for another time, but I felt like I could give them a little longer to change minds about my being chief. And I had no one I was willing to put in their place yet if it came to it.

"I will go with you then if you would be willing?"

Marta inclined her head and with the matter settled, attention turned to taking our seats.

This time, I was given the head place that had been Inge's for as long as I had been sneaking to their lodge. I tried to argue, but her look quelled it. Marta was ushered to the spot on my right, and a faint redness tinged her cheeks.

The others were making no excuses for us to at least sit like we were chief and *dronni* in one place.

But I still deferred to Inge to give thanks to the spirits before we began to eat.

"Marta made the flatbread," Janne piped up as I took a piece.

Marta's cheeks turned even redder, and she stared fixedly at her soup.

"And she's teaching me better stitches."

"So it might look like a person made them instead of a bear trying to wield a needle?" Michal asked and took a mighty shove from Janne with a laugh.

Marta chuckled and the easiness swept back around her. "It is not that bad," she reassured.

"I was always better with stitching wounds than cloth," Inge admitted.

"The kitchen has always called me more," Mother said. "I did not have much more to teach than basic mending."

"My sister is the same, and more than content to leave it all to me." Marta smiled. "But I do not mind. Sometimes it makes more sense than people."

It made me smile slightly. That was a sentiment I understood.

The others were content enough to carry on conversation as we ate. A part of me was relieved to see Marta welcomed into it and not looking like she was holding herself apart. And every time my eyes drifted her direction, I focused just as fast on something else. Emil's warning rang through my mind. I could give nothing away to Makar, but it almost frightened me more to think that I might have something to care about after years of keeping myself apart.

Thirty-One

DAVOR

"The problem will be clearing it all off, Chief. It will be a mighty task in itself. You sure you want to keep it here?" The chief woodworker from the lower village rubbed his chin as he surveyed the ruins of the lodge beside me.

"What would you need to make it happen?" I asked.

He cleared his throat, hand rubbing harder against his jaw. "Well...plenty of strong men, but there are many who cannot leave their duties for so long, Chief."

I looked at the charred ruins again, thinking I understood his hesitation. Beyond him, the five other craftsmen who had been brave enough to come looked anywhere but us.

"There are plenty of warriors who have nothing to do. Would they be strong enough to suit your needs?"

The man coughed and his copper skin faded a shade. "It would be no trouble, Chief. I can call for others."

"No, the warriors will do. Battlelion?"

Alik flashed a smile as I turned to him. "I know just the men, Chief. I'll be around to make sure they follow your direction," he reassured the craftsmen.

Now all the men were staring at the two of us in disbelief, but when we showed no signs of joking or reneging on the promise, they shared looks.

"And I'm sure you might need help cutting and hauling wood for building?" I asked.

The woodworker nodded again, new calculation in his eyes as it seemed he was now seriously considering the task ahead.

"It would make the work faster. We could focus on the building and the carving. You would want it in the same design, Chief?"

"No." It blurted from me. I forced calm back. "Perhaps we could make some changes."

Changes so that the new lodge would not remind me so much of the old.

The man studied me a moment and nodded, pulling out a piece of birchbark and charcoal. "I've helped build many lodges. What are you thinking?"

By the time we settled on the design and what patterns I did not want to see etched into the wood, my throat almost ached from how many words I'd said. The other craftsmen had come in and out of the conversation as they walked more freely about the ruins, exchanging ideas with us as they went. Alik shared laughs and easy conversation with them as the woodworker carefully rolled up the designs.

"You are sure about the warriors, Chief?" he asked again.

"Yes," I said. "Some have gotten too comfortable in their positions."

Agreement flickered across his face before he quickly ducked his head to hide it. I almost smiled.

"And if you have any difficulties with them, come to the battlelion or to me."

He tapped fist to his forehead along with a slight bow. "We will be ready to start tomorrow."

I nodded. "I look forward to seeing your work."

Alik came to join me as the man returned to his fellow craftsmen. They stood in a group, heads bent together and occasionally looking at the ruins.

"I think you just gained their loyalty," Alik said.

My thumb knuckle pressed against my forehead. "How difficult is it going to be to get warriors out here?"

He chuckled. "I'll start with the men who actually like the two of us. But I have a long list of warriors who could stand a few days of hard labor."

A huff escaped me. "I can make an official order."

"Official order? The power has gone to your head already." He shook his head. "It's tragic, really."

My lips twitched. "I can still name a new battlelion."

He scoffed. "Like that will get rid of me."

We turned and I hesitated at the sight of the two figures walking the path up to join us. Janne hurried a few paces ahead of Marta.

"A new one is going to be built?" she asked.

"Yes, with plenty of room if you feel like walking up and down a hill."

Janne bounced up on her toes. "Really?" She flashed the hopeful smile that just might convince me to do anything.

I dipped my head and her grin spread.

"Janne." Alik gave a smile. "You look nice today."

Redness spread to Janne's cheeks as she looked to him. "Battlelion." It practically came out a squeak.

I flashed a warning glare at Alik, but he clapped a reassuring hand to my shoulder. Janne ran her hands down her overtunic, something seeming different.

"I'd recognize Marta's work anywhere." Alik gestured to Janne.

Janne seemed to return to herself. "Yes, she's been very kind." But she beamed at Marta.

"*Dronni.*" Alik tapped fist to forehead.

Marta rolled her eyes. "I do not know if I can take it seriously when you say it, Alik. We've known each other too long."

Alik always had a ready supply of smiles. "What brings you both up here?"

"We are going to the gathering," Marta said. Janne's excitement was brighter than I had ever seen, and something dangerous softened in me as I looked to the woman I'd bound myself to.

"You should come with us, Davor." Janne turned the look on me that she knew would get me to agree. My half-sister was a schemer, if nothing else.

"A chief at the gathering," Alik mused. "You should go, Davor, and really give them something to gossip about."

That did not help assuage some of the constant tension bunched up in my shoulders, but all three of them were looking at me.

"For a little while," I allowed.

Janne bounced on her toes again before comporting herself back into something more solemn.

"I'll send a guard." Alik tapped my shoulder and moved away, but there was a suspiciously evaluating look in his gaze as it swept among all three of us.

Janne led the way back down the hill, and Marta fell in beside me, her hands wrapped around the strap of her bag.

"Did the meeting go well?" She broke the silence.

"Yes." My hand fiddled at the hilt of my sword. "We'll find extra help from among the warriors."

I could almost hear her eyebrows raise. "The warriors? That is a bold move."

The half I trusted, I needed in the village for when Makar moved to battle. The other half, I did not trust enough to send on boundary patrols if they dared to scheme or follow Makar's orders away from the villages. I did not need the Greywolves incensed so soon after the truce, or the Pronghorns to the south to get any ideas.

"Things might become even more tenuous with it."

"I might begin to think you like starting trouble." But she softened it with a smile.

A faint one tugged my mouth in return. "I'm starting to remember why I've avoided it my entire life."

A question lingered about her, but she did not give voice to it. I turned away, sure that I did not want her to know anything else of me.

Noise gathered as we moved through the upper village, and as we stepped out into the fields, the sounds of hundreds of people burst over us. I balked before it. I rarely went out among a gathering, and the amount of people was usually why.

It would cause a stir for a chief to be there, much less with a *dronni*, and maybe this time I would be able to directly stop any open hate directed at Janne. But from the open excitement on her face to be walking in a crowd *with* someone, I did not regret my decision.

"Thank you for inviting her," I said to Marta as Janne pushed a few steps ahead of us.

A fond smile tugged Marta's mouth. "She has been so welcoming to me. And I saw when she came for prayer cloths how hard it is for her to come out here."

I almost asked what she had thought in stitching my rune in the cloth for Janne, but something else caught my eye.

The crowd slowly parting for us in a way it had never done. From the way Marta's hands gripped the strap tighter, she was unnerved by it as well. Janne fell back to Marta's other side, face falling into more severe lines.

Most were staring at us and it took several pounding beats of my heart in order to return them with an even look. So many expressions flashed back that I stopped trying to pick them out.

"Where did you want to go first?" I asked Marta. She had her bag and it seemed she carried it when she needed something.

Marta stared straight ahead. "We had just come to look, but…" She raised on tiptoes to see above the crowd. "Let's go this way."

She angled our path, and again it began to split for us. There was a faint gasp from her when a not so quiet *coward* and worse came after me, but I kept walking out of long habit. One of Makar's men vanished deeper into the crowds, and I had my answer for the disturbance and the agreeing murmurs following. My hand twitched as she closed the larger gap between us.

"Together, right?" Her question was quiet. I nodded.

We came out of the path created for us to a long table filled with fabric.

"Lene," Marta greeted the woman behind the table. Grey streaked through her hair, and her dress was bright cloth and stitches along the seams.

"Marta!" the woman started warmly. It faded slightly when

she saw me. "Chief." She tapped fist to forehead.

"This is Lene." Marta looked from me to the woman. "She makes the best cloth in the villages."

Lene gave a modest smile, but it was clear she knew her own skill. "And this is…?" She pointed to Janne, hovering a few steps away.

"My new sister, Janne." Marta's voice rose a little and those around us turned to each other as Marta took Janne's arm and pulled her close.

"Ah, congratulations on your marriage." But Lene's eyes were sharp as they looked between us. Marta released Janne and I hid my flinch as she wrapped her hand around mine.

"Thank you." Marta's chin was high. "I would like to barter for some cloth. Janne, come and we'll make something for the summer festival."

I did not contradict her even though a summer festival might not happen, at least not with me as chief if I could not hold the position.

As Janne and Marta turned over pieces of cloth and discussed with Lene, who was gentler with a bargain in front of her, I half turned to look out at the crowd.

One of Alik's pack stood guard nearby and he tapped fist to chest. I nodded and kept looking. Most of the tribespeople had begun to turn back to their conversations and bargaining, but there were still eyes on us.

The smile on Janne's face was worth my discomfort, and there was that same flicker of dangerous something when I looked to Marta. Eventually a pleased smile settled over Marta's face and Lene folded up a piece of cloth. But before the women could step away, I came closer.

"Lene, what village do you hail from?"

A guarded look came back over her, but she answered readily enough. "The lower, Chief."

"As you might know, the chief's lodge is being rebuilt. I have interest in new tapestries being made for the lodge."

A new expression settled over Lene's face. Calculating and some respect.

"You would stoop to cloth from the lower village?" Familiar challenge laced the words.

"My wife said it was the best in the villages," I returned, not daring to see how Marta reacted to the term.

Lene crossed her arms, no less intimidating than a warrior.

"I am entrusting this task to Marta, and I hope she might find other women to help with the stitching as I have no experience in it."

A faint smile flickered over Lene's face, and I returned it with a slight one.

"You chose well then, Chief. Marta's skill and my cloth will make fine tapestries for the lodge. And as much as I dislike offering competition for myself, you might also speak to Zora from the middle village. She does some fine weaving for embellishments."

"I know her," Marta said.

"Thank you." I inclined my head to Lene. She gave a more deferential salute to me and a nod to Marta. And after a moment's hesitation, something of the same to Janne.

We moved on and I waited until we were out of earshot from Lene to say, "I am sorry for surprising you with this task."

"No, it is a good idea." Her voice was musing. "But I have a question."

I paused, and she went a step before turning to face me.

"It seems you always have a purpose in doing things." Her arms folded over the cloth, tugging it to her body.

"What you said about the women talking had me thinking. Most of my fights will be against the men and warriors. Would something like this help bring together the wives?"

Understanding broke over her face and if I did not know better, a sly smile. "I think it just might. Leave it to me."

I might have almost worried if she had not immediately turned to asking me what designs I wanted for the tapestries. But I shrugged.

"Whatever you want. Just nothing like what hung in the old lodge." I could not quite contain the harsh edge, and she regarded me a moment.

"I do not know what was in the old lodge. Might I ask you sometime so that I do not copy a pattern?"

I jerked a nod and kept walking. Men and women were pausing around us and I did not want to give them ideas for gossip. Janne came up on my side. She said nothing, but pressed her arm against mine in silent understanding before moving away.

"When do you want me to start?" Marta asked.

"Whenever you feel ready to." I had no idea the length of such a task, and was content to leave it under her care, hoping that it might serve its purpose.

We wove our way back through the crowd, Marta again coming close beside me, but this time it felt a little more reassuring and it seemed she felt more at ease as well.

THIRTY-TWO

MARTA

The days began to settle into something of a routine over the next counting. I would help with preparing meals, assisting Janne in keeping the benches neat and the floor swept, with plenty of time still for my stitching which was something my fingers ached without.

Davor and I kept our distance within the lodge, but if for some reason we had to step out together, I was usually the one closing the gap between us. But we never did more than walk side-by-side. He usually offered nothing of his day, except for the weariness creeping up around his eyes and quiet silences that lasted longer and longer. Sometimes he would say nothing at the evening meal, just staring at his plate as he barely ate.

We all wondered why sometimes he came from the back door in the morning or the evening when no one had seen him go out, but always coming back more worried than before. His mother watched with a frown that grew day by day, but I did not feel brave enough yet to ask if I might do something to help.

Michal came and went with him most of the time. He did not seem much more willing to share things, but I often saw him and Janne whispering together. They all seemed to know more than me, and when it came to Davor, I sensed a certain protectiveness from all of the women in the lodge with something of the same emerging from Michal. They had been welcoming but it appeared they did not quite trust me yet.

When the day came for my normal trip to the lower village, Davor waited silently for me to gather my bag. A warrior fell in behind us in a pattern that was starting to become depressingly familiar, like I had forgotten what it was like to not have someone shadowing every step I took.

We walked through the upper village, the tribespeople out and about offering some respect, others scowling at Davor and sometimes me as well. And more than once I heard pointed words and whispers that made my ears burn. But Davor always walked like he did not hear it, though once I caught the tightening of his fist at a curse and a *coward*.

I did not dare ask why he did not retaliate, but that might frighten me more than the asking of it.

It was different walking the worn path from the upper village down to the lower across the field, instead of over the swaying bridge, but like other things, it had started to become familiar. Though I still did not like passing the training grounds.

Only the day before I had seen Alik engaged in a fight with another warrior. It did not look like a sparring match and iron clashed against iron. I'd been rooted to the spot until Alik had won, and I did not like the unfamiliar anger twisting up his face.

Later I had seen him and Davor engaged in conversation

with Alik sporting a bandage around his arm.

Silence dogged our steps, and this time I could not bear it for long.

"How are things really?" I blurted.

Davor flinched under the suddenness of it. "Nothing to worry about."

I swung around to face him, and he came to a guarded halt.

"I find myself worrying about things, and about you." The confession rushed out. "You seem more and more troubled every day."

He shifted like he was just going to walk around me, but I moved to match. Irritation flickered in his eyes, but I willed myself to hold my ground.

"It will be fine." Though the reassurance came through gritted teeth.

I was not yet brave enough to keep pushing, so I stepped out of the way and we kept walking. As always, he accompanied me right to my destination.

The door flung open at my knock and the girl who answered shouted my name back to the lodge. I do not think Davor was prepared for the stampede of feet announcing half the lodge.

"Let me come inside first!" I laughed as I returned hugs and greetings from the children, some so small they barely came up to my waist. I beckoned Davor after me, and after a moment's hesitation, he followed me in.

The common room was chaos as normal, the open windows shedding light upon it all. A haggard looking Ione came to greet me, carrying a tearful infant with her.

"You might want to take the lesson outside, Marta," she said above the noise.

I winced a little under a piercing shriek from across the

room. "Can I help with anything first?"

She gave a hopeless shrug, and then noticed Davor behind me. "Chief!" The baby sobbed as she tried to juggle the infant to give the salute. He waved her off and her shoulders sagged in relief.

"I will find my husband." Ione hurried off before I could say anything else.

"What is this place?" Davor had to raise his voice a little.

I scooped up a toddling babe and cooed at him for a moment before answering. "These are all orphans or unwanted children. They care for them in this lodge."

He looked around with a softer expression that fled the moment Feliks came and gave a formal greeting.

"I am sorry for the mess. I'd rather be out on the battlefield than here." Feliks scrubbed a hand across the back of his neck.

"What can I do to help?" I asked again.

He just shrugged, as helpless as his wife. "Some war has been declared this morning, and no truce has been accepted by anyone."

Davor shifted by my side and I followed his stare to a young girl sitting on a bench, knees curled up to her chest, well apart from everything going on.

"I don't know her." I shifted the infant on my hip, letting him play with the cord of my river-stone necklace Vanda had given me years before.

"She came to us a few days past. I still do not know what lodge she was from. She has not said much, but…" Feliks shook his head sadly, and my stomach turned. Davor's expression did not change, but I thought he tensed.

He moved, cutting a path around the chaos, avoiding two younger boys wrestling on the floor. Feliks stiffened in alarm, but I held out a hand, sure Davor meant no harm.

We watched as he went to the young girl. She curled up a little more, but he crouched in front of her. His lips moved, but they were too far away to hear anything. An edge of recognition reached between them.

She did not reply, and he said something again. This time she nodded. Another question and she answered something. My heart squeezed a little, watching as she started to reply quicker. There was something kinder and more gentle about him even though not much about him shifted. A slight smile creased his cheeks and a tentative one emerged from her.

He rose and came back to us.

"If anyone comes for her, let me know immediately and I will take care of it." Davor's tone was harsh, and Feliks nodded wordlessly.

"You know where she's from?"

"Yes, and I will deal with them." There was no forgiveness in his face, and a shiver ran down my arms. "If you need anything, come speak with me."

Feliks promised with wide eyes.

"I will come find you when you are done. I have other business," Davor said to me.

I nodded. As he turned to leave, the girl darted over and flung her arms around his waist. He froze, and when she did not immediately let go, his hand came to rest tentatively on her shoulder.

She gave another smile then vanished into the confusion. Davor said nothing else, disappearing out the open door. I watched for a moment, turning over what I thought I had discovered about him.

Feliks helped me pick out the girls and usher them outside. It took several more minutes to get everyone settled on benches or blankets on the ground, with several trips back inside to gather forgotten needles or cloth.

The warrior on guard settled back against the shaded wall, hand on his sword as he watched. The girls said nothing, but curious glances were thrown at him. For a moment, concern spiked at the sight of him standing there and Davor off on his own. When I went to ask the warrior, he did not reassure with, "Chief can look after himself, believe me. I'm to stay with you."

"Where did he go?" I asked, not content with this loyalty.

"He is going first to discuss things with the *sjandsen*. And then he had some other business." The vagueness did not go unnoticed. I narrowed my eyes, wondering if I could use my position as *dronni* to make him tell, but the warrior kept his lips pressed tight and went back to scanning for any threats.

I tried to focus on the lesson, but my eyes kept wandering off to the paths, watching for his return. A light *"Dronni!"* had me returning a wave and smile from the young woman with the red cloth tying off her braid, as she walked by, basket on her hip.

The girl Davor had spoken to eventually came out and shyly took a seat against the wall away from us.

At the sight of the others working and chattering together, she edged closer. I beckoned with a smile, and she perched on the edge of the bench a safe distance away.

"Do you want to work with us?" I asked.

She tucked her hands in her lap. "I don't have a needle or cloth."

"Here." I pulled a bit of cloth and one of my extra bone needles from a small pouch and extended it.

She came to sit next to me and threaded the needle.

"Can you show me how to make those?" She pointed to the

yellow violets edging my overdress.

"Perhaps in a few lessons," I said. "Let's start with something a little simpler."

She let me help her work the needle through the cloth. And I finally gently asked, "Do you know Davor?"

A bit of regret speared at the way her shoulders tucked down again. "I'm not supposed to say anything."

The alarm the words should have brought didn't come with the way I'd seen them interacting.

"He's my friend, too." I hoped that wasn't too much of a lie to the child. But she sat a little taller again, stabbed her needle in the cloth, and spoke so quietly that I had to lean close to catch the words.

"He brought me to the nice healer one time when…when I didn't feel well."

So many things pushed at my heart that it quelled my words for a few moments.

"That was very kind of him."

She nodded, and lips clamped shut, and it seemed like she put a little space back between us. I only spoke again to praise her work and guide her into a new stitch. It brought a smile back and she kept happily on beside me.

Two hours passed and one of my looks around finally yielded the sight of him coming down the path. My shoulders dipped in relief, and he seemed taken aback by the smile forming on my face. As his shadow fell across us, the girls all scrambled to their feet and pressed fists to forehead. He gave a nod and they all seemed pleased to have been noticed by the chief.

"Did you need to stay longer?" he asked as they settled back down.

"No, we are almost finished for today."

"If you have time, I would like to speak with the young man you mentioned," he said.

I had forgotten, but it was starting to become clear that he did not forget anything.

At my instruction, the girls began to tuck away their stitching, some coming to show me progress one last time. Davor waited patiently, after a moment, going to the warrior. Their low voices caught the edges of my ears no matter how I strained to hear.

The girls made no more secret of trying to eavesdrop. Even orphans and unwanted children knew the rules. Things adults whispered about were bound to be more interesting than those loudly discussed. I gave a sharp noise and waved them inside like I had not been trying to do the same thing.

The new girl gave a shy wave to Davor before darting inside. That same softening around his mouth came and faded as I stepped up to his side, adjusting my bag over my shoulder.

"You have a friend," I observed.

His sharp eyes lingered on the door. "Perhaps."

"You know which lodge she came from?" Hesitation locked up other questions, especially at the harshness forming around his eyes.

"Yes."

I did not need the warning look the warrior gave me, instead turning up the path towards the smaller spirits' lodge. "It's this way. Kir is probably there. If not, he might be out in the fields."

A distance sprang back between us as we set off. I gnawed at my lower lip, alternating watching my boots appear and disappear under my hem or the path before us. At least the air of tension and suspicion was not as thick as it was in the upper village. There, I felt like I could cut through it with a knife. Here it fluttered and shivered like a sparrow in the wind.

Davor moved through it all silently, a sablecat intent on whatever it was he was hunting.

I'd never considered myself a person who needed to fill silence with words, but walking beside Davor was sometimes like standing in the silence of midnight, with nothing stirring except cold starlight.

But I had no idea what to say to break the silence that might not bring a storm rushing in.

The spirits' lodge saved me, and I sent a small prayer their way for bringing Kir toward us.

"Kir!" I raised my hand.

The young man flashed a smile and jogged over, stumbling the last step when he recognized who I walked with. He folded into a bow, threatening to knock himself unconscious with the fist that came up to smack against his forehead.

"Chief!"

Davor cleared his throat, the sound only making me want to laugh more. But I mustered an even expression.

"Kir, the chief wanted to speak with you."

Panic took over the boy's face until I hastened to reassure. "It is about the spirits' lodge."

"Oh." Kir looked doubtfully to Davor.

"Marta tells me that you go to offer prayers there frequently." Davor's voice was even as if he was no more than discussing the turning of the seasons.

"Yes," Kir hedged.

"A noble thing," Davor said, and the boy relaxed though I wondered at the statement since it did not seem that Davor held much in the way of regard for the spirits or the All-Father. "Would you perhaps want to serve them in another way?"

"What way?" Caution had Kir leaning back.

"The *talånd* will not live forever. I had thought to help him find a new apprentice."

Kir's face lit up with joy so bright it brought a smile to mine. "Yes! I would…that is…it would be an honor." He seemed lost for more words than that.

Until Davor leaned a little closer. "It might not be an easy path for now."

Kir looked back at him and there was a shift in his eyes like he understood already. Davor's head tilted slightly.

"A *talånd* is meant to be a bridge between the spirits and man," Kir said slowly.

"And I fear the *talånd* has long lost sight of that path. We have strayed in many ways, Kir," Davor said. "It will take years before you would be ready to become *talånd*, but would you be willing to walk the path?"

I watched Davor instead of Kir. There was a bit of urgent desperation around his eyes.

"In exchange for what?" Kir's question came a little sharp. Sharper perhaps than I had expected in a boy of fifteen when faced with a chief.

"I have seen some of the scrolls detailing a *talånd's* duty. I want you to be loyal to that and not to anyone else. If you say you serve the spirits, then serve them. I want you to be willing to stand against what is wrong, to not let anger and abuse take control of this tribe again."

Kir looked to Davor, and for a moment there was a shared *oldness* between them, an understanding I was afraid of.

"I understand, Chief." He brought fist to forehead again.

Davor inclined his head. "Meet me tomorrow at midday at the *talånd's* lodge. He will take you on as apprentice."

The return of joy to Kir's eyes overshadowed the wariness

lingering there and he bowed again before he left, a spring in his step before he disappeared into the spirits' lodge.

"You do not agree?" Davor's question shook the frown from my face.

"I…" My teeth grabbed my lip. "Might it not be forcing the spirits' hand?"

"Perhaps it would get them to look down every once in a while." His voice turned bitter as he began to walk away.

"Kir will make a good *talånd*." I knew this with certainty. "But what if the *talånd* does not take kindly to it?"

Davor scoffed. "I know he will not. But I think the Greywolf will help make sure Kir is kept in the right teachings."

"The Greywolf?" Doubt flared up.

He inclined his head. "He was intent once on forcing man's will, but now seems to be making amends where he can. I trust him more than ours, and that is barely enough."

I found myself walking a little faster to keep stride with him. "Why worry about an apprentice now?" Surely there was more to worry about.

"I need the *talånd* busy."

So things were not going well and his broad shoulders were set like he was struggling under a heavy load.

"Davor."

He paused at the insistence in my voice.

"If you have somewhere urgent to be, then go." I offered a smile. "But I cannot walk this fast."

I could, but would nearly be running and would rather have a voice to find a way to distract him.

His features shifted in surprise, and then the corner of his mouth twitched. "I am sorry."

I waved my hand. "As *dronni* am I not supposed to slowly

walk around with an air of grave importance?"

The twitch flickered again. "Perhaps." He matched my pace, and I searched for something else to say.

"You have been going to the lodge for a long time?" He surprised me first.

"A few years now." I tugged at the strap over my shoulder. "I stumbled into it by accident. One of the older girls asked me at a gathering to teach her, and then dragged me to the lodge. I enjoy it."

There was a certain calmness in teaching. A thought that what I knew would not end with me. It would live on in someone else's stitches and then pass to someone else as the years marched on. Perhaps I had a bit of someone from the past lingering in every motion of my needle in a way that meant we might always be remembered.

Some friendlier smiles were cast my way as we passed through the last round of lodgehouses, and I lifted a hand and offered a smile in return.

"You are good with people," he observed.

"It has been harder this last counting."

"I am sorry," he said before I could regret my words spoken in haste.

"It's not your doing."

The look he tilted to me screamed he thought it was.

"We are walking together, but the things people think and say are their doing alone," I said.

Him blaming himself for cold welcomes where before there had been nothing but warmth was nonsense. They had decided to change while I was no different.

Davor's focus shifted forward, and a brief moment of worry struck that I had offended him.

"Is there nothing more I could do to help?" I asked before my self-doubt could overwhelm me.

"With?"

I gestured around to the village.

Davor seemed to draw in on himself again. "No. Do not worry."

I treated him to a raised eyebrow and a tilt of the head. "I think I will, Davor. I am in this, no matter what you say."

His mouth opened, then slammed shut as I dared to place a hand on his arm.

"I meant it when I said I would prefer to be friends. And friends help one another. Especially when one is set on shaking the ways of an entire tribe."

The corner of his mouth tilted again, and a sudden wish blossomed to see the smile escape. It might be a more wondrous sight than the spirits' lights which sometimes danced across a summer night sky.

"I will think on it," he finally allowed, and his eyes followed my hand as I withdrew my touch.

I nodded, determined to be content with this allowance. It seemed like some sort of progress and the air was clearer between us as we walked back to the upper village.

THIRTY-THREE

DAVOR

"Y ou sure about this?" Alik asked under his breath as he matched me stride for stride.

Beneath the rage simmering since seeing the young girl in the orphans' lodge yesterday, I knew what he meant. I was about to do something perhaps never done in this tribe's history.

But I had a promise to keep, and I did not want another pair of helpless young eyes haunting the darkest parts of my mind.

"Yes. You have things prepared?"

A few tribespeople pulled out of our way as we strode down the main pathway in the upper village. Three other warriors followed behind us, hands on swords.

I'd asked a few questions of those who had always given me information and they had returned with rumors confirming what I had known since seeing her sniffing and cradling an arm in a lodgeway a year ago, and again yesterday. Alik made no argument when I'd come to him with the plan.

But now, doubts were rising. Was it too much, too fast? Would it make a difference? Would it be better to keep moving in the shadows and deal with it quietly? Should I even do such a thing?

The memory of utter relief in her eyes quashed the questions.

I halted in front of the lodge and Alik pounded a fist against the door before stepping back to my side. He rested hands on sword hilt and squared his shoulders up with a sharp breath.

We'd chosen just before dinner when most of the lodge would be gathering back together, and those from the lodges around would be making their way home.

The door swung open and welcome faded to concern in the face of the man standing there.

"Chief?" he said warily.

"I want to speak with the mother of Lera."

"Lera?" His face lightened. "You found her?"

"Yes."

The uncertainty came back at the flatness of my voice. He opened the door to invite us in, but I did not move. Alik stayed at my side, hand still on sword. The man eyed us again before backing away.

"You ready for this?" Alik murmured. Outwardly calm still held my features, but inside was a raging storm.

I had no idea what I was about to do. No experience in standing up for someone else. But I knew that look in the girl's eyes and I refused to let it stay there.

A woman came to the door, the man behind her again. Beyond them in the lodge, men and women were gathering to see what might be happening.

One of the warriors standing at my left side shifted, and I followed his quick glance to the tribespeople starting to gather around the nearer lodges. Makar leaned against a wall, cold calculating in his eyes. I held his stare for a moment, then deliberately looked back to the woman.

"Chief?" She raised a fist to her forehead.

"You are Lera's mother?"

Her eyes narrowed for a brief second. "Elik said you found her. Where is she?"

"Before I tell you anything, I want to know if it is true that you have left her with more bruises than can be counted, and broke her arm for not moving fast enough for you?" A dangerous crack emerged in my walls, heat like a geyser pushing at the weakness and ready to spew forth.

Her head tilted back, and offense coated her like a thick cloak. "You think I would do such a thing to a child?"

"I do not know you," I said. "Are there any in this lodge who might speak on your, or her, behalf?"

The man behind her suddenly found the floorboards more interesting as I looked to him.

She whirled around. "Elik, tell him!"

But Elik said nothing. Another woman stepped forward from behind them.

"Chief, I've cared for Lera once or twice. I…" She looked at the woman. "I'd believe the child."

Rage covered the mother's face.

"She could never!" another said, but it seemed rushed with a look to the mother.

Murmurs were growing behind me, and I did not have the courage to look.

"Battlelion." I nodded. At Alik's signal, two of the warriors stepped forward and rested hands on her arms.

"What is this?" Her anger did not abate.

"You will have a day to prepare a defense for yourself, then you will come before me at the *tâkn* for judgment. Until then you will be kept in a secure lodge."

"You cannot—!"

"I cannot what?" I snapped. "I cannot stand for a child unable to defend herself? I cannot be tired of cruelty pervading this tribe? What have children done here to be subject to the anger of their parents?"

Another breath tremored through me and a sliver of calm broke through the storm. "Do you have a husband or anyone who would stand with you?"

She tugged against the hold of the warriors. "He died of wounds from the Blackpaw war years ago."

I nodded to the warriors and they escorted her away, leaving me and Alik facing off with a lodge full of shock.

"I will pass judgment tomorrow evening if anyone here cares to speak for or against her."

Silence dogged my steps away before a rush of sound and voices broke. I did not turn.

"Well." Alik glanced back over his shoulder. "That'll have them talking for awhile."

"You say that like it is a good thing." My hands were still clenched no matter how much I tried to uncurl my fingers.

"I think in just a few minutes you showed them what kind of chief you want to be. More than rebuilding lodges or meeting with officials." Alik paused, forcing me to turn and face him.

"I think it is a good thing, Davor. I've seen things like this before in the middle village. Sometimes we take care of it, take the children, or women, sometimes even men, into different lodges, but no *sjandsen* in my lifetime has cared to do anything to stop it."

He did not have to tell me that.

"What are you going to do with her?"

"I don't know yet." The admission fell between us. I had survived the confrontation, and only now felt like I could look ahead to the next task.

"I'll stand with you, whatever you decide." Alik reached out and gently tapped my shoulder with a fist.

"You don't know what I will do yet." I rubbed my forehead to try to smooth some of the furrows from it.

"I trust you, Davor. You won't rush into anything." Alik began walking again and it took another moment before my legs moved as well to catch up with him. Belief was so easy for him and many times it scared me that it was placed in me.

Michal bolted up when we stepped into the lodge.

"Did it work?" he asked.

"Did what?" Janne immediately voiced the question in everyone else's face. My jaw locked back up, but Alik easily replied.

"Yes, and things will be set for tomorrow night."

"What things?" Janne pressed again.

Alik looked to me and it was all I could do to nod again, looking at some point just beyond everyone.

"There was a young girl at the orphans' lodge who ran from her mother, with good reason," he said.

The sudden shift of attention back to me had my fingers curling up, but Marta's questions softened to understanding.

"You took care of it?" she asked softly.

I jerked my chin down.

"Some others in the lodge were ready to confirm that the mother had been mistreating the girl. The woman has a day to prepare a defense," Alik said.

Mother appeared in front of me, her hands resting on my shoulders. Pain and understanding and pride shone fierce from her, rippling through me as her palms touched my cheeks for a moment.

She stepped away and turned to Alik. "Will you stay for dinner?"

"No. I will meet some others in their lodge to keep gathering support with the warriors. With guards," he reassured me. "Michal." He clapped the young man on the shoulder. "I'll see you on the training grounds first thing. You've been practicing?"

Michal nodded, a smile breaking over his face at the promise. It almost brought one from me seeing how easily Alik broke through some of Michal's barriers.

"Good." He tapped Michal's shoulder again and looked to me. "Midday tomorrow?"

I dipped my head in promise that I would be at our usual meeting place, and he left. As the door closed, our small lodge swept back into preparing for the meal. Before I could turn to my room to lay aside my weapons, Marta stood in front of me.

Her dark eyes searched my face a moment, then she tentatively placed a hand on my arm. "Thank you…for what you're doing for her."

I wanted to confess that it was something I should have done years ago. Something I should have been doing all my life. But I had been too much of a coward. So instead, I tipped my head and eased my arm out from under her touch and vanished for a few moments of quiet before facing her again.

Dawn came quiet and with a hint of chill that was coming less and less as spring marched on. A light breeze snuck around the corner of the lodge and tugged at my shirt sleeves as I sat on the bench, the thumb of my left hand working across the palm of my right.

The night had passed restlessly, plagued with nightmares of the past and hazily conjured fears of the future. It did not bring confidence with waking.

"Are you trying to get yourself killed?"

I jolted, my focus shifting up to Emil standing against the sweatlodge. My glare did not bother him, and he only moved further into the shelter of the lodgeway.

"You seem to be the only other one who cares enough to be up this early," I said. He also seemed to be standing closer than last time we had been there together.

"At least tell your guards that you come out here to look moodily at the ground." Emil looked from end to end of the space.

"I have told them to leave me alone."

He arched an eyebrow. "Does that not defeat their purpose?"

I leaned back against the wall. "Is that concern in your voice, Emil?"

A huff broke from him, and he settled more comfortably opposite me, arms crossed. "Only because you are doing something vaguely interesting, and I want to see how it plays out."

"Ah, so I am here for your amusement once again?"

The heel of his boot scraped against the lodge wall, acknowledging the lack of bitterness in my words with a lift of his shoulder.

"Only because you have been so good at it recently."

"Is this why I am honored by your presence today?" It had been days since the last time he had come, and the only times I had briefly seen him in the villages was always beside Makar, leaving me still doubtful about his true intentions.

"Perhaps I want to know why you are taking the side of a child you do not know."

I forced myself to hold his eyes, the light in them threatening to spill into a blaze. "We are meant to learn from our mistakes, aren't we?"

His face was unreadable for a moment before he shifted. "What are you going to do with the woman?"

"I don't know." I hated admitting as much to him, but it felt different between us in the space between lodges. "Alik says he trusts me to do the right thing, but I barely stood up to the old chief...and even facing her...what do I know of such things?"

He shifted, but there was no scorn building around him. "We both know what I would do." It came a bit wry.

"I do not think I want that."

Quiet lapsed, and my thumb kept worrying at the palm of my hand.

"This new way you are trying." The words came careful, like he was deciding as he said them. "Will you come for me because of what I did to the chief?"

I turned my hand over, my fingers sweeping over a scar on the back of my wrist. "When I think of it, I feel nothing but relief. Perhaps it was justice."

Emil said nothing, arms still crossed as he stared at something on the ground.

"What do you feel?" I asked.

He slowly looked up. "Many things, but regret is not one of them."

I nodded. "Perhaps we should see if I can even hold this position before deciding anything."

Faint motion stirred the corner of his mouth. "I think you might have a chance. It was a bold move, but I hear talk leaning towards respect for you. Makar does not know yet how to try to spin this against you."

"But he will try?"

"With everything you do until you or he is defeated." Emil's face held the closest I'd ever seen to apology. But it did not stop the low curse from breaking free as I scraped a hand through my hair.

He tilted his head in agreement with my coarse assessment.

"He is spreading rumors that you have overstepped by forcing the *talånd* to take an apprentice. And feeding on the unrest in the warriors following him at your orders to help with the lodge and hunt for themselves."

Alik was only barely keeping order among the warriors resistant to him and the orders I had given. But the work of clearing the ruined lodge was progressing at a pace agreeable to the craftsmen. Though perhaps not for much longer.

"And the *talånd*?" I asked.

"You think I regularly talk to the *talånd*?"

This time I huffed and tilted my head back to watch the rising sun chase away the greyness of the sky above. "I need him busy and the Greywolf will make sure he does not lead Kir astray."

"Some might not like that you are placing so much trust in the words of the Greywolf."

"Are you one?" I looked to him, and he shrugged.

"He at least sees this tribe for what it is," I said.

His words had returned to haunt me more than once since that blustery winter day he had spoken them, warning of a reckoning coming for the tribe. Perhaps it was the war, perhaps it was something that had yet to come. Perhaps everything I was trying to do was too little too late, and we were doomed for our pride and sins.

"And you think he would help you with this new way?" The scoff came back in Emil's voice.

"He has nowhere else to go unless he wants to try his luck with the Pronghorns or farther east in the high mountains." The Greywolf did not seem a man readily able to defend himself in the wilds. He had no sword or wolf. He understood well enough that this was his chance to build a new home.

Emil tipped his head. "Just be careful where you put your faith."

"Does that include you?"

His smirk flickered with a hint of challenge. "I never said you could trust me, Davor. Perhaps I am helping Makar just as much and am waiting for the two of you to destroy each other to pick up the pieces myself."

He did not flinch under my regard.

"No," I mused. "You want something else entirely."

I did not know what yet, but he had let his mask slip just enough in our last meetings. The familiar coldness swept back over him, edging his features in sharper lines.

"Always so sure you know everything," he said.

The barest hint of a noise around the corner brought our attention toward it. Emil slid a knife free and eased down the lodgeway with me right behind. He tipped a glance over his shoulder and I nodded, for once the two of us working in tandem.

Emil reached around the corner and hauled someone into the lodgeway, slamming them against the wall with knife to the throat.

"Michal?" we both hissed in unison.

Michal scowled back at us and shoved Emil's hand away.

"Emil? You're meeting with *him*?" Michal's full ire came at me.

"Hello to you too," Emil said wryly.

"No. You're helping Makar and he's a…" He called Makar some of the worst things I'd ever heard, stopping when I cleared my throat.

"Been teaching him things, have you?" I raised an eyebrow at Emil. That almost grin was back on his face.

"He is not wrong."

Michal crossed his arms and glared.

Emil rolled his eyes and sheathed the knife. "Yes, I am working with Makar. And, against my better judgment, with the *chief* here."

"Why?" Michal's posture did not forgive.

"It seems for once, the two of us agree on something, and that is to keep Makar from being chief," I said.

"Does Alik know?" Michal asked.

"No."

That brought his brows up.

"And you will not tell him," I said sternly.

I'd never known how ferocious a glare could be from Michal, but I was finding out.

"You don't trust him? You don't trust *me*?"

There was the hurt, the betrayal.

"Michal…" My hand lifted slightly between us.

"He doesn't trust me," Emil cut in. "I don't trust him either. And I don't want the entire tribe knowing my business here."

"I'm not the entire tribe," Michal muttered, scuffing his boot against the ground.

"No, but Janne would know within a heartbeat and then the entire tribe might." Emil rolled his eyes.

Michal opened his mouth to defend his twin's honor, but I lifted my hand higher, forestalling him.

"This stays between the three of us," I said, and Emil punctuated it with a flick of his knife.

Michal gave a scoff of agreement, but the betrayal still lurked around him. Emil stepped back and sheathed the weapon.

"Watch your back tonight, *Chief*." And he strode towards the opposite end of the lodgeway and disappeared around the corner.

"Is he who you're meeting out here every time?" Michal jerked my attention back.

"Sometimes I come out here for some quiet and to think." And Emil's words had my mind turning over many things.

Tonight.

"Davor?" Michal's quiet voice brought my attention back to him. "You could have told me."

"I'm sorry, Michal." I gestured in halfhearted apology. "I just…don't know how to trust…anyone, really."

The fight in his eyes faded away and he dug the toe of his boot deeper into the ground. "I know, but…"

"I will try."

He flashed a small smile and I thought I might be forgiven with it.

"What are you going to do if Makar tries something tonight?" Michal asked.

I tipped my head. He was catching on quick with many things. "Perhaps we go speak with Alik."

"Can we eat breakfast first?" he asked hopefully.

A faint smile tilted my mouth. "I won't be able to think without it."

He led the way back inside and I followed after a moment. I was getting used to having him around, seeing more of the brightness he still held tight inside him. It seemed many days like we might eventually have something like brothers between us. And thinking back to the moments in the lodgeway with Emil, as words came a little easier between us, the thought of a truce between us did not seem so unlikely.

THIRTY-FOUR

DAVOR

More people than I had expected trickled into the space around the *tåkn* grove. The *talånd* arrived shortly after me, his colorful robe sweeping around his shoulders. Kir was on his heels, cloaked in plain grey, and keeping steady despite how obviously the *talånd* was trying to ignore him. I waited under the head *tåkn's* shadow, Michal at my side, and wondered if I needed to accept something to wear other than a heavy cloak I avoided that might show my new place in the tribe.

The scrutiny of the gathering crowd began to wear on me even though it had only been five minutes of standing there. I turned my attention to the carved wooden pole beside me instead, taking a moment to actually look at it—the images of sablecats, spirits, the story of how the tribe came to settle under the shadow of Half Peak. It wound up and around the weathered wood until I could no longer see the images. A carved sablecat head dominated the top, declaring the spirit whose favor marked our tribe. Other poles spread out in lines behind it, telling the smaller and more recent histories.

"Sometimes I think we want to imagine we are all different, each tribe." The Greywolf came to my side. He held his grey cloak tight around him, looking up at the great *tâkn*.

"The Greywolf *tâkn* holds our story, the wolf head pointing to the north star, reminding us of the All-Father's place."

My fingers brushed over a few runes declaring a victory over a faraway tribe who rode giant eagles, the reason our bows had come into being. What deeds might this history omit, if our tribe had always been this way?

"We never want to remember the bad," he said, as if hearing my thoughts. "No tribe is perfect. Many things might not be recorded on the *tâkns,* but some of the more important things will be held in memory and passed down instead, weaving themselves into the legend of the tribe. The things you do here will live on for many generations."

I did not want to look and see if that faraway gleam was in his eyes, seeing if he spoke the truth in a way that only the All-Father granted to His holy men.

"Good or bad?" I asked instead.

"You are still weaving the threads, Davor. You have the choice to make it what you want."

"I do not know if talking to you ever helps." I finally turned to him with a faint smile.

His returning one was broader. "Ah, you met the battlewolf, I hear. He is much the same. Wanting easy answers and direction, but things are not always so."

I tilted a look up at the sablecat atop the *tâkn*. "I wish just once they would make it so."

"If life was not a constant battle, there would be no warriors' tables in the All-Father's lodge."

The bitter thought snuck out. "If the spirits cared so much, perhaps they would let there be peace sometimes."

"Perhaps you are their tool for peace." His words struck deep into my chest, and I had no reply. It did not seem fair that some might see me as a tool for peace when I was the one who had to fight—and maybe lose—bloody battles.

"Davor." Michal touched my arm, cautious eyes turned to me.

I eased my fingers out of their fist and turned to face the crowd. Raised torches had been brought out and set in a wide circle. Their flickering light danced across the packed earth, warning away any villager who might try to encroach closer to the place of judgment.

A stir through the crowd marked Alik's approach with the woman and her guards. They halted in the center of the circle. The woman stood with shoulders hunched over crossed arms, her hair an untidy mess, as if it had taken one day away from the comfort of a lodge to bring her to despair.

Another swirl of motion marked the arrival of Marta and the young girl. Trailed by two guards, they came to stand on the edge of the circle, five paces from me.

Looking at them, my breath lodged in my chest for one precarious moment. Marta had been at the orphans' lodge most of the day, helping prepare Lera for this. But now she wore a red dress and white overtunic embroidered with leaping sablecats and curling vines at the borders. Her hair was half braided along the crown of her head in a manner like the way any women warriors might wear theirs. The rest flowed down around her shoulders, smaller braids scattered through it.

She met my glance and smiled, which did not help my suddenly stammering heart. Lera leaned against her as she placed hands on the girl's shoulders protectively. Once Marta had asked what I'd intended to do, there had been a shift in her eyes, a resoluteness as she declared she'd stand with the child.

My effort to turn my attention away seemed like it must be painfully obvious to everyone gathered. As I had requested, the *talånd* came forward first, lifting his hands and turning face heavenward.

"May the All-Father and the Saber spirit bear witness tonight and guide our chief towards the right decision." His gaze fell from the skies to me as he finished, something like a smug warning there.

I gave a sharp nod and he stepped back. Kir gnawed on his lower lip, sudden anxiety in his posture directed towards me.

With a feeling that was more a curse than a prayer, I stepped forward.

The woman said nothing to defend the accusation I brought forth. Nothing but a glare at her daughter who pressed closer to Marta. A few declaring themselves from her lodge or from the upper village tried to defend her as a good woman, but others from the lodge refuted with quiet claims and glances at her.

But before I could move on, Makar stepped out, a bit of swagger through his shoulders as he flaunted the absence of a sling. A smirk settled across his features at my sharp look, and he moved easily, spreading both arms wide.

"I wonder, Chief, what you might have against this woman? Are we to so easily trust the words of those who might have issue with her? Or perhaps the word of a *child*? Do you know so well the difficulties of raising a child?" The last was said with a bit of laughter.

At this the woman raised her head, finally looking at me with the defiance I had seen before I'd ordered her taken.

"No, but I know the difficulties of being a child in this tribe. I know that a parent should not vent their anger on the innocent. That a chief and a *talånd* should stand for everyone in this tribe."

The *talånd's* face froze, and the flash of refusal shone about him.

"Anger?" Makar was not done. "The way of this tribe is strength, and we must raise up our children in that way. Something you might not know anything about." The sly sneer appeared.

"Strength?" The perilous weakening in my walls came again. I was getting tired of feeling it, of fighting it. "Was it strength to leave wounded to find their way off the field? To brutally punish those who do not move fast enough or perform a task to perfection each time? Is it strength to strike a child who cannot fight back?"

"The way of the battlefield is to pare the weak from the ranks. We do not need that in the packs." Makar tossed his hand to encompass the gathering.

The barrier broke.

"It is *cowardice*. There is no honor in leaving someone behind to die. No honor in turning a blind eye. I have made mistakes. I have turned away from those who needed help before, but no more. The strength you speak of, Makar, is *empty*. The pride you flaunt is hollow. And I will not tolerate any strikes like this against any man, woman, or child in this tribe."

Absolute silence followed my words and my sharp breaths

seemed to echo in time with the jolting torchlight. Before Makar could speak again, my feet brought me one step forward, keeping all focus on me.

"I declare you guilty here today," I said to the woman. "You will not be locked away, you will not be cast out, though it is easily within my right to do so. Instead you will lose your place in your lodge, in any lodge. If they feel like they may take you in, so be it, but you will take the lowest place always. Your task now is to serve the tribe in whatever way someone needs. But if someone is wrongfully using you, I will step in. You are not to speak to Lera ever again unless she so wishes it. If she enters into the same village as you, you will immediately leave those boundaries. This will hold until the day you die. Do you understand?"

"Yes, Chief." Her answer came subdued, eyes wide perhaps in shock that Makar's challenges had not swayed me.

"And what of the child?" Makar was apparently not done. "Are you going to take her, Marta, to prevent the chief from forcing you to bear an heir?"

Cold fury washed away the heat, but before I could say anything, Makar laughed again.

"No answer for me?"

Marta slowly turned to regard him, and though red flushed her cheeks, her voice came even. "We are not on familiar terms, so I will not acknowledge my name coming so freely from your lips. It is *dronni* to you, or not at all."

The anger faded away to a sudden rush of something that felt like pride. Pride that she was standing her ground.

This time, Makar's face showed signs of anger as some scatterings of laughter, quickly quelled, sounded from those gathered.

"As for Lera," Marta continued, sweeping her gaze over the tribespeople gathered, "it will be her choice where she goes, and

I will ensure it is a place where she will safely grow into a woman of this tribe."

"This gathering is done," I said.

Alik gently pulled the shocked woman away, giving me a slight nod as he went. We'd debated all day, eventually both agreeing that this might be the best way of things.

"Chief!" Lera ran to my side, throwing her arms around me before I could prepare. Fierce strength filled the grip of her small arms around my waist, and the front of my tunic smothered a faint sob.

Gingerly, my hands touched her shoulders. Her hug tightened and another sniff had some helplessness rising up.

"Thank you." The words were muffled.

It killed some of the anger still lingering, and I carefully rested a hand on her head. She pulled away and turned a shy smile up at me.

"She said she wanted to stay at the orphans' lodge for now." Marta joined us, arms tucked low over her waist. A fond look turned to the girl, and I forced my eyes away.

Michal leaned forward, hands on his knees, better to come eye-level with Lera.

"You were brave," he said.

Lera twisted side-to-side, hands tucked in her dress. "Marta helped me to be."

I followed Michal's look over to Marta. "She's very good at being brave," he said.

Marta's cheeks flushed again, but it was softened by a smile at the two of them.

"You did well," I told her softly.

Marta edged closer, unfurling her arms to show her hands. "I think they've stopped shaking."

My hand moved before I could think, gently touching her wrist before I withdrew.

"Did it trouble you much, what he said?"

She pulled in a breath, tucking her hands back after a longer glance at her wrist. "A little. But I have a feeling it will not be the last time we hear something like that."

Our glance met, awkward again.

"It will pass." She lifted her chin with a forced brightness. "People always find something else to talk about."

Perhaps not about this.

And as I looked at Makar, still glowering at me from across the gathering place, I knew that he was not going to let it pass.

THIRTY-FIVE

DAVOR

"You don't look happy about last night." Alik parried my swing, our wooden practice blades cracking across the training grounds. It was too early for many others to be out, dawn barely shedding its grey cloak.

"Should I be?" I backed up a step as we circled again.

"You did a big thing, making that judgment. Not to mention everything else you said." He probed forward, the medallion sliding across his armor.

"I've yet to walk the villages and see the response to it. I hesitate to call it a victory."

Alik scoffed. "Just take one when you can."

My lips tightened. I never took a victory unless it was fully assured.

"At least feel proud about it." He lunged forward and any reply I might have had was pushed aside in the barrage of strikes and blocks.

I did not feel like hearing anything else from him, so I pushed the mock fight until we both fell back breathless and sweating.

"You're stronger on your left again." Alik jabbed his wooden sword at my arm in question.

I moved it, trying to avoid the memory of the searing pain of the burn.

"So is Makar."

"I saw," came Alik's grim reply. "We think the fight starts in earnest now?"

I nodded sharply. Now he might be physically strong enough to start striking with iron instead of just words.

"How is Marta?"

Alik's question caught me off-guard, and as my startled look turned to him, he arched an eyebrow.

"She seemed flustered last night after Makar spoke."

I moved away to replace the practice blade in the bucket full of other blunts. "She did well in replying," I said.

Alik came up on my side. "And?"

"And what?" I snapped a little.

His huff only stoked some irritation within me. "From what some from the lodge were saying, it looked like the two of you might be closer than Makar and everyone else is assuming."

"Is that so?" My simmering anger was back.

"Davor," Alik said calmly. "She is a friend of mine, and I know that you would never do anything dishonorable, but I just want to know if she is actually happy enough in this new place."

A bit of defeat slumped my shoulders. "I don't know."

Because I did not ask, and I avoided her whenever I had the chance.

"I am trying to make it as easy as I can, but…" I shrugged.

The eyebrow lifted again. "Marta is the sort of person who is happier being active and helping others, no matter how much it seems she stays apart with her stitching. Don't push her away forever. She showed the tribe last night that she is strong enough to stand as *dronni* at your side. Let her."

My gaze fell to the ground, the uneven grass blades trying to beat back the constant press of boots and paws. I sympathized with them, still trying to grow even when they were stomped down again and again.

"My focus needs to be elsewhere." But it sounded empty to my ears.

He settled a hand on my shoulder. "Things might be easier if you let her, let the others in your lodge, help to shoulder some of your burdens. A chief is not meant to carry everything all alone."

I gave a nod, afraid to try and promise anything. He shifted and tapped fist to my shoulder before moving away.

"At least try."

Exactly what he had told me with Michal countings ago. I had tried then, so there was nothing stopping me from trying again.

"We need to start planning a defense for when Makar strikes." I scooped up my sword and buckled it on.

Alik did not argue the sudden shift. "You going to tell me who your spy is?"

But he did not look angry or upset. I gave him a wry look.

Alik gave a short laugh. "Michal was acting fidgety yesterday."

I shook my head. Exactly why I did not entrust many secrets to Michal.

"You trust whoever it is?" Alik asked, not pressing for more.

"More than I thought I might," I finally admitted.

He tipped his head, easy agreement in the gesture, and apparently content to let me keep the secret. I almost told him of Emil, but perhaps it was selfish and I did not want to destroy Alik's confidence in me, so I did not.

"Perhaps you need to start wearing armor," Alik said.

I had not so far, wanting to show that I was not afraid for myself, or did not see threats. But it was a dangerous gamble, especially with Emil's most recent warning. He had warned of something last night, and Makar was now healed enough to try.

I had been chief for almost two countings and nothing had challenged me except words. It would be soon.

"Not until he does something," I decided.

Alik scoffed, throwing a hand up. "So you'll let him kill you rather than wear something that might slow him down at least a little?"

"He has been playing games with words, seeing who will flinch first. If I start wearing full armor now, it might look like I am giving in to fear. The old chief started wearing armor many days when it was obvious he was not in his full mind."

"I understand you do not want to look overly cautious or paranoid, but you should also protect yourself."

I brushed away Alik's argument, to his disapproval.

"At least there's someone around who will put neater stitches in you when you inevitably need them."

A faint smile lifted my lips and he frowned to hide any of his amusement.

"Go on then!" He waved a hand towards the edge of the

training grounds. "Go with no regard for my poor health."

I rolled my eyes. "I think you'll be fine."

"Heartless." He shook his head. "Midday?"

I nodded. He'd see how the winds shifted in the warriors, especially with a new group supposed to help the craftsmen that day, and I would go on business to the *sjandsen* in the middle village to listen and learn what I could.

"Be careful." It was a needless reminder. We both were tired of looking over our shoulders.

"You too," I returned, and we parted ways, each with another warrior trailing our paths back to our respective homes.

The lodge was stirring as I entered. Marta seemed to always have a smile for me, and Alik's words did not have to echo back for me to muster up a short greeting to her.

Michal emerged from his furs with a groggy yawn, sounding more like a grumbling sablecat than a human.

I ducked into my room to rinse some of the training from my skin and don fresh clothes. Even with the training, my appetite was still dulled. Mother never hid her expressions around me and at least one look of disapproval leaked from her when I glanced up from my nearly full plate.

With an effort, I looked to Marta, surprised to see concern in her eyes as she clearly watched me.

"I am going to the middle village today, if you wanted to come?"

"I would like that," she replied.

She was ready, no bag over her shoulder, when I was. We stepped out and Tinek fell in behind us. He'd been a steady presence on many days, sometimes offering reassurance that I did not find annoying.

"I had a question for you today," Marta said, hands in pockets of her overdress as we walked. This seemed to be our routine when we were together—her asking questions. But I did not mind most of them.

I nodded to her to continue, though some apprehension sparked when she seemed more hesitant than normal.

"I wondered if…you had refused another necklace like the old chief's…I thought I might add something to your tunics or shirts to look…"

"More chief-like?" I asked wryly.

The faint red came and went from her cheeks, and she tilted her head. "Yes?"

A faint huff broke from me. "I do not have much since the fire took my trunk with it."

"I can barter for new cloth to make new things." She half-turned in step with me. "Though dark colors only, I assume?" There was a lilting tease in her voice.

My eyebrow lifted. "You are correct."

She smiled and settled back to walking forward. "Though red would suit you well, I think."

I did not know what to say to that. "Whatever you want to do." Though my voice seemed a little off to me.

"Whatever?" The tease was back.

I just gave her a faint glare, but her smile didn't dim. She saw through it well enough, and it made me a little pleased.

"How long will you be here?" she asked.

"However long the *sjandsen* is going to keep talking at me." The thought almost had me rubbing my knuckle across my forehead to stave off the headache that would surely come from speaking with him.

She chuckled. "Could you not aloofly announce that your wife summons you?"

"Would you?" Hesitant curiosity escaped.

She gave another smile. "If you needed an escape. I have pretended that Mother desperately needed Vanda before when she did not want to speak with someone. Usually an over-eager boy." She leaned a little closer.

Our boots scuffed against the bridge boards. Cords still fluttered from the railings, some already wearing away from the breezes or birds trying to worry them free to carry off for nests.

"And she would do the same for you?" I didn't care, but I couldn't stop the question, wondering how much I had upset her life by this arrangement.

She did not seem bothered. "Men stopped lingering around after I turned down my second marriage offer two years ago."

"Why?" Even I could see that she was a good match. I would have thought a few refusals would not have deterred every man in the villages.

"Perhaps I was waiting for a chance to grab a chief." She winked at me.

A half-smile tilted my mouth. Something changed in her face and I wasn't sure what had caused it.

"And how has that plan unfolded?"

Marta turned enough again to regard me. "I think I did well by waiting." Seriousness had replaced some of her levity, but I suddenly felt like I was on dangerous ground.

Her sudden touch on my arm had me almost jolting. "I am not lying, Davor."

I knew, and that, perhaps, was more frightening.

THIRTY-SIX

MARTA

I watched Davor stride away toward the *sjandsen's* lodge before slowly turning to my family's. The words we'd exchanged had been more friendly than ever before, and then he'd almost smiled.

I'd been right. Even seeing half of one changed him so much. There was some brightness still hidden within him, and I wanted more than anything to draw it out again.

But perhaps I had ruined that chance by my words, meant to be reassuring, but seeming to shut him off again. I sent a quick prayer to the Saber spirit to protect him before stepping through the door.

Vanda was first to greet me, hurtling forward to hug me. I laughed and returned it just as tightly.

"It has only been two days since we last saw each other."

"I know!" She pulled away. "But after years of suffering with you as a sister, it is strange to not have you around."

"Blessedly freeing, you mean?"

She poked me in the stomach, and I hopped backwards to avoid another strike.

"What's the latest news?" I dodged again and made my way towards the cook fires to find something to eat even though breakfast had not been long ago.

"You tell me." Vanda darted up to my side, wiggling her eyebrows. "From what everyone said, you and Davor seemed very friendly after the trial last night."

I froze in the middle of taking a fruit-filled flatcake from a bowl. "What?"

Vanda plopped down at the table, leaning forward to prop her chin on her hands. "You heard me."

I slowly joined her, picking a crumb free from the flatcake, appetite suddenly diminished. There were not many others around in the lodge, but Vanda had not exactly been quiet so there was a good chance they were ready to try to listen in.

"We're getting along," I said softly.

"And?"

I frowned at her. "And I thought you were against all of this?"

"Perhaps he's not as terrible as I once thought." She shrugged. I supposed I should be grateful at least one argument between us was settled so easily. "I cannot make sure you are happy?"

I sighed and took a bite to stall my answer. Vanda knew my ways, and waited patiently, not moving on until I swallowed the driest cake I'd ever eaten.

"I think I am."

"You think?" She frowned.

I set to picking at the cake again, crumbs falling away under my fingers to scatter on the table. "It's just...he's very reserved. We get along, but he keeps everyone, not just me, at arm's length. It's hard some days."

It was suddenly spilling from me, the doubts and hurt that had been building up, festering a little in the darkness of the lodge as I lay on my bench.

"Do you want him to bring you closer?" Vanda asked just as quietly, sisterly teasing gone.

"I don't know." My hands fell into my lap. "I suppose I didn't know what to really expect, so maybe I shouldn't be surprised. And...and I never thought too much of marriage before this, but I always thought maybe it would be someone I would feel close to. But..."

But that half-smile flashed in my mind again, and my heart skidded over the next beat.

Vanda's brow arched. "But?" The bit of tease was back.

I sighed, half-heartedly tearing at the flatcake. "Could we talk about something else?"

My sister smiled and did as I asked. Even after two days there were tales to go around. She made no secret of listening in or engaging in conversations that would lead to Davor or to me. It seemed at least the middle village might be throwing in behind him.

We slowly moved our way outside, watching for Father to come back from hunting, hoping he would arrive before Davor returned.

But Makar appeared before either of them. I pushed to my feet, Tinek coming closer to my side. Three other warriors pushed between us until Tinek looked ready to pull a blade. I raised a hand and he stilled.

"Wise choice, *Dronni*," Makar sneered.

Vanda pressed behind me, and I kept an arm half-outstretched in some slight protection.

"What do you want?" Anger stirring at the way he and his men pushed forward around us, trying to intimidate, helped my voice stay steady.

"To become better acquainted with you." He was close enough for me to smell the venison he'd eaten not long ago.

My hand strayed to Davor's knife on my belt.

"This seems a strange way to make introductions." I kept my chin high, holding his gaze though he was trying to glare me into submission.

"The chief seems taken with you. Perhaps I want to know what kind of woman you are."

It almost made me flinch and I wondered that a few moments of conversation between Davor and me had caused such a stir.

"One tired of smelling your breakfast."

His hand closed around my wrist, squeezing tight, keeping me from pulling the knife.

"This is your sister?" Makar looked past me. Tinek stirred again, but the warriors pushed back. I did not dare look around to see if anyone was close enough to help.

"She is."

"How lucky am I to meet the *dronni's* family?" A smile spread over his face and his hold on my arm tightened. My fingers were beginning to tingle.

"I want to know a few things, *Marta*."

I hated my name coming from his mouth.

"And what is that?" I asked through gritted teeth.

"Why a woman like you would subject herself to a man like Davor? Surely you do not want to submit to him. I know what kind of man his father and Kamil were. Help me and I can help you."

Some gentleness crept into his voice, and he loosened his hold to accentuate it.

The same heat as the night before rose to my face in response to his suggestive comments, but there was a probing edge to them.

"If this is what your help would be like, perhaps I do not want it."

A mocking half-smile turned up his mouth. "Then perhaps I will just move on to asking what you know of him, his plans?"

"You expect him to broadly announce his plans to everyone?" This time I forced a scoff. "No wonder you cannot find a way to beat him."

"So he does not trust you?" The pity was back, and my skin crawled under it. "Does he only have one use for you?"

Words locked up in my throat this time, and the triumph was shining in his eyes, thinking he had a victory, something he could hold over me, or over Davor.

"Makar." Davor's deep voice cut in, and a new chill rushed down my arms at the tight fury contained there.

Makar smiled at me and stepped away, turning his attention to Davor.

"Chief." He bowed mockingly.

"Is there something you need, or are you intent on pushing your way into places you are not wanted?" The iron had not fallen from Davor.

Makar stood more relaxed, perhaps more confident with his

men still keeping Tinek back and me still in reach of him.

"Just getting to know our *dronni* a little better."

Davor looked to me and at his slight nod, I nudged Vanda into motion with me, sliding along the wall until we were closer to Davor.

The warriors gave way, letting Tinek have a clearer path to us.

"And just making sure that her honor stayed intact." Makar cast a loaded look at Tinek, the older warrior not hesitating to show his angry scorn with the comment.

Stillness shrouded closer around Davor and I edged back another step, worried that violence might explode if someone moved too suddenly.

Makar broke off first, signaling his men. They moved away, Makar still facing off with Davor. It left me with a sickening feeling that he might have figured out something about Davor from the words exchanged.

There were several others around, watching. Some I knew were among those trusted by Davor and Alik. I was tired of the looks, tired of the words said aloud or left in expressions. Of the way many were judging me, judging him, for the actions of others.

I touched Davor's arm. I'd give them something different to talk about. Show them how different he was, that I was not afraid of him.

His attention swung to me, halting at whatever he saw in my face. A crease appeared between his eyes.

"Are you—?"

I pushed up slightly on my toes and pressed my lips to his. His stillness rushed around me, not faltering as my hand brushed his chest. My heart raced like it never had before. There was a faint touch of his hand against my elbow before he pulled away.

And there was nothing but terrifying storms in his eyes as I looked up at him.

"Do not," he said softly, "play games with me."

Before I could protest, he signaled to Tinek. "We are leaving."

Vanda cast a wide-eyed look at me. I hugged her quickly before Davor could leave me behind.

"Are you all right?" she whispered in my ear.

"I will be fine." My arm still stung from Makar's hold, but not as much as my heart did from Davor's response.

He waited a few paces away and let me step up beside him before beginning to walk away. Makar hadn't gone far, sharply watching us both.

We did not stop until the bridge. Tinek fell well behind at my look and I halted.

"Davor."

He whirled on me and I very nearly flinched.

"Why did you do that?" he snapped.

I refused to draw back. "I thought it might help. I thought—"

"No. You didn't think!" Anger blazed in his eyes. "Now they will freely target you. Now they think there might be a weakness in this house."

"Or maybe others in the tribe will see us standing together." Makar's words, Vanda's speculations had stung more than I'd thought, making me doubt everything more. "See us being different from your brothers and father. Did you not think of that?"

His eyes narrowed. "And who is to say they think that?"

I tossed my hands. "Everyone. Perhaps I am tired of walking these paths and hearing that there is only one use for me in your lodge!"

"It's just words."

His dismissiveness stung again. "It is not to me."

Suddenly he loomed closer. "So you would give them more to throw at you with your actions just now? You cannot give anything to anyone."

I shook my head just as sharply. "Perhaps you need to trust, Davor. You cannot spend your life planning and scheming!"

"Do not tell me how I should live my life." A chill ran through me at his voice. Colder than iron and just as sharp.

It had never been directed at me, and I suddenly understood some of the fear the tribe had for Davor, son of the chief.

Some wordless order passed from him to Tinek, wisely still standing away from our argument. And then he strode away, leaving me on the bridge.

I had half a thought to just go back to my family's lodge, but that might look like defeat. Instead, I forced my feet to move and went straight to Inge's lodge. It had almost started to feel like a new home in the last counting, but now stepping inside, I felt out of place once again. Something with an awkward edge making things uncomfortable with how it didn't fit.

Tinek fell into place outside as I gently shut the door.

"Marta?" Nina's quiet voice brought me slowly turning, shoulders hunching up towards my ears. Davor's mother stood at the table, flour dusted over its surface and her hands as she mixed a new batch of flatbread in the light of the afternoon sun streaming through the open windows.

"What's wrong?" she asked, rubbing her hands together, flakes of dough falling to the table like odd snow.

"Nothing." I certainly did not want to tell his mother of all people what I had done. I did not want to lose her kindness for she would surely be on her son's side.

"I do not believe that." Nina smiled softly. "Come." She pointed to the bench on the other side of the table from her.

I inched forward as she went and poured two cups of hot water over dried leaves and petals.

She set one in front of me and returned to her kneading while letting hers cool. I traced over the etched surface of the cup.

"Is it Davor?"

I looked up to find a bit of wryness there. "How did you know?"

"You two left together, and you came back alone with a look about you." She dusted her hands and picked up the mug, blowing curling steam gently away.

It took a moment, and nearly scalding my tongue on the hot tea, before I could make myself slowly tell her everything that had happened from Makar to my perhaps ill-advised kiss.

But Nina was not angry. Instead she nodded and took a seat on the bench across from me, the dough forgotten a moment.

"There might have been a girl once." She smiled sadly. "But it did not take him long to learn that she was working for Kamil. But maybe not soon enough for the damage to be done. He guards his heart so tightly."

I stared at my hands, wishing I knew why I felt so spurned by his response. There was a moment where I thought he might have kissed me back.

"He has learned over his whole life to not trust others. To see motives in every small thing."

"I thought it might help," I whispered softly to my cup.

A scuff brought my head up to find Nina leaning on the table, hand extended. I took the offer and let her squeeze my hand.

"And?" she gently prompted.

"And perhaps I am tired of everyone thinking that I am be-ing…used, and them thinking the worst of me…of him."

Her fingers tightened around mine. "I know what you feel, except it was true of me."

My heart broke at the look in her eyes.

"It has never truly gone away for me, but I did not have someone who might care for me."

"I think I ruined any friendship we might have started."

Nina shook her head. "I don't think so. Don't be afraid to talk to him. Davor has a gentle heart buried in there still. Per-haps you could help bring it out again."

Heat rose up to touch my cheeks.

"He does care about you. I can see it. He will not stay angry for long. Talk with him, be honest. Just…never lie to him." Nina squeezed my hand again and released it to curl her hands around her mug.

"I don't ever want to hurt him." I needed her to know that. Understand him a little more, maybe see that smile one day. But never hurt him.

"I know," she reassured.

"How do you do it?" I blurted after a moment. "Walk through the villages every day with people looking at you like…" My gaze fixed on the tea again.

"I suppose after twenty-seven years, I am used to it." Wry weariness surrounded her.

"I'm sorry," I whispered.

Her shoulders lifted. "It's what I taught Davor. Sharp words are intended to stick in you, to carve at your heart until you are as bloody and miserable as the ones who spoke them. But they cannot hurt you if you wear armor of iron."

Her smile flickered sadly. "It caused both of us to shield our heart from many things. It took me time to learn how to care for him like a mother. At first, all I saw was—the chief in him."

I curled my cold fingers around the mug.

"He was eleven months old, bravely pulling himself up onto a bench. I watched, wondering if I would care if he fell or hurt himself, when he smiled at me. Just a wide smile, proud of himself, babbling like he was demanding my praise." A faraway look took over her face. "I felt then what the earth must feel when winter suddenly gives way to spring."

She looked to me again. "And I knew that I was not going to let him go the way of his father."

"I've wondered what he might be like if he smiled," I confessed, that warmth sneaking up to my cheeks again.

Nina smiled fondly. "Guard your heart on that day."

The heat grew upon my cheeks and I took a hasty drink of tea.

She chuckled lightly and pushed up to standing. "Would you like to help me finish?"

She hadn't directly invited me to help her yet, both her and Inge keeping me out of some of the tasks they had clearly formed into years-long routine.

"I would like that." I smiled and stood to join her and plan out what I might say to Davor the next time I saw him.

But he did not return the rest of the day. Or for dinner. It was just Michal and Janne and I at the table, Nina having gone to help Inge with a birth in a lodge across the village.

Michal looked to the door as often as we did, the frown creasing deeper between his eyes as minutes passed without sign of Davor.

"Where did he go?" I finally asked.

"To discuss things with some pack leaders here in the village. He said I did not have to stay." Michal frowned at the door.

Janne and I turned to clearing the table and putting away the food. After a moment and a silent agreement, we filled a plate and covered it with a cloth, leaving it on the hearth for him.

Finally I settled on a stool by the fire with a piece of cream-colored cloth, needle and thread in hand, stitching cornflowers along the edge. It would go to one of the women from the lodge next to my family's who would have her first child any day now. Janne dragged Michal to help scrub the plates and mugs.

I fell into the rhythm of the stitches, needle sinking in and out of the cloth as I hummed a slow lullaby every child in the tribe had heard.

The tune died on my lips as the lodge door creaked open and shut. My fingers clenched around the cloth, needle stabbing harder through the cloth. I did not dare look up yet to see if he might still be angry with me.

A thud jerked my attention up.

Davor leaned heavily on the table, head bowed, and one hand pushed up against his side. Firelight glinted off red staining his tunic. He shifted and kept walking, finally collapsing on one of the benches against the wall. A faint gasp escaped as his head thudded back against the wall. I sat frozen. Biting his lip, he looked down.

Blood had followed him from the table to the bench and seeped through his fingers. The needle fell from my hand and I strode towards him.

"Davor?" Janne's breathless gasp halted me. She rushed to her brother's side, gripping his shoulders.

Paleness rushed across his face. I pushed in.

"Janne, when will your mother be back?"

She looked at me, eyes wide and fearful. "I don't know. It's the woman's first birth. It could be minutes, it could be tomorrow…" She trailed off, looking back at Davor.

"Can you help instead?" I nudged her gently.

"I…"

Davor shakily lifted a hand away and a flicker of lightheadedness prodded me at the sight of the spreading blood.

"Davor!" Michal was there in an instant. "What happened?"

"Ambush leaving the lodge." Davor's bloody hands were slipping and shaking.

"What about Alik?" I asked. There were no cloths nearby except for what I was working on. I ripped the thread and tucked the needle through my skirt before reaching toward his side.

His fingers closed over mine, arresting the motion, but not hurting. A glance up showed his lips pressed together and a look in his eyes I couldn't quite decipher. He suddenly let me go.

"I am sorry." And he pushed his hand back against his side.

I offered the cloth. "For the bleeding. Until we can get some help."

Davor slowly nodded and let me press it against his side. I sank to a knee to better push against the wound. Gingerly, his bloody hand set over mine to keep it in place. But I did not relinquish my hold.

"Alik?" I asked again.

"I'll go find him." Michal headed for the door, vanishing out into the darkness. Janne turned a look of fear to me, one that I felt. What if there was another ambush coming?

"Do you know what to do in the meantime?" I asked her.

Davor's head tipped back against the wall, eyes closed again, but his hand didn't falter over mine.

Janne nodded and headed for Inge's supply room. She went

in and out several times, drawing water from the barrel in the corner and setting it to heat.

I did not move and eventually Davor's eyes cracked open. Something hovered between us, threading between the sounds of the crackling fire and the echo of his trembling breaths under my hand.

Janne came back to stand with us, arms crossing and uncrossing, until she finally set a hand on Davor's shoulder. He turned that half-smile up at her, reassuring, but his grip faltered.

I opened my mouth to ask what to do next, when the door slammed open. I jumped, pressing harder on his side as I whirled around. But it was just Michal with Alik on his heels. Dirt and some blood spattered Alik's face and armor.

He strode over, grabbing Davor's shoulder.

"You all right?" His normally even voice had a hoarse edge.

Davor nodded. "You?"

"Of course I am. I'm wearing *armor.*"

Davor huffed, but had no other reply.

"Let's see." Alik gently touched my arm, nodding in reassurance. I slowly moved away, releasing my hold and letting him peel away the soaked cloth. "Doesn't look too bad."

A noise caught in my throat. "There's so much blood."

Alik touched my hand to bring it back to press over the cloth again.

"Could be worse. Janne, what do you have?"

The two of them moved to drag a bench closer to the fire. Michal stood back by the door, hand on sword, still on guard. Alik and Janne took over, helping Davor up and to the other bench and getting his shirt and tunic off.

I stood back with bloody hands hanging limp by my sides. Three bulky scars raced each other in ragged lines across his back. He painfully got feet up on the bench and lay down, turning his head to the fire, showing a shorter one across the back of his neck where the collar usually hid what his short hair did not.

Alik started cleaning as Janne held another lamp higher. Davor's hand clenched the side of the bench. I could barely watch Alik thread a needle. They both knew what they were doing, but I felt so helpless.

Davor flinched as Alik touched his side.

"Steady," Alik murmured.

But Davor shifted again. The sight pulled me forward. I turned my back to the sight of Alik and the needle and scooped up Davor's hand instead. Drying blood stuck our palms together and I might have gagged at the sensation if Davor had not been staring up at me.

I gently squeezed and he turned his head away from me. That sting of rejection came again, but he did not let go of my hand and I did not release my hold either, letting him clench as tight as he needed as Alik stitched and Janne handed bandages.

As they finished, Davor lay back on the bench, eyes closed. I gently freed my fingers and rested his hand on the bench beside him. Janne squeezed out a fresh cloth and dabbed away at some of the remaining blood. Alik scrubbed his hands clean and beckoned me over.

"Wash up. I know you hate blood." He poured fresh water.

"I…" Red covered my hands and my stomach flipped uncomfortably.

"I don't want to clean up vomit tonight." Alik ushered me forward, taking my wrists and dipping them in the water.

My stomach settled enough for me to scrub with the soap he handed me.

"Thank you for your help," Alik said.

"I didn't do anything." I lifted my hands out, relieved to see clean skin.

"I think you did," he said thoughtfully. "I need to go, but there will be a few extra warriors outside. Make him rest here for a little while."

Janne and I promised our obedience, and Alik disappeared back out the door after a brief whispered aside to Michal.

"What happened?" We both went to Michal where he pulled on armor.

He shrugged. "I don't know much yet, but it sounds like Makar finally made a strike."

A shiver raced down my arms and I hugged them to my stomach. Would he have done something to me earlier if Davor had not stepped in? Did Davor regret stepping in?

I looked back over to him. His eyes were closed, and his chest rose and fell evenly like he slept.

Michal cinched up his breastplate and I was suddenly looking at a man older than seventeen and full of more anger than I had ever seen.

Janne reached out, softening his edge for a moment.

"I'll be outside." He buckled on his sword and drew bow and quiver over his shoulder with a rattle of arrows, then stepped through the door. The two of us were left to look at each other.

"I need to clean things." Janne rubbed her arms.

"I'll sit with him for now." I touched her arm. She mustered a smile, and I pulled her into my arms like I might for Vanda when she was trying too hard to be strong. Janne returned it fiercely, shoulders shaking with a faint sob.

"You did well." I rubbed between her shoulder blades.

"No, I froze. I could have helped him…I…" She hiccupped, tucking her face more against my shoulder.

"It's all right, Janne," I hushed. "You knew what to do when Alik came."

"What if he hadn't come?"

"You don't have to think that, because he did. And I think next time you'll be ready."

Janne pulled away, tears still streaking her face. "You think so?"

My hands rested on her shoulders. "I do. Now, go clean up."

She scrubbed her sleeve across her cheeks and moved slowly away, pausing by Davor again. The small lamp had been left on the table and I shifted it a little to better see his pale face.

His discarded shirt and tunic lay on the floor, ripped and bloody. I picked them up one by one, gingerly turning them over. His undershirt lay beneath them, the lighter grey covered in dull scarlet. Turning it over in my hands, I risked a glance at his bare chest, feeling that odd heat rise to my cheeks again.

A bundle of cloth lay by his feet. With a short sigh, I recognized the blanket I had been working on, but there was not much regret in me at having used it to stop the bleeding.

It was irreversibly ruined, covered in blood that no amount of soaking would bring out.

"I'm sorry." Davor's voice, quiet and a little hoarse, almost had me jumping.

"For what?" I turned to him.

There was a bit of haziness in his eyes, but each blink was bringing clarity back. "You've been working on that for two days."

My fingers tightened on the cloth. He'd noticed?

"It's all right." I smiled. "But I think I can salvage some of your clothes."

A grimace tightened his face as he slowly started to sit up. My hand hovered beside his arm, not sure if he needed, or wanted, my help.

"Are you sure you should move?"

He did not answer, instead asking his own question. "Where is Alik?"

"He had to leave, but he left a few warriors here. Michal is outside as well," I said.

Davor's head flew up. "Michal?" Question furrowed his brow.

"He's all right," I said, thinking I knew the reason for his concern. The lines of his shoulders eased, and he looked down at himself, fingers gingerly brushing over the bandage. I tried not to follow the look. I'd never cared about such things, or joined in other young girls' giggling when faced with young men and muscles, but for the first time I understood some of the fascination.

"How do you feel?" My voice squeaked a little.

The frown was twisting up his face. "Fine."

That might have been the most blatant lie ever told to me. "Do you need anything?"

His hands came down to grip the edge of the bench. I tensed, wondering if I could actually catch him if he fell.

"Water. Please."

I set aside the clothes still in my hand and went to pour a cup of water. "We saved some dinner. Would you want something to eat?"

His hands still braced on the bench, and after a moment, he gave a nod. I gave him the water first, exchanging the plate for the empty cup once he finished, and brought it back full. As usual, he only picked at the food, taking more bites of the flat-bread than anything.

I set the water down beside him and claimed my stool, tucking hands in my lap to worry at each other. Nina had told me to talk to him. With him sitting there looking more worn out than anything, it seemed like it should be easy to. But the memory of his storming anger was all too fresh.

He wasn't really looking at me either, and I hated the uncertainty clouding up between us. Gathering courage and squeezing fingers together one more time for strength, I started.

"Davor?"

His dark eyes turned up to me, and the firelight caught in them for a moment, a pinpoint beacon in the midst of the storm.

"I wanted to apologize for today. You were right. I wasn't thinking. Well, no more than what I said. But I do not plan. I've never had to. But I should have asked, and I am sorry."

He made no reply, and I almost couldn't hold his solemn gaze. I shifted to perhaps withdraw and maybe keep nursing my wounded pride when he spoke.

"I am sorry as well for what I said afterwards. You…you caught me by surprise. I was…harsh, and I am sorry."

I offered a small smile. "Start fresh tomorrow?"

"I would like that." The almost smile appeared again.

For two breathless moments, our gazes stayed on one another. Then he shifted, a grimace shadowing his face as he stood.

I stayed at his side, lamp in hand, neither of us saying anything as he limped to his room. It was the first time I had been inside, and I felt guilty to have invited myself in. A small table sat beside the bed, and I set the lamp atop it.

Davor eased down onto the bed—big enough for two, I nervously estimated—managing to undo the laces of his boots and shove them off. A bench against the wall had meager stacks of clothes, bringing back my promise to make more for him.

My heart stammered over itself as I nudged the lamp again like I was making sure it was set correctly before turning to him. He shoved back the blankets and started to lie down. I reached for the blankets, both of us pausing as I did, but he did not say anything as I drew them over him.

"Good night." My tongue very nearly tripped on the simple words, and I retreated, placing a door between me and him, like the action would shut off the nagging thought that my heart might well already be in danger from him.

THIRTY-SEVEN

DAVOR

"You look like *scata*."

I grunted, not bothering to open my eyes to see Emil leaning against the wall across from me. At least this time I hadn't jumped. It was finally something to distract me from the disgust at myself for causing the fear in Marta's eyes yesterday after she'd kissed me. It had followed me all day after I'd practically run away on the bridge. Left for a moment during the ambush.

Not quite quelled in the moment when she'd come to stand beside me as Alik stitched. Or the one after where we'd apologized to each other.

I opened my eyes, shoving the thoughts that had still come back. Heavy clouds promising rain kept the early morning darkness lingering.

"Is that concern?" I asked.

Emil's scoffs were holding less and less vitriol. Or maybe it was the exhaustion hanging on to every muscle that dulled my sense for it.

"I need you to stay alive for now. That's all."

"Of course," I solemnly agreed.

He rolled his eyes. "I am wondering if you have an aversion to armor."

This time I glared at him. A smirk lifted one side of his mouth.

"It's open war now," I said.

The faint humor vanished from him. "Close enough. He'll wait to see how you weathered last night. It was known that you left with a wound, and that was his intent."

Makar had not been at the ambush, so I could not accuse him directly. He would only deny it anyway. One of his followers had led it and was currently sitting in the guard lodge with a few other warriors who had not been able to flee in time, waiting for me and Alik to go question them.

I grimaced around a curse as I shifted forward, hand pressed against my side. Ache stabbed between my ribs and some blood had spotted the bandage when I'd carefully pulled new clothes on. Lightheadedness fluttered with every movement, and it took a second and a focused breath to keep it back.

When I looked back, Emil had shifted, watching me with wary eyes. And I finally realized what was different about him every time we'd met.

"No fox cloak?" I asked.

A confused frown twisted his face for a moment, then he gave a short laugh.

"No." He shifted his shoulders, but it did not seem like he missed the weight of the cloak that had marked him for years. "That was Kamil's order."

There was no missing over the name either. A bit of understanding crept in, making sense of some of his past words in this space.

"I always thought an eel might suit you better," I said.

Emil stared at me, then another short laugh filled up the space between us, something almost real this time. My own mouth tilted a little. Emil scuffed a boot against the ground, shaking his head.

"A fox was too obvious, I thought."

My feet braced a little wider against the ground and my arm pushed against my stomach and side, almost like I needed to ready myself for more words. I was so tired of fighting, of pointed words, of donning my armor over and over each morning. Perhaps this was another thing I could try at.

"You were right," I said, and his eyebrows shot up. "I didn't know many things."

After a moment he asked softly, "Would we have changed any-thing if we did?"

"I don't know."

A low growl of thunder followed up my words, a judgment from the sky itself on the mess between us.

He gathered a breath, then tilted his head, and said something maybe different than what he meant to say.

"Tell your *dronni* to be ready for more words." He pushed away from the wall. "She has withstood Makar well enough, but he is not finished throwing things her way."

He vanished around the corner, leaving silence in his wake. A few raindrops left fading marks in the dirt. More and more started to fall, and I slowly rose and made my way back inside.

Michal had come back inside sometime after my stepping out. He leaned one elbow on the table, straps of his armor half-undone, his eyes slipping lower and lower in exhaustion. With a faint smile, I went to him, and touched his shoulder.

He jolted awake, half to his feet with hand on knife before he recognized me. I tapped his shoulder, keeping him on the bench, and reached for the straps of his breastplate.

"You all right?" Michal barely smothered a yawn.

"Just tired. You?"

He helped me lift off the armor.

"Exhausted," he admitted and let me loosen his bracers and slide them off.

My fist knocked his shoulder gently. "You did well last night."

The pride lighting his eyes was enough for me.

"Go get some rest."

He yawned again. "I'll clean this first." He gathered it up and stumbled over to his bench, digging in his chest for oil to work into the leather.

The light clatter woke Janne. She bolted upright, looking around first at Michal, then to me. She was on her feet and throwing her arms around me before I could barely blink.

"I'm so sorry!"

"For what?" I returned her hug, trying not to wince at how tightly she squeezed my aching side.

"Alik had to come and do everything."

"Not as I remember it," I said gently.

"That's what I told her," Marta's voice interrupted. She sat up on her bench, blankets piled around her waist and shawl wrapped around her shoulders.

Janne sniffed and pulled away from me, turning a faint smile at the both of us.

"Is Inge back?" I asked.

She shook her head. "Nina came back in the middle of the night for more herbs. Said it was taking a long time."

I stiffened at that, ready to go out and make sure Mother had made it back until Michal spoke up.

"I saw her back to the lodge myself."

My shoulders fell in relief. He returned my nod.

"Then would you be able to check my side?" I asked Janne.

"Give me a few minutes." She moved away with purpose, any trace of her hesitation gone. Michal set his armor aside and lay down, pulling blankets up over his head.

I risked a glance at Marta, but she was looking down, a frown in place. Something lurched inside me at the way she gingerly brushed fingers over her forearm. My feet took me to her side before I fully realized, and fury washed over me at the darkened rings on her skin.

"What is this from?" I asked.

Her hand fisted as she lifted her forearm a little. "Makar I think." The slight tremor in her voice stabbed through me.

"May I see?" I tried to keep my voice even, but from the look she turned up as she extended her hand, I don't think I quite managed it.

One hand cupped under her wrist, and my fingers gingerly brushed over her bruised forearm. I froze at how close I'd gotten in my sudden concern, not sure what frightened me more—how quick I'd moved to her, or the way my fury at Makar had spiked even higher.

"Will I live?" Her voice was light.

And just like that, some of my anger washed away like the rain pouring down outside in a sudden rush. A faint smile lightened her face and I found myself returning it.

"It seems likely. Are you all right?" I asked quietly after another moment.

We both stared at my hand still cupped around her arm. Marta tugged her shawl closer around her shoulders, not moving from my hold.

"I think so," she finally replied.

"I am sorry it happened."

She lifted her arm away and before I could feel anything like regret, her fingers closed around mine instead.

"It was not your doing."

I did not see how that might make me feel any different.

"I never thanked you for being there and stopping him."

Earnestness lingered about her, and I did not quite know what to do with it.

Instead my fingers closed a little tighter around hers. "I do not think he will leave that matter alone."

Marta's lips dipped into a frown, but she did not release my hand or her determination when she replied, "I might refuse to give him the satisfaction."

That brought another faint smile and an emotion I did not quite understand. "Good."

Stillness wrapped around us, and I don't know how long we might have stayed there, hands twined together for the first time since the binding, but a clatter against the table brought our attention over to Janne.

She set bandages out, checking over her shoulder to make sure she had not disturbed Michal with the noise. I might have even imagined the regret in Marta's face or the same in my heart as I joined Janne at the table.

Even with her previous confidence, Janne still took a deep breath before unwrapping the bandage around my chest.

"What is that from?" she asked, lifting her chin to indicate the ropy scar above my hip.

"Also Alik's handiwork," I said wryly.

Janne's face twisted and she dabbed ointment over the stitches. "What on earth did he do?"

"Hot knife to close a wound." My throat locked up, and I avoided the way Janne stilled for a telling moment before resuming her work.

I held the clean bandage in place as she wound it around me and tied it off.

"How long has it been since you've been here for a rainy day?" Janne asked.

"Long enough." I smiled.

"You don't have to go anywhere, do you?" Pleading filled her face, but she knew what she was doing. I was already softening, and the rain was pouring down, thunder growling every few minutes.

"Not for a little while at least." I reached for my shirt.

Janne grinned and spun away to return the supplies to the healing room and then to the cook fires.

"Can I ask?" Marta paused beside me, tugging her overdress into place and straightening the belt with my knife.

"Inge, and my mother after she came here, started a tradition on rainy days." My side twinged slightly as I got my tunic on. "Opening windows and doors to watch the rain, baking whatever they wanted, spending the storm telling stories or playing games."

Marta's smile caused an odd shift inside me, like a storm was gathering outside and in.

"Vanda and I used to race each other through the rain to the river to see how angry the water was, and then back to the lodge where we'd make hot drinks and dry off." She rubbed her arms. "Sometimes we still do."

"I don't know when Inge and my mother will be back, but Janne is wasting no time."

Marta smiled. "Did you come here often to join them?" The expression faltered as I paused.

"No," I finally said. "No, I did not."

She backed away, summoning up the smile again, and opened the door, letting a blast of chilled air whip through. "Well then, perhaps I'll go make some pine cakes."

With a wink, she disappeared around the corner, and it did not take long for her and Janne's laughs to fill up the lodge. Michal did not stir. I slowly went to the windows, easing open one of the coverings to see if it could safely stay open without rain soaking the benches underneath.

The eaves kept it safe, and the freshness of the storm snuck through the open windows. I went to lean against the open door. The lodges across the square were squat blurs. Sablecats tucked up under the perches or under eaves, those that had not already bullied their way inside.

Luk raised his head from where he lounged against the wall under the eaves. He did not like being inside very often, and he kept his head up to watch the rain, tail flicking in and out of the shelter he'd claimed. Golden eyes turned to me as if asking me my thoughts on the storm before he turned back, mouth opened as he panted slightly.

He shifted to alertness and I tracked his attention out to the figure rushing towards the lodge under the shelter of a cloak. I stiffened and reached for the knife in the back of my belt. The figure turned into Vanda. She came up short at the sight of me.

"Chief?"

"Come inside." I stepped aside. She edged in, shaking out extra water from the cloak and holding it in an awkward bundle.

I extended a hand, flicking my fingers when she did not hand it over. Hesitantly, she did and brushed some damp bits of hair that had not escaped the rain away from her cheeks.

"Marta is by the cook fires." I pointed the way.

Vanda swallowed and hastily tapped her fist to forehead before hurrying away. I hung the cloak up by the door, unable to stop a small smile as a delighted shriek came from the cook fires.

Michal jolted awake with a muffled curse. He looked to me with blurry eyes.

"Are we under attack?"

I very nearly laughed. "No. But you can take the room if you want more quiet. Or just stay awake."

He rubbed his eyes. "Storm day?"

I nodded. He limped over to me, pulling a blanket around his shoulders.

"You staying?" he asked, like I looked ready to step right out into the storm along with all the other people.

I leaned closer. "Maybe only to beat you at Sabers and Shades."

We'd never done such a thing together, and for a moment, I was afraid he might refuse, but a grin took over his face.

"You're on!"

Within moments, he'd retrieved the hide painted with red and black squares and the pieces from his trunk and laid them on the table. I eased onto the bench and collected the rounded pieces with the dark woods' rune etched atop them, leaving the lighter ash wood pieces shaped like sablecat heads for him.

We were halfway through a game, me with more sablecat pieces captured by my shades, when the women emerged and joined us at the table with plates of fresh flatbread baked with fresh berries and smeared in honey, pine cakes drizzled with more honey, strips of smoked salmon, and beakers of tea.

Marta shyly took a seat by me and offered a pine cake. It took me a moment to realize that she'd remembered what I'd told her countings ago at this very table.

It was still hot, the honey soaking through the top of the cake, but I bit into it anyway. It crumbled perfectly and with her watching me almost anxiously for my verdict, I suddenly had another good memory to associate with them.

"It's good."

Perfect, really.

Marta's smile bloomed and she took her own cake. Suddenly we were so close our sleeves touched.

"I am not good at this game." She propped elbows on the table to watch.

Michal rolled up a piece of flatbread, neatly avoiding the dripping honey, and moved his next piece. It was entirely Marta's fault that I started losing. Or maybe it was Janne and Vanda chattering away like they'd known each other all their lives. Or the way pine cakes kept appearing on my plate, or pieces of dried salmon smeared in hickory paste.

In the end, I let him have the victory, and Janne claimed the next game. She and Vanda teamed up against Michal as he scooted down the table with the board and pieces, taking more food as he went.

Marta took half a pine cake before putting the other half on my plate.

"How much more food are you going to try to trick me into eating?" I asked.

Her eyes widened in mock-surprise. "You think I'd do that?"

I arched an eyebrow and she grinned. "It is the most I think I've seen you eat."

My half disappeared in two quick bites. There was not much point in arguing as even I admitted she was right.

"May I ask you a question?" she said.

I brushed crumbs from my fingers and leaned on the table. She adjusted on the bench to face me, seriousness surrounding her.

"Would you rather be caught in the rain or the snow?"

I tossed a hand, shaking my head as she chuckled. "What are these questions?"

Her laugh grew and she did not retract her question.

"How long am I stuck?"

She lifted her shoulders. "Three hours?"

"Why only three?" I countered.

She wrinkled her nose. "Stop trying to avoid my question."

I rolled my eyes. "Rain then. And what's your answer?"

"Rain, definitely. I hate being cold. Your turn."

"For what?"

"Welcome to the game Vanda and I will play. Think of the most ridiculous question and ask the other. But remember, you have to answer too." She waved at me to start and settled back with an expectant look.

I frowned. "I don't remember agreeing to this."

She placed another pine cake on my plate and held it up in front of my face.

"Fine." I glared, but she grinned again, seeing through the very thin wall I had up. "Fishing or hunting." It was the first thing that came to mind.

"Fishing. I have never liked helping Father clean the kills he brings back."

"Hunting. You can be alone in the woods and not have to answer ridiculous questions."

Marta laughed. "The spirits give you their blessing to turn into any animal at will. Sablecat or something else?"

"How long is this list of questions you have?"

"Infinite." She propped an elbow on the table.

Sablecat hovered on the tip of my tongue, but I paused. "Osprey."

Her head tilted and my reason followed.

"Easier to go wherever I want."

A soft smile played over her face. "Down your river?"

It wasn't my river any more than the forest belonged to man. But that hadn't stopped it calling to me many different times. "Perhaps."

"Otter."

"So you can be a pest even to the fishers?"

She gasped and gently nudged my shoulder, followed quickly by another smile. I crooked one and she stared at me a moment before prodding me again. "Your turn."

"You have to give up one of your senses. Which one?" I asked.

A breath exploded from her and she sat back, mouth puckering in thought. She picked at the pine cake on her plate, still musing. "Not taste." She popped the piece in her mouth. "Maybe feeling? I've pricked myself too many times with a needle." She held up her fingers, showing the callouses on her fingertips. "And maybe then I would never feel cold."

I'd thought I had an answer to my own question. Hearing, so I would never hear *coward* or worse, again. My ears would not betray my heart by gathering all the ways I was feared, hated, derided.

But suddenly that meant not hearing her laugh, her questions. Giving up something else meant not seeing her smile or the way she sometimes looked at me, like perhaps she might care to see past the front I showed everyone. Losing the way she wasn't afraid to reach out and touch me.

"Taste," I finally said.

She leaned closer. "Do you always barely eat?"

"Only when suddenly loaded with responsibility I've tried to avoid all my life." Some bitterness still snuck out.

The teasing left her face and her hand brushed mine on the table. "I think you are doing many good things."

My attention fell to the worn tabletop between my arms. "Well then, I hope I won't disappoint you."

That seemed like it might be unbearable. Her hand hadn't shifted from mine and she squeezed a little.

"Only if you don't like dancing."

I lifted my head and just fixed her with a look which brought another laugh.

"We will work on that," she said.

"Oh, we will?" It was a word loaded with promise I'd never thought of. *We.*

"Yes." And it seemed there might not be much room for argument there. "I don't know how it's done here, but in the middle village we have dances and fires on summer and autumn nights for any reason we can think of."

That was not the way of the upper village for certain. But perhaps with her as *dronni* she could change it. And if it was something that might make her happier in this place, then I might just see it done.

THIRTY-EIGHT

MARTA

"I suppose he is not awful." Vanda leaned her head against my shoulder.

"High praise." I nudged her. The eaves dripped as some bits of sunlight tried to push through the clouds that still threatened more rain.

Davor and Michal had left almost half an hour ago when the rain had slackened to sporadic drizzle. Both in full armor this time, a sight that reassured me in a deeper way than I thought I might ever feel.

"You know why."

I tipped my head against hers. "I do."

Vanda might be coming around to the idea of me being married to Davor—a thing I was slowly getting more comfortable with myself—and seemed to like Michal well enough after the morning, but there was another son of the chief neither of us might be able to forgive.

Just as well that I had barely seen him since coming to the upper village. Had not heard his name mentioned, so perhaps I would be able to avoid him forever. But I wondered if the day was coming that I might confidently ask Davor for some justice for Vanda.

She had not brought it up, and I did not think she would demand it of me, but surely she could not look on Davor and Michal for long and not think of the day Emil had caught her.

"You looked happy enough with him." Vanda's elbow dug into my side.

I huffed annoyance, but braced myself to admit it. "I think I might like him after all."

"Do you really?" Janne's breathless voice interrupted. I half-turned on the bench to see her standing there, cleaning cloth in hand. Hope shone in her eyes, and I softened a bit more. Davor clearly cared about her, and there was a sort of gruff affection emerging between him and Michal.

Vanda shifted to peer up at me from where she still leaned her head on my shoulder.

"I do."

My new sister released a relieved laugh. "Good. I…I just want him to be happy and…" The cloth twisted up in her hands. "I think you make him…less angry sometimes."

"I'll try." I did not have the heart to warn her against hoping for anything more than friendship between me and him.

"Janne, there will be a bonfire tomorrow night if the storm clears. You should come with us." Vanda sat up taller.

Janne's face lit up then just as quickly fell. "Oh, I…I'm…" Her cheeks flushed red. "I'm not usually welcomed at such things."

At least in one thing Davor and I were similar. We might just do anything for this younger sister.

Vanda made a scoffing sound. "You'll have to be now, the sister of the chief who everyone in the middle village is changing the beat of their tune for."

"Are they really?" Janne smiled.

Vanda nodded. "Marta, you are coming, right?"

I exchanged a glance with Janne, both of us thinking the same thing. "We'll ask Davor when he comes back."

"Ask?" A faint scoff filled Vanda's voice, like she did not believe that I needed to do such a thing.

"There is trouble brewing, especially here in the upper village, Vanda." In the minutes spent at Davor's side, I had forgotten about the ambush that had brought him home bloody.

"There is not in the middle village," she said cautiously.

I gave a mirthless smile. "Because Makar and his allies do not live there."

"Is it bad?" she whispered.

"Enough that all of us have a guard any time we leave this lodge." I had gotten so used to it that I barely thought anything of the warrior trailing me. "There was a fight last night."

"Oh." Vanda sat back.

"But we'll ask," I reassured Janne. She nodded, the hope coming back.

It did not fade through the rest of the day when Nina and Inge came back, bringing with them piles of cloths to be washed and new herbs to be crushed and prepared for later use. Vanda sneakily excused herself from the cleaning as she nearly always managed to do.

But the four of us threw ourselves into the work. The rain had brought a shift in the air and it almost seemed like there might be something good coming.

Davor was distant again at dinner. At least until I mustered my courage and said his name. The quickness with which his attention came to me almost knocked my breath away.

"There is a dance in the middle village tomorrow night. I wondered if Janne and I might go. Perhaps anyone else who wanted." I looked to Nina and Inge still sitting at the table as well.

Davor glanced around and halted on Janne where she leaned forward in her seat, hands squeezed in her lap. Then to me.

"I will find some extra warriors to be there."

Janne's grin brought one from me and I turned on Michal next.

"Perhaps Michal can come as well."

Michal's expression was equal parts terrified and interested, and I tried not to laugh too much.

"If you want to," Davor told him, but there was a twitch to his mouth.

"What about you?" Michal looked almost pleading.

"I have business in the lower village tomorrow." The iciness crept up around Davor again. "This could be your excuse to not come with me." A few bits chipped away.

Michal shifted on his bench, like he might not want to admit to either thing. I caught a look Davor gave me and thought I might understand.

"You should come, Michal. It will be fun. And since Davor does not dance, I will need someone in this family to join me."

Davor's lips flattened, but I was starting to know his looks. He was not upset, but was maybe trying to hide an annoyed sort of smile. I scrunched my nose back.

"All right." There was a little more confidence in Michal's voice.

"Perfect!" I leaned on the table and set my sights on the older women. "Now to convince the other two at this table."

"Oh, I don't know," Inge protested, waving her hands, but Janne immediately set in to persuade her.

Nina however, returned my look with a curiously evaluating one. I tipped my head, knowing she'd marked the small exchange between me and Davor—a thing that was starting to feel more comfortable again. But more than that, perhaps we were both thinking of the words we'd exchanged. How hard it was sometimes for us both to walk the villages, how ready we were for something different, though I had only experienced it for countings instead of a lifetime.

"Perhaps I will." Nina tipped her chin a little higher.

I nodded. I needed someone to show me how to carry myself with iron, and I wanted to show her that perhaps she did not need to wear her armor so tightly.

Inge was convinced quickly after and we spent more time planning what needed to be done. At some point Davor quietly left, but not before I managed a smile up at him and nearly got one in return.

I took another victory the next day when I convinced Janne and Nina to come with me to a lodge in the upper village that supported Davor to begin work on a wall hanging for the new lodge. Several women of the lodge, and a few from others, met me there and we began planning out the pattern on the cloth given by Lene.

Conversation was slow at first, some initially wary of Nina, but it was not the way of women with a group task at hand to ignore one member for long.

I wanted to see how Davor might react to his mother walking with more confidence, but he had been gone before breakfast. And no sign of him by evening as we left for the middle village. I tried not to worry. It was not the first time he'd been gone all day, but Michal had been in and out.

The village welcomed me at least, the others getting wary looks. But my old lodge followed mine and Vanda's example, and brought us all into their place around the fire in the lodge square.

Any movement on the outskirts of the gathering drew my gaze and it took many times before I admitted to myself that I might be looking for Davor.

Even then I was not prepared for the odd skip-thump in my chest when I saw him on the edge of the firelight, Alik beside him. Davor's eyes met mine. His expression did not shift, but it felt like something had sprung into place connecting us. I wondered if he felt it too. It drew me toward him as he also moved.

"You came." The obvious statement came a little breathless from me.

"Alik would not take no for an answer." A faint tug came at his mouth.

Alik laughed beside him. "I just like seeing everyone's reactions."

A grin lifted my lips at the vaguely annoyed look Davor shot him.

"Come." I beckoned them further into the gathering. As always, a path parted before us, but not many looks were of fear or anger. Instead, the warriors and huntsmen greeted him with that tap to chest, and a few others dared to mimic it. Davor's face did not shift, but he offered nods and the set of his shoulders eased a little by the time we made it to his family.

Alik pulled Janne into the circle of dancers and Davor's features softened more at the sight of her laughter. Nina and Inge stood with my mother and a few other women of the lodge, conversation flowing easily.

"Thank you for this." He looked to me.

I inclined my head. "I never thought about what it must be like for them until..." I rubbed my arms. The way Nina laughed made her look like her son. A touch to my arm brought me looking up at him. Regret formed in his eyes, but I shook my head.

"I wanted to make a change too, and that is what I will do."

My breath caught for a moment looking back at him and the way he seemed to look through me. I broke away first, afraid to hold it for long and maybe have him keep seeing bits of me I didn't even know I held.

The dance ended and Janne and Alik tried to convince Inge to join him with the dancers. Vanda pulled Michal out, his feet staggering a little.

"Are you sure you do not dance?" I turned a sly look at Davor that he returned with a flattening of his lips. I chuckled.

"You do not come to many of these?" I gestured out to the firelight and dancers.

"A few countings ago would you have welcomed me here?"

I opened my mouth, then shut it, so as not to tell a lie. "Well, if you *insist* on being right..."

But his lips tilted up.

"How was your day?" he asked after a moment.

"Good. The tapestry is coming along well. And"—I dared to nudge his arm—"from all the talk, many don't know quite what to do with you."

"There's a few who know exactly what they want to do," he said wryly.

"They don't matter." I waved a hand dismissively and he

arched an eyebrow. "Some of the women of the upper village were talking about how hard it is sometimes for widows to make their own place in lodges. I said I would speak with you on it."

But the look he returned was an evaluating one. "What would you do about it?"

I paused, hand reaching to tug at my overdress.

"You are *dronni*," he said. "Some of these decisions can be yours as well as mine."

"You think so?"

We had no way of knowing what a *dronni* might do, and knew all too well what a chief might.

He shrugged. "Why not? I do not know the way of some things, but you might."

There was no challenge in his eyes, just a steady look back at me like he really believed I could do it. And I wanted to for him. Wanted to show him that I would stand with him and help shoulder some of his burdens.

"I will think on it. Maybe I could ask you before I make a decision?"

He inclined his head, and we turned to watching the dancing in front of us. Michal escaped from Vanda and came to join us.

"It's not so bad, is it?" I teased. He'd grumbled a little under his breath the whole way across the bridge.

Michal wrinkled his nose. "Maybe not," he reluctantly admitted.

I grinned, and gently touched Davor's arm. "I'll get some ale."

I tilted a look over my shoulder as I threaded my way through the crowd to the food tables. Davor said something and Michal shook his head, shoving Davor's shoulder. It made the grin flicker. Michal returned the expression with an eyeroll and a broader smile.

SABER'S PRIDE

Alik joined them, and more words exchanged. Davor shook his head, but the smile was fighting its way out again. Alik's head tilted back with a laugh. I paused longer to watch. There was an easiness with how the three of them talked, and it seemed like some of the anger swirling around the two brothers faded away with it.

My father joined them, and it sent some warmth through me to see Davor give that almost smile and my father easily joining in their conversation.

"*Dronni.*" A voice jerked my attention back to my immediate surroundings. I gave Alik's father a smile and bowed my head respectfully.

"It's hard to know how to answer that when you've chided me for poor behavior many a time."

Lev chuckled. "Imagine how I feel calling my son Battlelion then."

Our laughs mingled and I asked the woman at the table for three mugs of ale. My father already held his own mug.

"Can I help you carry them?" Lev asked, even though he leaned on his cane. There was something in his voice that gave me a slight pause. "I would like to speak to the chief."

I nodded and took two of the mugs. Lev scooped up the third. My walk back to them was slower to account for his old battle injury, and I suddenly did not know how to talk to him. Alik's face shifted to something slightly guarded as we approached and I wondered at it. Davor caught the motion and stiffened as well, any hint of the easiness vanishing.

"Chief." Lev handed the mug to Davor and leaned on his cane.

I quickly handed one to Alik and the other to Michal, who had gone just as watchful as the others.

"This is my father, Lev." Alik made the introduction.

Davor and the old warrior locked in some sort of stare, then Lev shifted, stacking his hands atop his cane.

"My son speaks highly of you, Chief."

"He has been a good friend." Davor's voice stayed even, but a faint grin broke through Alik's wariness.

"That's his way." Lev cleared his throat. "I've had issue with you and your line, there's no denying it." He tapped the cane against the ground. "It's no easy thing for a man to admit he might be wrong."

Davor shifted slightly, enough for me to see some confusion. My father tilted his mug, watching Lev with a knowing expression, like he might know what was coming.

"Alik also confessed to something else, and I've been thinking on it for days. I will admit we have not seen eye-to-eye about you these countings."

Davor flicked a glance to Alik who shrugged, not denying it. If they had, it had been in private since word of it had not reached me through Vanda.

"I heard what you did for my oldest son in the Blackpaw war." Lev's voice caught and he gruffly covered with a clearing of his throat.

Davor's fingers curled up to his palm, then back out. "I wish it had been different," he said, and Lev nodded. Alik's gaze fell to his mug and his eyes closed a long moment.

"Alik is not often wrong in his assessment of people and things. It seems I should have listened." Lev stuck out his hand and it took a moment before Davor clasped it. Lev nodded again then stamped off.

My father tapped Davor's shoulder, holding for a moment like he sometimes did when reassuring us on some matter, then followed behind Lev, the two older men now locked in some conversation together.

Alik released a breath, covering maybe how his eyes glistened for a second. "I wasn't sure if he was going to punch you or not."

"Me neither," Davor said, glancing at his hand.

A laugh broke from Alik and he tossed back a drink. "If he's decided to throw in behind you, some of the other hardheaded old men won't be far behind."

"Was that your plan in making me come tonight?"

The battlelion shrugged and draped an arm around Michal's shoulders. "It was worth the chance." And he steered Michal away to join a group of other warriors.

The frown lingered on Davor's face but it did not seem upset, more like weighing.

I leaned closer. "Alik does not often scheme, but when he does, you should be careful."

Davor's brow raised as he turned to me.

"And yes, I know this from experience. Although, you should ask him about the time I got my revenge."

His look did not abate, and I grinned under it. "He could have shattered a rock with the force of his scream."

A smile twitched, and I tapped his arm.

"Come. I don't think you and my mother have formally met."

He paused a little longer, then followed me. My mother was gracious enough. Perhaps she had softened with speaking with his mother and Inge. And I did not miss the smile of thanks Nina shot me as I stood at his side when some of the huntsmen came over to greet him respectfully.

It did not take long for him to shift and tilt his empty mug.

His glance around the square held a flash of something. He jolted a little when I said his name, but gave me his attention.

"I am almost ready to leave if you are? It would be best to leave together?"

He nodded sharply, seeming to have lost his few words. I took his mug and returned it to the food tables, collecting a reluctant Janne from my sister as I went. Vanda pressed a kiss to my cheek and hugged Janne before we went. The guards fell in around us as we made our way with more farewells from the square and back across the bridge.

The quiet stayed between us as we entered the lodge, but before he disappeared into his room, he gave me a bit of a smile that left me with a sort of warmth that lingered long after I'd burrowed into my furs to fall asleep.

THIRTY-NINE

DAVOR

My lighter steps across the lodge square the next morning were halted at the sight of Alik nudging a bloody Michal along. Dread rose in my gut, not assuaged by the stubborn jut of Michal's jaw.

"What happened?" I demanded, reaching their side with strides much quicker than theirs.

Michal shoved arms across his chest, glaring at the ground when Alik turned attention to him. The battlelion waited a few seconds, but Michal did not relent.

"Caught him fighting with a few other warriors. I got over there before knives were drawn."

I turned a sharp glance to Michal, but he did not move.

"Michal?"

His shoulders tensed but when he looked up, there was only frustrated anger. "They were saying things about you."

"Things have always been said about me." I wanted to deflect the way I felt about this half-brother stepping to my defense.

Sharpness filled the shake of his head. "You didn't hear them."

But they were always meant to be heard.

"Just because you pretend not to care, or don't do anything about it, doesn't mean I don't have to." The spark in his eyes was growing brighter.

"You cannot react to every little thing." I did not want to be having this conversation in the lodge square in full view of curious villagers.

But his jaw only jutted more. "They were saying things about Marta too."

Despite myself, I jolted a little. "What things?"

"It is not to me," her words echoed back just as clear as the day she'd said them on the bridge. It did not seem fair that words meant to cut and score might be thrown her way.

Michal's look was one of slight betrayal that I'd care more about Marta's honor than mine. Alik shifted to mirror my alertness. Michal glanced around, digging his boot into the dirt.

"They were saying…they were calling her things…"

"Our mothers have heard all our lives?" I finished wryly.

He nodded, and Alik softened slightly.

"You all right?" I finally asked.

Michal scrubbed a bit of drying blood from the corner of his mouth. "You should see them."

Alik huffed. "He's right, but I have already assigned them to working on the lodge for the next four days. I did not know what you wanted done with him."

Michal immediately stiffened and Alik winced, seeing the change his words had wrought on both of us.

"That's not...he's technically your heir."

Michal edged back a step, caution filling up the lines of his shoulders. It brought a clamminess to my palms I hadn't felt in a long time.

"Ah, Chief, I'm glad I found you and the battlelion together." Makar's unwelcome voice cut in. I slowly turned, my fingers curling into fists.

"I'd heard tales of Michal instigating fights on the training grounds. One of my packmates was hurt in the scuffle. I came to see what the punishment would be."

His voice was loud enough to bring further attention to us. Michal turned his glare to Makar. A few other warriors began to circle up, along with Tinek. A brief flash of concern spiked through me before remembering that Artem was on duty with Marta in the lower village.

"Unless you will forgive him his actions?" The challenge came again. "Clearly the battlelion can't control his own warriors."

Alik settled a hand on his hilt, but I shook my head slightly.

"Yes, tell your runt to stand down." Makar leaned closer to keep the words between us.

"Want to see how sharp my teeth are, Makar?" Alik edged his sword slightly out of the sheath. Makar raised an eyebrow, and the scraping of iron against leather sounded around us.

I lifted a hand. Michal's focus honed in on me, that fear still lurking.

"Battlelion, you have assigned the other warriors involved to labor with the lodge?"

"I have, Chief." Alik's voice rang back clear though his focus did not leave Makar.

"Then it is best that Michal is kept apart to prevent any further fights. Two days' work in the fields should do it."

Michal ducked his head but not before relief flickered. Alik nodded. Some around turned away, satisfied maybe for the moment, but Makar was not.

"A pithy punishment, Chief. Your father would have chosen something to remind everyone of their place within the villages and packs."

My boot scraped the dirt as I turned deliberately to face him. "I am not my father."

"So you keep reminding us," Makar sneered softly. "You're nowhere near strong enough to be him."

He strode away with the confidence of victory. I did not have to look around to see the flashes of agreement in the warriors and villagers still lurking about.

"Davor." Michal stepped up beside me.

"No more fighting." I forced myself to meet his gaze.

His scowl came back full force. "So you want me to just stand back and do nothing when they demean you?"

I tried to muster patience. "It only gives them more to throw at you."

But he shook his head, stubbornness radiating from him. "Maybe they won't have anything to say if they don't have teeth."

"Michal." The sharpness leaked out anyway. Alik's eyes were full of questions I did not want to answer.

"Try not to be too bored in the fields."

Michal rolled his eyes, but the action seemed forced. Alik tapped his shoulder and brought him away, and I turned away as they glanced back. Makar caught my attention again, his calculating gaze turning from Michal to me. It was a look I'd seen too many times in Kamil's face when he'd figured out something about someone and how to use it against them.

Brawls on the training grounds were not technically forbidden, sometimes encouraged by battlelions past. Another way Alik and I might be seen as weak for stopping such fights and assigning to labor instead of beating any dissenters.

And I did not like the way Makar lingered on Michal, like he might be planning something.

I forced my feet to continue toward my original destination. A man pushed by me, almost knocking my shoulder and a "coward" was spat loud enough to be heard. My feet paused, shoulders tensing, heart calling for a fight. The warrior trailing me set hand on sword, waiting on my signal, but I kept moving, my face set forward.

Coward I might be, but I could not let them think they had anything more over me.

Michal did not return to the lodge until just before dinner, covered in dirt and sweat. The others stared in surprise to see him with armor dangling from his hand and clearly from the fields.

"What happened?" Inge asked.

Michal's scowl threatened me again. "Davor said I had to go work the fields for two days for fighting on the training grounds."

Inge glanced between the two of us. "Why were you fighting?"

I said nothing as Michal looked pointedly at me. "They were saying things about Davor, and Marta." Her name came a little hushed and with an apologetic look to her.

Marta offered a faint smile. "The talk still runs then."

"Are you not going to do anything about it either?" Michal growled.

I tilted my head warningly, but he ignored it. Inge did not and tapped her son's shoulder, nudging him away to go wash. When he was safely away, Inge came back, my mother not far behind.

"Do you want me to show favoritism and give them more weapons against all of us?" I asked before they could.

A short sigh cut from Inge. "I do not think it a bad thing for him to be defending your honor, or Marta's."

Marta offered a faint smile, and I had a feeling she'd be thanking Michal for it later.

Defensiveness rose in me. "There are other ways."

"Not for him," Inge said almost sadly.

"Then maybe he needs to learn," I snapped and turned away before I could fully see the look in her eyes. No more was said about it, and Michal had nothing to say to me through dinner or the next morning.

The door shut a little harder than normal behind him, and it stung though I tried not to let it. Marta gently touched my wrist. I pulled away.

"I will be going to the middle village today."

She offered a smile. "We'd planned to work on the tapestry today. Janne and Nina will be coming with me again."

Janne's eagerness brought back some peace. My mother hid her excitement better, and that dangerous softening prodded my heart again at the sight of Marta conversing easily with them.

A frantic knocking sent a jolt of alarm around the table. Inge was up first to answer. Janne rose to her feet, ready to help her mother with whatever injury was at the door. But it gave way to an older woman, wringing her hands and looking past Inge.

"*Dronni*, you'd better come." She saw me and hastily signed respect.

"What's wrong, Sif?" Marta pushed to her feet.

"It's…you'd better just come. Chief, you as well. You will need to see this." Sif's hands knotted around each other.

Marta's wide eyes turned to me.

"Wait." I went to pull on my armor and weapons.

When I returned, Marta had tied her belt with the knife around her waist. Janne stood beside her, the same stubbornness as her brother filling her up, silently declaring she was going with us.

The two warriors on guard fell in with us as Sif led the way across the lodge square. Marta gasped and stumbled to a halt, realizing what had happened before I did. A pile of cloth lay outside a lodge door, torn edges fluttering in the light breeze. A few women stood around, others gathering faster.

Marta crouched and gently picked up a strip of cloth, turning it over and showing bright stitches through the grey. It hit me and my gaze jerked up, looking around for Makar. He was not there yet.

"What happened?" Marta beat me to it in a gentler voice.

"It was gone from the frame this morning, *Dronni*," Sif said. "Everyone claims they saw nothing when it went missing." But her glare around called out the lie.

Marta slowly stood, the torn edge falling from her fingers. Janne placed a hand on her arm and Marta gave her a small smile, but a glint caught her eyes. She mustered a breath and lifted her chin.

"We will start it over."

The women tapped fingers to forehead.

"What of this, *Dronni*?" Sif pointed to the mangled tapestry.

Marta bent again and picked it up, running some of it between her fingers. "Perhaps some of the unstitched cloth can be used for something else."

"Who would want cursed cloth you have touched?" a new voice asked.

Marta whirled, dark eyes wide. I was slower to bring my focus to the woman. The one I had sentenced for her crimes against a child.

"Cursed?" Sif jolted forward a step, elbows tipping wide as if ready for a fight.

The woman sneered. "She denounces others' lives, but hides her own."

Cold rushed through me. Marta's brow furrowed as she stared at the woman.

"You turn down marriage offers, then no one comes near you. And you have a special interest in the orphans' lodge. Why is that... *Dronni*?" Bold suggestion filled the words.

Marta's face flushed, and one of the women closer to her edged away. It took another moment for me to catch the meaning.

"You think I have something to hide in that lodge?" Marta asked, but she did not quite keep the tremor from her voice.

The woman shrugged. "You spent much time with the battle-lion a few summers ago. Everyone in the middle village knows it."

Marta's jaw dropped before she mustered herself. I stood frozen, not sure what to do, what to think. Hating that I doubted her for a second. That I doubted Alik.

"And you know so much about the middle village?" Janne pushed forward, glaring at the woman.

She sniffed, turning a condescending look to Janne. "Like calls to like, I see."

My sister drew herself up, fury leeching from her. I touched her arm and the betrayed glare she sent me was too much like Michal's.

But murmurs were already filling up the lodge square where more had gathered with the news of the tapestry and the much more interesting sight made by the accusation. Some were looking at Marta with disbelief, scorn, pity, and much of the same at me.

Her hands were trembling in the folds of her skirt and I did not know whether to reach out to her or unleash my gathering anger on something or someone else.

"I have nothing to hide in that lodge or in any other," she declared.

Sif came up next to her, glaring her own defiance at the others. Janne joined them and another woman tentatively edged closer.

The outcast was not quite done, and flicked a glance between us.

"Perhaps it's not the battlelion's then. There's a tale of you two together years ago." Her hand flicked from me to her. "You aren't the only one to have tasted a chief's son."

"That is enough." My voice cracked across the square, bringing a hush in its wake. The woman jolted and the quick spark of fear in her eyes was nearly enough to kill my resolve.

"The *dronni* is a woman of honor and I do not doubt her words."

The woman's eyes narrowed. I held the look, not letting anyone see the tumult still trying to rage inside.

"As for this." I pointed to the mess of cloth. "The ones responsible will be found, and judged accordingly."

A growl punctuated my words as Luk prowled up, twining around Marta, teeth bared at the threat of those staring at her. Her hand bobbled as she set it against his side. The motion was tracked by many and that seemed to settle the matter for some, especially as his snarl slackened slightly under her touch.

The woman's glare did not falter and she stepped back to vanish into the dispersing crowd.

"Davor." Marta drew my attention to her. The others gave us a little space. Redness rimmed her eyes and her chin quivered. My fingers brushed her elbow before I could stop myself, and her hand fisted into my shirt sleeve.

"Are you all right?" I asked softly even though it was clear she was not. But I did not know how to help her with this. I had years and years of armor worn against words and accusations.

She pulled in another breath, not quite stilling the tremors. "It is true, what I said. I have nothing to hide. And nothing between Alik and me. Ever."

I almost pulled away from the desperation in her eyes, like she was afraid I wouldn't believe her, or might believe instead the words of a bitter woman. And for a moment, it seemed she might be right to fear as my walls were trying to re-erect at the sight of the pleading, the touch of her hand, my mind whispering it was a way to manipulate. Distract me from the way they exchanged words and smiles so easily.

"Davor?"

And it vanished. She hadn't lied to me, though perhaps she should be doubting me instead.

"I know."

Her relief stung almost as much as the previous fear.

"Are you all right?" I repeated, needing to hear her reassurance. Show her that I did believe her.

Her eyes shuttered closed for a moment and when she opened them again, the tears were receding, and the proud tilt of her chin came back. It pained me in a way I did not understand to see her pulling on her own armor.

"They are just words," she said.

They are not to me, my heart nearly screamed back.

Marta unlatched her fingers from my sleeve and gently tugged the cloth smooth again. My hand came slowly away from her elbow.

"We will start fresh on the tapestry today," she said. "Lene will have new cloth."

"We will go with you, *Dronni.*" Sif stepped closer with one of the other women. Janne nodded her intent as well.

I searched Marta's face, and she offered a faint shadow of her normal smile. "It will be fine."

I stepped back, giving her room to move away, but flicked a signal to Luk. He rumbled and fell in at her side as they moved away with the warrior escort. Marta rubbed behind his ear and tilted a glance and a more natural smile at me before walking on.

It took longer for me to move, and only when the warrior still at my side stepped up beside me with a quiet "Chief?"

A shrug ran through me, helping me shift into motion. We made it as far as the river bridge before Alik found me, running with Dariy hot on his heels. They both slid to a halt, waiting for me to finish crossing.

"Where's Marta?" Dariy demanded.

The weight settled heavier in my gut. "The rumors have reached the middle village then?"

"Where is she?" Her father did not back down.

"She went to get more cloth to start a new tapestry. There are guards and some women with her. She is all right."

Dariy did not look too reassured, and grabbed his quiver strap, preparing to push past me. But Alik was in his way.

"Davor." The hesitation in his eyes almost had me drawing back. "What they're saying about Marta and me. It isn't true."

Dariy paused, caution in his stance that had not been there since the first day we'd come face-to-face in the war.

I would not doubt them, not like I had been so quick to doubt her.

"I know. She told me the same."

They both eased, and I wondered what they thought I might have done if it *was* true.

"When did you hear it?" I asked.

"Someone came just after breakfast to tell us. Apparently they'd heard it last night." Alik frowned.

"Makar?" Dariy questioned.

"Who else?" Alik glared past me at the upper village as if he could find Makar right then. "It should not surprise me he decided to go after her. You two appeared comfortable together at the dance. Everyone could see it. No doubt he had spies there as well."

I jolted. But Dariy was nodding some agreement and it only made the lurking guilt worse.

"I did not want to bring her into this." The words almost came out pleading to her father.

He offered a bare smile. "Marta is strong. She can endure this."

I did not want her to have to. He reached out and tapped my shoulder, a surprisingly comforting gesture.

"I do not blame you for this. I blame Makar. But what I need from you, Davor, is to make sure she will weather it and for you to keep working to put an end to this." It was gentle, without reproof, filled with a little belief that I could keep my feet under me on this path.

I almost wanted to lean into the belief, ask if he had any advice for this matter or others, but it seemed too dangerous to look toward a father for anything. Instead, I nodded, and he squeezed my shoulder before letting go.

"Vanda is ready to go to war right now. We'll find Marta." Dariy tapped fist to chest.

"Thank you."

Alik stayed as the huntsman left. "Davor?" he asked as I didn't immediately move on. "You all right?"

"Me?" This wasn't about me.

"You look shaken. What else?"

The guilt crept forward again, and I found myself confessing. "For a moment, I...I know I shouldn't have doubted. She's been nothing but honest. But I..." And I braced for him to react to my doubt of her and maybe even him.

"How many times have you been lied to in your life?" His question held something almost mournfully understanding.

I looked away, focusing on the river instead.

"I won't blame you for the reaction. But you chose not to embrace it. For her."

The probing edge kept me from looking back to him as I replied. "She doesn't deserve to be singled out like this. I don't want her hurt."

He nudged my arm. "Like Dariy said, she's strong. But talk to her, make sure she's not just trying to push through it."

I managed a nod, and he heaved a short breath, reading my desire for this conversation to be done.

"Should we head to our next battle?" he asked wryly.

"What now?" I rubbed my thumb knuckle across my forehead.

"Some of the new hunters from the upper village have been bringing back next to nothing and have started to demand from the middle again. A huntsman from Artem's lodge finally confessed to giving up his entire hunt after some cornered him two days ago."

The near constant headache blossomed into being at the news. "I was going to see the *sjandsen* anyway. I'll talk to the huntsmen after."

I wanted the day to be over already, but the morning had not even reached its middle. I wanted quiet, but there were too many words ahead of me to wade through. I wanted to make sure Marta was all right to dispel the concern still beating inside. But what I wanted was never what mattered most.

We walked in silence, and I tried to ready my thoughts for the day ahead.

FORTY

DAVOR

The *sjandsen* professed ignorance of the issues of hunting, so I left him and went to find the truth from the huntsman. We found him with his sablecat, another two hunters nearby. Their brows twisted in worry that only deepened when they saw me.

"I hear you have been having trouble with the hunters from the upper village," I began without preamble.

The hunters hastily saluted, glancing between me and Alik.

"The *sjandsen* said nothing has happened but I'd rather hear the truth of it."

One of the men swallowed, his hands tugging at the quiver strap across his chest.

"Chief, I…it's not my place."

My boots scuffed the ground as I tried to hold in the irritation swirling through my entire body.

"Tell me the truth so I can see this matter put to rest." It came through gritted teeth.

He bobbed his head, but still hesitated, enough that I waved my hand.

"Four men came when Taras and I were back from the hunt." He nodded at the younger of the huntsmen. "They had weapons pulled and threatened to accuse us of stealing or worse to the *sjandsen* if we did not give them our catch."

"All but said they were too good for demeaning work like hunting," Taras spoke up, his frustration more open. "No matter that we both helped guide their packs through the valley plenty of times in the war."

"You think you'd recognize the warriors?" Alik asked.

The frustration melted to confusion, like they hadn't really expected anything to happen.

"Perhaps we could," the huntsman replied carefully.

"Did you take this to the *sjandsen*?" I asked.

His feet nudged the ground, head tilting. I wondered if he'd ever had to lie in his entire life.

"*Sjandsen* said not to argue. That it was a foolish law to make the upper village help hunt their own meat." Taras had no such compunction, even at the warning glance the others shot him. But I saw in him the need for something to be changed, to be different.

"Has this happened to anyone else?"

"Yarik gave up his catch earlier in the counting. They took everything to feed their sablecats too. He didn't go to anyone about it, but we all knew." Taras shrugged.

"Has anyone gone hungry because of it?"

This time a bit of scorn filled up all of their eyes.

"We've always taken care of our village," the older said, and only a little regret followed it.

"Battlelion, come with us to find the warriors responsible."

Hesitation filled salutes, eyes wide like they did not believe I was serious. It was a look I was tiring of. But they followed in silence as Alik and I strode back through the middle village and across the bridge, drawing more stares towards us.

It did not take long to find the warriors. They, like many others who still looked to Makar, stood or sat outside their lodges, sablecats lounging with them as they ignored duties or avoided orders as they could.

"Chief." The huntsman pointed at one of the warriors, a burly man who stood a hands-breadth taller than others around him.

The rider saw us coming, smirk in place as he shoved away from the wall and swaggered forward to meet us.

"Chief." A mocking hand touched to forehead, and nothing given to Alik.

My patience was fast deserting me. "There will be no more stealing of catches from the middle village. The responsibility for hunting for the upper village now lies with the packs here."

"We only caught one elk." He shrugged. "The hunters know how to do it better."

"Unfortunate," I said.

"Indeed." The smile tilted again, and he made to push by me.

I slammed a hand into his chest, halting him. His eyes narrowed a fraction, but I didn't blink.

"Unfortunate that you will not be eating by a lodge fire until your pack manages to learn how to hunt effectively." I tilted my head. "I'd hate to think that they would need to lose warrior marks and spears over poor hunting skills. The tribe can't survive a battle with a poorly prepared pack."

His features darkened into a scowl. "You wouldn't dare!" he hissed, trying to lean over me.

I gave no answer but a steady gaze at him.

"They will pay for this." He sneered at the huntsmen behind me.

"Then you will find yourself walking the plains without cords or sablecat."

He backed off slightly at the threat. "Perhaps if you weren't so cowardly as to deny us battle, we would not struggle so."

My hand curled up and I almost pulled a knife to give him one right there. "All the more reason for you to keep your skills and sablecats' senses sharp by hunting."

The warrior scoffed slightly and signaled to his men. I did not move until they rode from the village with sablecats and spears.

Alik had not shifted from my side, and the huntsmen stayed in a tight group. They slowly gave salutes and made their way back to the middle village.

"Others are realizing we have not sent out patrols yet." Alik kept his voice between us.

I scraped my knuckle against my forehead. "Is Makar offering his men?"

Alik huffed. "What do you think?"

It was a decision we'd circled around and around. Neither yet feeling we could send out patrols to scout the borders without stabbing ourselves in the foot. Both hoping the Pronghorn tribe would not realize we were staying within the villages, come home in defeat from our newest war. Hoping the Greywolves and Blackpaws might not try to take advantage of our weakness.

And every time we discussed it, I was reminded of my promise to meet the Greywolf chief at the border stones at midsummer to broker peace if we could. And every day that passed with peace coming no further to my own tribe only stoked the desperation inside.

"Chief?" a hesitant voice asked.

"What?" I growled forcefully. The man standing there drew back. Mustering myself, I brought a more even cadence to my voice. "What do you need?"

"There's a dispute, Chief. We've tried to work it between the lodges."

"I will come." Even though the woods and a small cave holding silence and walls bearing bits of charcoal smeared in my rage beckoned. Alik tapped my shoulder and a warrior fell in as we followed the man.

Well over an hour later, things were settled, though disgruntled looks filled both sides, leaving me doubting myself again. The sight of Marta and Janne stepping into Inge's lodge coaxed a quickness to my steps.

I paused with hand on the latch, wondering if she might even want to see me, but Dariy's words and the prodding from before to make sure she was all right sent me inside. My mother had wrapped her in a hug, and Inge touched her shoulder comfortingly.

At the sound of the latch clicking soft behind me, she lifted her head, exposing redness in her eyes.

"How was it?" I asked softly.

She pulled away from Mother's hold, rubbing her arms. "The rumors have spread to the lower village. But there were plenty of others there to speak against them."

"I am sorry."

Marta shook her head slightly. "It's not your doing. I might be nearly as tired of Makar as you are." Her smile trembled, but it was there. Mother wrapped an arm around her shoulders again.

I did not know what to do, what to offer.

"Thank you," she said. "For before. And for trusting me. I told several the truth of what happened that day in the woods. I did not want to let them say anything else against you either."

A nod seemed all I was capable of. "Are you all right?"

She nodded, but did not seem in a hurry to pull away from my mother's hold. "I might stay close to the lodge for the rest of the day."

"That might be best." I hated the almost shame in her eyes, my words barely staving it off. Mother's look held a promise that they'd look after her and try to keep the words at bay in her mind. Reluctance prodded me as I made my way back outside to face the rest of the day.

Michal was last to the lodge again that night, but fresh anger lingered about him. He went first to Marta, barely believing her reassurance. The frustrated anger had not left his eyes as he turned to me.

"Alik said I'd served the time." Michal's jaw tensed belligerently.

"Then you have," I said evenly. It seemed to only make it worse, but I had nothing more to give after the day.

Dinner passed in quiet, nothing on my plate appetizing in the least. A restless night chased any peace away. I nudged breakfast around my plate, the table quiet again, but I perfectly sensed the looks passed around.

"I was going to work on the new hanging today," Marta spoke up.

I nodded, forcing a bite of hash. "I'll walk you there."

"So you can do nothing again if they throw something else at her?" Michal muttered.

My hands clenched on the table, but I pushed back my chair and went to don armor. By the time I made it out, Michal was pulling out his armor. I shook my head.

"You are going with Dariy today on the hunt." Alik hadn't agreed with my request, but Makar's look burned in my mind.

Anger flared up around him. "No."

My jaw tensed, but he did not heed the warning in my look. "Makar—"

"Makar can take himself to the dark woods. I'm not afraid of him. I should be with you. Don't send me away!"

"You are heir, Michal. I cannot risk you in the same space as me."

Refusal twisted up his face. "Yet you can risk yourself? You can't be that foolish."

"What do you want me to do then?" My voice rose. "You, Alik, everyone else…what do you want from me? To hide or to fight?"

He leaned back a little from the rising anger. "You should fight. I want to help. I'm not a boy."

"You are, Michal!" I neared a shout. "There are some things I will not drag you into—"

"I'm not stupid, Davor!" he shouted back. "Was this all just a show to keep me close, to buy my loyalty to give you one less obstacle?"

"No—"

"So what? You think you can do everything yourself?" Hurt rippled off him in waves. "You lied about Emil; what else are you keeping from me?"

"Michal…" I tried, but he was just as angry as I.

"No! I'm not getting caught up in one of your games."

"Enough!"

He recoiled from the sharpness of my voice, the word cracking through the corners of the lodge. My fingers dug grooves into my palms, every muscle rigid. At the sight of the fear in his eyes, I deflated, but he was already moving. Spinning on his heel and throwing open the door to disappear.

Janne darted after him, something very nearly like reproach directed at me, before she, too, vanished out the door.

A curse exploded from me, and I fled from the lodge.

Alik stopped me from finding one of my hiding places, coming toward me across the lodge square.

"Don't," I growled at the question in his face.

He raised his hands. "I'd hoped to catch you in a better mood, but seems not."

"What now?"

"Those warriors didn't bring anything back, and took from the huntsmen again. The *sjandsen* was even there and watched them do it."

Another growl lingered in my throat.

"Where are we going?" Alik fell in beside me.

"To clean up this mess."

He did not question what that meant, just waved to a few other warriors. Alik, blessedly, kept silent as I stalked my way down the path.

Tribespeople moving about the middle village fell back from our approach, whispers following along in our wake.

My fist pounded against the *sjandsen's* door. Alik settled by my side, hands folded over his sword hilt. The question was there in his face, but he did not ask, and I did not give an answer.

The door cracked open, showing one of the women who helped tend to the lodge.

"Chief?" Her voice wobbled.

"Move."

She swung the door open, stumbling back in her haste to let us in. Our boots thudded against the planked floor, sending a hush through the sparse activity in the common room. The *sjandsen* shot up from his seat at the table, paleness rushing across his face.

"Chief! I—"

"Sit down." I strode forward.

He obeyed like his legs had been cut out from under him.

"You are going to tell me everything you know about hunts being stolen."

His mouth flopped open and closed much like a startled salmon caught in a net.

"Everything."

The man quailed in his seat. "There are many unhappy in the upper village with your changes, it's true!" He held up his hands. "Makar, he came and told me to not interfere with warriors taking what should be rightfully theirs. It is the way of things."

"And what do you get in return?" I slammed hands down on the table.

He jolted. "Things go back to normal, and I would get a bigger share. He said he wouldn't interfere in the way of the tribe if he was chief. No one is happy with you in the position," he babbled, staring up at me with frantic face, the fear there near enough to kill my anger. But not quite.

It rushed back like a flash flood.

"Your place as *sjandsen* is not safe anymore. And men, women, children, they can shout all they want, but this is the way of the tribe now," I said. "And it is not going to change. You will continue to follow the paths I set, or there will be someone else in this lodge come next counting. Do you understand?"

His head bobbed up and down.

I straightened, but did not leave yet. "If Makar comes back with honeyed words, you come to me immediately. Remember that he is even less likely to keep his promises than the old chief."

The official's jaw slammed shut. That, at least, he did know. The old chief played games with more people than just his sons.

He promised obedience, and I swept a cold glance around to the others standing in frozen silence.

Murmurs of "Yes, Chief," sounded until everyone had said something or brought hand to forehead in salute.

Everything inside twisted up the more at the sight of their fearful subservience.

Fighting another curse, I turned on my heel and strode away.

"Davor," Alik said quietly once we were outside. I pulled to a halt, hands aching in fists. Concern drew deep lines across his face, but before he could say anything, someone screamed my name.

FORTY-ONE

DAVOR

Janne sprinted toward me, skirts clutched in her hands, one sleeve torn and blood beading her mouth. My heart dropped to my toes.

Dirt crunched under my boots as I raced to her, catching her as she tripped into my arms.

"Davor!" She gasped for breath. "They have Michal—I was just able to get away—they have Michal!"

"Janne! Slow down!" I tried not to grip her arms so tight as my own panic roared up around me.

She gulped a breath. "I followed Michal. We...we..."

My hand finally unlatched to rub her arm instead of hold.

"We didn't go far. He told the guard to leave us alone."

Alik gave voice to the curse bounding across my tongue.

"Then Makar...he ordered others...there were too many." Tremors rocked her and I wanted to take her home, to sit down, breathe through it, but I needed to know.

"Where are they?"

"I don't know." It whispered tearfully from her. "Once I got free, I ran. I…"

"Janne, it's all right. We'll find him."

I turned to see my fury mirrored in Alik's face.

"Get her back to the lodge," I said.

Alik shook his head, about to refuse to leave when a new voice broke in. "I'll take her, Chief."

Vanda wrapped arms around Janne, peeling her away from my hold. Alik called two men over to accompany them.

"Janne, where did this happen?" I asked.

She lifted her face from Vanda's shoulder. "We were headed up the mountain. Not far from the chief's lodge, toward the river." She shook her head, afraid that might not help.

Unfortunately, it did.

Alik and I shared another curse. I took off running before Alik could say anything else.

My feet took me across the bridge, skidding across the last planks before turning uphill. The tributary river came from one of the valley lakes, wound through the forests before whipping itself around Half Peak, clawing its way through part of the mountain in a narrow gorge before dumping into the calmer great river that flowed under the bridge on its way south.

Up mountain, where the banks were carved from stone and leaned towards each other, was a spot whose memory sent a chill through my bones.

A sablecat's scream drew me on around boulders, and under grasping pine branches, following the sounds of the angry lion and men's shouts.

I skidded to a halt, breaths rasping loud enough to hear, but the six men standing at the edge of the rocky gorge were focused on something else.

Two held back Michal's lion with spears, as another nursed a bleeding forearm and kicked at a limp form with a curse. Another laughed and gestured. Two warriors hauled Michal up and my anger roared back at his bloody and dazed features.

I threaded my way through the trees, working my way closer as they started dragging him to the edge. A look back over my shoulder showed no sign of Alik. I couldn't wait. Michal was not struggling, not even as the one giving orders pulled a sword.

His sablecat screamed again. My cursing could have stopped the river in its tracks if it had bothered to hear me over its own noise. Yanking a knife free, I did what I would have never done countings ago, and charged.

Small rocks burst from under my feet, skittering over the edge I raced along. The leader turned, mouth open in shock. But I went for the nearest man holding Michal. Stabbed into his shoulder, grabbing at his breastplate collar and throwing him out of the way as his knees buckled with his surprised scream.

His companion faltered under the sudden weight of Michal. Until I grabbed my brother and dragged him a step backward.

The warrior retreated a step, recovering himself and drawing a sword. Michal's limp form pulled at my arms, and I silently cursed again.

No way forward, not with two armed men and a third swinging to face me with spear in hand. Still no sign of Alik and his men.

"Well, we were supposed to just kill him." The leader flicked his sword at Michal. "Throw his body in the river to wash below. But now, maybe *I'll* kill the chief and the heir, and see what that brings me."

My foot scraped the gorge's edge. The men laughed.

"No escape, Chief."

Michal jolted suddenly, incoherent sounds coming from him, and his hand scrabbled against my armor, trying to scrape my cheeks. I twisted my face away.

"Michal!" I shouted, hoping to reach him. Apparently I was not yet done being foolish.

The frantic motion paused long enough for me to tell him, "Hang on to me," as I wrapped arms around him and sent us both over the edge.

Cold punched through me, the shock trying to steal my breath and a few beats of my heart. I slammed against Michal, crushing him to the rocky wall, before we were thrown downriver, no more than leaves in the torrent.

Sky, rocks, and foaming water competed against each other until, with one last shove against a rocky outcrop, the river dumped us out into calmer waters.

Spitting out water, I unlatched an arm from around Michal and grabbed at one of the bridge poles as we passed. The slickness of my hand against damp wood slowed us long enough for me to get a foot against the pebbled bottom of the river and push out of the current.

We drifted, Michal still wrapped up in my arms, until the bank rose under my boots and I pulled us to it. He sputtered and bucked in my hold, but I did not let him go, hauling until we both collapsed onto the ground.

He lay prone in the sand, lips blue and hair plastered against his cheeks. I pushed to hands and knees, about to touch him when his body spasmed and he coughed out half the river.

"Michal?" I rested a hesitant hand on his shoulder.

Shaking arms pushed him up, halting when he saw me.

"D-Davor?" His brow creased in confusion. I tugged at his shoulder. A sob accompanied his next breath as he kept staring at me.

"I thought I was going to…I didn't think you'd come…"

"I'm here."

He threw himself forward and I caught him, wrapping arms around him as he sobbed into my shoulder.

"I'm here. I'm here." It seemed all I could repeat. One hand slowly unclenched from his sodden tunic and set gently on the back of his head.

He renewed his grip on me. A burst of anger drove away some of the river's cold worming its way under my skin as my fingers carded through ragged strands of shorn hair.

"Chief!" Dariy's welcome voice had me craning my head up to see him hopping down the short embankment followed by Michal's sablecat.

Michal shivered harder and tucked closer to me. The lion rumbled, nudging at Michal with soft chuffs.

"A-Alik?" The chill was sinking its pale fingers into me as well.

"We saw you come downriver. Tinek went up to retrieve him. Here." He unfolded a blanket and put it around Michal. It was a harder task to let go and tuck the cloth around him.

Michal slowly raised his head.

"Can you walk?" I asked.

A mumbled sound came from him in answer, and Dariy helped me pull him to his feet. My leg clenched around sudden pain as we slipped and stumbled our way up the bank and back onto the path, circled round and round by the sablecat.

Luk bounded to meet us as people gathered and pointed, but I ignored them all, my arm still wrapped around Michal's shoulders. Dariy helped more than me as Michal's legs faltered, keeping him going through the upper village with gentle words.

But it was me who pulled us to a halt in the center of the lodge square at the sight of the figure walking away.

"Makar!" I shouted.

He spun around, taking in the sight of us with shock that turned to a scowl.

I spread my arm wide, holding his gaze, fury giving me a new sort of courage.

"Here I am, you fanging coward."

His hand flew to his sword, but I ignored him, turning Michal toward our lodge. Luk and Michal's sablecat circled us, growls threatening. Three warriors from Tinek's pack drew up to cover our flank as we stepped inside.

Janne hurtled forward, throwing her arms around the shivering form of her brother, nearly knocking Dariy and me backward.

A muffled sound came from Michal, and Inge gently peeled her daughter away, directing her to go build up the fire. The warriors shoved benches closer to the fire at her order and then stepped outside. We limped to the bench and a whimpering cry came from Michal as we lowered him down.

I didn't want to let him go, but Inge gently touched my arm.

"Go change into dry clothes, Davor."

My joints had already stiffened, making movement difficult. A hand slid under my elbow and helped me up. Marta was there when I stood on my feet, open worry for me spilling across her face, and I stumbled back from the sight.

Doffing armor and changing clothes hadn't been so difficult since I'd challenged Kamil over the wounded. When I finally emerged, bundles of wet clothes in my hands, Inge was covering Michal in furs. Even across the room, I could see him shivering.

Mother gently took the bundle from me, directing me to the hearth where I sat against the warm stones. Marta brought a blanket, helping tuck it tight around my shoulders.

Inge sat on the benches beside Michal, briskly rubbing over the furs. Janne knelt by his head, tears streaking her face. Michal shifted, mumbling my name.

Inge looked to me, but I was already struggling up to go kneel by the bench. My hand tentatively touched his shoulder.

"I'm here."

The blue had left his face, but bruising had already begun to show, even with the cold of the river.

"I'm sorry." His voice hitched over the words. "I'm sorry." A tear escaped and trickled down his face.

"Me too." I set my hand against the side of his head. He turned into the touch, hand snaking out from under the blankets to wrap cold fingers around my forearm.

"And I'm sorry I let this happen to you," I whispered. Another sob jolted from him. "No one is ever going to hurt you again, I promise."

He nodded, gripping tighter.

I tapped my forehead gently against his. "I promise."

I stayed there until his fingers lost the intensity of their grip, and his eyes fluttered closed, letting more even breathing pass through half-swollen lips.

A touch on my shoulder brought my attention to Inge. Tears were finally welling up in her eyes.

"I'm sorry." The whisper shivered from me. "I'm sorry this happened. I should have done something years ago for him, for so many people...I..."

Inge sank to her knees, pulling me into a hug that terrified me a little.

"It's not your fault this happened to him."

A shudder wracked me, cold leaving only because it was making way for latent adrenaline and the realization of how scared I'd been to maybe lose Michal.

"I could have done so much before." The words came stilted and frantic against her shoulder. "I'm too much of a coward and…"

Her arms tightened around me. "You stop that right now, Davor."

Another sound escaped me.

"Spirits know I saw how all four of you boys were hurt and used," she said. "But you didn't go the way of Kamil, or the chief. And Michal, he saw that, and I know sometimes he tried to be like you, no matter how hard it was. It's not cowardice to survive, Davor. It's not cowardice to decide you've had enough."

Heat trickled its damp way down my cheeks, soaking into her overtunic.

"You protected your mother all these years. And the stories of your bravery in battle, or how you stood up to Kamil, are spreading more and more every day. So don't you dare tell me you are a coward. Understand?"

I nodded, feeling wrung out and empty with my next breath. Inge held me another few heartbeats, gently rubbing my shoulder. When I lifted my head, Janne leaned close and pressed a kiss to my temple.

"Thank you for finding him."

I reached up and took her hand. "You all right?"

She nodded, then her face fell. "You're not. Mother, he's bleeding."

Inge shifted, tugging at my shirt. The motion conjured a strangled noise in my throat. She pulled away and different hands swept under my arms to help me up to a bench. Pinpricks of pain ran up and down my legs, vanishing as I stretched them out.

"Let's get this off."

Startled, I looked up to see Alik there. A grim smile flattened his lips as he helped me get my shirt overhead.

"I'll take care of things. You need to rest."

Inge undid the damp bandage still around my ribs. The stitches Alik had put in me nights before were broken, the cut messy once again.

Alik nudged my arm. "And I'm going to need you to tell me your plans first from now on."

But wry humor softened the words.

"Sorry," I said, but he shook his head, ignoring the apology.

"I'll be back later. I'm glad he's all right." Alik's fist knocked against mine, and then he was gone, taking Dariy with him.

A rustle marked a bright dress and overtunic coming to stand in front of me. Slowly, I lifted my eyes up, afraid of what I might see in Marta's face. But it was only concern in her dark eyes. Her attention shifted away and she picked up my shirt.

"Good thing I have another one nearly finished for you the way you keep showing up bloody." Her lips tipped up at the corner, coaxing a dimple in her cheek.

Inge tapped my arm to lift it as she wrapped a new bandage around me. The jittering had started to leave my muscles.

"I'll try to keep it to a minimum." I managed a faint smile back.

Marta's fingers gently brushed my bare shoulder and then she was gone.

"Time to rest," Inge said. "Do you want to stay here by the fire, or your room?"

I levered to my feet, weary and spent and wanting time away from the eyes that had seen my weakness break through. Mother followed me, tucking me in under some extra furs like I was still a small child sleeping next to her. Her kiss brushed my forehead as my eyes closed and I fell into an exhausted slumber.

FORTY-TWO

MARTA

A muffled noise woke me sometime in the night. I rolled over to see Davor sitting by Michal, leaned forward on his knees and just staring at the younger while he slept. Firelight flickered, casting deeper shadows across his features. I slowly sat up and wrapped a shawl around my shoulders. Once Nina had helped him to his room, he hadn't come back out, even for dinner.

"Davor?" My whisper floated between us.

A startled glance up sent the shadows receding to show different emotions lurking around his eyes I hadn't seen before—confusion and loss. It was enough to send me to his side.

"What's wrong?" I looked first to Michal, but he still slept, burrowed in the furs.

"He thought I wouldn't come for him…" It carried a little of the same loss and confusion, enough to have me reaching forward and resting a hand on his.

"I'd come for you—if anything happened. You know that, right?" He looked to me, a bit of desperation there.

I slowly sank to my knees, keeping my hand over his. "I do."

I'd thought he might before, but after today, I believed it. And from the way the talk ran, more of the tribe was starting to believe in him as well.

"I'm sorry."

"For what?" I asked.

"For bringing you into this. If it wasn't for the *talånd* telling me, I wouldn't have chosen anyone."

I shifted a little. "As I recall, I offered my hand freely. But you didn't have to take it."

I'd wondered that day, and many nights since, why he had when he so clearly did not want to. For a moment, I didn't think he would answer, but he did.

"I have always admired you."

It sent a prick of something through my heart and a bit of red across his cheeks in the firelight.

"Ever since that day in the forest. You always seemed...kind, gentle, unafraid. And you are. I didn't want someone who would give up, or be afraid of...me."

His fingers clenched and I softly brushed a thumb across the back of his hand.

"It seemed like you could stand tall beside me and not break. I did not want someone who would silently suffer through... duty...and hate because of it."

My head tilted as I kept studying him. His eyes were fixed on his fists and my hand atop them.

"What about love? Did you not think of that when you chose?" I asked quietly. Had he thought nothing for it?

He gave a sort of broken scoff. "Who would love me? I might be worse than a bastard, born to an unwilling woman outside of a bond. The stain of my father is over us still, and I have not done enough to distance myself from it."

His words, spoken softly to Inge, but we had all heard that morning, came back to me. I'd never thought him a coward, and it sent an ache through me that he thought of himself that way.

My other hand rested atop his and the tightness of his fist relaxed. "More and more of the tribe is starting to see what you are doing. And even before, it was known that you were not like them, what little you showed everyone."

His hands shifted slightly, and I took the almost invitation, sliding one hand into his. Each time I held his hand, it felt something a little closer to...I did not know.

"I have needed to plan three steps ahead my whole life. Love has never been a factor." It was said with a certain resignation that prodded my heart again.

"What if it could be? What if there was room for it?" It seemed a dangerous thing to ask. Perhaps it was the darkness around us broken only by a golden pool of firelight, the absence of the mask on his face, or that odd feeling in my heart, but I wanted to know if this might be dangerous ground I was suddenly standing on. If I could maybe see him as something different than a friend one day.

He shook his head, a sharpness in the short laugh. "I have been angry for as long as I can remember. Shoving down my pride until I thought I had kept nothing for myself. I do not know if there is room for anything else."

His eyes turned from me to the fire, the flames catching at their darkness but unable to pierce through it.

"Perhaps I could learn one day to give a part of my heart, but I do not know if even that could be worth anything."

"I think it is," I said quietly. The truth was there—I already wanted a part of his heart.

His head shook a little, perhaps trying to deny it.

"Davor." I did not let go my hold on his hands. He slowly looked to me, and it seemed a part of his walls were back up in readiness for what I may or may not say.

"I do not have any regrets about marrying you. I don't think I ever will. You are a good man. And I think…I think you should be angry a little. I don't know your story and you don't have to tell me, but I heard many things. My parents are not perfect, but they are good…the way parents should be. And that was stolen from you, from Michal. I don't…"

I stared at our hands, aware of how he still watched me. "I don't know the right thing to say, but there are many things wrong in the tribe, wrong with what the chief did and how he brought you up. And it takes strength and courage to make a change."

I finally looked back up to find his focus on our hands.

"What if I don't know what I'm doing? What if I'm doing everything wrong?" he asked, voice low.

"I suppose that means you are human."

He tilted a look up, like he was not sure whether to be annoyed or amused.

I offered a slight smile. "It also means you should sleep some more." I eased up to my feet, still keeping a hold on his hands. "Perhaps things will be better in the morning."

"I doubt it." But he let me tug him up.

I let him go, my hands feeling colder without him. He did not move, staring once more at Michal.

"Inge said he will be all right." I tugged my shawl tighter around me.

He didn't say anything for a long moment, then turned and made his way back to his room. I followed, bare feet hushed against the floor. No word passed between us as I halted in the doorway, making sure he lay down.

But he curled on his side, back to me. Something about the sight drew me a few steps closer.

"Davor, do you want to be alone right now?"

Threads of firelight stretched their tentative way into the room to illuminate the shake of his head.

"No." The admission came hushed.

Even a day ago, I would have never dared. But right then I did not hesitate. I nudged the door so only a crack remained and made my way to the bed's empty side.

He did not move or protest as I lay down, pulling the blankets over me. Only once beside him did I pause, wondering if this would make him angry again.

He said nothing, and I caught another shaky breath. I rolled, keeping a small space between us as I reached my arm over his side. The muscles in his stomach tensed as I gently set my hand there. I almost pulled back before his calloused fingers brushed my skin but did not knock me away.

FORTY-THREE

DAVOR

I woke warm and with a comforting weight draped across my side. My hand brushed something as I shifted. A muffled noise came from behind me, and the warmth pressed closer as the heaviness over my side hugged tighter. I froze, trying to remember, the tension immediately leaving when I did.

Slowly, I looked over my shoulder. Enough light crept under the window covering to illuminate Marta. She slept, mouth slightly open, hair a tousled mess across her cheek and splayed over the pillow.

It weakened some of my walls in a way I didn't quite understand.

"I do not have any regrets about marrying you. I don't think I ever will."

I did not have any either, except for bringing her right into the trouble surrounding me.

But when she was around, things seemed different, hopeful. Brighter. Like maybe I could one day have a future, one I would be happy enough to have if she was there.

I wasn't sure what had led her to stay with me, but I did not mind that she did. Just as quick, doubt crept up. Perhaps she'd only done it out of pity.

At that, I began to ease out from under her hand, wanting to be gone when she awoke for fear of what might be in her face when she did and saw where she was.

My boots were still damp from the jump into the river, but I put them on anyway. Marta had given me back a shirt two days ago, cleaned from bloodstains, and I pulled it on.

She did not stir as I slid a knife into my boot, and then eased out. The common room was quiet, Michal still sleeping when I tiptoed over to check. Reassured, I went to the back door.

As I opened it, the sight of Emil standing there brought me up short, and nearly coaxed a curse from me.

"How is he?" Emil demanded without pretext.

"Michal?" I asked dumbly.

He scraped a hand over his jaw. "I was in the lower village yesterday morning. I didn't know…" He backed away a pace like he'd realized finally how close he was. "Makar summoned me and wouldn't let me out of his sight the rest of the day. I was about to knock."

I'd never seen this half-brother so self-conscious or worried. My mind seemed to be spinning in circles, so much so that I latched on to the first thought I could.

"Do you want to see him?"

Emil's focus turned down to his boot, scuffing against the packed earth. "I…yes." It came hushed, like he didn't really want to be admitting it.

"Everyone is still asleep." I opened the door further, giving him room to enter.

He hesitated, then cautiously stepped in. We made our way over to Michal, one glance making sure that Janne still slept and the door to the room our mothers shared since we'd all moved in was still closed.

I built the fire back up. Emil stood at Michal's side, expression unreadable in the firelight. Slowly, he reached down to gently touch Michal's blanket-covered shoulder. I stayed back, half-afraid to intrude. There was almost care in Emil's face.

"He's all right?" Emil's gruff whisper brought me closer.

"Inge said he would be with rest."

Emil's features shifted and cold fury took over. He gently tucked back the blanket to show the shorn ends of Michal's hair.

By the warriors' estimation dishonored.

"I will kill Makar right now if you want me to." His burning look pierced me through, but for the first time in a long time, it wasn't directed at me.

"If *I* want?"

"You said it yourself yesterday from all accounts. He's a fanging coward and I don't see you doing much to stop him."

"He's aiming to draw the packs to battle, and I want to avoid war in the villages," I said. "And I need to be the one to deal with him. If you do, maybe his men will seek to follow you instead."

His scoff broke. "They will have no luck."

It relieved me more than I cared to admit hearing him say it.

"If it comes down to death, it should be me that does it."

Reluctant understanding came with his nod. "Just challenge him then."

"I'd rather him do it."

Emil considered me. "Make him look desperate?"

I inclined my head, and I might have imagined the bits of respect in his eyes. Michal stirred and Emil backed away like a spooked deer. At the lift of my hand, he halted, seeming torn to stay. Michal's eyes fluttered open and fixed on me.

"Davor."

"You all right?" I leaned a little closer.

A mumbled noise of assent came as he scraped at his eyes. "Hungry."

I gave a faint smile, looking up to Emil. He hadn't left, hovering still on the edge of the firelight. Michal shifted, following my look over his shoulder, blinking owlishly. Emil stilled, throwing a narrow glare at me, then around the lodge, poised like he was ready to pull a knife. I did not move, not wanting to spook this side of him that was maybe showing some caring.

"Emil?" Michal's questioning tone had bits of welcome in it, enough to bring him edging closer when I did not threaten.

Emil's hand hooked on the belt across his chest. "Several of the men had wounds. Wanted to make sure you didn't break your knife on their hard hides."

Michal grunted. "I tried."

"Good." That almost smile flickered on Emil's face.

"I used the move you taught me."

Emil's gaze flicked to me, faintly guilty, then back to Michal. "So you did pay attention."

Michal rolled his eyes and yawned. "You staying?"

Emil tensed, darting a glance at me which I returned with some of his same caution. "Best if I don't."

He retreated without another word, and I followed him outside.

Emil's focus turned down the narrow lodgeway. "Make sure he does not feel any dishonor."

"I will." I'd had no one to do it for me, but I would not let Michal walk this road alone.

"Makar is planning something bigger. I don't know when, but he'll keep testing until then. I made sure the story of four men against one spread in Michal's favor." He still did not look at me. "Some agreed with the words you said. Likely they will stay quiet for now, but you have more support."

I nodded, on the verge of thanking him, when his dark eyes snapped to mine.

"Thank you," he said abruptly, and strode away.

Eventually I broke out of my shock, and turned inside. Janne commandeered my attention where she sat, arms crossed, clearly waiting for me.

"Emil?" I could not see her face clearly, but the affronted in-credulity was plain.

"And you will say nothing about it." I tried to keep a bit of gentleness in with the stern words. She raised her hands and hopped up from her bench. I sank onto the bench nearest Michal, easing out my leg, a faint ache stirring now that I had been up and about.

"Where's Marta?" Janne whirled to me.

Awkwardness seized me, and I cleared my throat. "In the room." The fire's heat leapt across the room to warm my face.

The twins traded identical looks of surprise that faded to near-fiendish delight. Mouths opened in mock-*oohs*, not abating under my glare. Janne gave a sound that was more cackle than laugh as she danced away to the cook fires before I could protest.

Michal smirked as he levered himself into sitting, pushing

away some of the layers of furs. He reached to straighten his shirt and faltered. My heart twisted and I could barely watch as his trembling hand combed the ends of his shorn hair.

A sharp breath escaped, and he pulled knees to his chest, wrapping his arms around and hiding his face. I moved to the bench in the space at his feet, and leaned onto my knees.

"I thought it might have been just a nightmare." His voice came muffled.

"There's no shame in it." The words scraped raw from my throat. "They did it to be cruel. It was not in punishment for anything you did."

He sniffed and lifted his head, enough to show redness in his eyes.

"How did it happen to you?"

My fists clenched tight around each other. "How do you think?" It came out a bitter scoff.

"Kamil?" His voice was small.

I could barely force a nod. "The chief—he'd been setting us against each other with tasks in the villages. It was play the game or see Mother get hurt. So I did. And was doing well, enough to make Kamil worried for his place. He followed me up mountain one day. There's a spot I would go."

My fingers worked around each other. "I don't know if I was careless that day, or maybe just caught up in the fact the chief had been proud of what I'd done." I tilted my head to see the understanding in his face.

"Kamil surprised me. Cut my hair and sliced my neck." I brushed fingers over the spot.

"Why didn't you grow it back?"

My shoulders rose and fell with a short intake of breath. "Because then he could never do it again."

"Oh."

"The rules changed that day, so I shifted my pieces and carried on."

"Just like that." He shifted, frustrated again with the side I showed the world. The only side safe enough to show.

"It hurt, Michal. It stung *so much*." My admission came strangled. "And they made sure I knew it. I didn't have anyone to shield me from it, so I did what I do best."

He grabbed my sleeve, pulling me into an awkward hug even though I'd been meaning to comfort him. I shifted to better get arms around him as his forehead rested against my shoulder.

"But you've got me, if you want." I gently touched the back of his head.

His nod came smothered against my shirt.

"Maybe even Emil. He said he spun it in your favor yesterday."

Michal lifted his head slightly. "He's not all bad."

"I'm finding that out." I tapped his shoulder. Emil helping me was a rogue piece on the table I would never have predicted.

He sat taller and I pressed a hand against the side of his head. "Listen to me, Michal. You've done nothing wrong. Don't let anyone make you think otherwise."

He nodded, lips pressed tight.

"And I'll try and be better about telling you things."

"You better." He swiped under his eyes and then tapped a fist against my chest. "And now you have me. It's no bad thing to have someone fight for you."

Stinging threatened my eyes and I nodded, afraid of the knot in my throat. He jerked a small nod, understanding passing between us in that brief moment and settling us both into something steady again.

I lightly nudged his shoulder. "Why don't you get up and move around for a bit."

He slid back under his blankets. "Can't. Too many blankets. Too heavy."

I rolled my eyes and flipped one over his head before standing and making my way to the cook fire to help Janne, needing to do something and not yet willing to go back into the room to see if Marta was awake.

It was not much longer before she emerged.

Unfortunately, right as I set empty plates and cups on the table. We stared at each other, each trying desperately to figure out what to say.

"Sleep all right?" I asked finally.

A snicker came from Michal's direction, but Marta chuckled, freeing herself with the sound and going over to shove his shoulder.

"Someone is feeling better, I see."

Michal gave a noise of complaint, but Marta kept poking.

"And I only went in there to get away from your snoring."

"I don't snore!" He emerged.

Marta backed away, picking up her dress and tugging it on. "You were last night. Your nose must have been full of river water the way it was burbling."

"You did," Janne confirmed, coming around with a plate of fresh flatbread. "At least you know what you'll sound like at eighty."

Michal scowled in annoyance, tugging up a blanket around himself as Marta chuckled. Janne waved me down to my seat, and I obeyed, stretching out my leg, bruised from smashing against a river boulder, and trying not to pay attention to Marta tying her belt and then passing a comb through her long hair.

Inge and my mother appeared soon after, taking turns fretting over Michal who accepted it like a pleased sablecat. A small smile played across my face. This was part of what I'd wanted: family, a lodge of people living in harmony, caring for each other. Marta sat next to me, sparking something else inside.

The others gathered, Michal wrapped up in a blanket, and turned to eating. Something in me had eased since the last time I'd sat at the table, and the sight of my empty plate had even me blinking in surprise.

"Do you have to go back out?" Michal asked in a hushed voice, his shoulders tucking forward. The lightness wicked away, some still tenuously holding on.

"I do," I replied. "But you stay here until you feel up to walking about the villages."

He nodded, turning his mug between his hands.

"Whenever you feel ready." Inge reached over and tapped her son's hand. He took a deep breath.

"Maybe…maybe you could make this better?" His fingers brushed his hair, and it was my mother who replied.

"I can help if you want."

We exchanged a look. She was the one who kept mine short and in order ever since that fateful day.

"I want to go with you today, Davor," he said with more certainty.

"I need to check my armor, and then I'll be ready."

He set the cup down and stood from the bench, sliding off the blanket as he did. The rest of us shifted to go about the rest of our duties.

Marta's hand on my arm paused me. "I finished the shirt yesterday, if you wanted it?"

At my nod, she went to her bench and picked up a bundle. A

shirt of dark grey unfolded, red sablecats standing out on the high collar. Knotted vines and thistles tumbled down on either side of the slit and laces. More red adorned the sleeve edges.

"I am almost done with an overtunic." She pressed the shirt into my hands. My thumb gently brushed her work. The red was certainly brighter than I was used to—the entire thing finer than anything I'd ever dared to wear.

"Thank you." My voice caught over the words. It seemed a foolish thing to feel such a way about a piece of cloth.

Her hands twisted at her waist, but she wore a softly pleased smile. "It won't take me long to finish the tunic, if you wanted to wait?"

"I can."

She flashed a brighter smile that left an odd hitch in my breath and whirled back to her bench. I took myself to my room to change and gather my armor and hope my heart was not about to seize the way it was flipping.

I slipped the shirt on, tightening up the laces, before smoothing a hand down the front. I had no idea if it made me look more chiefly, but it felt different to wear a thing someone had cared enough to make me.

Picking up my armor and kit, I returned to the table. Michal sat with hands clenched over the edge of the bench, Mother behind him with shears.

Mother ran her hand through the tangled ends, humming like she had done the first few times she'd trimmed my hair. It worked, and he unlatched one hand from the bench.

I sat at the table to clean and oil the leather. It should have been done yesterday after the river, but my mind had been anywhere but that. Marta claimed the seat directly across from me, cloth and needle in hand, giving me another smile.

It took extra effort to turn to my task, made more difficult when she started humming along in time with Mother. I wondered what she was doing, but when I risked a glance, her brow was furrowed in concentration, needle flashing in and out of the cloth.

A knock at the door, even in the all-clear signal, had me grabbing a knife. But Alik stepped through the door.

My greeting died instantly and I shoved to my feet, the bench scraping loudly.

"What happened?" I demanded.

Alik's hair had been cut close, much like mine. There was no other sign of injury about him, no matter how hard I looked. But he shrugged like nothing had happened.

"Thought it was time for a change."

Willingly? My mind screamed trying to reason through it.

"Why?"

"If there is to be dishonor in this, then it's something I'll gladly bear." Alik's stance was unflinching.

"Alik." I shook my head, wishing I knew how to make him understand. He'd cut his warrior mark, perhaps not fully grasping what it would bring.

"Makar has been spreading tales of honor and dishonor around. Perhaps I'm also just tired of him."

I had no reply and Alik moved to tap Michal on the shoulder.

"All right?" he asked.

Michal turned wide eyes up at him, nodding wordlessly. Dangerous emotion welled back up into my throat. Alik had done it just as much for Michal as to spite Makar. And as Michal started moving with more confidence, I could not be angry at the battle-lion.

He joined us at the table as Michal gathered his armor to oil, chatting aimlessly with Marta and my younger brother. I'd finished with my last bracer when Marta stood, coming around with the tunic.

Black cloth, this time with white thread mixed with red along the wider collar, sleeves, and bottom edge.

"There." She tugged at my collar after I pulled it on, brushing invisible things from my chest and shoulders. "You look very chiefly. Though red cloth would still look better."

Her grin was back, and I fought against one.

"No."

She handed me a bracer. "Then stop coming home with bloody clothes or I'll be forced to make you one."

I took it from her hands. "I'll try."

"Good." She smiled again, and it took a moment to remember what I was even doing. Michal finished with his armor, and Alik helped him arm up.

We stepped out into the morning sunlight to find another surprise. The two warriors on duty around the lodge had also cut their hair. They offered salutes like it was any other day and they had not disregarded tradition for some unfathomable reason.

Tinek jogged up, a smirk on his face, hair also cut.

I was beginning to think I'd entered some odd afterlife.

"Makar does not know what to say." A bit of savage triumph shone on Tinek's face.

"Perfect." Alik draped an arm over Michal's shoulders. "Michal, feel up for a bout on the training grounds?"

Michal nodded, new determination taking over his face. We fell into step together, Alik not giving up his hold around Michal, much like a brother who might know what he was doing.

The day passed without incident, the calmness a dangerous illusion. I still saw plenty of Makar's supporters out and about, and there was plenty of speculation as now half the warriors wore their hair short. Alik had hunted down the men who had attacked Michal, and they sat in the guard lodge, waiting for me to be a little less angry before passing judgment. The *sjandsen* in the lower village had quicker replies for me, perhaps hearing of my threats in the middle village.

I saw Emil once, and just briefly, to catch him checking on Michal from a distance, approval on his face for the confidence Michal carried.

As the day wound to a close, Alik accompanied me back to the lodge. Marta sat outside with Janne, both with needles and thread. She looked up and flashed that heart-changing smile with a slight wave.

It was suddenly getting easier to offer something closer to a real smile, as if somewhere in the last hours, something had been knocked loose inside me.

"You like her." Alik's voice held a delighted tease.

I frowned at him, holding up my wrist of marriage cords. "I thought I might try since we're stuck with one another for life."

"But you like her."

The conversation seemed to be going nowhere.

"I will see you tomorrow," I said.

He tapped fist to chest, grinning like an idiot as he backed away.

Dinner passed quietly, and I had just divested my armor and sat on the bed when a tentative knock sounded. At my call, Marta stepped in, one hand still on the door. I sat a little taller.

"I…I left my shawl." She indicated the bed.

"Oh." It lay by the pillows and I scooped it up, proffering it.

She crossed over to take it, twisting it up in her hands.

"Actually, I wondered…it was more comfortable in here."

Redness tinted her cheeks, but she still looked steadily at me.

"We can trade if you want," I said.

"No." Her flush deepened. "It was more comfortable in here…with you."

"Oh." My heart forgot its steady duty and hopped around my chest instead. But whatever had happened that day, it was with some unexpected confidence I replied. "There is room then, if you want."

She smiled and backed away to nudge the door closed. I took the far side of the bed, turning my back to her, focused instead on pulling off my boots and shirt and tunic, leaving my undershirt. The dip of the bed marked her already under the blankets.

She doused the lamp as I slid under the blankets, not yet rolling on my side as she squirmed and tugged a little, trying to get comfortable. A touch against my lower leg drew a yelp from me.

"Your feet are *freezing*."

A muffled laugh came from her. "I'm sorry. They always are."

"Have you never heard of stockings?" I craned my head to try to see her through the darkness.

"I hate the way they feel under blankets."

I snorted. "Then how do your toes not fall off from frostbite?"

Another chuckle. "Sometimes I sleep by Vanda, and she lets me tuck them around her stockings."

"Your sister deserves a place by the All-Father," I muttered.

She prodded my side. "You are very dramatic."

A smile touched my lips, and I rolled to face her.

"What are you doing?" She sounded confused, maybe concerned.

"I am not waking up all night because of these icicles. Come here."

She tucked a little closer to me and stuck her feet between my lower legs, trousers taking some of the cold.

"This explains your hands." I had fingers around hers before I quite knew what I was doing.

We both paused, a breath away in the darkness, but she did not pull away.

"What about my hands?" she asked.

I rubbed them like I might any other person in the dead of winter with a need to get warm. "They are always cold."

The little chuckle came from her again, and she scooted closer. "Perhaps we balance each other out. It's like I have my own hot rocks next to you."

I gave her fingers another squeeze and released her, but she had tucked in even closer, a contented hum sounding. And for once, I did not want to pull away from another's closeness. We said nothing more, and her breath eventually evened out. I stayed awake for some time after, half-trying to convince myself to pull away from the foolishness. The other, bigger half convincing me to stay, close my eyes, trusting enough to fall asleep.

FORTY-FOUR

DAVOR

The rasping of a knife against whetstone drew my eyes open.

"Well, well."

Cold rushed over me at Kamil's voice. I turned my head to see him standing by the bed.

"You're dead," I whispered.

He laughed, drawing his knife across the stone. "You thought it would be that easy to get rid of me?"

I blinked and he leaned over me, shimmering point of his blade hovering over my chest.

"You cannot be free of me, Davor." It sank into my chest, dragging through my skin, until a cry locked up in my throat.

He laughed and backed away. I gasped, feeling heat soaking my chest. A whimper drew my gaze back over to him. Kamil's laugh grated against my ears as he pointed at the ground. Horror drew another sound from me.

Marta huddled on the ground, blood soaking through the back of her shift in three red lines.

"The coward found someone to care about," Kamil mocked. "You know what will happen to her, right?"

But this time, fight surged through me. I pushed up. Hands grabbed me, slamming me back against the bed. The battlewolf leaned over me, blood dripping from the cuts on his face.

"The bond of brothers may break the sins of fathers."

Then he was gone, leaving me confused. Kamil laughed again and this time I heard the sound of weeping. I wrenched upright, confronted by a new figure. Shadows blurred the lines between him and the full sablecat pelt draped over his shoulders and head, trailing to the ground. The sablecat's long teeth curved over his face. His eyes were hidden, but tears ran down his cheeks.

"Davor." His voice sent a shiver through my bones. "Keep fighting. Help my people. Bring them peace."

He vanished, my father taking his place, holding a torch up high. I recoiled from it, and Kamil seized his advantage, plunging a glowing knife at me over and over.

"Keep fighting." The words pummeled me with each knife strike, but I couldn't. My joints were frozen, unable to stop Kamil.

"Davor!" A new voice broke through. One that seemed familiar.

I latched on to it, dragging myself away. Kamil's knife flashed, and I threw my hands up. It pierced my palms as I closed my eyes. I cried out, opening my eyes again to darkness. I lurched upright, finding the softness of blankets around me.

Brightness flared to my left, illuminating a looming figure. I wrenched away, arm up to shield my head as I tore free from the blankets, bare feet stumbling on the floor, until I hit the wall.

"Davor?" The quiet question brought me fully back to

awareness. Slowly, I lowered my arm to see Marta kneeling on the bed, lamp in hand, her eyes wide with concern.

A sound escaped with my next breath, my hand against the wall and feet against the floor bare spots grounding me to the truth that I was awake. I blinked and she was in front of me. I jerked back from her reaching hand.

She stopped, but her eyes never left me. The open concern had my gaze falling to the floor, palm still pressed almost desperately against the wall.

"Are you all right?" The soft question brought another shaky breath from me.

Still not looking, I turned to the bed, peeling off my sweaty undershirt.

"Sorry I woke you." I tried to keep my voice even, practical, but it still held a tremor.

"It's all right."

My fingers clenched in the folds of the shirt, residual adrenaline running rampant through my muscles. Movement brought my attention wrenching up to Marta. I tracked the hesitant reach of her hand all the way to my shoulder. Then looked away when her fingers absorbed some of the heat from my skin.

Gently, her hand moved to settle between my shoulder blades, rubbing in small circles. The motion drew out the last tremors and a faint almost sob escaped with my deeper breath.

"Why don't you sit down." Her voice hadn't lost the quiet timbre. Her touch lifted as I obeyed, turning and half-collapsing down to the bed. My shirt fell from my hands as I leaned forward and pressed fists against my head.

Her hand re-settled between my shoulders, resuming the soothing rhythm. "Sometimes Vanda has nightmares. It would wake me up when I slept next to her. Some nights she wanted to talk, and others she just wanted to sit in silence. What do you need from me?"

"I don't know…I…" My voice still hadn't steadied. "I'm sorry."

She hummed. "Don't be sorry. Do you want me to stop?"

I mutely shook my head. It was slowly bringing me back to earth after feeling like I'd been cast adrift amidst a blizzard's anger. Finally, I pulled in another chest full of air, holding it, before slowly letting go, straightening as I did.

Her hand shifted, and in the split second she paused, I could feel the space between her hand and the knotted edge of one of my scars. Then her hands were in her lap, and we sat next to each other in silence.

"Thank you." My voice came low, like it might break if I spoke more than that.

"I'm sorry if I overstepped. You seem like you don't really like to be touched."

I almost winced at the honest assessment. "No. It helped."

"I'm glad." Her hands worked together, a short breath drawing past her lips before she spoke again. "I just… You are not alone, Davor."

A laugh broke from me, sharp and brittle. I did not look up.

"Everyone says that. But I am. I have been for so long…it's just easier…and I…I don't know how…"

My fingers and wrists curled up into fists, tendons straining, until her hand touched my wrist. I wished I might figure out a way to give something of myself to her, to anyone, but it felt locked too tight inside.

"The reasons why are all over me." Even that hurt to say, and I still could not meet her gaze, not wanting to see if it was pity or horror since my scars were on full display.

"Sometimes my left ankle will wobble from the time I badly sprained it in the woods and a boy who everyone was afraid of, was kind, and helped me home."

My breath lodged in my chest. I didn't know where she was leading this.

"And sometimes, when it aches or does not feel steady under me, I think about that boy. Sometimes it makes me sad to think of him so distant and cold when I was sure I'd seen some warmth in him." Her hand hesitantly touched my shoulder again, bringing a spot of heat to my skin.

"All I know are the rumors and stories of what happened in the chief's lodge. I don't know how true they are, but that does not matter. What matters is that it probably happened and that was not fair to you, to Michal, to anyone. Alik says you wall yourself off with thorns, and I think that is true. Because you were trying to protect yourself when no one else would. And there is no shame in that. But sometimes I think I see you past the thorns. The kindness, the smiles you almost let out. It makes me want to see you start living and not just fighting to survive day after day."

"What if I don't know how?" The fearful admission wrenched hoarse from me.

Her hand lifted and before I could regret the loss of her touch, her fingers touched my fist, opening my hand. Her palm settled against mine.

"I'd like to think we are friends at least, Davor. I'll help if you want. I know Alik will. Your family here. You don't have to walk any part of this road alone."

A shaky breath escaped, and I blinked hard to steady my vision.

"And you deserve to be happy. To be loved."

My trembling fingers tightened around hers. Her other hand closed over our entwined fingers, willing me to hold her words even closer.

We sat there until I'd willed my eyes dry and the lamp guttered and spouted fainter sparks of light. I lifted my hand and she released it, her look holding some of my own regret. She touched my shoulder again and moved to the other side of the bed, giving me room for one more breath before I sank back under the blankets.

The lamp extinguished and she moved in beside me. I rolled on my side out of long habit. It seemed she had to toss and squirm a little first. Then warmth tucked up against my back.

Something like a smile pulled at my lips before I closed my eyes.

FORTY-FIVE

DAVOR

"*Keep fighting. Help my people. Bring them peace.*"

The words turned over and over in my head as I stared at the ground, hands working at each other. They'd come back to play throughout my dreams once I'd fallen back asleep.

"Davor!"

I jerked upright, finding Emil standing in front of me, frown on his face.

"What?"

"I've said your name at least three times and you haven't moved. You all right?"

I stared up at him, confusion drawing my brows together.

"I know. I'm just as unsettled asking you." But there was a faint tugging at his mouth.

"*The bond of brothers may break the sins of fathers.*" The

battlewolf's words came back. I thought it might be about Michal, but a different option lurked in front of me.

If I was indeed giving consideration to words from frantic dreams. The other origin of the dream, I was perhaps too afraid to consider.

Emil still looked at me for some response.

"Do you know if...the chief...ever had dreams?"

A puzzled look crossed his face. "Dreams?"

I nodded, and tried to believe it when he sat on the bench, though a wide gap still existed between us.

"From the spirits?"

"If that's not some sort of legend from the past to make us look to chiefs with more awe." This time bitterness was rampant in me. I didn't know if I wanted anything from the spirits, and I surely didn't want to share anything with my father.

Emil settled back against the wall. "I don't know. If he did, he never said anything. And he did not consult the *talånd* about many things."

I did not want to take this to our *talånd* at all.

"If it's real, they're meant to be a mark of favor from the spirits or All-Father. You think they'd give it to someone like him?" Emil's bitter tone matched mine.

"Perhaps you need to believe in them first to wonder such a thing."

His short laugh was full of sharp agreement. Believe in them, or perhaps it was the trusting in something that did not seem to care that I had difficulty with.

But I did believe what I saw with my eyes—that something had changed in the last day. Between us, between others. I felt different since waking up with Marta's arm draped over me.

And it made me hesitantly ask. "Do...do you ever wonder if

you—if we—deserve something different than what we were cast upon our entire lives?"

He looked steadily at me. "You are giving something different to Michal. To Janne. You think you could not have it either?"

I could not hold that gaze, for once not full of hate or disinterest.

"You tell me. You know what I am, perhaps better than anyone."

"And what is that?" Challenge was back in his voice, but something gentler this time.

And it made me softly answer, "A liar and a coward."

"No." He looked at the lodge opposite, jaw tensed. "I have been thinking on what you said here before. I also did many things to survive. We might not understand each other anymore, the two of us, but at least we can both admit that. You perhaps have some things to be proud of over the years. I do not."

A feeling prodded at me, faintly like the one when reassuring Michal whenever he thought he'd done something wrong. Was this what it was to be an older brother?

"Michal says you are not all bad."

Emil shook his head, leaning forward on his knees and scraping his palms together. "Sometimes Michal still sees things in the hopeful light of early dawn."

"You don't?"

He scoffed. "There is not much hiding all the things I've done."

"Perhaps you could make reparation for some of it."

"And you know about that, do you?" The scoff returned, its bitter edge scraping raw against me.

I focused on the spot the earth mounded up against the opposite lodge. "I am learning it."

The tenuous peace sprang back between us.

"What did you dream?" he asked.

It rushed from me, almost desperate. "A man covered in a sablecat cloak. He told me to keep fighting, to bring his people peace."

Emil sat back, staring with wide eyes. "And you don't believe that was the spirit himself?"

I lifted a shoulder almost helplessly. "Why would he come to *me?*"

"Maybe because you're trying to do something about this fanged place." His weariness was back, and I felt it all the way in my bones.

"There was one other thing." Hesitation slowed my tongue. "I saw the battlewolf. He said... 'The bond of brothers may break the sins of fathers.'"

A bit of fear shone in his eyes, the same that ricocheted through me. *Brother* had never been a word I looked with longing toward.

"Well," he finally said. "I'm only here to make sure his legacy is overturned."

"Right," I agreed.

"We part ways after this."

I nodded. Though that annoying nudge prodded me again.

"You don't call him father." His quiet question brought me back. There was a curious edge to it, like he needed to know.

So much twisted up inside me, but I pushed through to answer. "He might have had a part in making me, but he was *not* a father."

Emil nodded, almost to himself. Then abruptly pushed to his feet.

"Makar is holding his plans close, but whatever it is will be soon. He took your words to heart. He's coming straight for you this time."

"I will make sure Michal stays out of it as much as I can."

His boots scraped against the ground. "Be careful."

And he vanished around the corner.

It took an extra moment before I levered to my feet and went back inside with one more look over my shoulder at the place he had disappeared.

"What's your plan for today?" Alik nudged his plate aside. He'd arrived for breakfast and claimed the spot next to me and across from Marta.

"It's the day I promised to hear questions from this village," I said.

"No doubt Makar will be there making his voice heard."

"Or more." I left my meal half-finished.

Open concern flitted around the table from the others, but Alik's face was grimly set.

"You want extra warriors?"

"Not noticeable." I hated discussing things so openly in front of the others, but they needed to know. I feared Makar might still take a strike at any of them like he'd done at Michal. "Perhaps increase the guard here."

A noise came from Mother. She leaned on the table reaching for Marta as if to protect. "You think he would come here?"

"I don't know. It might be his next move if he doesn't openly come for me next."

Michal sat taller. "Am I coming with you?"

"If you want to."

He nodded. "I'll be ready."

"Where were you planning to hear the questions?" Alik asked.

"I'd thought the square, but with things changed so much, I might ask for a lodge. Not this one," I said before Inge could offer. Makar might barge his way in, and I did not want him to be anywhere near this place.

"Tinek's lodge will be willing," Alik said, and it was decided.

We started to move from the table, stacking our plates together. Marta caught my hand. She half-turned on the bench to look up at me, eyes wide in concern. I squeezed her hand and mustered a small smile of reassurance I did not feel.

She squeezed back, not believing me one bit from the look in her eyes, but perhaps appreciating my attempt.

Makar was nowhere in sight when we stepped out of the lodge. Emil leaned against a lodge across the square, talking with one of Makar's followers. The other man gave a dark look my direction, carrying some of Makar's vengeful weight. Emil flicked a dismissive look at me, the faint and familiar sneer back. But this time it looked out of place on him, like I could see some of the edges of the mask that perhaps he wore.

I ignored him like I had for years, and Michal muttered something under his breath. Alik sent a warrior ahead to Tinek's lodge. The tribespeople welcomed me, most saluting, but I still noticed a few scowls and two men who slipped away out the door with a look my direction.

Michal was shifting restlessly at my side by the time I'd heard two petitions.

"Do you want to go?" I asked quietly in the moment before the next person came forward.

"I will stay." But he looked longingly at the door.

"Michal, I know you do not want this."

We both shifted to look down at our hands.

"Dariy said he would take me hunting. We've been before. I…I think that's what I'd rather be. Not a warrior, or chief, but a huntsman," he admitted in a hushed voice, lifting the shoulder nearest me as if to protect from my reaction.

"Perhaps there's a way to do both."

He looked hopefully at me.

"If we can put the matter of Makar to rest, perhaps you will be more free."

"And you and Marta?" His eyebrow raised.

I risked a glance around the lodge, but no one was in earshot.

"Do not get your hopes up."

A disappointed frown turned his mouth. He might have been hoping just as much as Janne for something to come between me and Marta, but definitely hid it better than the hopeful looks in our sister's eyes whenever she saw Marta and I near each other.

We finished in early afternoon. Michal ran from the lodge, eager like a young sablecat finally free from training leads. Some men and women had come with earnest questions, difficulties that needed solving. Others came intending to confuse, to thinly hide insults, or clearly on a mission from Makar. And with all of them, I'd made decisions while tamping down doubt in my own choice.

Tinek stood guard outside, and Alik and I stopped next to him. Michal stood a few paces away with another young warrior, and it made me smile a moment to see them trading words like young boys, so much of Michal's seriousness melting away in the easy friendship.

"Saw Makar once or twice," Tinek reported. "Thought perhaps he might take a gamble to force his way in, but he left before trying anything."

"He'll try something before the day is up." A growing certainty had been building in me ever since Emil's words. And that nagging came back that I might need to see the *talånd*.

"Your spy?" Alik's wry question brought my attention back. He still did not look offended or betrayed that I had not told him, but there was a bit of frustration.

"Yes," I admitted. "And perhaps just a gut feeling."

Alik inclined his head.

"I said I'd go see the progress on the lodge," I said.

Three more warriors came and joined our group at Alik's signal, but Michal looked hesitant. If Makar was going to attack, perhaps he would be safer away.

"Go find Dariy if you want," I told him.

His face cleared and he saluted before running off.

"Smart," Alik remarked.

"I wish I knew how to do better for him," I admitted a little helplessly as we set off for the chief's lodge.

"I think you are doing well. My brother and I walked the different paths we chose, but he still looked out for me and I for him."

I had only a brief memory of his brother from the battle he had described. And I wondered what he might have to say about our alliance.

"You and Michal are finding your feet as brothers," Alik said. "That's what he needs more than anything. A big brother."

That seemed almost more terrifying than anything I'd faced so far, and it must have shown on my face because he chuckled softly.

"I don't think he's going to let you out of it."

But that somehow eased the panic inside and I nearly smiled. I was getting used to him around as a younger brother. I did not want to give it up either.

Our boots scuffed on the path up to the chieftain's lodge. Even with resistance from the warriors in helping to clear the ground, it had been done even sooner than the craftsmen had anticipated, and they had been spending their days cutting and preparing wood, arguing over building, and grumbling about the rain that might have set them back.

A skeletal frame now stood, connecting the remainder of the old lodge to what would be the new. Men moved about, the sound of their mallets striking iron nails rang across the mountainside.

The head craftsman raised a hand in greeting as we came, his weathered face breaking into a broad smile.

"Chief!" He switched the hammer to his other hand to give me a salute.

I nodded in return, content with letting him fill up the spaces my words did not. The others paused in their work, saluting as well, most abandoning their work to trail us as he showed us around the outline of the new lodge.

They had taken my words to heart, and the new lodge would sit crosswise to the old, not even the corners in the same place. Another rush of relief swept through me at the sight of the next way the former chief would be scraped from the memory of the tribe the way the burned lodge had been cleared.

"The walls have started." He indicated where narrow logs, stripped of bark and cured in the sun, were now being nailed into place on the inside of the frame, positioned carefully to connect with others in the corner. Once it was built high enough, the exterior would be covered in resin and then another layer of bark-covered logs would cover it.

"You are working fast." I turned slowly to look up at the

open frame, my gaze sweeping from there to the blue sky.

"Some of the warriors stayed on to help with the building."

I glanced to Alik.

"They are still keeping their duties as warriors," he reassured.

The craftsman looked a little chagrined. "I should have asked you, Chief."

I waved my hand. "The battlelion has charge over the warriors. I am glad you have the extra help."

He bowed his head, not quite hiding his relief. They followed as my feet took me to the top of the lodge where one day the seat of chief would be. Perhaps it might even be me sitting in it.

I turned and looked down what would eventually be the great hall. It faced toward the village, the peaked roofs standing in their proud squares. The lower village was barely visible in the shimmering warmth of the afternoon.

"It will be a good place." Alik came to stand beside me, hands resting atop his sword hilt.

"I think I will have even more doubt in my ability to lead standing here," I confessed.

He chuckled. "You are only a few countings in. Things get easier with more experience."

"How do you stay so confident in your position?"

"Oh, I cry myself to sleep every night," he said easily.

I flattened my lips in a glare at him. He only chuckled again.

"Perhaps I'm learning a thing or two from you about how to hide the absolute panic that I am ruining the position of battlelion by wearing this." He tapped the medallion.

A short laugh echoed in my chest, and we kept contemplating the land before us. Then, slowly, I told him of my dream.

"And you do not believe it was the spirit himself, because…?" Alik asked before I could even admit my doubt.

My shoulder lifted. He nodded like he understood all that motion encompassed.

"When my brother died, I turned from the spirits for a time. I did not see how the All-Father could allow a war like that, the deaths of innocent people."

"What brought you back?"

He gathered a breath, rubbing his chin before replying. "I'm not sure. It was a few years after he died. My mother dragged me with her to the spirits' lodge while she burned a cloth in his memory. I didn't want to go. Father had grieved in his own way, as she had hers. I don't think I'd let him go yet. Maybe it was hearing her pray, believing so much that they still watched over us, even though so many things went unpunished in the tribe. And I began to see them in small things after that. The way some people tried to do good, even though it was like a salmon fighting its way upstream."

I felt his gaze settle on me and I dared not look.

"Perhaps the All-Father's will is not a mighty thing that settles heavy over us, forcing us onto paths. Perhaps it is up to us and how we choose to live here on this earth—ignoring or following it."

"So why choose me when I've ignored it for most of my life?"

"Because I think you have at least one foot on His path, though you realize it or not."

"I don't know."

"Perhaps you should go talk with the *talånd*."

I scoffed before I could hold it back. "You think he would advise me in any way?"

Alik huffed. "But we have another *talånd* here, one you've spoken to before."

I arched an eyebrow. "You would not have issue with me consulting the Greywolf?"

"He spoke for you in the lodge at the naming. He's spoken with you since."

"How do any of us know that he has not been attempting to sow further seeds of discord by that?"

"What do you think of his words in the past?" Alik challenged.

My mind immediately went back to a winter's day when he warned of a reckoning. And it seemed he had spoken true of that.

"I'll go with you." He clapped my shoulder as if it was already decided and my silence had been reassurance enough.

With one last farewell to the craftsmen, we started across the hill. A worn path wound from the place of chief around the mount to the open space that housed the lodge of the spirits and the smaller dwellings of those who would serve them.

Sounds of chanting led us around the corner of the spirits' lodge. Tall pines sheltered the houses from winds that would come sharp down the mountain. Benches were set around a fire pit in a wide clearing.

But it was not our *talånd* who sat on the benches with the apprentice. It was the Greywolf. He patiently corrected Kir through the rise and fall of words, pausing every few moments to nod and join his deeper voice to the supplication they practiced.

He looked up and the chant cut off. Kir sprang to his feet, and I did not miss the quick pass of fear in his eyes.

"Chief." The Greywolf was first to welcome us, pushing more slowly to his feet and offering a hand to his forehead.

Kir followed suit but stayed in silence. I cast a glance around, waiting to see our *talånd* and not just the two in grey cloaks.

"Where is the *talånd?*" I asked.

Kir scuffed a boot against the ground and looked almost helplessly at the Greywolf.

"He has found himself occupied with other matters."

"And you are teaching Kir?"

The Greywolf gestured to the small pile of scrolls on the bench. "Our ways are not so different from each other. What I know to be similar, I have taken it upon myself to teach."

"Kir?" I softened my voice to let him know it was not his fault.

He looked up, shame coating his cheeks in red. "The *talånd* has all but refused to teach me. This is the only way."

I nodded. "I see. And do you know where the *talånd* is right now?"

Kir shook his head, gaze back on his boots. The Greywolf tucked his cloak around himself though spring was giving us days of glorious warmth.

"I say this with no ill intent," he began. "I say it as a man who also sought to force the will of the spirits, to try to force the tribe in ways I thought were best."

My jaw set, tension rushing back through me. The Greywolf nodded and we understood each other.

"But I have repented what I did. Their ways are inexorable and not for man to try to thwart. Reidar perhaps thought to push their hand by taking another woman. They gave him two sons, and we saw what came of that." He gestured vaguely north.

"I learned from that mistake, and perhaps they were at work all along. Exile brought me low, and then closer to them than perhaps I had been in a few years. Perhaps I was meant to be here to help Kir. He reminds of me my apprentice back home." He gave a fond smile to the boy, who brightened under it.

Alik exchanged a look with me, one shoulder rising in a shrug. The Greywolf had smooth words, but at least he was here teaching instead of away plotting.

"Perhaps you can advise me on the matter of dreams," I said.

The Greywolf did not seem surprised, though Kir's expression turned to something of awe. I took the bench the *talånd* beckoned toward.

He folded his hands in his lap, and I almost smiled to see Kir hastily emulating the position.

"Dreams are often sent by the spirits, perhaps sometimes the All-Father Himself, to *talånds* and chiefs alike to guide the tribe. Tell me."

Even though I had already told two people, one of whom I never thought I'd ever confide in, it still took a moment to bring the words forth.

As before, I did not speak of the role Kamil had in the dreams. Or my father. I did mention the battlewolf this time, and Alik stirred at my side.

The Greywolf only nodded. "And this troubles you, why?"

His dark eyes were gentle, pressing an answer from me.

"I've never felt much of anything to them. Why should they come to me?"

"Has there been any time you might have turned to them?"

"Other than to curse them?" I asked wryly.

This did not shock the Greywolf, but it did Kir. Alik did not stir. The *talånd* took a moment. A breeze stirred through the pines, prodding the low flames of the fire. He freed a hand and gestured around us.

"The All-Father brought all life into this world, and He set

His spirits to watch over it."

I nodded, content enough to agree with this tale.

"The breeze, the earth, the fire, even the heavens; we see them, feel some of them. Each of these have a spirit as their guide. They are all around us, watching us, and doing the will of the All-Father."

"If they are here, why do they not step in when they see injustice?" I asked. "Surely the All-Father, Who was said to have sung songs of peace at the making of the world, must hate war and violence."

The Greywolf nodded, not denying it. "The seasons turn, the stars spin in the sky, the moon waxes and wanes. Fire burns, wind blows, and green things grow. Yet they have no will of their own. When the All-Father made man, He gave them something else. Something to help them live in this world He created. He gave them the freedom to make their own way. For good or for ill."

It seemed like a way to avoid responsibility to me.

"But He never has, and never will abandon us. His guidance is all around us, flowing like a river, waiting for us to take and use. To my people He promised the Greywolf spirit in protection, and the Saber spirit here. I do not doubt it was the Saber spirit you saw and heard in your dream."

Why?

"You say he instructed you to keep bringing peace. I told you once in this very spot to expect a reckoning, did I not?" The Greywolf gave a wry smile.

I had nothing more than a nod to give.

"As you said, the All-Father sang songs of peace in the making of the world. That is what He wants, more than anything. But He does not disgrace those who have fought in battle. Though perhaps one day we might find that He honors the champions of peace more. Even if you do not believe in the spirits, you have decided to pursue this thing. I think that makes them look favorably upon you."

"Only now because I am doing something they like?" I challenged again, still not seeing why only now, they should care.

The Greywolf sighed and his head bobbed, though not yet in defeat.

"I think if you look back on your life, you might find times they looked on you then."

A scoff tore from me and I pushed to my feet. The Greywolf did not shift, though Kir looked worried.

"I know enough that I will not overstep in telling the *talånd* what he must or must not do in training his apprentice," I said. "But perhaps you might warn him what happens when *talånds* try to force their will on chiefs."

The Greywolf inclined his head, and I left. Alik said nothing at my side. The afternoon had worn on, but I felt like I had not moved forward at all since waking up.

"I need some time," I said abruptly.

Alik nodded easily. "Any chance you might tell me where you're going?"

I hesitated, and then shook my head. I did not want to give away my hiding spots. But Luk trotted up to my side from the direction of the villages. His tongue swept around his fangs and he yawned. Probably just back from hunting.

"I suppose I'll have to be content with him," Alik said wryly.

"I will be careful," I promised. "And will be back for dinner."

"I'm holding you to that." He raised a finger in warning, and I mustered a faint smile. After he made his way down mountain,

I waited in the silence for a few minutes until sure I was alone. The forest to the west called, and I was tempted, but it was too far. I had another place nearby that I could haunt.

Luk padded beside me, every now and then turning golden eyes up at me. He knew my spots, and he would not tell.

Though once safely inside a fold of stone created over years by winds or dripping rainwater, quiet did not seem to be what I needed.

The restlessness that was usually quelled by a few hours in this spot or another still swelled, perhaps even more than before. Luk settled at my feet, tail twitching as he kept watch for me.

I leaned on my knees, hands twisting together, pausing only to rub at the base of a thumb, as I tried to make sense of this new feeling. It wasn't the *talånd's* words, though part of me still rebelled at maybe trying to find evidence of the spirits throughout my life.

No, it was that I'd found out I wasn't alone, and so perhaps, I did not entirely belong in the silent and dark spaces anymore. Perhaps even more terrifying was the thought of gentle brown eyes if I went back to the lodge.

Luk gave a low huff as if he could read my mind. I looked at him.

"What do you think?"

He'd heard more convoluted questions and arguments from me, though perhaps this one I wanted an answer for.

His sides rose and fell in light pants, but he did not look away.

"I know." But I did not want to admit it to myself. Caring for her seemed a dangerous and untamed thing. My fingers fell to the marriage bands around my wrist. It was an easy thing to wear them in alliance only. But I had no idea how to be a true husband.

She claimed we were friends, and perhaps we were. I trusted her where I might not have trusted someone else before. Certainly, no one had ever slept that close to me before.

"She makes me want to laugh," I admitted softly, feeling foolish as I said it. But Luk heaved himself up to shove his great head onto my lap. No betrayal in his eyes as the last one who had truly made me laugh, the two of us alone and taking a tumble in a snowbank.

The golden eyes challenged me again.

"And like maybe I could be…more." It came even softer, afraid to even admit it to myself.

He lifted his head, sitting taller, and looking at me. The rustle of the pines stopped, and abrupt silence fell. I could not look away from him, that same feeling of *other* coming over me as from my dream.

Even my heart seemed to pause, until Luk blinked and turned away, stretching and kneading his paws into the earth.

I gulped a breath and the world returned to its rhythm. The Greywolf's words echoed again, reminding me that the spirits were all around if I dared to look. The Saber spirit's own animal lay at my feet, now purring contentedly.

A shiver raced down my arms and I rubbed across my sleeves to ward it off. Spirits ignoring men who turned against the oaths of the world, I could understand. Trickier, perhaps, was spirits caring for a man who had cursed them more than once.

The *talånd* seemed confident in their stance, but he did not know my whole truth. Luk growled lightly, the sound he made when grumpy with me for not bringing dried meat for him.

"I do not want to go back and ask," I told him.

He huffed. I shook my head, pushing to my feet before I could think more on having a nearly coherent discussion with a sablecat.

We wound our secret way down the mountain, my steps faster than they had ever been coming from that place at the promise of going home.

Home.

The thought brought me up short. The chief's lodge had always been a place to sleep, a place to eat, a place to survive. But Inge's lodge, the meals around the table, Marta finding her place, and making one beside me, laughter, no fear.

It made me walk even faster.

And the thought of Marta waiting there made my attention flounder as I turned between two lodges. Movement shifted and Luk's warning growl came too late.

FORTY-SIX

DAVOR

I barely got an arm up to block a blow, but the heft of the attacker threw me into the lodge wall. My head snapped back to impact and for a moment the twilight sky faded to black.

When my vision refocused, I saw another warrior coming for me. Luk's reverberating roar spurred me into action. I drew my sword, meeting another blade, the iron shrieking against iron.

Shouts filled up the lodgeway, and spears drove Luk away from me. Torches flared, trying to dampen my vision again. A spear thrust toward me, and I twisted away, desperately trying to find my bearings.

"Again!" Makar's voice rang out.

I battered the spear away, getting my feet set under me. Luk roared, swiping heavy paws at the spear points holding him back. I hoped his noise would bring someone.

A shiver ran down my back. I spun, ducking low and

swinging my sword in a tight arc with me. I cut through a warrior. I continued the motion, coming back around to see the spear coming again. Barely dodging, I fell back a step, my shoulder slamming into the lodge wall.

Triumph shone in Makar's face. Both arms spread, flaunting strength. Biding time under the guise of healing. Two more swordsmen rushed forward. I charged to meet them in the narrow way. Expecting me to maintain a defensive position, they gave several steps, one falling behind the other in the narrow space.

Instead of pressing the attack, I turned and ran down the empty way. Shouts followed. I'd barely turned the corner when something slammed into me. The force of my back meeting the lodge knocked the breath from me and buckled my knees.

Hands hauled me up and I stared into the wide eyes of Emil, his bloody sword poised between us. For a moment, it was just the two of us, breathing harshly, and I didn't know if he was there to help or wield the blade himself.

I started to lift my sword and he moved at the same time, shoving me around a dead warrior, hand still on my breastplate collar to keep me on my feet.

We turned down another lodgeway, boots skidding to a halt as two more warriors and a sablecat charged us. Emil cursed and pulled me back the way we came. We tore around another corner, the path free into the lodge square.

Makar shouted behind us. Two warriors closed off our path. Swords raised, we charged together. My opponent went down with a wounded leg. Emil's would not rise again.

"Davor!" Emil threw himself at me, knocking me sideways.

My arms came up around him as I heard the thud and saw the grimace contorting his face. His sudden, heavy weight tumbled away from me, and battle found me again.

Heat scored across my arm, and a sword point skidded across my breastplate. A savage growl announced Luk jumping down from the rooftop to land atop two attackers. An unfamiliar roar sounded and two sablecats prowled forward, followed by more warriors.

I shifted my grip on my sword, mouth suddenly dry. I did not have a spear, and swords were poor defenses against lions. A grunt and scraping announced Emil levering himself up against the wall, face pale but determined.

Something whirred beside my ear, sending me flinching away. A sablecat died with an arrow in its throat. The other bounded forward. I brought up my sword in desperation. A knife embedded itself into the lion's shoulder, but it still came on, now more enraged. Another knife whizzed by, missing this time.

Its feet ground against the earth, springing at me. Weight knocked against me, taking me out of the path, and my mouth dropped in horror at seeing Emil torn away by the sablecat. The force of their fall threw me to the ground.

Shouts filled the narrow way and boots pounded past. Alik led the charge, and my attention fell to Emil.

The sablecat had rolled past him, knife in its throat. He sprawled on his stomach, broken arrow stuck in the back of his shoulder, angled oddly where it had hit the breastplate strap.

Blood had started to pool around him, but his limbs jerked.

A sound broke from me, and I pulled him onto his side. His glazed eyes locked on to me, then to my bloody sword.

I risked a glance away. Alik seemed to have it in hand. All I could think about was this half-brother in front of me. Jumping to save me.

Sheathing my sword, I grabbed under his arms and pulled.

He cursed and swore as he struggled to get to his feet.

Once up, with his arm around my shoulders, I forced my feet to carry us away.

Get away. Get safe. The words echoed with every scuffing step forward.

He managed to lift his head. "If I die from protecting you, I am going to *haunt* you from the dark woods."

"You are not going to die," I told him. He couldn't. Not before I could ask him why.

Emil hung heavier on my arm with each step, until finally the familiar door loomed in front of us. He folded forward, pulling on already straining muscles, as I freed a hand to shove open the door and stumble in.

Janne was first on her feet, rushing over, then darting back a step with a gasp when she saw who I held. Inge's face stayed more reserved, not flinching at my hoarse: "*Please.*"

At her nod, the others sprang into motion. All except Marta who stared at Emil with anger and heart-stopping fear.

"Here!" Inge came and helped me half-drag him to the benches. We got his armor off, the motions bringing him back to consciousness. He half-screamed as Inge cut his shirt off, jostling his shoulder.

Gouges over his arms and some on his legs from the lion's claws were draining blood all over him. Inge wrapped bandages tight around them, drawing another sound from him. She brought a cup towards his lips and he jerked away, nearly sliding from my hold.

"Drink." Her voice was stern but not unkind.

Emil looked to me and something of almost pleading was there.

"It's all right," I said. "You're safe here." And I meant it.

His eyes, though glazing with pain and blood loss, still studied mine, looking for deception. Then finally he nodded, and let Inge pour it down his throat. We got him on his side and she went to work, him now largely unresistant from the draft.

The door burst open and I whirled with sword drawn, but it was Michal, and behind him, Alik. I lowered the blade as Michal charged across the room, throwing his arms around me in a ferocious hug that rattled the arrows left in his quiver.

"You're alive!" It came muffled against my armor.

I nodded, though stinging pain was beginning to make itself known now that adrenaline was fading. Michal stiffened, pulling away and studying the half-conscious form of Emil beside me.

Alik was right behind him, but more scorn and less wonderment in his eyes.

"He saved my life," I said.

"No matter," Alik said. "There's still business to attend to out there." He jerked a hand over his shoulder.

I finally had the presence of mind to wipe my sword blade clean on my trousers. Alik stole some of Inge's bandages and wrapped my wounds.

Some sound came from Emil, and it had me bending toward him. His eyes flickered open and closed, flinching every now and then as Inge stitched. The confused stare finally settled on me again, and there was that question and request all wrapped up into one.

"Michal." I turned to the youngest.

His hand tightened around his quiver, torn between staying and coming with us even though I wanted to order him to stay anyway.

"I will stay." He gave a firm nod. I would make sure Emil was safe, but I also needed someone to watch him as well.

Michal pulled up a stool, looking longingly at me and at Alik already impatiently at the door.

"Davor!" Marta halted me.

She was in front of me in a whirl of color. Her hand settled on my chest, and she searched my face.

"Be careful."

My fingers brushed the back of her hand and I pulled away. "Do not go outside for anyone or anything."

She nodded obedience, and we stepped back out into the chaos.

Tinek and another warrior stood outside the door, spears in hand and blood spattering their armor. Luk stood with lashing tail and teeth slightly bared as he looked out at the village. Night had well and truly fallen in the frantic moments between lodges, no moon to brighten the villages. I should have seen it coming tonight.

"Fights all over, Battlelion." Tinek lifted his spear. "We're getting spread out."

Alik cursed and I heard my own frustration at being surprised in such a way.

"You two stay here," Alik ordered. "I'll try to send more men this way if I can. We don't know what Makar will try next."

I looked over my shoulder at the lodge. If Makar attacked the lodge, I would forego any planning or waiting and take his head myself at the first chance.

The two warriors saluted and Alik clapped them both on the shoulder before striding away. I paused only to give them a nod and followed, Luk my dark and vengeful shadow.

A burst of shouting and clashing iron took us at a run towards the far end of the square. Some doors opened, but Alik shouted for them to stay inside. A few lodges already had a few men out in front with spears, glowering at us. At least they were watching after their own people.

We slowed at the same time, and Alik beckoned me behind him. With a flash of irritation, I obeyed, letting the battlelion move first, stealing from wall to wall, making our way towards the fighting.

Torchlight flickered and gusted in the lodgeway. The sounds died out and at Alik's nod, we turned around the last corner to find the remains of a battle. Our men lay bleeding or dying on the ground, some of Makar's warriors with them. At the sight of us, one ran and the two remaining charged us to cross swords.

Luk sprang forward and took one to the ground. Alik made short work of the other, catching him off guard with a cut and then slamming sword hilt against his head.

"Can't bring myself to kill our own people," he said apologetically. I shrugged, understanding the reservation, but with every passing second, rapidly losing it.

I stood guard at one end of the battleground and Luk at the other, while Alik went around bandaging what he could. He whistled one of our signals, and another answered. The back door of a lodge creaked open, and we both raised blades at the threat.

An older woman and two men stepped out cautiously.

"We heard it all," she said. "We've a woman here who knows enough about wounds to see them through this." She gestured to the wounded.

Alik and I exchanged a glance.

"You've nothing to worry, Chief. Most here are coming around to your ideas." She brought hand to forehead.

I inclined my head. "Very well. All the wounded then."

Alik arched an eyebrow, but I did not waver. Makar had

wounded there too, but perhaps it was habit to not leave any on the field. Three of our warriors joined us, taking in the sight with somber eyes.

More men and women slowly edged out to help carry wounded in. The dead we left. We stayed long enough to receive another reassurance from the elder woman, before ghosting away.

Another sablecat came to join us, a bit of white splotched on its left ear. Luk greeted Emil's lion with a guttural chuff, and they prowled together. We made our way back out to the main square.

Luk's warning growl stopped our feet before we left the shelter of the lodges. His ears flattened against his head and Emil's lion focused on the left lodge with teeth bared and a rattling growl.

The five of us stepped back from the waiting ambush, swords coming up as we fanned out to face all directions. I positioned myself to look toward the square, and had the displeasure of seeing Makar come around the corner.

"Chief," a low voice warned, and I risked a glance over my shoulder to see more men coming up behind us. Six men flanked Makar as he started walking forward.

"How lucky am I to find the chief and the battlelion in one place?" He freed his sword from the sheath as he came.

I gave several steps until Alik's tap against my shoulder stopped me. This time I kept the forward position.

"I don't care about the others," Makar called to his warriors. "But we'll keep these two alive for now." His face carried vengeful promise.

Alik cursed softly and I agreed.

"Lost my horn somewhere," he muttered. Makar kept advancing. I did not have mine on me.

"Battlelion?" one of the warriors behind us asked.

"Fight to get away," Alik ordered in a low voice. "And for spirits' sake, get some more warriors and come back for us."

A strangled noise of protest came from the man, but another somber, "Yes, Battlelion," came from another.

I tipped a look to Alik. Grim focus settled around him, and he gave me a nod.

"Same goes for us." A faint bit of humor dared escape with his next words.

A mirthless smile tipped my lips.

Makar halted ten paces away, he and his warriors caught in the same waiting as us, seeing who would break first.

Boots settled against the ground with a faint crunch. Hands gripped weapons. My heart steadied. I blinked, and then charged.

Makar blocked my swing, and another warrior came up at his side to thrust at me. I stepped away from it, and both kept coming. Battle raged all around me, the sablecats yowling and roaring. A slash across my leg sent me stumbling. A spear butt crashed into my stomach, and I folded forward as it stole my breath.

Someone smashed their boot against my wounded leg and it gave way. Another strike followed, keeping me on my knees while my sword was torn from my grip. I tried to pull in air, get up to my feet, but couldn't stop the boot coming for my chest.

It slammed me back into the lodge wall. My hand slapped against the ground, the coarse dirt tearing at my skin. Two more blows from a spear fell before shouts filtered in and hands yanked me up.

Alik was on his knees, held in place by two warriors as a third pummeled a fist across his face. But the battlelion was undeterred, especially as he saw me on my feet. It took all three to hold him down as Makar approached me.

My arms were twisted behind me, painfully tight, the warriors yanking against me as I tried to move in their grip.

Makar's hand smashed into my face, throwing my head sideways. I came back around, spitting blood as I did. He stepped away for a moment, allowing me a view of the lodgeway, and my heart fell to see the dead bodies of two of our warriors. The third slumped against the wall, breath laboring as he clutched at his arm.

Alik still somehow managed to look apologetic from his position. It faded to pure menace as Makar approached me again. He reversed his sword and smashed the pommel into my stomach. The arms holding me kept me upright, and I couldn't stop the sound that escaped with my gasp.

"This is familiar, isn't it, Davor?" Makar looked past me and a hand in my hair yanked my head back.

"You know, Kamil often lamented that he hadn't killed you yet, but you were too pitiful to just get rid of."

Makar tilted his sword to catch some of the torchlight.

"Though you playing chief might be more pathetic than anything."

I shifted, boots scrabbling for purchase, but the hands had too tight a hold.

"Although, I never thought I'd see the day you cared about someone." He turned away, set the sword against Alik's cheek, and cut.

I swore, jerking against my captors. Alik slowly brought his head back up, blood gushing from the wound, but he steadily glared at Makar.

Makar laughed and kicked him in the stomach before turning back to me.

"Now." His face turned serious. "What did you do to turn Emil?"

I did not answer.

"Where is that thrice-cursed traitor?" He leaned close. "If he's not dead, I'll finish the job. Care to watch?"

I did not break his gaze. His upper lip curled up.

"I hear you're not man enough to take your wife. Perhaps I'll show you how it's done, make sure she knows her place."

Ice filled my veins, and I yanked a knee up to smash into his stomach. He swore and punched my face again. Stars burst across my vision as something crunched in my nose and blood cascaded over my lips.

He staggered back to compose himself. Then a change slipped over him, and he beckoned the warrior holding a torch closer.

The ice melted, replaced by fear, as he held his blade in the flame. He studied it then looked to me with a smile.

"We've been here before, haven't we, Davor?"

The hold on me turned to keeping me upright as my knees threatened to buckle. The iron turned red, glowing brighter and brighter.

Noise filled my ears, blurring out any other sound. Alik struggled again, his lips moving soundlessly as I looked to him. Makar took the sword out and approached me.

Breath left me and my stomach flipped over and over. He laughed but I could not hear it. His lips moved, but my eyes returned over and over to that red glare. It swept up toward my face, heating my cheek with its closeness.

The man holding the torch crumpled, an arrow in his throat. Makar paused.

The tension pulling my left arm faded away and I staggered. Makar pulled away, shouting soundlessly. A sablecat leapt from above and I was shoved to the side. My legs gave out and I slid to the ground against something solid, focused on the bloody ground between my boots sprawled out in front of me.

Dirt sprayed, boots and paws thundered back and forth, and then nothing.

Breath still hid from me. Boots stopped, and hands grabbed me. Panic finally freed my limbs and I struggled as I was hauled to my feet.

"Davor!" My name was muffled, becoming clearer every time it was repeated, and I finally recognized Alik, bloody and battered, holding me upright.

"Davor."

Breath swept in and my hands clenched around his upper arms.

"It's all right. It's all right," he repeated over and over.

A sound tore from me and I pushed against him. He did not let go, his reassurances falling on my partially deaf ears.

"No," I finally heard myself repeating.

"Davor."

A scream shook my chest and all the way down to my hands. Everything stilled and I tried to pull in air.

"Davor?"

My hands worked themselves free from their grip on him, and another helpless sound escaped. Resistance fell away, letting me retreat.

A touch on my arm sent me cringing away, arm halfway up to protect my face before I registered Alik.

"Just leave me alone," I begged.

He came a step towards me. I slammed hands into his chest.

"Leave me alone!" He did not flinch from my shout and did not let me go. Another pleading sound caught in my throat.

Then I was pulled forward, his arms wrapping around me. My shaking arms pushed until his quiet, "It's all right, Davor. It's over," broke through and I slumped against him, relief breaking free and trying to settle me back.

Until a touch against my back and another flare of torchlight set my heart back to racing. I wrenched away, pulling out from under the hand he tried to put on my arm, and fled into the lodgeways.

FORTY-SEVEN

DAVOR

I stumbled blindly until I found myself on a bench. My entire body shook and I folded forward, pressing arms against my stomach.

A sound burst from me in the silence, my eyes closing like that might help me resist my body's urge to vomit.

"Davor?" A quiet voice brought my head whipping up.

Michal stood at the entrance to the lodgeway, torch in hand. I turned away from the fire.

"Can I sit with you?"

I jerked a nod, not moving from my position. He didn't say anything at first, perhaps waiting for my breath to even out from the rasping, jerky inhales it had started again.

"I saw the hot blade, and I...I'm sorry."

"I c-couldn't move..." My arms pressed tighter. "I...I just... Makar h-held me down when Father...when he..."

My back spasmed with the memory and I tucked closer on myself. I had no idea why the words were coming. To Michal of all people. But it wasn't like he didn't know what happened the night the chief stuck his blade in the hot flames of the fire to punish me.

A hesitant touch settled on my shoulder, light like it wasn't sure if it should be there.

"I couldn't move," I whispered again.

"It's all right."

"I couldn't…"

Michal pulled me into an embrace where he was supporting me more than anything.

"I know," he said softly. "And it's all right. I know exactly how you feel."

His voice didn't sound right. But I didn't have the strength to see why. My head rested against his shoulder. He said nothing for the long minutes we sat like that. And finally I lifted a hand to rest over his forearm.

One last shaky breath came, and with its escape, I felt clearer, like I'd finally torn through the fog. I tapped his arm and he released his hold. I straightened, lifting a hand to my face. He gently stopped me with an apologetic smile.

"I wouldn't touch your nose yet."

I scrubbed my eye instead, brushing away flakes of blood, and finally realizing where I was. Somehow my feet had taken me home. Michal's torch was in the bracket by the door. And Alik leaned against the corner of the lodge, Luk beside him. At my look, Alik limped forward.

"I worried you might have disappeared on us."

"Sorry."

"It's all right. Just glad you're safe." Blood and dirt crusted over him, and he kept one hand against the wall.

"I yelled at you." Some things were starting to filter back, helped by Luk's comforting nudge against my leg.

Alik offered a crooked smile. "The worst you said was to get away from you, so I think my pride can take it."

I looked to my hands, barely able to see skin under the mess of blood and dust.

"You were there?" I turned to Michal.

A chagrined look crossed his face. "Emil woke up and told me to go after you. I found some other warriors and we got there just in time."

"The arrows…?"

"Me," he said a little self-consciously. I rested a hand on his shoulder, and he gave a faintly proud smile.

"And then I followed you here."

I offered a nod before he could apologize for it.

Alik limped a step closer. "Davor, I mean this in all sincerity and friendship, but you look like absolute *scata*."

A laugh burst from me, almost desperate in its sound, and I took his help to stand.

"Makar?" I asked.

He got a hand against my upper arm as I staggered a step before finding some footing.

"Got away. Barely. I have some warriors looking for him. Artem is getting count of wounded and living right now. Though it looks like we might have gotten a few new men."

My brow wrinkled.

"Some defected. I've already gotten their vows. We're getting the others who aren't as intelligent into the guard lodges."

I managed to stand a little taller, but he shook his head.

"Don't even think about it, Davor. You need to lie down before you fall down. Inside."

Michal opened the door, and we stumbled in.

Inge directed my mother and Janne around the room to care for wounded men on the benches. Most didn't look too injured. Tinek stood at the main door and snapped to attention as we came through.

It brought focus to us. Marta was there first, standing in front of me. She shifted cloths in her arms to lift a tentative hand to touch my chest.

My head dipped to touch her forehead before I quite knew what I was doing. She let me stay there, hand sliding around to cup the back of my neck, until I felt strong enough to move.

"Come." Inge took my arm. Marta slipped a hand under my elbow. I pulled to a halt, looking around the warriors.

"Where is…?"

"Come." Inge inclined her head. She led me into the smaller healer's room. A cot holding an unconscious Emil took up one half of the room. A tightness in my chest loosened.

"We thought it might be better to hide him in here once wounded started coming in." Inge pointed me to the bench.

I slowly sat, raising arms with an effort to the buckles of my breastplate. But Marta gently tapped my hands and I let her take over. Inge worked around her, prodding at my wounds.

A low grunt escaped as the armor came off. But I shook my head as Inge reached for me.

"Will you go make sure Alik is all right?"

She looked down at me, hands on her hips, like she was about to refuse. But then she inclined her head.

"Let me set your nose before I go, since that will bleed again."

After a brief flash of pain that sent my eyes watering and sudden openness through my nose, she pressed a cloth to my face. Marta held it in place against the fresh river of blood as Inge left.

"Is this something I should get used to?" Marta quietly asked. "You coming home bloody and spent?"

Lightheadedness swooped and darted.

"Mm," was all I could manage. I was getting tired of it too.

"Is it all right out there? Men have been in and out, and we heard the healer from the middle village was up in a different lodge."

I didn't know how long I had been distant from the world, but Alik would not have lied about things settling.

"I think so."

"Some said Makar had you and Alik." Worry was free and clear in her voice.

I nodded. Her little gasp tore through me, and a pressure on my cheek turned my face toward her. I touched her wrist in reassurance. It seemed she believed me, turning back to making sure the bleeding had stopped.

Carefully, she pulled the cloth away. Apparently satisfied, she set it aside, and indicated my bracers. Exhausted, I let her undo the laces and slide it off. She removed the other, then the greaves.

Inge had still not returned. Marta studied me a moment before declaring she was getting more water to wash some of the blood away. I was left gripping the edge of the bench.

Emil had not stirred, breath coming evenly. I levered up and limped over. Bandages wrapped around his arms and chest, those not quite hiding the scars tracing his skin in silvery streaks.

A few strips like permanent bruises were laid across his back in a pattern I had felt before. It was all too many for him to have not felt the wrath of the chief or Kamil over the last sixteen years.

My eyes closed for a long moment and when I opened them again, I saw a young boy in front of me, eyes pleading for help. My hand stopped just shy of touching his shoulder, taking the blanket instead and tucking it up over him.

When I turned back, Marta was in the door, bowl and cloths in hand, and that same dizzying look of hate and anger and fear in her eyes as she looked at Emil.

I waited until I was sitting again, and she had wrung out a cloth, to ask, "What is between you two?"

She gave the cloth another savage twist, before setting it gently against my forehead. "He hurt Vanda." Her voice had me pulling away and touching her wrist again. She glanced over her shoulder, perhaps making sure he was still unconscious.

"He caught her in a lodgeway and kissed her. When she tried to push him away, he beat her. She was seventeen." Her jaw trembled and more tremors rocked her hands, white-knuckled around the cloth.

"And so perhaps I wonder why he is here." Challenge filled up her eyes, perhaps even a little anger at me.

"He has been helping me these last countings," I said. "I had my own doubts about him, but he saved my life tonight." I did not release my hold on her. "But I promise you, when things settle, I will speak with him, and will figure some sort of reparation for her."

Her eyes glinted bright in the lamplight. "You will?"

"I promise."

She inhaled and looked down at our hands which had at some point become entwined.

"I believe you."

I nodded and I might have even imagined the reluctance with which she freed her hand to return to her task.

Inge came back, moving with the efficiency of years of practice. Alik's bandages from before were removed, my tunic and undershirt carefully lifted off. Deeper wounds stitched, and aching ribs wrapped. Marta disappeared and returned with fresh clothes.

I insisted I was well enough to change myself. Inge brought another bucket of lukewarm water and soap. She turned to check Emil while I carefully washed more blood and sweat away. With one last admonition to be careful, she left.

I barely managed to get into the clean clothes, taking a few minutes to gather new strength to open the door again. The common room had emptied except for a few warriors on the benches, and Alik wearily giving in to Mother and Janne's convincing to stay.

Most of the blood was gone from his face, a stripe of stitches covered in poultice on one cheek. We gave each other exhausted nods.

Inge paused by me. "Janne will sleep with us to make space on the benches, or you can sleep in your room."

I gestured vaguely towards the room and made my way there. A hand under my elbow steadied me as I stumbled, and Marta was there again, staying with me every step of the way until I eased onto the bed.

"I can see if there's space for me to share with Janne tonight." Her fingers messed with her belt.

I looked up at her, filled with the sudden certainty that I did not want to be alone.

"No, there's room here if you want."

She gave a little smile and went to shut the door.

I managed to lie down, turning onto the side that ached less, leaving me facing her. An odd heat filled me at the sight of her just in her shift as she extinguished the lamp and crawled under the blankets. She moved with more caution, coming closer to me.

"Tell me where's all right to stay," she whispered.

"I don't *think* I'll break," I said, though my head was throbbing. A muffled chuckle accompanied her wiggling closer.

"How many times did you wade through the river before coming in here?" I grumbled, but let her stick her icy feet between mine.

"Only twice." Her reply coaxed a small smile from my aching face.

She shifted again and then a gentle pressure came against my shoulder along with a tickle at my chin. I froze for a second at how close she was. But if she felt my hesitation, she did not show it, or move away. I carefully set my arm over her, hand away from her back.

A contented hum came from her. Silence settled over the lodge, and she did not shift away. I let my eyes close, sleep pulling me under with almost vicious intensity, but for that moment, I felt safe and secure.

FORTY-EIGHT

MARTA

Warmth cocooned me, and I regretfully opened my eyes. A contented feeling pooled in my chest as I realized I was tucked up against Davor. He still slept and I tipped my chin up to look at his face in the dim light. He was usually gone by the time I woke.

I'd admitted to myself at the beginning that he was handsome. Even now with his nose swollen and bruises spreading across his face. Sometimes when I caught his faint smiles or when we talked, there seemed to be something dangerous between us.

But not here, the place it seemed there should be, with his arm wrapped around me. It seemed safe and warm and hopeful.

Even with him jolting awake twice in the night. Once not even fully coming awake, just muttering something incoherent and a little panicked until I'd guided him back down. I shifted so my forehead rested against his chest again.

We'd settled, barely blinking, into this new routine. And I was more than content to let it be. Somewhere along the last few days, other moments had sprung up where it seemed I might want something more than our friendship. But spirits only knew if he felt the same.

Davor jerked awake with a faint gasp. His arm moved from around me as he pushed up on his elbow, eyes bleary and confused. I slowly sat up, drawing his attention to me.

"Good morning," I said softly. Something pulled at my heart, realizing this was the first time I'd seen him wake up.

He stared at me another moment, then made some sort of inarticulate grumble and slowly lay back on the pillow. I bit my lip to keep in my chuckle.

"How are you feeling?" I tried again. The dim light from the window coverings wasn't showing much, but I had a feeling he'd be trying to hide anyway.

Another mumble that sounded like, "Awful."

This time I smiled, and gently stopped him from rubbing his face. "Be careful just yet of touching your face."

He obeyed, setting a hand on his forehead instead and the other on his stomach, grimacing again. I scooped his fingers from his head into my hand. His eyes cracked open again, watching me. But I frowned and gently pressed the back of a hand to his forehead.

"You're burning up."

"'M cold."

He still didn't seem fully awake yet.

"I'll go get Inge." I gently freed my hand, and pulled on my clothes. He turned his face away while I did, and it made me softly smile again.

The lodge was stirring as I stepped out. Inge was sending away a few of the warriors who'd stayed with firm instructions to come back for bandage changes that night. They promised obedience, most giving me the *dronni* salute when they saw me. I might have felt embarrassed for coming out of Davor's room, but just then I was more than happy to give them the illusion of a marriage.

I smiled and saw them to the door, thanking them quietly for their efforts the night before. Some looked embarrassed at the praise, others just nodded, and went their way. When I closed the door, Inge was bickering softly with Alik. He was half in armor already, not swayed by her frown and hands propped on hips.

Finally she scowled and raised her hands in a sort of vengeful acquiescence.

I went over to them. "He's always this stubborn."

"He's lightly fevered and could barely walk last night, yet insists on going back out." Inge's scowl did not relent.

Alik's expression faltered to something of betrayal when I looked to him. "I have to make sure Makar didn't take over in the night!" His bruised and swollen fingers struggled with fastening his bracer. I raised an eyebrow and took over the task.

"How is Davor?" he asked.

"I'd just come to get Inge. He's feverish himself, and probably needs something for pain."

"I'll get something for him." Inge left us.

Alik touched my arm. "How is he really?" His voice lowered to between the two of us.

"What do you mean?" I was almost afraid of the concern in his eyes.

He moved slower than I had ever seen up from the bench

and beckoned me to a more private corner.

"Last night…Makar would have done something awful to him if Michal and the others had not gotten there."

My stomach clenched. "What?"

"You've seen the scars on his back?"

I nodded. I thought I might know what had caused it.

"Makar helped the chief put those there years ago, and would have done it again last night."

My hands pressed tight over my stomach like it might hold in the disgust and horror.

"He was in a bad way before we came in. I think Michal talked him through the worst of it, but I wondered if you might know anything else."

"He woke up twice, but it wasn't…" Wasn't like before when he'd been wide-eyed and shaky for long minutes. "He was fine with me staying last night."

My cheeks suddenly burned under Alik's steady look. "I don't mean…we don't…"

His mouth crooked slightly, and I glared.

"I know," he said.

It didn't make the fire fade from my cheeks. "I just started sleeping in there after everything with Michal…I didn't want him to feel alone."

"Good."

"We're friends at least, but I don't think he trusts me to tell me much," I admitted and tried not to let it sting.

"I think you might be surprised." Alik didn't shift from a sort of knowing look. "Look after him today when you can."

I nodded. I didn't need anyone to ask me that. "How are *you*?"

"Oh, I feel like *scata*, but we've got a mess out there that needs sorting, and I'm not dragging Davor back out yet."

I rested a hand on his arm. "You're a good battlelion."

His smile was crooked.

"And stubborn, and still an idiot who doesn't listen—"

"All right!" He raised his hands in surrender. "Tell Inge I will be back later, and she can lecture me then."

I chuckled and made the promise. I closed the door after him as he limped away, and hesitantly went to Davor's room, nerving myself up to go through the open door.

Inge was helping him sit up, and his faint groan drew me over. He sat slumped over on the side of the bed as Inge lit lamps. Behind the bruises on his face, utter exhaustion and near defeat lingered.

I sat beside him and dared to touch his hand. His fingers curled around mine for a moment and he squeezed before letting go. I offered a smile to let him know I understood.

I helped Inge get his shirt off, him not quite hiding the grimace as his arms settled back to his sides. Or as she undid bandages and pressed around the bruising spread in dark blotches over his skin.

"You really do look awful," I said.

His lips crooked and a faint huff escaped that might have even been a laugh.

I looked to Inge. "Alik said he would be back later, and you could lecture him then."

Inge shook her head. "Oh, I will."

Davor's smile twitched again. "He's all right?"

"He's upright," I said. "But he's not going to let that stop him from checking on things."

"Don't even think about going out." Inge settled a hand on Davor's shoulder. "You are going to the hot spring. It will help pull some of the soreness from your muscles and ease the bruising."

He nodded obedience.

"I'll get Michal to help you. An hour at least in the spring." Inge got another nod from him. She softened and dropped a kiss on the top of his head.

"I'll send him in."

I watched her go, then looked to him with a light smile. "I think you ended up with two mothers."

"She's always helped look out for me."

"See?" I leaned into his shoulder. "Not alone."

He regarded me from the corner of his eye, then huffed again, but it came as some amused defeat. Michal knocked and entered, his constant energetic motion not quelling his concern as he regarded Davor.

I surrendered Davor's hand I'd somehow taken again, and left them together. The common room was empty but for the scent of breakfast coming from the cook fires. I headed that way, stopped by Inge calling my name.

Hesitation slowed my path to the open door of her healer's room. She was wrapping a new bandage around Emil's arm.

"Come help me with this."

I stopped in my tracks. Emil looked back and he *knew* why the anger was swelling inside.

"Marta." Inge's voice held gentle command.

The two of us did not break our stare as I crossed over to stand beside him.

"*Dronni*," he finally said and lowered his head in deference. It only made me angrier as I held the bandage as Inge instructed so she could better wrap it.

She made me stay as she finished with his other wounds,

sometimes helping, sometimes handing bandages, or holding a bowl full of paste she spread over the stitches.

Finally, she wiped her hands. "Marta, will you get him some food?"

We both looked to her to protest, but she shook her head.

"You are staying here for now. Davor asked me to look after you, and I am for him."

Emil's mouth slammed shut.

"You need rest, but I will find ways to keep you here until he decides what to do with you."

An angry look flitted across his eyes, and I stiffened, apparently ready to take on this man I knew to be dangerous with my bare hands if he threatened Inge. But he inclined his head. Inge turned on me next with an unwavering look. I held it for as long as I dared, then swept from the room.

Both Nina and Janne looked up in surprise as I stomped to the cook fires.

"Marta…?" Janne began warily.

"I've been tasked with bringing Emil food." His name tasted bitter in my mouth.

They both looked at me, wide-eyed, never having seen this side of me before.

"He is…"

"I do not care what any in this lodge might think of him." I cut Janne off. I'd seen the way Davor and Michal were worried for him last night. "He hurt my sister and I will never forgive him for that."

Nina wordlessly handed me a bowl of hash and a piece of flatbread, along with a cup of water. I whirled, almost spilling the water, and forced myself to go back to the room.

He was still sitting there and it made me even angrier to

realize he wore a pair of Davor's trousers I had just made.

"Here." I shoved the bowl and cup at him. The water splashed over the edge as he struggled to get his arms up to receive them.

Emil's mouth opened again, but my finger in his face stopped him.

"Do *not* say anything to me. I do not care if Davor or Michal trust you, I do not. And if you even think about hurting either of them in any way, I will come after you myself."

Like I had any way of hurting him, but my anger would not be contained.

He had the audacity to scoff. "Davor does not trust me."

I scowled back. "He would not have brought you here if he did not."

He seemed taken aback by the words, and broke my glare to look down at the bowl in his hands.

"You have hurt my family enough. Do not do it again." I swept from the room and out the front door to stand in the open air and wonder when family had spread to include everyone in the lodge.

"*Dronni?*" Tinek came to my side.

I drew a deep breath and relaxed my fists. The warrior had dark circles under his eyes, and he seemed to be propping himself up on his spear.

"Did you leave at all last night?" I asked him.

He shook his head. "Ordered to stay here."

I gave him a look at the longing in his voice.

"You'd rather have gone off to fight?"

He gave a sheepish smile. "The way of the warrior, *Dronni.* Most of us do not do well with sitting still while there's a promised fight. That's why so many are resistant to the chief's way of things."

I shook my head. I did not understand this. Did not see why they would rather be off fighting than at home. But perhaps they never looked back to see what they left behind in the lodges when they went.

Except with the anger still jittering through me, maybe I could understand the need to move about. And maybe I could do some good while I did.

"Where are the other wounded?" I asked.

Tinek looked at me, but I did not waver.

"I have no idea what the duties of a *dronni* are, but this feels like it might spite Makar, and help Davor all at once. So I want to go see those who fought last night."

Tinek threw back his head with a laugh. "Never let anyone say you are not a warrior." He lifted his spear and led me on.

I hastily ran fingers through my hair and tugged my dress and overtunic straighter in a quick attempt to look like I had not barely dressed and stormed from the lodge in a fury.

In the first lodge, there were five wounded. Two were separated off and from the glare the others and Tinek gave them, I gathered they were Makar's men. But they had been tended and given some comfort.

I glanced at them while I stopped by the other three.

"Chief ordered them cared for as well," one muttered. But it seemed not all of his companions felt the same resentment.

Tinek's words came back relating how Davor had not allowed men to be left on the battlefields either. And I looked around the lodge again with clearer eyes. The men and women, some of the older children, had that same division among them.

Not sure if they should follow the new chief, or cling to the ways of his father. I'd hated the division of rank among the villages for as long as I could remember, so who was I to stay on one side and perpetrate this one?

I stepped over to the two warriors. Now closer to them, one was young, perhaps a few years older than Michal. The other older, and sitting like he might try to protect the younger from anything.

"And how are the two of you?" I asked.

The wariness in their eyes faded to something like confusion at my question.

"You know what side we fought on last night?" the older returned.

"I do." I did not break his gaze. "And I hear the chief still asked that you be cared for after being left on the field."

They both nodded, neither seeming to know what to do with that yet.

"And I wanted to thank this lodge for caring for *all* of them." I turned slowly to encompass the people.

Most brought hands to foreheads. One man hesitantly stepped forward.

"How is the chief? We heard rumors…"

I didn't dare ask what those rumors were. "He was injured last night in Makar's cowardly attack, but will be fine with some rest."

I did not give them time to reply, instead leaving as a strange quivering set into my muscles. But Tinek's low laugh helped settle me once we were outside.

"The two of you are going to turn these villages upside down." He shook his head. "I see why he chose you."

I nodded, feeling it was best to not tell him I had chosen Davor just as much as he had me.

"Where to next?"

He guided me on, standing silently with me as I stopped in two more lodges with mostly the same response. And each time reassuring that Davor was fine and not hiding my disdain for Makar's attacks.

By the third, my stomach was kind enough to remind me that I had not eaten before storming out. To my embarrassment, the head of the lodge heard it, and offered me some food with a faint smile.

Alik caught up with us at the next.

"I heard rumors flying that our *dronni* was out and about this morning. What are you doing?" Light exasperation mixed with pride.

"If you can stagger about like a corpse, can I not be out as well?" I retorted.

Alik folded his arms across his chest, winced, and then scowled at Tinek's chuckle.

"Perhaps I am tired of blood and war haunting these lodge paths."

Alik nodded. "I was just on my way back to talk to Davor. Makar is nowhere to be found, and from reports I've gathered, it seems many of his followers were injured, killed, or switched sides at some point. Most of the huntsmen and warriors from the middle villages were up here last night as well once they heard the fighting."

"An end might be in sight?" I asked.

He tilted his head. "Perhaps even closer with the work you've been doing this morning. You make a good strategist, Marta."

I grinned, face heating a little in pride.

"And now no one will loudly question you and the chief standing united," Tinek said quietly.

"Good." My voice carried a bit of iron that almost scared me.

"I'll go back with you," Alik said. "Tinek, go get some rest."

The warrior saluted, and a bit of shame pricked that I had not dismissed him and found someone else to go with me, but Tinek waved it off.

"I am always willing to serve, *Dronni*." He offered a bow before leaving.

We made it back to the lodge, Alik pretending like he really didn't need my hand under his elbow for the last half of the walk. Inge had a righteous "I told you" look as he took a seat on one of the benches.

"Davor is asleep," she said in response to my quick look around. The door to the healer's room was closed, and I turned away before I could become angry at Emil again.

I went to Davor's room, smiling at the sight of Luk sprawled next to him on the bed. The sablecat had a bandage wrapped around his foreleg. His head lifted when I came around, greeting me with a soft chuff and laying his head back down. Davor was tucked up on his side, back to his lion, face smoothed out in sleep.

I gently touched his shoulder, and when he didn't stir, pressed fingers to his forehead under the damp bits of his hair. The fever had fallen, and his breath came a little easier.

It was enough for me to slowly back away, and return to the common room, pick up cloth and needle, and set in to work with that same contented feeling settling around me.

FORTY-NINE

DAVOR

A low thrumming and touch of something cold and damp against my cheek pulled my eyes open. Luk's nose drew back and butted my shoulder instead. I grunted. One great paw set atop the bed and he nudged again. I got a hand free from the blankets to place against his broad chest and the rumble of his purr. He rubbed his head against my shoulder, his other forepaw coming up on the bed.

"No." I warned him away from trying to fit all of himself on the narrow space between me and the edge of the bed and tipping us both over. His nose pressed against my cheek again before his rough tongue swept through my hair.

"Stop." I tried to turn away from the affectionate attempts to groom me, but he kept on, looming over me as his paws kneaded the blankets. "Luk!"

He paused for a brief moment before starting again. A clear

laugh startled him enough to drop one paw off the bed. I pushed up on my elbows before he could resume his attack. Marta stood in the doorway, a smile brightening her whole face.

Luk went over to her, twining around her, and butting his head against her shoulders until she sank hands into his fur and scratched around his jaw and ears. I took advantage of his distraction and sat all the way up.

I had never seen my lion so affectionate with anyone other than me. She crooned gently to him until he dabbed her cheek with his tongue. Her nose wrinkled and she laughed at the sensation. The open sound pulled a smile from me, widening as he kept half hopping on forepaws to try to get her face as she twisted and turned.

Finally she got her hands on his cheeks and kissed between his ears. I'd also never seen Luk so pleased. He lowered to the ground and rolled over. A laugh escaped me.

"You've done it now," I said.

She grinned up at me from where she crouched to scratch his belly. Something snapped in my chest as we smiled at each other. The broken piece darted around my chest as she sidestepped Luk and came over.

"How are you?" she asked.

"Better," I admitted. The ache was still there, but had faded into the background.

"You look better." She reached out and brushed some bits of my hair. I froze, looking up at her. Her smile didn't falter, but turned a bit self-conscious as she lowered her hand.

"Inge sent me to ask if you wanted to come out for dinner."

"Dinner?" I frowned in confusion. Last I remembered, it had been early morning. My stomach rumbled as I was newly alerted to this.

Her grin returned. "You fell asleep before breakfast, and then right through lunch."

"I'll get up then."

She found a shirt and my boots at my request, then accompanied my slow walk out. Janne and Michal broke out in identical smiles to see me.

"Alik was just here." Michal carefully tapped fist to my shoulder. "I'm supposed to tell you a few things."

"We'll talk in a bit."

He nodded, not put off by the words.

Mother came and pressed a gentle kiss to my cheek. "Good to see you up. Dinner will be soon."

I squeezed her hand, and she gave a wavering smile as she looked at me again before retreating.

"Where is...?"

"In there." Michal pointed to the healer's room. No one said anything as I limped my way there.

I knocked, and a gruff "Come in," replied. Emil sat on the cot, leaning up against the wall, a blanket tossed carelessly over his legs. Caution filled up the space between us.

"Still here?" I finally said.

"It was implied I was not to leave until you gave permission." A sneer threatened.

I edged further in and took a seat on the stool. This was new ground, more tenuous even than the space outside on the bench. I cleared my throat.

"Thank you...for last night."

He looked down at his hands. "Why did you bring me here?" he asked abruptly.

"It was the safest place I knew."

"To better keep an eye on me?" Confused anger flashed

across his face. I might not have understood it either had the positions been reversed.

"No." I forced myself to meet his eyes. "No," I said with more certainty. "You've been helping me and…and I couldn't leave you behind again."

He wrenched his gaze away. "*Scata.*"

But he didn't sound like he quite believed himself.

"How do you know I'm not playing both sides?" His jaw set to match the challenge in his voice.

"I don't," I said simply. "But if you were, I don't think Makar would have so angrily asked where you were and threatened to kill you."

A pause, and then he scoffed. "Well, angering him makes it worth it."

I almost smiled. "You all right?"

He shifted, like he could avoid the question. "I'm fine. Sable-cat didn't cut too deep."

"Good."

Neither of us knew what to say to the other, both so very unsure of what came next.

"What did he do to you?" he asked abruptly.

I tilted my head in question.

"You look worse than when you left, and Michal's been by, and he can't keep his mouth shut."

I wanted to curl my shoulders in, sheltering myself from the question and the almost concern.

"I…" Words faltered on my tongue. Emil gave me a knowing look.

"He'd heated his blade and would have…" My voice died again as my memory flitted dangerously close to those moments.

Emil cursed softly. He shook his head, and I watched in

confusion.

"There were many times seeing you hurt felt like a kind of vindication to me…but not that. Not that." His voice hardened. "That was just cruel. And he did not have a reason for it."

A sound broke from me, and I focused on my hands clenched together. When I dared look up again, his face stayed turned slightly from me. And it seemed that I found an air of loss, of loneliness around him. His life had been upended, perhaps more than mine, since Kamil's death and that night in the chief's lodge.

I'd found something I dared call belonging in this lodge, but I did not know what or who he had.

"Where does that leave us then?" I wondered if he might give me an answer.

"You tell me," he returned. "Your battlelion and *dronni* don't like me."

"I hear there might be a reason for it," I said carefully.

His jaw tightened as he looked to his hands. "Would you care to hear it?"

"Perhaps I can find a way to try to understand."

He shook his head even before I finished speaking, already dismissing the words. But a knock at the doorframe cut him off.

"Davor, someone here is asking for you." Michal looked as confused as he sounded.

"Who?"

"A woman."

I made my way out to find a young woman standing just inside the door, hands twisting together, watching the others warily. A cloak wrapped around her shoulders, and a loose braid tied off with a bit of red cloth hung over her shoulder.

"Chief." She hastily signed respect. "I…I'm from the lower

village. And I…we heard about the attacks last night, and…" Her hands wrung faster. "The way he talked about you recently, I thought it might be safe to come ask…"

Confusion robbed me of any words. Marta stepped towards the woman, hand raised in comfort, when she blurted, "Have you seen Emil?"

Marta stumbled to a halt. I stared at the woman, trying to sort out the meaning behind the question.

"Do you know where he is?"

But before I could manage to speak, a voice brought my attention around.

"What are you doing here?" Emil leaned against the door-frame of the healer's room, his voice holding a rasp I'd never heard. "Get. Out."

Fear.

She didn't say anything, just looked almost pleadingly at him. I lifted a hand, stopping the words he almost spoke.

"Marta, will you wait with her?"

Marta's gaze searched my face but finally she nodded and stayed the woman with a touch to her arm, but the look Marta threw Emil was full of warning.

Janne and Michal watched with open mouths as I made my way back to Emil. He fell back into the small room, braced in wariness, the fear not far behind it.

Just when I'd thought there was no new ground to tread with this half-brother. I slowly closed the door and took a seat again. He mimicked me, taking the edge of the bed, poised to spring up if he needed.

"I have no interest in using people against each other. You know this. But if she, or you, needs protection from the other, I'll see it done."

He stared at me a long moment, then half scoffed.

"No interest in using people? Then how does Marta feel every night?"

I tilted my head, giving him an even look. The scoff came again, but this time the fear was leaving, and I might have imagined the respect.

"I wondered," he said.

His look turned to the floor, hands gripping the blankets at his sides. I waited.

"She's...Yelene is my wife."

FIFTY

DAVOR

Five heartbeats sounded, slow. Then my "*What?*" filled the space.

No marriage cords around his wrist, no indication ever. Stories of him in other lodges, some women claiming to have been with him.

His knuckles showed white, and he still didn't look to me.

"Willing?" I asked.

He gave a sharp laugh. "I would not do that to her."

I leaned forward on my knees, searching for words but he beat me to it.

"She's from the lower village. I met her years ago when…my mother had a lover from the same lodge. She was with child and Father found out. He…he killed her for it." A tremble snuck though.

No one had ever known for certain what it was that killed

Emil's mother, but perhaps I should have guessed.

"I knew which man it was. I'd seen them before and sworn I wouldn't tell, but…there are some things you can't hide." His smile twisted bitter. "After she was dead, I went, ready to kill Nikon for getting her killed. But…but I didn't and somehow was there for a meal, let him talk to me. I kept going back when I could. He turned out to be more of a father than ours."

A slight pang of jealousy flared.

"And then I met Yelene. She helped me break free from some things, they gave me a place to hide when I needed. She's good. Innocent. I thought I never would, but two years ago, asked her to marry me and she said yes."

His shoulders lifted with a breath, and his hand twitched like he'd rather be messing with a knife than with the unraveled bit of cloth under his fingers.

"Two years?"

He'd hidden a wife for *two years*?

"The Coyote *talånd* married us. I snuck away when I could, many times going over a counting before I could safely get away. It worked until…she's with child."

I could barely sort through my own confusion, much less the odd sort of fear and pride in his voice at this new pronouncement.

"How far?"

"Far enough she won't be able to keep hiding it for much longer. I panicked when she told me. If…if Kamil found out, or if others in her lodge or in the village did…" He looked to me for a brief instant. "I thought maybe we could run, but Kamil would track us down, and…and then came the war."

My hand scraped over my jaw. Of all the things Emil had to admit to, this was not it.

"She would get trouble in the lower village?"

Emil scoffed. "We don't wear our cords. She wouldn't be the first to appear to get pregnant out of a bond, but once they know I'm the father…"

Marta heard enough for just being married to me, but Yelene might have it much worse for being tied to Emil.

"You said you wanted to be free," I said softly. "Is she the reason you helped me?"

It took a long moment before he jerked a nod. "Partly at least. The last few years with her…it showed me that there might be something different. But Father and Kamil…theirs was the only way I have known. Then…your words turned out to be more than just hot steam from a geyser. And…and I thought if I helped, maybe I might be free enough to take her from this place…"

He trailed off, and I recognized that deep longing for things that could never be.

"And if you stayed?" I asked.

Emil shook his head with a short laugh. "There's no place for me in this new way of yours."

The odd tugging came at my heart. "What if there could be?"

"You don't know half my sins, Davor. And you would have to judge me for them, or be condemned yourself."

It was only the truth, and what once might have been something simple now lay tangled before me.

"For now, perhaps, helping me might be punishment enough," I said.

He looked to me, then scoffed again, but it was losing its edge.

"And no one knows about her?"

He shook his head. "Besides her father and…Nikon."

"I would like to speak with her first," I said. Emil jerked a nod, wariness back.

"Perhaps we could make room here. And there would be room once the lodge is finished."

He looked silently at me. Whatever happened, I would not let her be shunned for any of it. Not like our mothers and not like Marta.

"I've no idea how to be an uncle."

Something like a broken laugh came from him. "I don't know how to be a father. Other than to do the opposite of everything he did."

"A good enough plan."

Understanding passed between us before I stood. "I'll speak with her. And, Emil, you are free to go, or stay, whenever you want."

He nodded, the caution back. I left him. The others still stood, darting glances to the woman who remained by the door, hands knotting her dress anxiously.

Marta tipped a questioning look as I beckoned both her and Yelene farther away from prying ears. Janne and Michal took the hint, frowning as they went to the far end of the common room. Inge and my mother stood at the entrance to the cook fires, a sort of knowing in their faces as they watched Yelene.

"Emil told me." I kept my voice low. "But I want to hear it from you. No lies. What are you to each other?"

Yelene lifted her chin, and I already admired her steady resolve. "We married two years ago, and I willingly put my hand in his."

Marta inhaled sharply, but Yelene did not flinch.

"I know who he is and what he has done." She looked between both of us. "And I have no excuse for any of it. I know where he came from. I bandaged his wounds and soothed his hurts plenty of times. And I pray every night to the All-Father that he might find his way out of it. He's different around me, around Nikon. We both tried so hard to give him a place where he could find some peace."

Marta had not shifted once, and I knew her thoughts lay with her sister.

"And I know he has many regrets." Yelene looked to me. "He does not speak so harshly of you anymore. I know he has been helping against Makar. He has done so much to protect me over the years, and this is another way he is trying. I do love him, faults and all, and...I would just ask that you give him a chance to keep trying."

"I will try," I finally said. "But much of it depends on him as well."

She nodded, and I inclined my head for her to follow. Emil was on his feet the second I opened the door. Yelene darted past, sliding arms around his neck.

"Rumors were flying that you were dead. You didn't come back. Teren did, but you didn't..." Yelene's voice trembled. Emil pulled her closer, a softness about him that I had never seen.

"I'm sorry," he whispered.

I turned away, maybe finding the last proof in their words. His lion had gone to her, perhaps when it couldn't find Emil. I pulled the door closed to give them some privacy. And faced off with the room.

"She's his wife." I lifted a hand helplessly.

Silence, and then Michal's "What in fangs?"

"Michal!" our mothers reprimanded.

"Sorry." He didn't look the least bit chagrined.

I shrugged again, but the motion of Marta crossing her arms

drew my attention to her. There was a new rigidness to her features and stance.

"You're angry," I said, and I knew why.

"Confused, maybe." Marta did not relent. "When you promised me something last night."

"I know." My leg was aching again and I eased onto a bench. "I do not know what to do with any of this. But I will find reparation for Vanda."

Marta barely softened, but she would hold me to my word, that much I was sure of. And I was proud of her for it.

"Do we set places for them?" Janne asked carefully.

I shrugged, looking to Inge and my mother for help. A wordless exchange flew between the two of them, and then Inge nodded.

"If they want."

Marta did not look happy, but I reached out to her. It seemed a small blessing that she took my hand.

"It might be much to ask, but can you trust me with this?"

Her focus fell to our hands, and then she squeezed gently. "I do, Davor. It's just…"

"I know."

She paused again. "I will trust you with this."

She might never know how much those words meant to me right then. "Thank you."

The door creaked open and Yelene paused with Emil in the door. Their fingers were twined together in a way that might never be torn apart.

"There is room for both of you for dinner," Inge said.

They looked to her, Emil shifting like he might be ready to put himself in front of Yelene.

"I don't know that I should." Yelene shook her head.

Inge looked more gently at her. "Have you seen a midwife yet?"

Emil moved, tugging her hand and glaring at me.

"He said nothing, Emil," Inge said gently. "I guessed."

Yelene's cheeks flushed, and her free hand fluttered to her stomach. "No. I haven't dared to."

Inge stepped towards them. "I knew about your mother, Emil. I kept her secret and did what I could for her. I'll keep this one."

Emil appeared taken aback, that same crack forming around him like when he'd told me only a few minutes ago.

"Come." Inge beckoned Yelene. "Go sit down." She pointed Emil over to the table, shooing him when he didn't move. He scowled but obeyed after Yelene gave a small smile and released his hand. The two women disappeared into the room and Emil cautiously sat across from me.

Marta glared down at him, but he didn't flinch.

"*Dronni*," he said.

Her expression didn't abate, and she walked around him and to the cook fires. Michal slid onto the bench beside me, leaning on the table and looking between the two of us.

"Don't get your hopes up," Emil warned wryly. "I'm helping only until Makar is dealt with."

Michal slumped back, some of his disappointment echoing in my heart. The others brought the food out. Janne took the seat beside Emil and he edged away.

An awkward silence fell, no one sure what to do, though Emil seemed perhaps the most discomfited. The door opening to show Yelene and Inge brought everyone shifting in relief. Yelene rested a hand on Emil's shoulder and that odd softness shadowed his face as he looked up at her.

"I should go," she said softly. He nodded, and their wistfulness had me darting a look to Marta. She'd barely softened.

"I can have someone walk her back," I said.

Emil looked torn between accepting and refusing.

"Emil, you should not be walking anywhere besides back to bed," Inge said, and helpless frustration welled around him.

"I can go," Michal piped up. "I'll take her back."

Emil's jaw worked as he stared at Michal, and only the gentle touch of Yelene's hand on his shoulder broke it. He nodded sharply and Michal stood and began to pull his armor back on.

"Straight there and back," I told him. "Take your lion."

He gave a sharp salute with a bit of a grin and pulled his quiver over his chest. Emil's hands curled helplessly on the table, watching them prepare to leave.

"Wait." Marta pushed back as Michal set a hand on the latch. Emil stiffened, wary, but I did not know what she was doing either. She went to her trunk and pulled a bright strip of cloth from a pouch.

"I've traded these to many expecting mothers." She offered it to Yelene. "If you want it."

Yelene darted a look between Marta and Emil. Marta's posture eased from stiffness.

"I pray only for peace and health for children and the women who carry them," she said softly.

Yelene gently took it. "Thank you, *Dronni*. I'll keep it with me."

The women exchanged a tentative nod before Yelene stepped out with Michal. Marta checked the latch as it shut behind them and came to sit next to me in the silence.

"Thank you, *Dronni*," Emil said quietly after a moment.

Marta sniffed, still not really looking at him, then dipped a short nod. The others joined us, and Inge offered the prayer to the spirits. Emil shifted during it, but said nothing.

As we finished the meal, the door swung open and Alik stepped through.

"Still here?" He scowled at Emil, whose hand closed around the small knife nearest him. I shot him a cautionary look, but he didn't relinquish the hold.

"Michal told you yet?" the battlelion asked. I shook my head, having forgotten completely. Emil's warning latched on to me.

"I sent him on an errand."

Alik look askance at me, then, ever-trusting, took the seat next to me.

"We can't find Makar," he said without preamble.

Emil gave a quick glance at the women, but I lifted a shoulder. I had not adopted the old chief's way of discussing things only in private. But they began to move anyway, gathering plates as Alik declined food.

"I have men watching those who defected to us last night, but so far nothing. A few have been willing to talk, but no one seems to know where he is." Alik turned a piercing look on Emil.

"And why do you think I know?" Emil sneered.

"Because you seemed deep in his graces. You've always been following violent men." Alik leaned on the table.

"Not speaking very highly of your chief here." Emil flicked the knife my way, keeping it spinning around his fingers.

Alik's glare turned slowly to me. "*He's* your spy?"

For a terrifying moment, I wondered if the betrayal in his eyes might be the end of our friendship. Emil seemed grimly pleased by his surprise.

But Alik just turned back to Emil. "So what does the eel know?"

"Plenty. Have you been looking with your eyes or just irritating people into ignoring you with that mouth?"

Alik's hand was on a dagger, and I cleared my throat. They did not ease from their aggressive posturing, but fell silent.

"Emil made the decision himself to give me information on Makar, and I decided to trust him countings ago," I said.

Emil startled like a deer, wide eyes flicking to me for a moment before focusing on Alik.

"Doesn't mean I have to," Alik growled.

"I am not asking you to." I lifted a hand between them. Alik finally grumbled and released his knife, jerking his hands wide in a sign of peace, though his face said the opposite. Emil narrowed his eyes with a scornful huff and set the knife down.

"He's been sending others to attack, wear you down while he heals," Emil began at my look.

"We figured that one out."

I gave a slightly exasperated look at Alik who didn't look chagrined at all.

"He found less support than he thought these last countings. That and his wound slowed his challenge. He planned last night to kill one or both of you."

"And no warning of that one?" Alik said.

"Makar did not entirely trust me either."

Alik muttered something under his breath that sounded like sarcastic surprise. I almost rubbed my temples.

Emil glared at Alik. "He finally gave the plans yesterday noon. I'd been trying to find Davor to tell him all day."

This time I winced. I'd vanished for some peace and then walked right into it.

"But you didn't think to come tell me?" Alik growled.

"Would you have believed me?" Emil retorted.

Alik glared. "That doesn't answer where he is now."

Emil tossed a hand up. "Do you have any patience?"

A grin almost broke my face, and a strangled noise came from Alik.

"He won't be in the villages," Emil said. "If you really depleted his forces, he'd head for safety."

"Where is that?"

Emil shifted in his seat again. "My guess is the *talånd's* lodge."

Alik and I both sat back.

"The bastard would try to claim protection from the spirits?" Alik spat.

Emil shrugged. "I'd seen him and the *talånd* talking many times. Never got close enough to hear anything interesting, other than them trying to figure a way to denounce you within tribe rules, maybe in place of going for a kill."

"Don't trust him?" I asked wryly.

"I did tell you." Emil scooped up the knife again. Alik tensed, but Emil just started fiddling with it, passing it from one hand to the other.

"So he claims protection and we can't do anything to him?" Alik said.

"And I doubt the *talånd* would do anything to help us," I finished. "The Greywolf couldn't as he's not of the tribe, and Kir is still only an apprentice."

The knife spun on the table under Emil's fingers. "I can go scout."

"So you can go straight to Makar? No." Alik shook his head.

"I think we're both more interested in killing each other at this time." Emil spun the knife faster.

"A theory maybe we should test," Alik muttered.

"No," I said. "I doubt Inge would let you go." I tried to lighten the words.

Emil's scowl was much like Michal's when he was about to try something anyway.

"Or I can find someone who can," Emil said.

"Our men aren't good enough?" Alik butted in. I was about ready to push him out the door.

"No, you have men who loudly declare their loyalty. I know some who still might be able to walk undetected through Makar's men."

"And you trust this, Davor?" Alik scoffed.

Emil's jaw was tightening, and I was fighting frustration myself.

"Alik…"

"No." He shoved from the table. "No, I know what he's capable of."

"Do you?" Emil's voice had a deadly edge.

Alik's hands slammed down on the table. I flinched despite myself, and Emil's grip turned white-knuckled around the knife hilt.

"Vanda is like a sister to me, and that is only one of the many things I know you've done." Bright anger filled Alik. "Do you even remember her among the list of your sins?"

"I do," came Emil's soft reply.

Alik didn't break his stare. "Does Davor know what you've done, or have you lied to him as well?"

"He knows plenty." Emil's knife ground into the table. "And where do you think I learned to lie?"

I flinched again, looking away for a moment, then mustered my own words.

"I know, Alik. And there will be reparation made." I looked to Emil, and he hardened himself under the promise, but did not shy from it.

"Alik." Marta's quiet voice drew Alik's fury up. She came around the table, touching his arm. "A promise has been made to me already."

Alik wrenched away, and I could barely look at the betrayal still bright in his eyes. He scoffed then turned for the door. I forced myself to follow, stepping out into the falling night and calling after him.

His feet unwillingly halted, and he bowed his head, hands on hips, before turning around to face me.

"Just let me be angry for a few minutes," he said almost wryly.

"I'm sorry." Pleading threaded my voice. I didn't want this to be the way I lost him.

His shoulders rose and fell in a great sigh. "I know. I just… wonder how the two of you made an alliance."

"We might not be as different as you think."

He tilted his head. My boot scuffed the dirt.

"He has walked a different path than me for many years. Once we were closer. Until I abandoned him to the chief and Kamil and never looked back."

Alik shook his head. "So, what, you feel like you owe him something now?"

"Perhaps. Tell me how some of the making of him wasn't my fault? I have a long history of turning my back on people, Alik."

"Not anymore." The stubborn loyalty came back to his voice.

"Maybe. If I was…my father, or Kamil, I would have killed him as soon as I became chief. Maybe before. Kamil intended for most, if not all, of us to die in the war. But I'm not them, and maybe I want to give him a chance to break free too."

Alik sighed again, his boots scuffing as he crossed his arms.

"I know what he's done. Believe me, I know more than you," I said as he gathered a breath.

He let it out with a huff. "Fine. I don't trust him, but I trust you."

The relieved rush wasn't even blocked by the continuation of his words.

"I'm a little angry with you right now, but I'll get over it."

"Thank you." I hoped he didn't hear how almost desperate it came from me.

He stepped forward and gently tapped my shoulder with a fist. "I'll send out some men and bring their report tomorrow. Get some rest, Davor."

I nodded and waited for him to disappear into the darkness before turning back inside. Emil was on his feet as I shut the door.

"I should just go," he said.

I shook my head.

His face twisted up in refusal. "I don't belong here, no matter what Michal wants to think. You're dividing your lodge by me being here." He backed away.

"Emil." I kept my voice gentle. "Tell me honestly. Do you have somewhere else to safely go right now?"

His walls fell again, showing the loss and confusion. "No," he admitted finally.

"I know my word doesn't mean much, if anything, to you. But you'll be safe here."

He slowly lifted his gaze to me. "As soon as Inge says I can, I'll leave." It was almost a threat.

I inclined my head. "All right."

He backed away, the small knife still in his hand, and I didn't ask for it. He vanished into the healer's room, and I turned to mine, sinking onto the bed and wondering silently at all the things that had been revealed that night.

FIFTY-ONE

DAVOR

I was already in bed, lying with back turned to the door when Marta slipped in. I'd half expected her not to. The soft sounds of her moving about, folding her dress and leaving boots by the bench still holding my spare clothes came, and a bit of calm found me. She extinguished the lamp and tugged the blankets up over herself. But did not move closer.

I did not know what to do, to say. I'd never been this close to anyone to see betrayal from my actions. Never let myself care when they inevitably did.

Having slept all day, I was still wide awake, mind more than happy to keep replaying every word, every action of the evening. Marta tossed and turned. I did not know how to speak to her when I knew what was troubling her.

Finally, she sat up.

"Davor?" The cautious question flitted through the dark.

"Can't sleep either?" I asked.

A faint laugh came. "No."

The blankets over me tugged, then. "Can I ask you a question?"

"Yes." My arms pressed tighter over my aching stomach.

"Why do you trust him?"

It was not the harsher question I had expected.

"I did not at first, when he came to me a few countings ago," I admitted. "But..." I braced myself, suddenly about to tell her. Maybe it would be easier in the dark, unable to see her face, but I wanted—needed—her to understand.

"When we were children, we got along. I remember being excited when I realized he was a younger brother, not really understanding the reason why. Kamil...he already had accepted some of the chief's ways, young as we were. And I...I thought I could teach this brother to be different."

Her steady breaths filled the space as I paused.

"I taught him what I knew then. How to sneak around the lodge, avoid certain people, how to lie..." My arms pressed tighter against my chest. "I'd already mastered it well. I taught him how to play Sabers and Shades, how to cast sticks and count their runes. I could beat grown men by my eighth year. But one thing I could not teach him was how to stay strong under our father's wrath."

A tremble edged her inhale.

"I did not know how to do it, so I avoided it as much as I could. And one day, we had been playing together, and Father came with Kamil. They had demands and I could not meet them, so I turned away and they took him instead. And I let them."

"How old were you?" she asked quietly.

"Ten."

I could not tell from her faint gasp if she'd expected us to be older.

"I could have perhaps salvaged something between us, but did not. And three years later…" This time shame pricked. "I let the blame for my actions fall squarely on him and did nothing to stop it or the punishment that came with it. I…I couldn't."

A breath lodged in my throat. "He has hated me since that day. I took the coward's way to survive, then and many days since. And he also did what he had to. There was no resisting Father for long." Burning prodded the back of my eyes. "And it was because of me that he was thrown onto that path."

"No." Her certainty came with a hand on my arm. "It was because of them. You were a child. How could you have stopped a grown man?"

"We never got to be children," I said, my voice shaking. "We never…it's always been a battle, one way or another, and…"

Her hand tightened over my arm. My chest suddenly felt like it was going to collapse on itself. I wrenched upright, throwing my feet over the edge of the bed.

The burning grew hotter in my eyes and I swept a hand across them.

"Everything…all this since the day we rode out for war, until now, has made me confront many things. As I got older and stronger, I could have done something. I saw much, but ignored more. I did not see what he still went through to survive. So I feel like I owe it to him to give him a chance."

The bed shifted and her warmth pressed up against my side. Her fingers touched my arm and I let her trace down until she found my hand, leaving a tingling trail behind.

"I might have been the same." The words wouldn't stop coming. "There was a day that I broke under my father's hand

and enforced his cruelty on someone else. He looked proud. I felt sick. Even more so when I saw my mother's face when she heard."

I'd vowed that night to never see those looks in either of their faces again.

"She told me that day that violence begets violence. And the only way to stop it is to choose to be different. To not give in to its chaos. Even if it's painful. Even if it seems it will destroy you. I thought it meant to avoid it whenever possible, so I did. Until these last countings. I know what he's done, but I also know what I have, and could have, done. I don't know my end in all this, but maybe I thought I could make it a little better for one of my brothers."

"You are for Michal," she said softly.

A choppy breath escaped. "And I still abandoned him at least once to Kamil during the war."

I scrubbed my eyes again, making them water more as I hit a tender spot at the bridge of my nose.

"I just...I want things to be better, to have a home, to have peace, but I don't know how to do any of it. Now I'm destroying one thing trying to fix another. I—"

"Davor," she said gently. "I'm not angry at you for anything. I understand now, more than I did, so thank you for telling me. It's...I'm angry at him."

Her hand tightened around mine. "You are changing this tribe, day by day. Changing yourself in many ways. Good ways." She leaned into me.

Her words only made me shake more.

"But you cannot take responsibility for what others do or do not do. That is up to them. They, and they alone, own their actions. Your father could have chosen not to be cruel. So could

Kamil. I do not think men are born evil. I think it is a choice made every day. The *talånd* could have stopped it. Any member of this tribe could have stopped it, took you or the others into a different lodge. No one made you help Lera. You chose that because you knew it had to be stopped."

A sound caught in my chest. Her hand touched my shoulder, and then she was pulling me around into a hug. My arms slowly folded around her as I rested against her shoulder.

"Kindness and courage are choices made every day, and you are making those." Her words hummed against my hair. "I see you making them, and so does everyone else."

She held me for a time, fingers gently combing through my hair. When I finally pulled away, my hand found its way to hers again.

"Marta…"

So many feelings swirled around me, weighted heavier by the sudden sense of expectation between us at my next words. I did not know where we stood, but I was finally figuring out how much she meant to me. But I had just confessed so many broken pieces of myself, and it did not seem like anyone would want to risk cutting themselves on them.

"Thank you," I finally finished.

She squeezed my hand and moved away, and I blessed the dark for hiding if she was relieved or not. I turned back on my side. The blankets tugged, and then she was tucking up against my back, shoving freezing toes between my legs, and wrapping her arm over me with an intensity that dared me to say different.

But I only smiled and rested my hand over hers. It brought her snuggling closer, and my muscles eased. I might not dare yet to ask where we stood, but this was becoming something I did not want to give up.

FIFTY-TWO

DAVOR

Alik arrived early in the morning, fully armed and grim. He did not bother sitting at the table with the rest of us.

"He's at the spirits' lodge and calling for you."

I took the news in silence, then nodded. "I'll get my armor."

"I'm going," Emil and Michal said almost at once, the younger already shoving to his feet.

I focused on Emil instead. Alik had no argument, maybe content to follow my lead.

Emil gave a bitter smile. "I want to see his face when he sees me walking with you."

I tipped my head. "Get your armor."

He brought hand to his forehead, but it only vaguely mocked.

Marta followed me back into my room, watching silently as I armed up.

"What does this mean?" she asked. We'd woken with me turned over in the night, arm draped over her. Despite that and my jagged confession, the easiness stayed between us.

"It means the end might be coming one way or another."

"I do not like the sound of that." She rubbed her arms.

I gave a mirthless smile. "I've long known blood will be the only way to settle things."

Her hand reached halfway between us, then drew back. "Be careful."

I paused beside her, briefly touching her shoulder. "I will."

Michal did up the last strap over Emil's shoulder, his movements hampered by the bandages under his shirt. Emil buckled on his sword, and the knife belt across his chest. His hand hovered over the three empty scabbards, a frown in place.

Michal went to his bench and picked something up. He extended two knives to Emil. "I found these in a lodgeway while helping clean up."

"These are mine." Emil looked sharply at him.

"I know." Michal shrugged. "I notice things."

A faint smile tugged the corner of Emil's mouth as he checked the edges and sheathed them, satisfied.

Alik waited by the door. He and Emil exchanged a glare but did not argue. Outside, three warriors fell in behind us. I steadied the sword at my side as we walked, trying to find a way to bring the same to my heart.

Makar was backed into a corner, and he was more savage than a sablecat. He'd be using every weapon he had.

The chief's lodge was a skeletal structure, walls half built, the new wood pale in the rising light. It had seemed hopeful, full of new promise a few days ago; now it just stood like a child's effort to play at great things and falling short.

I turned my gaze from it, and to the spirits' lodge where a fire burned in a freshly dug pit.

The *talånd* waited before it, leaning on his carved staff. Kir stood well away, cloak wrapped tightly around himself, looking sick under a spreading bruise around his eye. My anger roared up, snapping walls back in place.

"What happened to Kir?" I asked before the *talånd* could say whatever smug thing he had planned.

He cast a distasteful look at the apprentice. "Boys who know nothing should stay out of the way of their elders." He finished by looking at me, then pointedly at Michal.

A seething hiss came from my brother's direction and Alik tugged at his arm to keep him still.

The *talånd* ignored it and dragged his staff in a line in front of himself, dividing us from the fire and lodge.

"I call the spirits' protection on this place to ward against any ill intent," he announced.

I crossed my arms. "Where is Makar?"

The *talånd* tilted his nose higher. "Do you swear to abide by this law, or will you further meddle with things above you?"

"I do. Now where is he?"

Makar stepped out of the lodge, fully armed as we were. Four warriors circled around from the back to join him. They stepped up with the *talånd*, keeping the fire between us, out of easy reach.

Makar's gaze swept over us, settling on Emil.

"You live." He spat into the fire. "Cowardice must run in the bloodline then."

"And stupidity in yours," Emil replied, undeterred. "You really thought I would so quickly follow you?"

Fury filled Makar's face at the open pity in Emil's voice.

"I will kill you after I'm finished with the coward."

A gasp of mock terror came from Emil, before he hardened the next instant. "Try."

Makar focused on me. "Perhaps I underestimated you, Davor. You have some of the same resilience of a beetle under a crushing boot."

"They get rid of refuse, do they not?" I returned calmly. Emil did not hide his snicker.

"Enough," the *talånd* cut in. "This is a matter of the chief's position, not squabbling children."

I lifted an eyebrow. "Interesting you should say such a thing, *talånd*, when you declared me chieftain in front of the tribe and the spirits."

He drew himself up, reminding me suddenly of a porcupine trying to puff itself up to deter predators. "And it has been made clear to me that was in error."

"Convenient," Alik muttered.

"The scrolls declare a chieftain should have a wife. Which means any son who inherits must be of that bond, making no room for bastards to hold the place."

"Well," I said slowly. "Perhaps that keeps Makar from taking it from me."

The *talånd* turned on Makar whose fury fell to me. "A wild claim. You have no proof."

I shrugged, leaving him with just enough doubt. The *talånd* paused, caught between the two of us.

"I have once again consulted with the spirits," he announced. "Perhaps they will show us the way."

He dug a hand into a pouch and brought out a handful of powder. He began chanting as he threw it into the fire. The flames roared higher a moment before shifting colors, the smoke thickening as it rose higher.

I had no idea what he would do with this. If he declared it the will of the spirits, how quickly would people turn? There was no way to disprove him.

The Greywolf stood beside Kir, disapproval in his face as he watched the *talånd* continue to chant. Makar's sneer flitted in and out through the puffs of smoke. He knew what would be "discovered" in this prayer.

Emil shifted and a knife slid free. I held out my hand to stop him, and earned a look of disbelief. I needed something other than murder or a fight to stop this.

The *talånd's* chant reached a peak and he lifted his arms to the sky. A tremor rocked the ground under our feet. His words died. The ground shook again, a groaning ripping through the mountain. A hand grabbed my arm to steady me, and then the earth stilled.

We waited in the hushed silence, but it did not come again.

The Greywolf strode forward. "The spirits have spoken."

"Those happen here from time to time," the *talånd* spat, but his pale face belied the words.

The Greywolf flung out his hand. Dirt had been knocked from the side of the pit to smother the fire. Smoke escaped in thin tendrils. He pointed again at Makar picking himself up off the ground.

Emil released his hold on me, but I did not dare to speak, barely dared to breathe. I was not sure what had just happened, maybe not daring to admit that the spirits had just shown themselves.

"You are meddling," the Greywolf accused the *talånd*. "You have turned your back on the spirits. You discard the one they sent to take up the staff after you." He pointed to Kir. "You convince yourself of words the scrolls do not say. Our role is not to please man, it is to serve the spirits and the All-Father. I learned that lesson harshly myself. Do your duty here, now, and perhaps you might stave off their wrath."

The *talånd* quailed before the words, shock and disbelief still circling him. He cringed away from the smoking logs, half bent under some invisible weight.

Makar grabbed his arm, shaking him, but the *talånd* pulled free to stumble to the ground. A curse brought our focus back to Makar. He stood at the edge of the line.

"If he will not do this, then I will. A challenge, Davor. An *alakti.*"

Silence fell again, sweeping all the way through me. A challenge against all comers. Until the one warrior yielded, or challengers stopped coming.

Michal exploded. "You're not brave enough to take him on yourself?"

Emil held him back, but he added a curse to Makar as well. I did not move. The Greywolf looked somberly at me. The *talånd* rocked back and forth on the ground, muttering to himself.

"It's been generations since one has been called," Alik said.

"In a time of strife when a chief had to defend his position, so the *tåkns* say," Makar replied. "It is not just me who thinks this chief should be replaced. Would you disregard tradition, Davor?"

It hardly seemed a fair tradition. He would not be the first in the ring to face me. It gave me an odd sort of triumph he was that scared of facing me head-on.

Keep fighting. Bring my people peace.

The words whispered on the breeze carrying away the last of the smoke.

It would end in blood and death. A thing I had always

known. But this way, it could just be me facing it and I would spare my people, my friends.

"I accept."

Makar's smile shifted to triumph, but before he could say anything else, Emil stepped forward.

"You would call an *alakti* against an injured man? Your cowardice must run deeper than I thought."

Makar's fists clenched. "Very well. I will see you on the field on the last day of this counting, Davor."

I nodded. Four days. Four days and this would be over.

"Greywolf, see this done since this one can't seem to gather his wits," Makar said roughly.

The Greywolf slowly turned his gaze from Makar to me.

"An *alakti* has been called to settle the matter of chief. Blood and iron." He looked between us.

I took a knife and cut my palm. Makar did the same. We squeezed out drops of blood onto the ground before the *talånd*.

"Iron and blood, man's justice invoked. May the spirits give their own blessing on this fight."

He stooped and swept his hand over the bloody earth, mixing the grains and binding Makar and me together in this thing.

Makar stepped back, satisfied. "See you in four days... Chief."

I made it two steps away when Emil grabbed my arm.

"Why would you say yes to that? How foolish are you?"

Michal was right beside him, angry and scared all at once.

"Davor?" Alik's gentler voice broke through. He had the same questions.

"One fight ends this," I said.

"You think he won't wait until you're half dead from facing however many men he'll throw at you first?" Emil hissed.

"I know he will." A detached calm was settling over me. This was where my path was going to end.

"Not if we're there with you," Michal butted in. My look swept to him, and then to Alik nodding.

"They'll have to fight more than you," he said. Even Emil seemed ready to agree.

"No." It whispered from me. "No, it will just be me."

"Davor." Alik's hand stayed me as I tried to move on. "You're not alone in this. You've changed the rules, changed tradition. We can change this."

"He's right." Emil crossed his arms.

Frustration burst out. "So more men can die? No."

"We're not letting *you* die," Alik stubbornly persisted.

"Don't be stupid," Emil said. "Change the law."

"*No.*" I sucked in a breath, trying to still the mess raging inside. "No. The *talånd* has already bound Makar and me together. The *alakti* is part of our history and Makar will make sure the rules are well known. If I come with more men to fight on my side, then what do you think he will do? He will say I'm going against the spirits, or afraid, or trying to twist the rules for my own gain, or a dozen other things."

A brief curse whispered from Emil and at least he understood. Alik took a moment longer, and he was no less happy.

"I'd take the help, believe me," I said, a poor laugh escaping. "But this has to be me."

They might have had plenty more arguments to throw at me, but I forged on.

"The villages will have felt that tremor. Make sure they know what happened here."

"I will, Chief," a new voice broke in. Kir stood with the Greywolf, resolve tightening his features.

The Greywolf settled a hand on his shoulder. "We both will."

I inclined my head. "Makar will likely try to find anyone who still supports him, even from the sanctuary of the lodge."

"Leave them to me," Emil said darkly.

"No killing."

He scowled.

"Or stabbing."

"Then send the battlelion to talk them to death."

Alik crossed his arms, but did not react. Emil relented slightly under my look.

"I'll take care of it."

"I'll tell our warriors," Alik said.

"What about me?" Michal looked almost desperately at me.

"Prepare to become chief." My voice wavered slightly.

"Davor." Disbelief knocked him back a step. "You can beat him. I know you can."

The earnestness was a balm and a blow all at once. "Just in case." I found a smile, faint though it was.

My muscles felt stuck as I looked to Alik. "I need…"

"Go," he said softly in understanding. "I'll find you later."

"I won't go far."

He pressed my shoulder, giving me a nod, before backing away. The others slowly did the same, moving away to their various tasks, leaving me alone on the path to find a place to loose the storm building inside.

Emil found me later, sitting on the bench between the lodges, leaned forward on my knees.

"Do they always let you go off without a warrior or knowing where you are going?" He settled against the wall opposite me, arms crossed.

"They don't often have a choice," I said wryly.

He dragged the heel of his boot a few times through the dirt. "Why did you agree to that?"

I rubbed the edge of my knuckles. "One fight ends it all. Maybe I spare men this way."

"At the cost of yourself? Why not take the help? You have plenty who would step into the ring with you."

I shrugged. "I've always known it will end in blood, maybe death, for me. I knew it months ago when I made this choice. Maybe it's easier for me to pay it alone."

He huffed. "So you think no one cares about you or what might happen?"

I swallowed. "Michal might since he will become chief after me."

Emil shook his head. "You have a lodge full of people who care about you. A wife who cares for you maybe the same as you do for her."

I tilted a look up. I knew the confusing way I felt about her. And it did not seem fair to ask where we stood when in four days, I might be dead.

He gave a short laugh. "I cannot believe I am the one to tell you this. I spent one night in this lodge and can see it all." He tipped his head back against the wall. "You found family, people to love you." It wasn't scornful, maybe a little wistful. "You would throw it away?"

"I don't know how to have it all." My admission came hoarse.

He shifted, scuffing his boot again. "I don't know what Yelene sees in me. I'm too many jagged pieces, and many times I fear she is going to cut herself irredeemably on them. But she told me once that she knew my edges and chose to love me in spite of them."

His arms tightened over his chest and he didn't really look at me. "And if I can figure out a way to love her and make myself better in some small ways because of her, then you can. I know they are all bright-eyed enough to do it with you."

"What if you were here too?" I asked.

He pulled back a little, but didn't immediately lash out at the words. "What, you think you could drag me onto this high path you're walking?"

"Would you want to?"

He tilted his head to look down the lodgeway for a long moment before focusing on me. "Only because I can't let you be better than me."

A smile tugged my mouth. "It's not a competition."

A faint grin speared across his face. I nearly broke off my gaze at the sight of it, and the reminder of different times between us. And before I lost my chance in four days, I knew I had to say it.

"Emil, I am sorry."

He pulled away from the words, readying himself for a fight.

"And I'm sorry I never came back."

His face turned from me again, and a smothered sound came. Slowly, the tension in his jaw eased and he looked back.

"I am sorry too."

It hit me in the chest, the not knowing how much I'd wanted to hear it too.

"Maybe blaming you was easier than cursing myself for everything I did."

We weren't quite looking at each other. I did not know what the right thing to say was, but I did know something.

"We were children, Emil. None of us deserved what happened to us. We never asked to be made into what we are. Right or wrong, we made our choices to weather what was thrown at us because it was the only shelter we had. But we're free now. Free to maybe be what we could have been all along."

"I don't...I don't know what I am without them," he admitted in a hushed voice.

"*Better.*"

Emil looked at me through red-rimmed eyes.

"I'm figuring out myself with each new day," I said. "If I survive this, and if you want to stay after it's all over, I could help if you wanted."

He said nothing, and I was almost afraid he would angrily refuse, when he nodded sharply before abruptly striding away.

FIFTY-THREE

MARTA

Michal was first back, storming through the door, sending us all jumping. I nearly stabbed myself with my needle.

"What happened?" Janne leapt up, hands balled like she was going to go fight if needed.

"Makar is a coward, that's what happened. He challenged Davor to an *alakti* and like an idiot, he accepted."

I set my work aside. "What is that? Why is it bad?"

Michal dragged a hand through his short hair. "It means Davor has to fight whoever wants to challenge him until either he yields, dies, or challenges stop coming. And he won't let us help."

My stomach twisted. Janne had gone pale. Something smashed to the ground behind us, and Nina stood there, hands clutching at air, the remains of a clay bowl at her feet. I moved to her side, taking her arm, even though her same shock had muddled my mind.

"Where is he?" I asked.

I wanted to look him in the eye, ask him why.

"He sent us all off to spread the word how we wanted. He's somewhere quiet." Michal lifted a hand.

I could imagine him calmly doing all that. But what was happening with him by himself?

"When?" Nina asked in a hushed voice.

"Four days from now." Michal's voice held chagrin, like he hadn't meant to so bluntly announce this to Davor's mother. But his apology encompassed me as well.

Four days. Four days to…what? I thought I knew how I'd started to feel about him; this pounding fear at the thought of maybe losing him to the *alakti* had to mean something. But where did he stand?

Nina shook, and I guided her to a seat. She gripped my hands tight.

"He'll win," Michal said confidently, and I wanted to share his desperate belief. That Davor would conquer anything after making it through battles so many times, no matter how battered and bloody. Nina offered a shaky smile.

"You should go find him," she said to me.

"Me?"

Nina tilted a smile with tear-filled eyes, and patted my hand. Some heat crept up my cheeks.

"Do you know where he went?" I asked Michal.

He shrugged, apologetic again.

"Davor has many hiding places, but it might not be safe for you to wander about looking," Nina said.

"I'll go with you," Michal said.

"All right then, Michal." I smoothed a hand down my skirts as I stood. "Tell me what happened, and perhaps a *dronni* and a chief's heir can fight in their own way while we look for him."

Michal grinned and saluted. We stepped out together, making our way through the upper village where tribespeople gathered in groups. Some stopped us, asking about the truth of the challenge. And we answered, Michal more loudly than I, but I did not stop him.

We crossed to the middle village where Nina told us of a place he might be. Part of me wanted so much to run straight home to my family and maybe try to sort through it all in their safety. But others stopped us, and finally Alik joined us, small smirk in place that meant he was up to something and was proud of it.

"I heard you'd joined the fight, Marta."

"Michal has been assisting admirably." I wrapped an arm around the young man's shoulders, and he beamed at me.

"Have you seen him yet?" Michal asked. "We haven't found him."

The battlelion shook his head. "I was hoping either of you had. People are talking and he should be seen." Alik rubbed his jaw. "The Greywolf and Kir are at the lodge here."

"Lead the way," I said.

He grinned and we made our way down the main path to the smaller spirits' lodge positioned at the highest point of the village.

It had been all but abandoned by the *talånd* over the years, so it was strange to see someone standing there with people gathered about. The Greywolf saw me and signed respect. I bowed my head, and I pulled a prayer cloth from my pocket, asking for a blessing for strength on it.

The Greywolf beckoned to Kir, and together they said the words. I slid it back in my pocket.

"I would request offerings to the spirits on the chief's behalf," I said.

"We will see it done, *Dronni,* along with anyone who desires to offer their own supplication." The Greywolf inclined his head. I nodded sharply.

The tribespeople melted away before me.

Four days. Four days of this. I did not know how I would stand it.

I paused, taking in a suddenly shaky breath. Michal looked to me in concern, but I gave a smile. My reply was cut off by Alik stiffening beside me.

"What do you want?"

Emil stopped a few paces from us, and it was the only time I'd ever seen him hesitate.

"*Dronni*...I would like to talk to your sister."

My spine snapped straight and Alik bristled.

"Your parents should be there. Him too." Emil pointed at Alik.

"Is Davor making you, or are you trying to avoid punishment somehow?" Alik asked.

Emil's shoulders twitched and he drew a hand from a knife. "I'm here of my own choice. This is a thing she needs to hear from me."

I eased my fingers out of the tight fists they had formed. "Very well."

Before I could talk myself out of it, I led the way to my family's lodge, barely looking back to see Emil and Michal following.

"Will you go ahead and warn them?" I asked Alik. He gave me a searching look, but jogged off at my "Please?"

Alik waited at the door as we arrived. Emil stayed Michal with a light touch.

"This is between us," he said.

Michal nodded, giving me a look that asked if I was all right before he leaned against the wall.

The few people in the common room drew back at the sight of Emil. We followed Alik into the private room where I had met with him and Davor countings ago.

Emil slowly followed me inside, and Alik closed the door, taking up a stance and blocking Emil from leaving. Vanda and my parents stood at the far end of the room, their arms around her. A small sound escaped her at the sight of Emil and she pressed tighter against my mother. Father stepped in front of her, hand on knife.

"What it is you think you have to say here?" He glared at Emil. The only time I'd seen him so angry was when Vanda had been carried back and she told us what had happened.

Emil shifted, glancing at me and around the room. I realized then what he'd done. Put himself completely at our mercy for whatever was coming, and it almost made me respect him.

"Two years ago," he began, and heaved a short breath. "Two years ago, you caught the eye of Kamil."

His gaze never left Vanda, even through the surprised hush.

"I was with him the day you did. I knew what happened to women he wanted." A bitter laugh escaped. "I know my sins, but I never could stomach that. So I found you first. He…he did not like things spoiled before he got to do it himself. When you pushed back, it gave me an excuse to beat you for…for not giving me what everyone would assume I wanted. He was furious when he saw, but left you alone after."

Vanda stood silent, tears dripping down her face. Our

parents looked at him with horror and confusion.

"There were a dozen different things I could have done, but that was the only way I knew then that would stop him. And I'm sorry. Truly sorry. That is the truth of it. I won't beg for something you likely don't want to give, but you deserved this. I'll continue to stay away and take whatever Davor sees fit, but if you, any of you"—he encompassed us all in his look—"need anything, ask me, and I'll see it done."

He turned, hand on the latch as Alik stood aside, when Vanda shifted.

"Wait."

Emil halted, shoulders rising slightly as if bracing for a blow. He looked back over his shoulder.

Vanda stepped forward, tears still cascading, and hands trembling by her sides. I reached out to her, but she did not pull her gaze from him.

"I forgive you."

With those words, a look came over him. Like he was afraid and relieved all at once. He sharply jerked the door open and left. For a moment we all stared at each other, then I followed.

He was out on the path before I caught up.

"Emil!"

He paused, hesitantly half-turning to me. I did not know what to say. His words, the things Davor had said the night before, realizing that Emil had given us a favor from him, a thing that placed him in our hold if we so chose.

He waited, and I finally found my voice.

"You may call me Marta."

A faintly understanding smile tipped his mouth, and he inclined his head in acknowledgment before striding away.

I watched him go, barely feeling the dampness trickling down my cheeks. I brushed it away, and turned back inside, going to Vanda and holding her as she wept against my shoulder.

⌒

Michal walked beside me as we made our way back to the upper village. He hadn't asked, other than to see if Vanda was all right. His open concern made my heart warm, and I thought maybe it wouldn't be so bad to have a brother.

A figure stopped in the path ahead of us, and we hurried to greet Davor. He smiled a little when he saw us, and let me take his hand, but it seemed like he pulled away.

"Are you all right?" I asked.

He nodded, but the weary lines around his eyes that had been gone that morning were back. "You heard?"

"Michal and I have been out trying to find you and conveniently have stopped to speak with others about it along the way."

The depths of his dark eyes lit with his amused expression. "Maybe I should just leave the running of the tribe to the two of you."

I might have laughed, but it could be a real future in four days if he did not walk out of the ring. I mustered a smile for him.

"Perhaps you should."

Michal frowned like he'd tasted something bitter. "Don't you dare."

The faint smile tipped and for a moment his features shadowed Emil.

"Did you have somewhere to go?" I asked, not yet giving up his hand.

He shook his head. "I'd heard you were down this way, and had come to find you."

It was near enough to dinner that I turned us back up the path to the lodge. "Something else happened today."

We walked and I told him what Emil had done. He paused, face unreadable for a moment, then something near enough to pride flashed.

"I'm glad to hear it. How is Vanda?"

"Shaken. It's something she'll carry all her life, but perhaps now, there might be some peace for it."

He gently squeezed my hand, and I returned it. But once we reached the lodge, he gently untangled his fingers and ushered me in before him.

Dinner was quiet, the others like me not sure what to say as he lapsed back into his silent ways, barely touching what was in front of him. Emil did not come back that night or the next two.

And with every passing day, Davor seemed more distant. He was gone in the mornings before I woke, and off in the villages during the days with Michal. A warrior still went with me when I went out. Vanda seemed happier than she had in a long time, and I was glad to see it, even if my heart weighed heavier as each sunset brought us closer to the fight.

He still let me curl up beside him at night, but he did not reach for me. Even when I felt him wake up in the night. It drew the odd vice around my heart tighter and tighter.

The evening before the challenge, Alik came back with him. Dirt and sweat from the training fields covered them both. Nina pointed them right to the sweatlodge to go clean.

A tentative knock took me to the door, opening it to Emil.

"*Dronni.*"

Old feelings were a gut reaction to seeing him, but I smoothed them away with an effort. He had offered a change, and I could extend it back to him.

"Come in." I opened the door further.

He slowly stepped inside.

"Emil." Inge came around the table after setting a stack of plates down. "How is Yelene?"

He seemed afraid of existing in the space, and offered a shrug. We both stared at him.

"You have not seen her since?" Inge asked softly.

He mutely shook his head, curling his shoulders a little as if afraid Inge would be angry about it. "I do not know what will happen tomorrow," he said, voice a little gruff. "I cannot risk her."

And for another brief moment, I found some sympathy for him.

Inge softened. "How are you feeling?" she asked instead.

"I'd...I'd wondered if you could look at the bandages?" Again, he hesitated like he was so unsure of the ground he stood on. Perhaps he was.

"Of course." Inge beckoned him to the healer's room. "Has anyone looked at them since you left?"

"No." His voice kept the tentative edge. "But I kept them clean."

Alik stomped back in, followed by Davor, hair damp and armor dangling from hands. Michal flitted to their side as they took one of the benches along the wall to start cleaning the leather.

Davor caught my glance his way and offered a slight smile. I did the same and went back to helping finish dinner preparations. Emil and Inge emerged as I came back with the plate of flatbread.

"Emil." Alik greeted him.

"Battlelion." But there was no scorn in the slight tap of fingers to chest Emil gave him.

"You staying?" Davor asked Emil.

He shifted, glancing around. "No, I…"

Inge gently touched his arm. "There's enough for dinner."

Emil studied her face, then eventually nodded. "All right."

I brought extra plates for him and Alik. Nina came around and touched Emil's arm with a soft welcome. He seemed wary of it, but gave the slightest incline of his head before moving over to Davor and the others.

"Any change?" Davor asked.

Emil flicked a glance over at me, but answered, "No, he's stayed there the whole time. Plenty of coming and going. *Talånd* seems to still be shaken by what happened. He's barely gotten off his knees by the fire."

My feet brought me closer. Michal stood beside them, arms hooked across his chest, sharing the same grim expression.

"Haven't heard any other talk in the lodges, but word got around that I turned on him." Emil shrugged, hanging a hand on his knife belt.

"I haven't heard anything either." Davor set aside a bracer.

"You think it won't end tomorrow?" The question was out before I could stop it. Emil swung around to bring me in his eyeline, some warning flashing and dying as the others did not react to me being there.

Davor did not immediately answer, scrubbing a cloth across his other bracer. Alik studied him a moment then spoke.

"Trying to be prepared for anything." His smile was not in the least reassuring.

Emil flicked a glance between me and Davor when he did not say anything more.

"Are you ready for tomorrow?" he asked Davor quietly.

Davor's hand twitched. He cleared his throat and took up his breastplate next, attacking it with focused intensity. "As I'll ever be."

We all heard the edge to his deep voice and exchanged a look. Even Emil appeared concerned, and he rose slightly in my esteem. Michal's lips parted but Alik gave a slight shake of his head. The younger subsided, worry swirling around him.

At Inge's call, we moved to the table, Emil and Alik finding places among us. Alik did his best to keep the talk light, Janne and Michal jumping in to help. But Davor stayed silent beside me. I touched his arm gently and he let my hand stay there a moment before shifting away.

Each bite weighed heavy in my stomach, until finally I pushed my plate away. Davor did not eat much more than I did. After the meal was finished, he and Alik turned back to cleaning their armor and sharpening weapons, the sound of iron on stone grating on my ears, a horrible promise of what was coming.

I finally retreated to the room to get away from it. Through the door I heard them tell Emil to stay, benches shoved from the table, and boots moving about. My fingers ran over and over the prayer cloth I'd kept in my pocket since the Greywolf had blessed it.

I did not have a prayer for the spirits other than *please*. I begged so hard my hands shook around the cloth.

The door creaked and I swallowed the terror that was setting in. Davor shut the door gently and came over to me.

"What's wrong?" he asked.

I almost laughed in disbelief. How could he ask that?

"I just worry for tomorrow. For you." I did not reach out. It seemed he did not want it. "I've barely seen you."

He edged away to set down his armor and pull off his boots. He did not answer no matter how I waited as he pulled off his tunic and shirt, leaving the undershirt behind.

"Are you all right?" I whispered.

He paused at the foot of the bed, just out of reach of the strongest lamplight. "I cannot see past tomorrow. I've known it could come down to this—a challenge. But there is no other answer, no other way out. No matter how I look."

He's afraid. The realization sent a shiver through me. I put the prayer cloth away and folded away my dress and shoes, and wrapped my shawl around my shoulders before going to sit back on the bed.

He lay on his side, back to me, but I reached out still.

"Davor?"

He tilted his head just barely.

"I don't know if you're supposed to tell me it will be all right, or if I'm supposed to say it to you." An odd laugh broke from me.

Davor rolled over to better look to me. "What would you rather hear?"

He let me take his hand. "I don't know. I just…I don't want to think about maybe losing you."

His thumb brushed the back of mine. "I don't know what's going to happen tomorrow."

A bit of heat was growing under the pattern of his thumb. He stopped, but I did not let him go.

"We're friends at least, Davor. Could you not lie to me just this once?" I managed a smile.

"I don't want to ever lie to you." The low rumble of his voice sent another shiver over my skin. But he softened as he said it.

"Perhaps we could pretend then."

"What?"

"That everything will be fine." I could not let him go.

Sadness lingered in the crook of his smile. "Perhaps."

He shifted his arm and I took the invitation, and daring more, rested my head on his chest and tucked arms up between us. I could feel his muscles tense.

"I'm cold."

He huffed and his arms came around me. I might have smiled, but this felt too much like *last*.

We said nothing, and eventually the pattern of his heart steadied under my ear. I must have fallen asleep, for movement startled my eyes open. Davor was moving and sudden fear took me that it was already time for him to leave. My hands clutched his shirt.

"Just the lamp," he murmured, twisting over me. The room plunged to darkness, and I settled closer again, my hold on him still unbroken. "Go back to sleep."

I closed my eyes, reassured by the feel of his arms coming back around me, and something pressing against the top of my head before sleep took me.

FIFTY-FOUR

DAVOR

I was awake long before dawn. Only the warmth of Marta curled around me stopped me from going out to pace the lodgeway. The hurt in her eyes when she'd confessed concern after barely seeing me over the last days had stung. As had her gentle reminder. *Friends at least.*

It was only because I could not see past today that I had not said something different. Tried to give voice to the way my heart snared every time I saw her. How I couldn't help but hang on to her every word and smile.

My arms tightened around her, stealing one more moment where I could pretend that maybe she might feel the same or it would be a day that would see me alive at the sunset. A day where I might feel brave enough to take her hand and ask if she might be willing to look on this marriage as anything more.

But fate was against me, and the sun was rising.

I began to pull away. She stirred, pulling on my undershirt, eyes fluttering as she mumbled something incoherent. My hand closed over hers. Her breath fluttered across my skin.

"It's time?" she whispered.

"Yes." My voice came hoarse.

She released her hold and pulled in a breath. In the closeness of the moment, our eyes met, and my fingers brushed bits of hair away from her cheek.

I pulled away before I could do anything more foolish. She said nothing as I dressed in the dim light and slipped out the door. But even the quiet of the lodgeway could not soothe me. I paced back and forth, trying to banish the shaking in my muscles.

Once I might have looked evenly back at death, but not anymore. Not when I had a promise of something to finally live for. This fight wasn't just for my survival. If I failed, I left the tribe to Makar. Left Michal and Janne and Emil to his mercy. Alik would be killed without hesitation. Marta...his threats came back all too clear in my memory.

I'd never been able to fail in my life, but now I surely couldn't.

My feet would not stop. *Please. If you've ever cared anything for us...for me...if you truly care about this tribe...*

If the rumbling mountain had truly been the All-Father intervening...

"Let me be strong enough," I murmured to the dawn.

A light breeze trickled down the lodgeway bringing the fresh scent of pine. I closed my eyes, breathing deep, and a bit of peace wormed in. When I opened my eyes, Luk stood in front of me, gold eyes solemn.

I did not dare move or speak. He gently set his head against my chest, pressing for a moment, before drawing away. His purr broke the silence, and he pushed under my arm, knocking me sideways until I scratched under his jaw.

The calm stayed with me as I stepped back inside. Through barely choking down some breakfast. The others did not say much as they dressed and armed. Marta disappeared back into the room and re-emerged in the red dress and white overtunic she had worn the night of the trial.

I tore my focus away and back to one last check of my armor before pulling it on. The familiar actions of tightening buckles and checking blades brought steadiness back. When I looked up, Alik, Emil, and Michal stood by the table, armed and waiting. Alik held a bowl of paint.

"Ready?" he asked.

I stepped over to him. In the war, I had done my own paint. But Alik had asked the honor of painting the lines today.

It spread cool across my skin in the pattern I had not worn since the day of my naming as chief. He stepped back, nodding once.

Emil and Michal exchanged a glance, then Emil dipped a finger in the paint and took my arm, turning it to paint a rune on the surface of my bracer.

Strength.

Michal did the same on my other arm.

Honor.

He did not let go of my wrist after he finished, blinking suddenly, before throwing his arms around me. I returned the embrace just as fiercely.

"I don't want to lose you." His words came muffled against my shoulder. I set a hand on the back of his head.

"It will be all right."

His shoulders shook and I did not let him go until he felt steady enough. Michal pulled away and I rested hands on his shoulders. He sniffed, scrubbing the back of his hand against his eye.

"Be strong for me," I said.

Michal nodded, piecing himself back together.

I nudged his shoulder. "I'm glad I have you as a brother."

A grin split his face, not quite banishing the watering in his eyes. He knocked his fist against my chest. "You too."

"Go on." I nudged him.

Emil wasn't far, watching us with careful eyes. He shifted and focused on me.

"Don't die."

A smile tugged. "Is that concern?"

His eyes narrowed but there was no threat there. "Caution."

"Ah." I nodded.

I thanked the spirits for the understanding we had found before the end. I flicked a glance to where Alik helped Michal with his warpaint.

"If anything happens, look after them?"

Emil swept a glance around the lodge, then his shoulders squared and accepted the weight of the responsibility I asked.

"I will."

He stepped back to make way for Janne, no less tearful than her twin. Then Inge, and then my mother.

Mother's fingers touched lightly to my forehead around the paint.

"I am proud of you. So proud." Her voice shook.

I pulled her into my arms, pressing a kiss to the top of her head. Neither of us had ever dreamed a day when I might take chief's place, much less a day like this. She finally stepped away, and Alik was there, face painted and battlelion medallion gleaming atop his armor.

His honest features cast the lines into a different shape, and I could not remember what the same pattern looked like on Kamil.

For once he had nothing quick to say, just resting a hand on my shoulder. My hand grabbed his shoulder. The last four days had been spent with him on the training grounds, every spare minute around the last duties I was seeing to, making sure things were set for Michal to take over if it came to it.

"Not too late," he said. The same thing he'd said to me for the last four days. Wanting to step into the ring beside me. I shook my head, not giving voice to the same argument I'd given back.

I was not risking my family, my friends. Not when the life I'd dreamed was within their grasp.

"You're a stubborn idiot." But the words were softened by his rueful smile and little shake at my shoulder. "But one I'm proud to stand beside. I'm with you every step of the way, brother."

My hold on him tightened. His fist slammed into my arm as he nodded sharply.

"So are we." Michal drew my attention to them, and my hand fell away from Alik's shoulder. Both Michal and Emil's warpaint was that of the chief.

"He wants to fight a chief," Alik said. "So we'll keep giving him chiefs to fight until he's done."

I tried to shake my head, fighting the feeling that was pressing against my chest, trying to burst out of me.

"He's not making it out of that ring," Emil softly promised.

"But if you die, I'm going to kill you." Michal crossed his arms, returning my faint smile.

Alik tapped his fist against my breastplate. "We'll be outside," he said.

I almost questioned it until I saw Marta. She stood back, waiting for everyone else. Her hair had been pulled back into a warrior-like braid at the crown of her head, and she wore my knife on her hip. The door closed and it was just the two of us.

Something tentative hovered between us, pulling us a step closer. She placed a hand over my heart. I did not dare move.

A breath trembled over her lips. My hand covered hers, and it seemed I could feel my heart beating through the leather and our layered hands. *I love you* seemed like too little.

"I find I am selfish, Davor," she said softly, lifting her face to me. "I do not want just a part of your heart. I want it all."

Hope rushed through me, and my hold tightened over her hand. "Do you?"

She nodded. "And I would give you all of mine, if you would accept it."

I bent closer. "There is nothing else I'd rather have. And nothing I'd rather give."

We were barely a breath away. Eyes met and I saw in hers everything I felt. My lips brushed soft against hers, once, twice. Then her arms were around my neck, fingers in my hair, as our lips crashed together. My hands cupped her face, just as desperate.

We finally parted, breaths a little ragged in the space that dared exist between us. She moved slightly, her fingers brushing the edge of my jaw.

"Good. I didn't mess up any paint."

I smiled faintly. Her chin trembled, and a tear spilled out from the corner of her eye. My thumb swept it away.

"No tears," I said gently.

She inhaled shakily, trying to lift her chin higher. "Perhaps I do not want to watch my husband die. I am too young and beautiful to be a widow."

"You are." My thumb skimmed her cheek again. "Beautiful."

Her smile faded and the tremble came back. Her hands cradled the sides of my head.

"Promise…promise me you'll walk back out of that ring."

I did not want to lie. Not to her. But maybe it didn't have to be a lie. Maybe it could be truth. For the first time, I saw something past all this. A life with her at my side. With family around me. I wanted it more than anything I'd ever wanted.

"I promise."

A ragged noise escaped her, and she pressed her lips to mine again, slower this time, like she was memorizing the touch, the taste. I smoothed her hair as we pulled away. She drew something from the pocket of her overdress and I did not stop her as she tied the prayer cloth around my wrist above the marriage cords.

I pressed a kiss to her forehead. "Be strong."

She nodded, and I waited for her to gather herself, wiping her face clear of tears and tilting her chin up. I took her hand in mine, and we walked out together.

FIFTY-FIVE

DAVOR

Alik stood outside with hands on sword hilt, a sort of smug look settling across his features. Warriors lined a path to the field, and I nearly stumbled.

Every warrior had the pattern of chief painted across his face. That feeling pushed up again and I did not know what to name it. Hope, pride, gratitude?

Marta squeezed my hand and when I looked to her, it was pride for *me* in her eyes. Tinek stood first in the lines, and he brought hand to chest.

"Chief."

Each warrior did the same as we passed. Other tribesmen and women began to fill in the spaces. No paint on their faces, but the same hand to chest, or hand to forehead, the same naming of me as chief.

I'd never seen such a thing, never heard of such a thing. And it did not stop as we walked through the village to the open fields where the *alakti* would be fought. Benches and raised platforms had been brought out over the last few days, and it had not helped watching it from the training fields.

All three villages began to converge on the ground, a small path remaining to the center where a broad circle had been cleared. Emil and Michal had gone ahead, and they waited for me there, with the same triumph as Alik's at the tribe's support.

The Greywolf and our *talånd* waited in the ring. The *talånd* stood with shoulders hunched, his colorful cloak hanging limply around him.

Makar and his men stood on the opposite edge of the circle. A thin sneer graced his face at the sight of us—battlelion and three chieftain's sons standing together.

A rustle marked warriors pushing forward. Fully armored and faces painted like mine. They knew they could not interfere, but they were there, nonetheless. Makar's fury only grew at the sight, well over half the entire tribe standing with me, and sending uncertainty through his men.

But he did not back down.

The *talånd* stirred and beckoned me forward. My hand caught against Marta's. She stood, chin high, but with a telltale quiver. I squeezed her hand, but before I could let go, she kissed me again.

When she regretfully pulled away, the promise I'd given shone bright in her eyes before she released my hand.

Alik lifted an eyebrow with a faint smile, before raising his spear in salute. I stepped into the circle, stopping by the *talånd*. He gave a hesitant look to me, and I stared back evenly.

"Chief...I—"

"Do your duty here." My voice did not travel beyond the two of us, but he still flinched from its harshness.

The Greywolf did not look sympathetic in the least.

"An *alakti* has been called against Davor, chief of the Saber tribe. His honor as chief and the strength of his leading has been called into question by a member of the tribe." The *talånd's* voice echoed across the gathering.

I did not break my gaze from Makar.

"Chief Davor, you accept this challenge?"

"I do." Perhaps it was the brothers and the tribe behind me that lent extra strength to my voice.

"You will fight until there is no one left to challenge or you yourself fall?"

"I will." The words tasted like sharp iron across my tongue. "But let each man who comes forward declare if they will fight to their death or to their yielding. I have no desire to keep spilling the blood of this tribe in foolish causes."

It was not the way of an *alakti*, but I was tired of blood and fighting and death. And this one thing, I would change.

Makar shifted restlessly, but some with him looked to each other in relief. A murmur rippled through the gathering like wind through pines as my words were spread to the farthest reaches of the field.

"Let it be so." The *talånd* raised his staff, brought it down, and it was begun.

I drew my sword as they both stepped out of the ring. A warrior came forward. He glanced over his shoulder at Makar, then to me.

"To yielding," he said quietly. I inclined my head.

He charged, and I sidestepped, blocking his swing. Half-hearted attacks followed, until I kicked his legs out from under him. He hit the ground and I pressed the point of my sword to his throat.

"Yield." It came almost as a question.

I tapped the blade against his breastplate. "You might wish to join the Battlelion once you get off this field."

He cast a glance at Makar then nodded. I stepped back and he hurried from the circle. The next warrior boldly declared death.

He fought with more intensity than the last, and sweat soon stung my eyes. My left bracer helped block a blow. His sword skidded off the leather to slice into my arm. He pushed a new attack as I pulled away. The sting of the wound faded away as our swords slammed against each other. His next lunge brought him too close, and my sword found his throat.

He fell and I stumbled away from the body. I curled my arm up to look at the wound, but another warrior charged into the circle.

Our blades locked and he used his momentum to push me back until I dug my feet in. He disengaged and swung again. I ducked and stabbed. He wrenched out of the way. Our blades shrieked against each other as he kept coming in close, drawing a knife in his other hand.

I thrust, and he trapped my blade between his arm and breastplate. His knife wormed against my side, trying to get through the overlapping leather to my ribs. My left hand grabbed a dagger from the back of my belt and stabbed deep into his shoulder.

He fell away with a scream, intensifying as I pulled my knife free. He went to a knee, and I kicked him in the chest.

"Yield," he half-sobbed, trying to stop the bleeding.

I stepped back. Felt a tugging against my side. One of the straps had broken under his blade and another hung desperately on, presenting a weakness in my armor.

A fourth warrior stepped in. His grip shifted nervously on his sword, but he did not declare, following the lead of his comrades and charging me. The steady flow of blood from my arm was finally making itself known. I wavered under several strikes, and his blade cut across my thigh.

I stumbled and he more boldly attacked until I caught his sword between my sword and dagger. I twisted with his attempt to pull away, keeping it imprisoned. His knee buckled under my kick.

"Yield!" He threw up a hand as I pulled my sword back to strike. Again I stepped back, but the fifth did not let the defeated warrior hobble from the field before he attacked.

Pain scored across my right shoulder from a knife strike, further loosening the straps of my armor. A snarl caught in my throat. Not that I had expected a fair fight from Makar, but this was no more than chasing a bison and striking with arrows and spears until its blood was spent and it fell to its knees, finished, and ready for butchering.

The fury gave me a burst of strength, and I stabbed, slicing his leg, pushing forward as it buckled, and plunging my knife into his throat. I stumbled with him, coming down hard on my knee.

A breath labored from me, and I scrubbed the back of my left hand across my face, smearing hot blood in its wake. I had to use my sword to lever back up to my feet, and when I stood, Makar stepped into the ring.

"Death," he declared with a sneer.

He prowled forward, and my leg clenched around the wound as I matched his circling pattern.

"You don't look so good, Davor."

I shook my head. "If you had any honor, you would have made this between just you and me."

"I'm giving you a chance to prove you are not such a coward."

"You are doing what Kamil would have done. Sacrificed warriors in pointless bloodshed so you do not have to pay a price."

His face contorted, and he brought his sword up. "I'll make this quick."

"Please do."

I took a limping step forward to meet his attack, arms shaking under the blow. The yellow of the prayer cloth caught my vision, and new strength burst through me. I shoved him away, but he came right back, hammering blow after blow at me.

I deflected each strike until my injured shoulder could no longer hold correctly, and his blade scored my leg again.

Breaths jerked short and hot from my lips, and both hands closed around my sword hilt.

"Just give up." Makar swung his sword at his side.

He brought it crashing down and I sidestepped, but was too slow to return it and he blocked.

"I'll kill them all," he promised with a sickening smile, and it gave me another frantic burst of strength, driving him back and finally inflicting a wound on his arm. He snarled and swung for my injured shoulder. I batted it away more with bracer than with blade, and struck his throat with my left hand.

He staggered back, gasping, and I limped forward. He recovered in time to spare himself several more wounds. But a faint sound escaped from me, blood slicking my hands and trying to loosen my grip on my sword.

The world tilted, and as it righted, I saw Makar coming for

me. I swung my sword up. He dodged around, passing me by. I stumbled forward as something battered my side at the breast-plate edge.

My guard faltered, left hand pressing against the searing pain.

His hand curled around the back collar of my breastplate, and his breath whispered hot against my ear.

"You should have remembered your place, Davor. Cowards have no place in this tribe."

The word sent my hand clenching tighter around my sword, pain forgotten in the rush of vengeance for years of hearing that word.

I lifted my sword, reversing grip, and stabbing down into his leg. His hold did not falter, even as I ripped the blade free. I twisted, and he knocked the blade from my hand, drawing me close as his face drained of color.

I grabbed the strap of his breastplate and for a moment we stood, locked together by our desperate hold on each other. My left hand, coming up to try to push him away, brushed a knife instead. Fingers closed around it, and I yanked it free. His eyes widened, shout starting before I plunged it into his throat.

I staggered as his hold turned desperate in death. He crumpled to the ground, taking me with him.

The impact knocked the little breath I had from me. I rolled once, coming facedown to the bloody grass.

My wheeze barely stirred the green blades beneath my lips.

My heart thudded, trying to break free of my chest.

Give up Get up Give up Get up Give up Get up.

Blood drained from me with each beat. *Give up Get up.*

I lifted my head, muscles shaking and screaming. My blurred gaze settled on a figure in red and white, hands clenched tight by her sides, head lifted proudly.

Get up. Give up. Get up.

Another breath strained from me. I'd promised. My hand slammed down on the hilt of my fallen sword.

Get up.

I couldn't.

Give up.

This was where it ended. My head bowed. Yellow fluttered around my wrist where my hand clutched the ground.

Get up.

I'd promised.

Get. Up.

I dragged a knee forward, pushing up on shaking arms. Head bowing, muscles straining, I lurched upright, feet barely keeping steady underneath me.

Silent warriors and tribespeople stared back. Movement stirred and Emil stepped forward, drawing his sword. My heart fell.

He knelt, laying his weapon on the ground, and pressing fist to his forehead. Yielding absolutely to me.

Alik sank to a knee, bare sword crossed with his spear before him.

Then Emil charged.

Caught me as I fell.

His voice, uncharacteristically gentle, whispered, "I've got you."

He repeated it as a ragged sob escaped me and I held on with all my waning strength. Someone pulled my sword from my hand. Emil shifted his hold, wrapping his arm around me and pulling mine over his shoulder. Alik took my other arm, and they pulled me forward.

Shouts filled my ears, but I could not lift my gaze from my stumbling feet. Darkness skidded over my eyes, and when it dissipated, I was leaning on Emil as something yanked at my armor.

The world spun. Voices echoed and hands kept tugging. Heat flashed and gave way to cold. Blurred faces appeared over me, but not the one I wanted. Slowly, I tilted my head to the side, trying to roll over. It was too bright and confusing, and I'd promised. I was pushed back, and my name was called. I ignored it, turning again, reaching out.

Then Marta was there. Her hands swept mine up off the table.

"Hold still, Davor." Cold pressed to my forehead.

There were things I wanted to tell her, but my tongue wasn't working the way it should. She squeezed my hand gently.

White seared across my vision until her shaking voice called me back. She was closer, forehead nearly pressed against mine. Dampness hit my cheeks.

"Stay with me," she said.

I didn't want to go anywhere else.

Darkness closed in and I felt myself slipping away. As she vanished, I heard her whisper one last time.

"Stay with me."

FIFTY-SIX

MARTA

I slumped against the table, Davor's limp hand still cradled in my own. Someone had pushed up a bench for me to sit at some point after he'd lost consciousness. It could have been hours or days since Inge had hastily thrown blankets on the table before Emil and Alik had laid him down.

Alik had dragged a panicked Michal away almost immediately. Emil had stayed to help move him as Inge bandaged, and now sat hunched forward on his knees on another bench, blood smeared over his clothes and armor. Yelene had come at some point and now sat beside him, hand resting on his back.

I straightened, wincing at the creak of my muscles. Nina gently washed blood from around the bandages, dabbing gently at his face and neck. In some places it was hard to see where the warpaint ended and the blood started.

A ragged breath caught in my chest. He looked so different

lying there. I'd have given anything to hear his voice in that moment. Nina gently brushed my wrist, guiding me to release his bloody hand.

"Marta." She touched my shoulder. "You should go speak to the tribe."

My blood-crusted hands curled in my lap. He would say the same thing, gently ushering me to take the duty, dark eyes holding confidence in me.

"I should clean first." My voice came raw from the tears I hadn't been able to stop. Blood stained my sleeves and smeared across my overdress.

"No." Emil lifted his head. "Go like that."

I put a hand to my face, feeling the stiffness of tears and dried blood as I sniffed again. I was sure I looked a mess. But I thought I knew what he wanted.

"Make them believe in him. In what he did," Nina whispered fiercely as she pulled me up. I squeezed her hand and pressed my forehead against hers. For a moment, we drew strength from the other, united by love for the man beside us.

Then I pulled away and made for the door. Emil met me there. One more glance back at where Nina gently brushed a hand across Davor's forehead before turning back to washing, and I stepped outside.

Twilight hovered over the villages, but small fires had cropped up, torches filling in other spaces. Small lightwings danced over the roofs, and sablecat eyes reflecting the fire winked just as often. I stared in shock at the number of people waiting in the lodge square, taking up every space and spare bench.

"Marta?" Michal's quiet voice was filled with question and apprehension. I turned to the young man standing guard on one side of the door, desperation in his eyes. Alik had kept him outside to keep watch and make sure peace had come.

I reached out and touched his hand. "He's resting."

He sagged against the doorpost, eyes closing, before tipping a look back to the cracked door. Indecision warred on his face, then he straightened and waited for me.

I turned my attention to Alik. His anxiety was no less hidden, but he stepped back at my nod.

It took another moment to fight off a wave of exhaustion and tears before I faced the tribe again. Some had risen, watching me. Hunters from the middle village who had been the first to openly speak to Davor. Sif with her youngest boy propped on her hip. Some of the older orphans from the lower village. Men and women who had tentatively welcomed Davor into their lodges.

"How is the chief?" someone asked.

I did not know how many of these people supported Davor or if they were hoping for something different to come out of the *alakti*. It had been blurs of faces along the path we'd walked together to the ring. All I knew was my heart ached and I just wanted to sit at his side until he woke up.

"He is resting." My voice barely carried in the silence.

"The wounds looked bad," one of the warriors, still painted for battle, said somberly.

My bloodied hands clenched at each other. "Inge thinks he has a chance."

"Is that a good thing?"

I did not see who spoke, but it came clear anyway. A wild burst of anger snapped through me.

Make them see.

"I do not know how he did it. Survived years in this tribe

when plenty called him a coward for not going along with the cruelty of others. I do not know how he kept a bit of goodness in his heart when so many were intent on seeing it stamped out."

I lurched forward a step. "We all know what his father was. And we all might as well have put those scars on him and so many others, because we did nothing to stop it."

My voice gained strength, and bits of it echoed back from the narrow lodgeways.

"And somehow he still dreamed of a tribe who could be better than the sins of their fathers. Dreamed of a place where wives are not afraid of their husbands. Children not afraid of their parents. Sisters do not fear for their sisters, and brothers do not fear their brothers. And despite the hate and mockery he got for this, he still persisted. Gave his blood for it. The very least we can do is honor that."

Many nodded, and warriors did as well.

"Everything he does has started here in this lodge. From the beginning he has treated me with respect and courtesy. Never taking, never expecting anything from me. And it has left me free to see that he is a good man. Nothing like his father. It has left me free to give my heart to him."

A tremor finally snuck through, and the weariness rushed back. I looked out at the tribe through watery eyes. I did not have much more to give, my bits of fury and frustration spent.

"He believed we could be better. Do it."

I turned back to the lodge. Alik brought fingers to his forehead, small smile in place. Emil did the same, respect clear in the action. Michal was last, though he looked frail and like he would be swept away without warning. I brought an arm around his shoulders, holding him close as we stepped into the lodge together.

He slid from my hold and hurried to Davor, placing a hesitant hand on the table beside him. I hugged my arms over my chest, sniffing again. Nina came to pull me into a hug.

"Thank you," she whispered and pressed a kiss to my temple.

Yelene stood back, but she gave me a little nod. Emil left her side and eased tentatively towards Michal. The younger's shoulders suddenly hunched, and he twisted his face away. If I had not already exhausted my words, I might have been speechless at the sight of Emil pulling Michal into a gentle hug.

Ragged sobs ripped from Michal, along with a plaintive, "I don't want to lose him."

Emil rested a hand on the back of Michal's head. "I know," he said softly. "I know."

The door creaked, and Alik entered, followed by my family. One look from my mother, and I burst into tears again. She held me and Vanda's arms circled me too. When my tears were spent, I tilted my head against my mother's shoulder, finding Alik standing beside the table, resting his fist against Davor's shoulder.

Michal pulled from Emil, scrubbing his eyes. Emil's glance fell to me, and he took a step back, ready to leave. But Alik touched his arm. I did not see what passed between them, but Emil gave a nod. He still backed off to the farther side of the lodge to give Vanda more space.

Mother gently ushered me to the healer's room and guided me to the bench. I watched numbly as she washed blood from my hands. His blood. Vanda entered with fresh clothes. Next Mother undid the braid, using a cloth to remove some bits of dried blood from my hair, and combed it out like I was a small girl again, not quite able to do my own braids.

Vanda sat with me long after they were done. My clean hands

folded in my lap, and I could barely look up from them. Her arm circled my shoulders and I leaned against her, no words passing between us, just patient understanding from her.

Eventually, I made my way back out. They had moved Davor from the table to a low bed by the fire. More blankets covered him, hiding the way he seemed sunken and hollowed out. I took the stool by his side, reaching under the blankets to find his hand, my fingers the warm ones this once. And I stayed at his side while others moved around me, barely moving when food was brought, or a blanket draped around my shoulders.

All I wanted was to close my eyes, open them again, and find him looking back. But he did not, and so I waited.

FIFTY-SEVEN

DAVOR

A soft clatter and muted voices filtered in through darkness and strange dreams. The rattle came again, the sound curious enough that I gathered the strength to open my eyes.

This darkness was gentler, broken by strains of firelight. A low laugh turned my head to the left. Two figures sat on either side of a low table next to me. Light played across Michal's face. Laughter was gone, focused instead as he held up sticks in front of him.

He set down a pair, and the other figure shifted, laying down their sticks. Michal scowled and a faint huff came from the other, back still to me.

"Your face is giving everything away."

Emil.

"So I should be more like you?" Michal twisted his face up

into an expression that looked like he was on the verge of violently expelling his last meal.

A chuckle, a little rusty in sound, came from Emil and he tapped a stick against Michal's knuckles. Michal's grin made a sound catch in my chest and brought their attention to me.

Emil swung around to face me. A grin spread over Michal's face as he brought his stool closer.

"You're finally awake!"

Finally? My confusion must have shown because Emil said, "It's been two days."

Two days. My hand felt empty, and I tilted to look to the empty seat on my right.

"Marta?" My voice rasped.

"The others were finally able to convince her to go sleep."

"We said we'd watch." Michal shifted on his seat. "How do you feel?"

"Trampled."

Michal cracked a grin. Emil tapped my shoulder and stood. He returned with a cup.

"Here. We're supposed to give you this." He slid a hand under my head and lifted enough to help me drink. Bitterness hit my tongue and I flinched away from it.

"Is it supposed to be all of it?" Michal watched. Emil took a break from forcing me to drink to tilt him a look.

"No wonder you can't remember how to count sticks. Inge told us how much."

Michal huffed with a narrowing of his eyes. "And?"

"All of it," Emil said. "I think."

I tipped my head away from the cup rim. He smirked a little at my look.

"Relax. I know what I'm doing."

I finished the last of the draught and another cup of water, and he settled me back. I worked a hand free from under the weight of blankets.

"You stayed?" I said.

He set the cup down deliberately before returning to rest elbows on knees. "Thought I might." But his words held question.

"Yelene's been staying here too," Michal offered. "I like her."

A faint smile touched Emil's lips as he tilted a look to Michal.

"Good." I was glad to hear it.

"Michal's been taking care of everything else. Not even blinking."

Michal shifted a little under the light praise in Emil's voice.

He looked to me. "Hopefully I'm not ruining everything."

"I know you're not." I tried to move away from the uncomfortable pressure all around me, quickly finding it was a bad decision. A gasp hissed from me, but instead of blankets, my hand gripped Emil's. He and Michal leaned closer to me, their worry fading away as I eased back.

"All right?" I asked Michal, whose concern still hadn't quite vanished.

A pained smile flickered. "I thought we might lose you a few times."

"Think I might stay."

He leaned forward, hand resting against the back of mine, so it was caught between him and Emil.

"You'd better. I need you to show me how to be a good man."

Stinging filled my eyes, but the faint smile on his face never vanished, nor did his belief in me. Emil's hand tugged on mine.

"And I need someone to keep me walking a better path."

The stinging spilled over to track down my cheeks, and shaky breaths followed. Michal wiped at his cheeks with his free hand. Emil sniffed suspiciously.

"No one hears about this," he said gruffly.

Michal chuckled and I smiled, gripping Emil's hand a little tighter. He huffed and squeezed back.

"What are you teaching him?" My voice still had a rough edge, but they acknowledged the change, and shifted back.

"Everything you taught me about counting sticks," Emil said, bringing the stinging back for a moment.

Michal glanced between us, a sort of smile on his face like he was glad to see the two of us talking.

"But he has no patience." Emil turned back to Michal.

Michal stuck his tongue out, and another laugh teased my chest.

"Emil rubs the corner of his left eye if he has a good pair."

Emil twisted to glare at me, and I flashed a tired smile back. Michal gathered up the sticks, a new grin in place.

They started a new game, Emil every now and then reminding Michal to keep his voice down. I lay there, content to watch and listen to the soft sounds of their gentle bickering, until I slipped back to sleep.

When next I opened my eyes, daylight had come. And with it, gentle breezes through the open windows. But best of all was the sight of Marta sitting beside me, softly humming as she stitched bright shapes along the collar of a shirt.

Her hair tumbled free over her shoulders, light glinting off the needle as it dipped in and out of the cloth. I could have watched her forever, memorizing every soft angle and curve in her face, the only lines from the slight pucker in the corner of her mouth as she focused.

She glanced up, pausing before a smile blossomed. Putting aside her stitching, she scooped up my hand and leaned close. Her smile never faded, but her eyes glinted with sudden tears. Then she surged forward, and her lips were on mine.

My free arm was strong enough to slide through her hair. She leaned her forehead against mine.

"Are you always going to ambush me like this?" I asked.

She bit her lip as she laughed. "Every chance I get."

I stole another kiss. "Good."

She pulled away slightly, fingers tracing along my temple. "Inge said we might have lost you. But spirits' blessing the armor caught most of that blow. And she said the scar underneath helped protect."

The scar I'd gotten from Alik closing up a wound. A memory of a burning blade touched to my skin that now meant something good. Perhaps it had been the spirits looking out for me. And it seemed I owed a visit to the All-Father's lodge for more than one thing once I was free of the bed.

I caught her hand as it faltered.

She lightly kissed me again. "I should get Inge, tell her you're awake."

I didn't let go my hold. "I'm all right for now."

She laughed softly. "I'd rather have you up quicker. We've days and days ahead of us, Davor, and unfinished business, you and I."

Heat seared through me, and I kissed away her laugh. She pulled away, a little red herself, and went to find Inge.

Through the open door, the sounds of talk and laughter, interspersed with the merry sounds of children playing, eased another rough edge from my heart. There might be difficult days still ahead, but I knew with certainty, the Saber tribe had found something to be proud of again.

FIFTY-EIGHT

DAVOR

L uk pricked up his head as we came over the last rise and down to the grasslands. The warriors behind us lifted their voices at the promise of home a short ride away. Midsummer was two days behind us, and with it, a final treaty with the Greywolf tribe.

We'd met them at the border stones, their solemn chief and restless battlewolf, and a pack of wolves. Their chief held himself confidently, a far cry from last I'd seen him. The battlewolf's scars from Kamil were ropy and red on his face, but it did not stop him from contributing plenty of words to the negotiations.

He and Alik had a wary truce, and I'd caught Michal hiding a grin more than once at what he said. I watched those half-brothers and sent a prayer of thanks that I was getting something close to their obvious bond with mine.

And now we were home. The days in the saddle from the

village to the border and back had worn on me, even though I'd thought my strength back from the *alakti* countings ago.

Alik gave the order and our lions picked up their pace, racing the last mile to the village. We pulled to a halt just outside the upper village. It would not be long now until any returning packs would come to the completed chief's lodge. Hammers striking nails and shouts of the craftsmen echoed from the hill, the walls in place and roof nearly done.

My heart jumped at the sight of the figure waiting for us. I dismounted and pulled Luk over to Marta. He curled around the two of us, hiding us from watching eyes as we kissed.

"I missed you." Her arms were around my neck. My arm around her waist scooped her closer.

"I missed you, too."

Luk tried to nuzzle in between us. Marta laughed and scratched under his jaw, still keeping an arm around me.

"How were things?" I asked, as we turned into the village, arm-in-arm.

"Quiet." But there was a lilt in her voice.

"And?" I prodded.

"You'll see."

"That sounds suspicious." I pressed a kiss to her forehead as we walked. She laughed and leaned into my side.

With the death of Makar, the tribe had largely accepted me as chief. There were still some who disagreed, openly or privately, but it came with words and not with swords or attacks in the night. And for every one who did not agree, there were more who did.

The three villages were settling into a new rhythm, guided by the joint alliance of the two *talånds*. I had even finally allowed a rounded medallion to be made, etched in runes reminding me of my promises as chief, and inset with another red stone in the center. It tapped against my chest, but did not bring any dread as a sign of the chief.

Signs of Marta's plan were evident once we stepped into the lodge square. Tables and benches were set out. Garlands of summer flowers growing in riotous swaths along the river and in the grasslands lay across the tables and strung between torch poles.

"To celebrate midsummer." She spun to back away in front of me, almost as if afraid I would not love whatever made her happy. "And the new peace."

"Who is coming?" I asked.

She grinned. "The *sjandsens* said they would be here, and whoever from the other villages wanted to come. I think for autumn we should have a gathering out in the fields for the entire tribe."

I arched an eyebrow at her intent, but she was already back beside me, excited for the night.

As the sun began to set, food was brought out, torches were lit and the fire in the center of the square sprang to life. Eating soon gave way to dancing. I stood back by the head table, drink resting against the crook of my arm as I watched the tribe whirl to the beat of drums and strings.

Inge and Nina laughed with other women. Alik almost shyly spoke with a woman, a widow's band around her wrist as a young girl tugged and spun while holding on to her hand.

Off to the side of the gathering, Emil sat astride a bench, arms around Yelene, head bent low as they spoke to each other, marriage cords in plain view around their wrists. Rumors still flew about him, but this time it was said if you spoke to Emil, brother to the chief, he would find a way to help or bring your cause directly to the chief. He lived half in and half out of the shadows now, and was not quite done with the ways of chieftains.

Yelene suddenly straightened, and grabbed his hand, pressing it to her growing stomach. He jolted, then a smile of unabashed joy spread over his face, and they shared a look of happiness I was glad to see on him.

My gaze moved away, to Janne dancing with a young man, from there to Michal with some of the huntsmen. Dariy had taken Michal under his wing, teaching him the ways of hunting, and teaching both of us something about having a father who loved. Michal still stood at my side as heir, but perhaps might not always have to.

I found Marta next, coming to me. I set the cup aside as she slid arms around me.

"Still no dancing?" she asked.

"No," I said with bare apology that turned to confusion as she swayed side to side. "What are you doing?"

She laughed. "Taking what I can."

I shook my head and kissed her instead. Her hand swept around to card through the ends of my hair as my forehead pressed to hers.

"Someday," I whispered, letting her continue to rock a little.

We were learning, day by day, how to give, how to love, how to uphold each other as husband and wife.

"I'll hold you to that," she murmured against my lips. I returned her smile, knowing she would and proud of her for it.

She tucked against my side, my arms around her, as we watched the gathering. Many who passed by gave salutes to us both. And as the moon rose, I let her pull me forward into the gathering, fingers twined about each other's, swaying a little to the beat of the drums, and finding small places to exist in love and belonging with the promise of many, many days ahead of us.

THE END

ACKNOWLEDGEMENTS

This book was not supposed to happen. I'd finished Greywolf's Heart, and thought myself done with this storyworld—even writing—as I struggled through months of intense creative burnout. And then one summer day, Davor kicked down the door and told me, "this is my story."

From writing the opening prologue, to thinking and re-thinking everything I knew about Emil, to a line from the books of Samuel speaking to cycles of abuse needing to be broken and realizing that was the main theme of this book and that it was something important, to admitting that I do kind of like writing romance in this soft and subtle way...it was a journey of several months, learning that I wasn't done with writing, that I still loved to spin stories of laughter and longing, redemption and hope, finding love and family and mending broken things.

All my stories are special to me, but this one taught me a few good things. Things about not giving up, listening to my heart, about pressing on, and giving characters a chance.

Yeah. Emil was supposed to stay a villain. Then he was going to die helping Davor. Then he dropped the news on me that he was a husband and soon to be father, and I knew he needed a chance to stay, find his sharp and jagged way home into a family.

Thanks always to my family, for being amazing, and loving and supportive my entire life. We're not perfect, but we do love and forgive and move on. Love you so much.

Thanks always to my friends who are constantly supportive and don't bat an eye when I basically lay on the ground staring at ceiling cracks going through another existential crisis. Paige, for the debriefs and encouragement, and Mollie, for the conversations and support and just listening to me ramble and figure out my own plot problems at the White Rhino or across text. To Jenni for just being an amazing person. To Emily, for the check-ins and steady support. To the rest of the Inkwell crew, thanks for being amazing authors and friends. I can always count on all of you, and you have no idea how much that means to me. To all the others I've met since Greywolf.

Beta readers, Jenni, Anna, and Michelle. Thanks for coming back on this journey with me and for loving Davor and this crew. Jenni, thanks especially for all the encouragement, fangirling, music swaps, and letting me come in with super niche book-specific memes that I couldn't share publicly because of spoilers. For making a few of those memes yourself. And for loving Emil. <3

Writing is sometimes a solitary endeavor, but it takes a village to put a book together. Katie for the edits, Deborah for the line edits and bookish love, Fran Stern for the amazing cover, Selina for formatting, Kristin for the incredible chapter headings. The White Rhino coffee shop for all the lattes and not kicking Mollie and I out when we got too excited about writing and our books.

A special thanks to Fr. Mike Schmitz and the Bible in a Year podcast for hitting me with that discussion on ending trauma cycles on a day when I was doubting everything about this story. That was a God moment early on in drafting and it was a mighty shove to keep going with this theme.

And always, always to my Creator, for giving me this love of story, of giving these kinds of stories to tell, and for being there for me, even when I don't look, or stubbornly think I'm on my own. I never am. For each breath, and each word I'm given, I'm truly grateful.

And to you, reader, Thanks for making it this far. I can't do this without you. I hope you found something of yourself in these pages. And as always, stay courageous.

MORE BOOKS BY C.M. BANSCHBACH

Greywolf's Heart
Spirits' Valley Book 1
A man born for war. A bastard raised in contempt. Only
together can they defend their tribe from slaughter.

The Summons: A Dragon Keep Chronicles Prequel

The reclusive Mountain Baron receives troubling news from
mercenaries invading his territory. War is stirring in the lowlands, and the man he once called brother has been kidnapped
by a renegade lord. But are the bonds of blood enough to draw
him from his sanctuary to confront his past?

Meet the Baron in this free prequel short story, available to
newsletter subscribers!
Subscribe: http://eepurl.com/gwcGjD

ABOUT THE AUTHOR

C.M. Banschbach is a native Texan and would make an excellent hobbit if she wasn't so tall. She's an overall dork, ice cream addict, and fangirl. When not writing fantasy stories packed full of adventure and snark, she works as a pediatric Physical Therapist where she happily embraces the fact that she never actually has to grow up.

She writes clean YA/MG fantasy-adventure as Claire M. Banschbach.

C.M. Banschbach on Facebook
@cmbanschbach on Instagram
ClaireMBanschbach.com

Sign up for her newsletter and receive (sometimes) quarterly updates, publishing news, and behind-the-scenes details.

Sign up - http://eepurl.com/gwcGjD